"Your brilliance makes you careless, believing you can fix what's broken. Not this time."

– *Professor Richard King*

* * *

"Mommy, watch! Daddy is lighting another firework!"

Hearing her three-year-old daughter's giggles echo through the trees, Rachel bumps her wheelchair along a familiar root-infested brick path. Peering downhill past lightning bugs blinking on and off, a sparkling rocket bursts across the dark sky like a shooting blue comet from a clearing along the Hilltop property line where Hannah is having the time of her life watching her father light off unsafe and insane contraband fireworks, courtesy of the PTB.

Loath to sound like the family killjoy, Rachel hesitates before shouting toward the festive pair, "Owen, are you sure no one lives in the house next door?"

Owen's response resonates through the darkness, "It's been empty since the Gorks—don't worry!"

"Well, can you at least make sure Hannah stays safe?"

More laughter and another whooshing blue comet's harmless trajectory over the hill precede a sing-songy, "We will, Mommy!" duet.

* * *

by John Hopkins

THE POWERS THAT BE trilogy

The Golden Ellipse

The Lost Ship

The Blue Spark

THE POWERS THAT BE short stories

Operation Bigfoot

Firing Henry

Dog vs. Alien

Thundercorp No. 5

The Special

Big Shots Club

Doc's Brain

LOST CACTUS comic strip anthologies

Lost Cactus - The First Treasury

Lost Cactus - The Second Treasury

LOST CACTUS ARCHIVES short stories

Middle of Nowhere

The Pixel Pusher

Emmitt's Encounter

Warehouse of Secrets

The Gremlin

LOST CACTUS ARCHIVES graphic novels

Volume 1:
The Wormhole Particle Project (future release)

Volume 2:
Tank and Gremlin (future release)

Volume 3:
Fox Gambit (future release)

Volume 4:
Zint and Daphne (future release)

THE POWERS
THAT BE
BOOK
THREE

JOHN HOPKINS

a subsidiary of Hopart LLC

Publication Date: February 2024

Trade Paperback ISBN: 979-8-9862338-4-0

Hardcover ISBN: 979-8-9862338-5-7

eISBN: 979-8-9862338-3-3

Library of Congress Control Number: 2023913616

johnhopkinsauthor.com

Cover illustration and interior page design by Hopart LLC.

Dedicated in memory of my Dad

... and everyone afflicted with

Alzheimer's Disease.

Characters

Listed in alphabetical order

Alan Adamo	Thundercorp No. 5 drone technician
The Advisers	Pro-human alien cabal
Joe Alexander	aka Uncle Joe, Rachel's younger brother
Marcus Alexander	Rachel's deceased father
Miriam Alexander	Rachel's deceased mother
Neil Alexander	Hannah's Grandfather, 4x removed
Alpha	Multi-armed, one-eyed service bot
Chet Andersen	Ian Dury's producer and lifelong friend
Andrew	Long-serving PTB CEO
Fred Beaman	Pugilist turned viral podcaster

Willie Beaman	Fred's son, inherits the podcast
Dr. Jon Benz	St. Dymphna's administrator
Mrs. Calogero	Panarea bakery shop owner
Rico Calogero	Underworld operative
Sarah Carter	Las Vegas cocktail waitress
Oliver Comerford	Former Scotland Yard detective
Dwayne Cooper	aka The Cowboy, Chrysalis Air pilot
Simona Dixon	Bianca Valentino's Panarea Alias
Ted Dixon	Owen Haig's Panarea alias
Professor Ian Dury	Maverick archeologist and documentarian
Gordon Epps	Lena Jackson's VP successor
Amira Fisher	Sarah's friend
King George VII	English monarch
Terrence O. Flynn Gilliam	PTB field agent, aka Flynn
Edwin Goddard	PTB security
Hannah Haig	Rachel and Owen's daughter
Owen Haig	Rachel's husband
Rachel Haig	Reluctant superhero harboring a secret
Shirley Harkness	aka Aunt Shirley, Miriam Alexander's sister
Julius Hart	Thundercorp founder
Stanley Hobbes	Rachel's guardian angel
Lena Jackson	Black Independent U.S. president
Lieutenant Jane	Navy doctor stationed at Sigonella, Italy
Professor Richard King	Aka Doc, ageless PTB scientist
Mitsuo Kobayashi	World-renowned robotics superstar

Philip Larrson	Swedish munitions expert
Maddie LeBoeuf	Hannah's friend on Thundercorp No. 5
The Light Specters	Quintessential pure energy aliens
Lola and Sven	Villa St. Claire's robot caretakers
Edgar Lopez	PTB company man
Louie	Villa St. Claire's major-domo
Lucy Lufkin	Julius Hart's assistant
Nina Madsen	Former PTB administrator
Mildred Meeks	Lena Jackson's campaign adviser
Frederick Neumayer	Austrian woodsman
Number 1	The first of sixteen sibling sisters
Number 8	The eighth of sixteen sibling sisters
The Overlords	Imperious hybrid replicants of extinct alien race
Paddy	Andrew and Number 8's son
Lou Pastorini	Veteran Secret Service agent
Penelope	Bianca's German Shepherd rescue
Artemus Pennywell	Deceased former PTB CEO
Colonel Vadim Petrov	PTB special ops commander
Ping	Artemus Pennywell's confidante
Piper	Hannah's Spaniel rescue
Pope Pius XIII	Cardinal John Caldwell Montgomery of the Archdiocese of Chicago
Dave Poole	Rachel's bodyguard and caretaker
Nurse Rahimi	Neonatal nurse
Sean and Alec	Best friends

Madge Simpkins	Mayor of St. Louis
The Sisters	Collective name of sixteen identical replicants
Mr. Smythe	Newport coffee shop proprietor
Jaques St. Claire	French underworld heir
Amelia Stawicki	Thundercorp recruiter
Gwen Stevens	American actress
Oliver Thornhill	Bartender at The Back Nine
Bianca Valentino	Former Italian Carabinieri and art forgery expert
Ed Watson	PTB lead architect and engineer

The PTB Council (ages in year 2044)

Aldo Santamaria	66, Chief Operating Officer
Franklin Pierce	72, Chief Financial Officer
Mitsuo Kobayashi	94, Technology Guru
Vita Carrera	38, VP, Legal Affairs
Millard Lufkin	70, International Outer Space Consortium (IOSC) Administrator
Edward Laughton	62, PTB General Counsel
Viraj Patel	42, Global Logistics
Aisha Ayad	49, Intel Chief
Professor Ernest Gann	32, Mathematician
Olivia Paquet	52, VP, Communications
Dr. Gene Simmons	46, VP, Global Medicines and Charities
Anastasia Gabreski	38, PTB UN Ambassador

The Final Eight (ages in year 2052)

Hector Gonzalez	23, Spanish
Monica Grasso	32, Italian-American
Ada Hansen	17, Norwegian
Enes Kabek	28, Israeli
Hedy Olsen	21, Australian
Lucia Sandoval	38, Brazilian
Lamar Tate	26, Black American
Michael Tran	59, Vietnamese-American

Places

The Cabin — Remote Dolomite Mountains hideout

Cortina d'Ampezzo — Alpine ski village in Dolomite Mountains

The Farmhouse — Outback sheep ranch

Gobekli Tepe — Enigmatic ruins in Southeastern Turkey

Hilltop Estate — Alexander family estate

Lost Cactus — PTB laboratory and research base

Panarea — Aeolian Island at epicenter of PTB underworld

PTB HQ — Sprawling concentric multi-level underground base in Scottish Lowlands

St. Dymphna's — Former penetentiary for the criminally insane converted to PTB black site

South Coast Plaza — Erstwhile world-class shopping mall

Thundercorp Ranch — Paradigm smashing e-commerce corporation based on Texas Gulf Coast

The Turd — Nickname for architectural monstrosity on former Petronas Twin-Towers site

Villa St. Claire — French Riviera villa with a storied past

Prologue

Stanley Hobbes | Newport, RI
11:43 a.m. | February 3, 2020

Stanley Hobbes fancied himself something of a low-level superhero. Sporting rumpled secondhand clothes under trademark moth-eaten sweaters and Coke-bottle spectacles on his bald head, the affirmed bachelor with a keen eye for the ladies looked more like one of Superman's turds which suited him just fine. His God-given short stature and humble outward appearance proved invaluable superpowers, lulling a cruel world to overlook and underestimate his squat 5-2 frame.

Heat-packing guards and state-of-the-art security systems protecting Newport's notorious debauchery and high society hedonism from the prying eyes of mere mortals proved no match for Stanley. Quick-witted and resourceful, his chameleon-like personae infiltrated elite gatherings, extravagant weddings, bar mitzvahs, glitzy fundraisers, and outrageous parties, documenting the inevitable devolution into a shameful and embarrassing smorgasbord of drunken bacchanals, vicious fights, and fumbling awkward trysts.

After uploading salacious high-class hijinks reportage and reputation-damaging hi-res imagery to his editors via anonymous links, he scooped up thick envelopes of cash at dead drop locations, maintaining his secret identity, just like Clark Kent.

On rare occasions, pangs of conscience permeated Stanley's psyche, but a lifetime of derisive mockery at the hands of these same rich assholes assuaged his guilt. Post ten years of countless breaches and narrow escapes, he almost had enough to secure a down payment on a vacant Newport storefront that sold candy back in the day. Stanley's dream: convert the retail space wedged between an antique shop and a maritime art gallery into Hobbes Rare Books, specializing in comics and pulpy fiction from a bygone era. An impressive personal collection of books and manuscripts amassed over his 35 years stored in a climate-controlled facility will stock the shelves before a grand opening.

Stanley Hobbes made a solemn resolution: one more big score, and he would quit the cloak-and-dagger paparazzi racket for good. With his John Hancock on a thick stack of loan papers, his transmogrification into an upstanding business owner and pillar of the community will be realized. He even had half a mind to join the local chamber.

* * *

Through a reliable source, Stanley learned that socialite extraordinaire Miriam Alexander, wife of Marcus Alexander, the Newport-based entertainment mogul, was rushed to the Women & Infants Hospital in Providence. Recovering from an emergency C-section, Mrs. Alexander's condition is guarded, and the six-month-old preemie baby girl is tucked away in the neonatal ICU under heavy security. The mission, should Stanley accept, is to capture pictures of the mother and child.

This was a job for, well, Stanley.

Rachel | Providence, RI
11:43 a.m. | February 4, 2020

Stanley pulled his 2002 Chevy Malibu rust bucket into a handicapped spot in the hospital parking garage, popped the trunk, pulled out his crutches, and snapped a brace around his right leg. Patting the charged smart device in his trouser pocket, the conman hobbled to the elevator to breach the renowned birthing hospital, churning out pampered little brats like a factory.

Struggling through cumbersome glass doors into the lobby, no one offered Stanley assistance—a harmless runt with a bum leg birth defect—not too far from the truth.

Stanley scoped the scene, feigning reading the hospital's directory inside the well-adorned lobby, noting stone-faced men in black impeding access to the bank of elevators. His source was not kidding about the heightened security presence. An anticipatory prickle down the spine informed the veteran reporter that there is more to this story than snapping precious baby photos for slavish masses eking out vicarious lives through the privileged elite.

Limping past the security desk, Stanley waved at a guard and pointed toward the gift shop. The musclebound Black man stared right through him before turning his back to assist another visitor.

* * *

Waltzing down a central corridor like he owned the place, munching on a Snickers bar from the overpriced gift emporium with a pink "It's a Girl!" balloon tied to a crutch, Stanley spied an unattended emergency stairwell. Checking his six, he ditched the crutches behind a potted plant and climbed flights of stairs, huffing, and panting by the time he reached the sixth-floor Neonatology ward.

Dabbing sweat with a hankie, Stanley held the balloon close, cognizant of cameras up and down the quiet corridor. Walking past floor-to-ceiling glass-fronted intensive care units bathed in serene blue glows to prevent jaundice, he read the handwritten placards by each doorway: Rodriguez, Hoffman, Yang, Simpson, Palmieri .... No Alexander. Shit. Shit. And more shit.

Moving toward a centralized nurses' station, Stanley nodded past a weary couple and froze as elevator doors slid apart. Melding behind a metal trash can, he watched a distinguished fellow in a houndstooth sportscoat and red bow tie with dark-gray curly hair leading a team of important-looking white-coated men and women into a meeting room.

Connecting the bow tie wearer to the men in black standing watch on the main floor, Stanley assumed his cloak of invisibility and sauntered past the preoccupied nurses' station. Approaching the closed door to eavesdrop, he heard voices raised in angry tones, realizing it was some kind of high-level ass-chewing. Ducking into an adjacent storage room on impulse, Hobbes searched the tight space and pulled a stethoscope from a shelf crammed with supplies.

"Jesus, I know where to go if I ever need a caseload of rubber gloves."

Jamming the earpieces into his hairy ears, he placed the diaphragm against the wall adjoining the conference room and picked up the superheated conversation.

"... *don't care about your damnable ethics! The injections must proceed on schedule.*"

A woman's voice interjected, "*Professor King, you must agree that the premature birth resulted from your drug trial. If you do not tell me what these injections are designed to do, ethically, I cannot participate. I will not be a party to your human experimentation.*"

Red bow tie's authoritative reply resonated through Stanley's earpieces.

"Doctor, you are free to go, but please be mindful of your NDAs. The Powers That Be will not fuck around with whistleblowers."

A more conciliatory male voice interjected, *"Be reasonable, Doctor Shepherd. Professor King's organization made a sizable donation. It is just one little girl. And, from what I understand, she is doing amazingly well for a six-month preemie."*

"Really, Bob? We are so hard up for cash that this so-called scientist can waltz in here, write a check, and we have to inject his untested drug into a tiny baby's brain? I want no part of this. I quit. Professor King, you and your powers that be can go to hell."

Readjusting the stethoscope earpieces, Stanley mumbled, "Powers That Be," before the conference room's door creaked open and slammed shut, shaking the thin wall.

The room fell silent before Stanley heard the man adopt a more conciliatory tone to quell further debate, *"We do not require the close-minded Doctor Shepherd's approval to proceed with the injections. I assure you that no harm will come to the baby. Case closed."*

Stanley scrunched closer to the wall, listening as a softer female voice dared to ask: *"Does Mr. and Mrs. Alexander know what you are up to, Professor?"*

"If you must know, Nurse Rahimi, Marcus Alexander, the child's father, signed off on the procedure in exchange for exclusive rights to build his arenas on a portfolio of high-end properties. Quid pro quo. That is how The Powers That Be operates. By the way, did your mortgage pay-off check clear?"

"Yes."

"Congratulations. Now, Miriam Alexander is still in post-cesarean recovery. She was told that her daughter's NICU is listed under the last name Hoffman for privacy. Everything is above board as far as the mother is concerned. Proceed with baby Rachel's injections and ensure no unauthorized hospital personnel enters her NICU. I do not wish to post guards, but I will if it comes to that."

Nurse Rahimi ventured a follow-up query. *"Do these injections have a name?"*

Hobbes leaned in to hear Professor King's reply, *"Blue Spark is the codename for the experimental treatment. Miriam and Marcus Alexander's child is the first of a new kind."*

Seated atop a cardboard box in stunned silence, Stanley Hobbes removed the stethoscope as the meeting ended. "Blue Spark ... that is catchy." With his paparazzi task forgotten, Stanley Hobbes exited the storeroom and stumbled past the nurses' station, mulling the consequential eavesdrop in his active mind.

"Sir! Can I help you?"

Still clutching the balloon, Stanley snapped back to the present, wheeling toward the woman's familiar soft voice, "Uh, Nurse Rahimi, uh ... I am here with a delivery. Uh, yeah, I was told to deliver this balloon to the Hoffman baby." With a wide-eyed nod, he mumbled, "Yep, that is why I am here."

Fresh off her confrontational meeting and in no mood to play around with the blatant liar, Nurse Rahimi's dark gaze pierced Stanley's wafer-thin story. "Should I call security?"

Stanley Hobbes tossed caution to the wind, "Please don't. You are right; that was a lie. I would like to see the Hoffman baby. Is that in any way possible?"

With one eye on the elevator, ensuring that Professor King's mysterious PTB entourage had vacated the floor, Nurse Rahimi proffered a broad smile, "Sure. Why not? Let me find you a mask and scrubs—sized extra small."

Covered from head to toe, Stanley Hobbes followed the dark-complected nurse into the blue-lit NICU.

"Here she is. Isn't she a beauty?"

Bathed in a peaceful blue ambiance, overwhelmed with a dizzying sense of grace, Stanley Hobbes moved before the tall glass incubator, staring enrapt at the delicate creature ensconced within, lying atop a cute animal print blanket. "She is the most perfect thing I have ever seen."

As if hearing Stanley's words, baby Rachel's eyes opened, and her tiny head swiveled onto his watery gaze.

Swallowing hard, Stanley noted the miniaturized cannula and thin tube extending from the delicate preemie's left temple with a wince. Replaying the stern man's profound statement that this child is the first of a new kind, he proffers a delicate wave, "Hello, Rachel. My name is Stanley Hobbes."

Upon saying the words aloud, the nebbish little paparazzo knew his life was irrevocably altered in ways that would play out over time. Taking a deep breath through his mask, Stanley returned Rachel's mesmerizing gaze through his glowing reflection in the incubator glass, "I will watch over you, Rachel. That's a promise."

Perceiving the gravitational pull between the tiny baby and the strange little man, Nurse Rahimi remained vigilant while administering a prescribed dosage of Professor Richard King's mystery drug from an IV bag. Monitoring the blue fluid coursing through the thin tube and into baby Rachel, the veteran NICU nurse hears people coming down the hall, "Okay, Mr. Hobbes, it is time to go."

Stanley removed his thick spectacles and swiped more tears from his eyes before pivoting toward Nurse Rahimi, "Tell me everything you know about The Powers That Be and the Blue Spark."

Chapter One:

The Maverick

Professor Ian Dury | Gobekli Tepe
4:45 p.m. | August 7, 2034

Alien Disclosure Day in early 2034 confirmed once and for all what most people already suspected—we are not alone in the universe. For Professor Ian Dury, the official pronouncement from a historic gathering of world leaders in the Nevada desert also reaffirmed his POV that human civilization had reached a climax. His proof? Coddled within a technological ennui, the distractible world quickly tuned out the second most important story in human history. Absent little green men landing on the White House lawn—which no one said was forthcoming anytime soon—they returned to standard programming: politics, sports, entertainment, and the latest titillating scandal du jour.

Disclosure Day had another annoying after-effect for Dury and a new generation of fresh-faced, open-minded young archeologists.

Years spent studying geographical and structural mysteries for clues to advanced human societies that flourished for eons before vanishing off the face of Earth were defunded in favor of the sexier and more accessible alien angle. In the mainstream, proponents of theoretical former human civilizations were cast as borderline insane nutjobs, and their ridiculous evidence was deemed downright preposterous and unworthy of academic scrutiny. Case closed.

Despite maintaining his staunch beliefs, interview requests filled Ian's inbox, requesting his learned opinion on alien links to sites like Nan Madol and Gobekli Tepe. Total horseshit, but now almost impossible to refute. Turning down lucrative offers from news producers and podcasters like Fred Beaman with his twelve million+ followers, Ian seethed at his colleagues' greed, selling their souls to sit behind microphones, repeating ancient alien propagandized drivel.

Liberated from the consensus-driven herd and weary of the nagging requests, Ian hoisted a middle-finger salute to the unholy public-private alliance and their confounding desire to project Mr. Alien onto flimsy ad-hoc narratives and return to business as usual, whatever that is.

Countering the noise, Ian decided to fight fire with fire by bootstrapping a documentary spotlighting his controversial research on former human civilizations. On a shoestring budget, the maverick archeologist—and a thorn in the side of mainstream academe—hired a crew of eager-beaver film school students willing to work for peanuts and, better yet, had their own equipment.

Gwen Stevens, a struggling American actress, signed on as the documentary's moderator and interviewer. Ian knew she brought nothing to the project but knock-out good looks, a great voice, and a brash, outspoken reputation. Still, the last thing he needed was a passive milquetoast afraid to take on the big dog. With Ms. Stevens, that was not a concern—he was pretty sure she disliked him from their initial meeting in Los Angeles. So much the better.

To get the ball rolling, the renowned professor opted to throw all his cards on the table and take the film crew to the infamous archeological wonder, Gobekli Tepe, in southeastern Turkey to record the initial segments of his film. A sink-or-swim test for the team, and Gwen can break in her shiny new Italian leather boots as a bonus.

* * *

The low-budget three-vehicle caravan parked in the empty Gobekli Tepe visitor lot near a dead-quiet museum complex built for hordes of tourists that never materialized. By contrast, better-known wonders like Giza and Stonehenge had reservations booked out a year in advance to control throngs of ET acolytes flocking to the sites in search of aliens.

Noting the tattered remnants of open-air tented structures designed to protect the site and its surrounding digs from the harsh Turkish elements, Ian spit on the hot pavement, "It looks like we can leave the incidental release forms in the car. We are the only ones here."

Tuning out grumblings from the youthful film crew getting its first taste of the less-than-optimal Turkish climate, a dizzying headrush caused Dury to grab the nearest car door to stop himself from faceplanting on the pavement.

"Are you okay, Professor?"

"Yes, Chet. It's the heat; you would think I'd be used to it by now."

Leaving Chet Andersen, his de facto director/producer, to supervise unloading the equipment, Ian scouted ahead down a familiar pathway of weather-beaten planks into the sprawling ruins. With a dismissive huff, he shunned a nagging thought that his arrival at Gobekli Tepe fulfilled part of a larger plan.

Noting discarded tools and equipment scattered about aborted excavations eroding under harsh elements leaking through gaping holes in a ripped canopy stretched between bent and rusted stanchions, the

48-year-old mused, "It is easier to put everything on ET than to chisel away under the hot sun. Sensible, really."

Shaking off another dizzy spell, a voice called from behind.

"Hey, Professor, I think it is too hot to play outside today."

Ian turned his tanned visage onto Gwen's pleasant countenance as the inexperienced Spielbergian wannabes struggled to unpack equipment and stage a two-minute opening interview scene before a massive stone pillar near the site's concentric epicenter.

Wearing a floppy sun hat and sporting an open-collar white button-down tied at the waist over skin-tight khakis tucked into her dusty boots, the actress found her mark while perusing an outline of the first day's shoot schedule. "There is no way we will get all these shots in a day."

Ian smiled, avoiding staring at her pert breasts visible under the thin cotton blouse, "I know; shoot for the stars, settle for the Moon." Dabbing sweat from his forehead, "This opening bit is designed for me to riff on the alien angle, but feel free to interject. I am not remaking Citizen Kane. I want this documentary to have an unscripted quality to allow us the freedom to take the conversation where it leads. I just need to get my points across in a coherent fashion using this extraordinary location to buttress my view."

"Yeah. I get it, Mr. Dury."

"Please, Gwen, call me Ian."

Standing before a tall pillar adorned with exquisite animal carvings, they watched as a purple-haired young lady struggled to attach a reflector to a stand on the uneven surface to redirect the natural light. In the awkward silence, Ian noted Gwen's bored and aloof posture translated to an utter lack of interest in the production. He was not stupid. The actress had lost out on several roles and signed the contract under duress, nothing more. And to make matters worse, she preferred women, which left the prospect of sleeping with his co-star a non-starter.

Watching the company makeup artist touch up her model-perfect features, he proffered a broad signature smile, "Ready, my dear?"

Nudging back her floppy hat, she waved her script as a fan, "I guess. It is 110 degrees. I should have asked for hazard pay."

Signaling Chet to get this shitshow rolling, Ian leaned close and whispered in Gwen's left ear, "The joke is on you, sweetheart. I am flat broke."

Hearing her genuine laugh, he felt the tension evaporate into the dry air.

Chet checked the camera and called for quiet, "Okay, Mr. Dury. We are ready for you."

A veteran of on-camera appearances that made him a household name, Professor Ian Dury left his mark to check the scene through the viewfinder, "Thank you, Chet. You might want to redirect more light on that pillar."

"Uh, good point. Hey Teresa, grab another reflector from the bag."

Dury chuckled toward Gwen while retaking his place by her side, "They mean well."

"Uh-huh. How many days will we be out here?"

On the cusp of a cheeky reply, Ian bit his tongue as his young director yelled, "Ready on set," like the second coming of Orson Welles.

With the camera light blinking red, Ian adopted the authoritative yet accessible demeanor and Indiana Jones-style swagger that vaulted him from obscurity to a viral star and popular talk show guest. "As you can see by the deteriorated state of Gobekli Tepe, my esteemed colleagues have moved on from this important site. After years spent with their heads buried in the superheated sand, they still ignore the obvious: this place—and many others like it worldwide— were built by human civilizations with a superior grasp of technology well beyond our current understanding."

Chiming in for the first time, Gwen played her part to a tee, countering Ian's open, "Professor Dury, how can you be so sure that this pillar," she reached out and tapped the gritty surface, "was not the result of extraterrestrials?"

Eager to address the ET nonsense and progress to more important aspects of his extensive research, "You know what, Gwen? We don't have to guess." Nudging the pretty woman whose previous claim to fame was starring in a series of hammy Netflix romcoms, "Since we now have the official confirmation of aliens in our midst, someone should just ask them."

"Cut! Cut!" Chet scowled at his boom operator, "Shit, Loretta, watch that fucking thing. It dropped enough to cast a shadow right behind Gwen." After reshuffling the deck amid a chorus of groans, Chet plopped back into his canvas director's chair with a raised finger, "And ... action!"

* * *

After a long and tedious day-one shoot, the film crew staggered back to their hotel tired, grumpy, and covered in gritty sand.

Averse to wasting a second of valuable time, Ian blocked the corridor to the rooms, "Hang on, everybody, I know you are all tired, but let's meet down here in an hour to review tomorrow's schedule."

Taking the mean stares and muttered curses as an enthusiastic yes, Ian stepped aside, watching the young film students trundle past him to their triple occupancy rooms. "Good job today. It gets easier, I promise."

Trailing the rest of the group, Gwen stretched her long frame with a loud yawn and mumbled a halfhearted goodnight.

"See you in the morning, Ms. Stevens. Bright and early, 5:30 sharp."

Ian watched the tall woman head down the hallway, calling after her, "I meant what I said this morning, Gwen. The aliens know we have had previous civilizational incarnations for millennia. What about the Eye of the Sahara, otherwise known as the Richat Structure? We are heading there next."

Shaking her head, she waved back at her employer, "Yeah. Yeah. Too tired to care right now."

Alone in the darkened lobby, Ian turned to find the desk clerk staring at him with a slackened jaw, "Close your mouth, son. The flies will get out."

* * *

In total darkness, Ian Dury bolted upright in his bed, shivering, and drenched in sweat.

A disembodied voice shattered the stillness, *"Return to Gobekli Tepe."*

Unable to shake off his addled, dreamlike state, Ian answered, "Right now?"

* * *

Pulling into the empty visitor lot, Ian checked the time, "It is 2:30 in the morning. I must be out of my mind."

Recalling the weird hunch that he was brought here for an ulterior purpose; the archeologist grabbed a flashlight and retraced the path into the UNESCO World Heritage site. Taking careful steps, cognizant of snakes, scorpions, and spiders lurking in the dark, he stumbled to the tall pillar where they managed to record the two-minute opening interview in only twelve mind-numbing takes—the extent of the progress on day one.

Sleep-deprived and confused, Ian cast his light over the recognizable animal shapes carved out of the heavy blocks, noting their deep cast shadows playing across the sandblasted surfaces under the narrow beam of his high-powered torch.

Trying to shake off whatever had hijacked his consciousness, Ian yelled into the starry night, "I'm here. What do you want from me?"

A ball of light brightened from the ether as if in response, illuminating Ian's trembling stance in a brilliant glow before transforming into a tall, naked male human carrying a matte-gray one-foot cube.

"This is a test. This is not a test. But it is a test. You are so close. You are far away."

Swallowing back palpable trepidation mixing with sheer confusion, Ian struggled to form a sentence, "Test? What kind of test?"

"It is a soul cage. The one who can use it will use it as a last hope before the Overlords. The Overlords."

"Who are you? Who are the Overlords?"

"It is more important who you are: the messenger. Nothing more. Nothing less. The Overlords will return to reclaim what was. Your existence is in great peril. They will spare no one. The cube. The soul cage. It must pass from your hands to the one who can use it."

With its task completed, the glowing man disappeared into thin air, leaving the cube resting on the dirt at Dury's boots. Squatting down for a closer look, he studied it for a long time before smoothing his hands along its sides, "Good Christ, this thing is freezing cold."

After a backbreaking struggle, he shoved the heavy cube in the back of the Land Rover under a tarp, overwhelmed with a heady sense of purpose well beyond the fucking documentary, and floored it back to the hotel.

Grabbing his go-bag with the first glimmer of morning coloring the eastern horizon in purple, pink, and orange hues, Ian climbed behind the wheel and paused to consider the paranormal turn of events, "Let's see … I'm supposed to deliver the cube to the one who can use it. Who the fuck is that? First, I need to get it out of Turkey …."

* * *

His mind scrambled; in a dead panic, Professor Ian Dury took the main highway out of Turkey toward Damascus, Syria. Thankful he remembered his passport; he experienced nothing beyond the usual third-degree from dead-eyed guards at the border crossings—no one asked to inspect the back of the Land Rover.

Making the last few miles of the eight-hour-plus drive on fumes, the bone-tired scientist pulled the ticking, overheated Land Rover to a stop at an upscale downtown hotel.

Secreting the heavy cube to his room on a luggage cart in a fit of paranoia, Ian bolted the door, closed the drapes, and hefted the cube atop the room's work desk. Scrutinizing the perplexing mystery for the first time, Ian shook his weary head in wonderment, "What are you?"

Smelling his own BO, Ian pulled his gaze from the cube's magnetic presence to shower in the tight hotel bathroom. Letting the lukewarm water run over his head, the scientist replayed the previous 18 hours, "Oh shit. I better call Chet."

Leaving short messages for Chet and Gwen, Ian surmised they packed up and headed back to the airport. "Just as well. I will apologize later."

Taking a long pull from a pricey hotel room vodka, Ian recalled meeting an intelligence operative at a dinner party in Tel Aviv. The tall, angular Nigerian woman tried to recruit him to work for Mossad, an offer he declined, preferring to keep his head where it belonged, atop his shoulders. Swiping through the contacts on his smart device, he found the mystery woman's number under M for Mossad. Smart. "Maybe she can help."

After three rings, a resonant voice broke his paranoid reverie.

"Damascus House of Sweets. How may I help you?"

Taken aback by the gruff tone, Ian garbled a reply, "Oh, I think I have the wrong number …."

"Do you know your password?"

"My what?"

"Come on, Ian, you must know the password."

"Who is this? How do you know my name?"

"Wait there. I will come to you."

* * *

A loud knock broke Ian's spellbound gape, staring at the cube from the foot of the bed. Heart racing, he moved to the door. "Yes?"

"Open the fucking door, Ian."

Unlatching the bolt, Ian opened the door, revealing an imposing Black man sporting a thick GI Joe beard. Brushing past Ian, the man moved across the crushed pile carpet to the cube, "Who knows you are here?"

"I left a message for Chet. What's his last name? Uh, back at the hotel in Gobekli Tepe. I abandoned the whole crew …."

"The Turkish authorities have your team in custody."

"What? As in arrested. What the hell for?"

The bearded man approached the window and peered through the drapes, "How did you know to come here?"

Ian moved between the man and the cube, producing his phone from a pocket, "I am not sure how much I should tell you. I want to call Chet for myself."

The human beard snatched Ian's phone, removed the SIM card, and smashed it under the butt of his .45. "No more calls. You are in danger. I will take you and the cube to Aisha Ayad."

Awash with relief, Ian nodded, "That was her name! Aisha Ayad, She works for Mossad."

The man studied the cube, dismissing Ian's naive recollection, "She works for us now."

"Is that so? Can you tell me what is happening? Why is my crew locked up in a Turkish fucking jail."

"For a professor, you are one clueless SOB. Your midnight rendezvous was captured by our satellites—and at least five other governments competing to gain the upper hand in the new techno race brought about after Disclosure Day. Turkish intelligence arrested them at the behest of the CIA."

"CIA? I'm just an archeologist trying to make a documentary.

What does any of this have to do with the Americans?"

The man grabbed Ian's repacked duffel and dumped the contents on the bed. Pushing Ian aside in the tight space, "What was your plan? Sell the cube to the highest bidder?" Zipping the cube inside the emptied bag, he dropped it back onto the luggage cart with a thud.

Sensing the man's impatience, Ian rushed to grab a clean trash bag from the bathroom receptacle and fill it with his scatted stuff, "I did not have a plan. I carried out the glowing man's wishes."

"Yes. We know, Ian. Let's go. Ms. Ayad is waiting."

"At least tell me where we are going."

"Cairo International Airport. That is the closest PTB facility."

"PTB? As in The Powers That Be? Are they for real?"

"If they weren't, you would not have made it this far."

* * *

The swept-wing passenger jet taxied to a stop in front of the imposing PTB hangar in a cordoned-off section of the sprawling Cairo airport, allowing Professor Ian Dury to deplane, followed by GI Joe with his kung-fu grip on the duffel holding the cube.

Gawking at the PTB's extensive collection of vintage aircraft, from biplanes to supersonic jets filling the hangar's echoing interior, Ian followed the agent through a door and down a fluorescent corridor to a bank of elevators.

"How far down are we going?"

"You ask a lot of questions."

Ian smiled at his reflection in the metal elevator door, "I'm a scientist; that's my job. I never got your name?"

"You can call me Agent Flynn."

The duo's wordless traverse of a long underground passage ends at an expansive, darkened conference room, motion-activated lighting illuminating a long mahogany table surrounded by plush chairs.

"Have a seat, Mr. Dury."

GI Joe, aka Agent Flynn, dropped the heavy bag on the table, removed the cube, and left.

Alone in the well-appointed boardroom, Ian pulled out the nearest chair, sunk into the plush leather seat, and fell into a deep slumber.

* * *

Snoring like a freight train, Ian awakened from a dreamless sleep, hearing hushed voices. Forcing open bloodshot eyes, his bleary gaze focused on a host of faces in the SRO room, returning his stare.

With a loud yawn, he stretched stiff muscles in the cushy seat, "I must have fallen asleep."

At the far end of the conference table, a dapper Asian man with a long gray ponytail closed a binder and folded his hands, "You have had a long day, Mr. Dury."

Ian squinted past the cube still centered atop the long table, "Hey, I know you. You are the robot pioneer, Mitsuo Kobayashi. Can someone here tell me what in the hell is going on?"

Kobayashi paused, making eye contact with Aisha Ayad midway down the left side, sipping coffee from a paper cup. "While it is not your concern, we are searching for a relic." Gesturing at the cube centerpiece, "However, it is almost certainly shaped like an oval disk consisting of an element similar to gold, but not gold. I am sorry for the confusion."

Ian looked around at the poker-faced assemblage, "Can I keep the cube?"

Another woman in a white lab coat looks up from her stack of notes, "Most certainly not. While it is not the object of our search, its appearance from the Light Specters is undoubtedly significant."

A cascade of memories flooded Ian's brain, "Can you all spring my friends from the Turkish prison?"

Aisha Ayad, the PTB's Intelligence Chief, put down her cup and leaned in, "It is good to see you again, Mr. Dury. Your people were released on their own recognizance. It was obvious from the start that you acted alone."

Gathering what was left of his tattered wits, Professor Ian Dury leaned back, "I think the angels were on my side."

Mitsuo Kobayashi smiled, "Not angels, Professor, Light Specters."

Dury pinched the bridge of his nose to ward off a headache under the canned lights, "Uh, look, the being told me something … the cube is more than a fucking cube. What did he call it? Ah, yes, a soul cage."

Noticing Kobayashi's renewed interest, Dury's thick brow rises, "He said the one who could use it will use it."

Professor Richard King | PTB HQ
12:01 p.m. | August 14, 2034

Disappointed that the cube was another false lead in decades of fruitless searches for the elusive golden ellipse, Mitsuo Kobayashi shipped the mysterious object to his chief scientist, Professor Richard King, at the underground PTB HQ in Scotland.

"The archeologist referred to the cube as a soul cage."

Listening to his long-time colleague and intellectual rival's voice through a speaker in his gleaming new white underground laboratory, Richard studied the dull-gray cube atop a high lab bench under a bright color-corrected light, "Soul cage. That's a new one. Mitsuo, can you send the satellite recording of the archeologist receiving the cube from the glowing naked fellow?"

"Done, Richard. Anything else?"

Richard King tugged his white lab coat collar and reached for his tuna fish sandwich from a plate beside the one-foot non-reflective cube. Taking a large bite, he laughed with his mouth full of bread and fish, "You forgot to send the instruction manual."

"Okay, Richard, nice talking to you. Gotta run."

Richard King ended the call, leaning back against the counter with a shrug and another bite off his sandwich as a new voice resonated in his head.

"Richard."

Choking down the dry bite, Richard straightened and stared at an almost imperceptible presence near the cube.

"Who are you?"

"The cube is for you, Richard. When the time is right, you will enter its protection."

"How will I know what to do? The cube has no controls … or instructions of any kind … I need more information."

"You will know how and when, Richard, only when the time comes. It is how it is done."

"Why did you give it to the archeologist in Turkey? Why not just deliver it here?"

"You have it now and will use it. It is how it is done."

* * *

Gifted from the Light Specters—for reasons beyond the PTB's collected comprehension—the cubed enigma remained a mystery, like many other secrets held close by the PTB.

Only Professor Richard King knew he was the cube's purpose. He told no one except Mitsuo Kobayashi how it chose him to transcend its incalculable mechanisms and upload his essence at an indeterminate future moment.

Assured he would know when the time was right, Richard shipped the cube to Lost Cactus, his former research laboratory hidden in the southwestern American hinterlands, where it became the latest addition to an expansive warehouse filled to its rafters with crated mystery objects, secured from overzealous governments seeking an upper hand in a ruthless race for hyper-advanced alien tech and gadgets.

Professor Ian Dury | Fred Beaman Podcast
10:30 a.m. | March 13, 2035

Expressing effusive apologies and promises to double their pay, Professor Ian Dury convinced Chet to round up the film school students and continue the documentary shoot, minus Gwen, who had lawyered up and threatened legal action, refusing to take his call.

Over the next six months, Ian's film crew traveled the world, making a solid case that technologically advanced human civilizations flourished for millennia before disappearing. The crumbling structures these mysterious multitudes had left behind were used, reused, reimagined, rebuilt, and buried under newer stone monuments to societies, gods, and potentates coming and going through the ages, making it impossible to determine the original builder.

Satisfied with the final cut of his latest documentary, Professor Ian Dury made the usual rounds to promote the film. Visiting the uber-popular podcaster Fred Beaman's Los Angeles studio, he took the infamous hot seat behind a mike and donned the proffered headphones.

Sporting a fire engine red velour jogging suit over his wide girth, Fred Beaman, the pugilist turned podcaster, lit a signature Cuban, and blew a thick cloud of smoke into the air, "Welcome back, famed archeologist Professor Ian Dury."

"Thanks for having me back, Fred."

Fred crushed back in his custom ergonomic chair and proffered a wily grin tinged with sarcasm, "So, another documentary on past human civilizations from the world-famous archeologist." Clenching the stogey in his porcelain veneers, he poured a double shot of his private label bourbon with a throaty chuckle, "I hear the flick bombed."

Ian leaned forward, his eyes watering from the cigar smoke,

"It will break even, like my other projects, but whether it makes a dime is irrelevant. The documentary counters the myopic fascination with ET, which obfuscates a much more important story about past civilizations—human or otherwise—that no one but me and a handful of colleagues has the balls to investigate."

Fred cut Ian off at the pass with an incredulous guffaw, "Come on, Ian. Read the room, my man! The fucking ET disclosure the world has been waiting for finally happened last year. People can't get enough of that alien shit."

Puffing his cigar, Fred's dark eyes narrow on his guest's implacable expression, "Okay, I'll bite. We do have two hours to kill. Let's talk about your film. Enlighten my millions of followers on why it is more crucial to human fucking civilization than confirmation of other sentient life forms in the universe."

Accustomed to Fred Beaman's dismissive mockery from past visits to the famous podcaster's studio, Ian poured two fingers of Fred's over-priced hooch into a mug and took a long pull, waiting for the smoke to clear. "Okay, Fred, here it goes: In the not-too-distant future, a previous civilization far more advanced than us—that left without a trace—will return. And Fred, you and I, your millions of listeners—and billions more around the globe—are not invited to their homecoming party."

I saw the angel in the marble and carved until I set him free.

Michelangelo

Chapter Two:

The Subject

2028

From curious to uneasy to panic-stricken terror, the human race capped a geyser of sentient AI milliseconds before a countdown clock to oblivion struck absolute zero. With the AI apocalypse averted, for now, an international convention established a strict set of enforceable laws and placed guardrails between burgeoning tech companies flush with venture capital and bot-crazy businesses and consumers that turned into a silicon rush for AI-controlled automatons pervading every walk of life.

Multitudes of mechanized wonders filled every job, from housekeeping and short-order cooks to fire jumpers and law enforcement. Humans meanwhile sat back and watched, wide-eyed and slack-jawed, as their monthly government stipend chinked through digital bank accounts.

Brigades of bipedal robot soldiers marching under fleets of combat-ready drones transformed the military-industrial complex into a scene out of science fiction—an unsettling image for those old enough to remember the old Schwarzenegger popcorn flicks.

Meanwhile, a new breed of expensive and sophisticated replicants intermingled with humans on an intimate and personal level. The flawless male and female bots' dexterous multitasking abilities, instantaneous recall, and ambiguous moral and sexual ethics supplant blue and white-collar workforces that never returned to a previous normal harkening back to 2019.

The rise of the robot spawned an overcrowded and cutthroat industrial revolution unseen since the early days of the horseless carriage.

Like the automobile, a thousand wonky Edsels trundle off assembly lines from South Korea to South Africa for every impeccably coifed Ferrari-level replicant strolling out of a high-tech factory.

Within a few short years, cheap and glitchy robots flooded the marketplace, resulting in tangled masses of discarded anatomical parts filling garbage dumps and landfills. Unsettling to some, a majority became desensitized to heads, arms, and legs jutting out of recycling bins or lying discarded along a street. The issue bifurcated human discourse along moral and ethical lines: *"Their human appearance means they deserve to be treated with respect."* countered by *"They are not human. Fuck off!"*

Aside from six-figure price tags, polls of affluent consumers investing in the Ferrari-level bots viewed their acquisitions as no different than buying a toaster. The morality of owning a replicant scored way down on a list beneath practical and prurient priorities. Case closed.

The advent of robotics pioneer Mitsuo Kobayashi's A-Class and B-Class replicants crafted at the exquisite, heavily-guarded Kobayashi Replicant Plant in Milan, Italy, changed that paradigm. Fusing 3D-printed organs made from lab-engineered organic tissues embedded with alien nanotechnology, the A and B bots proved indistinguishable from their human counterparts, putting a decisive end to the robot morality debate. Still, a finger pressed to a handsome man's temple, or the elegant nape of a woman's neck opened their heads like a tackle box, revealing quantum brain cores suspended in a gelatinous goo. Definitely not human, but a rare necessity conducted only in clean room environments by skilled Kobayashi technicians.

Despite his celebrity status at the apex of robotics by 2038, reaping an enormous fortune for himself and his employer, The Powers That Be—the 88-year-old Japanese-American from humble beginnings was far from satisfied.

Mitsuo Kobayashi | Kobayashi Replicant Factory, Milan
10:38 p.m. | October 22, 2038

Alpha, a multi-armed, one-eyed robot, entered Kobayashi's inner sanctum at the ultra-secure Milan plant. Approaching the boss's massive teak desk, he paused, not wanting to disturb the master.

Engrossed in a thick volume, his empty tea service shoved to the edge of his blotter, Kobayashi rocked back in his plush chair before a gigantic window overlooking the factory floor where a line of half-finished B's dangle from a conveyor belt like human effigies. Marking his page, he closed the book and folded his hands atop the desk, "Yes, Alpha?"

"He is awake."

Mitsuo stood and stretched with a loud yawn, "Excellent! I will be right there."

Entering a high-tech recovery room, Kobayashi strode to an elevated platform dominating the center of the hexagonal space where a quintessential six-foot male lay naked and prone atop a dull gray slab.

From the shadows, Alpha watched his boss caress the chiseled creation, "Hello, Andrew. Welcome to Milan."

Kobayashi's paradigm-smashing C-Class model sat upright and swung his legs off the slab like Michelangelo's Statue of David animating to life. Casting deep-set gray eyes upon his manhood, Andrew's face reddened, "It is a bit chilly in here. Perhaps some clothes and a spot of tea would do the trick."

Kobayashi laughed, giddy and astounded by his creation. Superhuman in every conceivable fashion with an erection to match.

Mitsuo Kobayashi | PTB HQ
01:30 p.m. | October 31, 2038

Following a chopper ride from Edinburgh Airport to the PTB's hidden helipad and a Disneyesque tram ride through a two-mile tunnel ending at the underground receiving station hundreds of feet beneath the Scottish Lowlands countryside, Mitsuo Kobayashi led Andrew into the PTB complex.

Edgar Lopez, an eager young PTB intern with a tablet under his arm, trotted over to greet the new arrivals, "Happy Halloween, Mr. Kobayashi. You are early. The meeting does not start for another hour. Why don't you and your handsome friend follow me."

Wearing a professorial sport coat with patches at the elbows over a dress shirt and tie, Kobayashi ushered Andrew to follow the young man along a well-lit corridor to a posh lounge.

After the long commute from Milan, Kobayashi sidled to a well-stocked bar in the lounge to fix a drink, "Can I get you anything, Andrew?"

"No thanks, Mr. Kobayashi. I don't drink."

"Of course not. I was not testing you. It's just that people drink to relax. You can relax, you know. Loosen up."

Andrew proffered a warm smile on his perfect face and ran a hand through his short, auburn hair. Plopping down in a cushy leather chair, he crossed a long leg, showing off his signature western boots, "How's this. Casual enough?"

Kobayashi can't help but laugh, "Oh, man. You are going to blow their socks off, Andrew."

The young man returned, offering Andrew a flirty smile, "They are ready."

Mitsuo downed a club soda and gestured toward the smitten young fellow, "Shall we?"

Andrew stood, removing a tiny speck of lint from his black mock turtleneck, "We shall."

Artemus Pennywell | PTB HQ
03:15 p.m. | October 31, 2038

Acknowledging the familiar faces talking and reconnecting around the crowded conference table, The Powers That Be CEO Artemus Pennywell had to laugh. In all his years running the clandestine organization, he could count on one hand the number of times all twelve disciples, aka the PTB Council, appeared together in the same damn room.

Indeed, this was a special occasion.

Upon receiving Tech Guru Mitsuo Kobayashi's message announcing his latest achievement, Pennywell suggested in no uncertain terms that if his other eleven disciples liked their jobs, they would plant physical asses in actual goddamn seats. No excuses. No bullshit virtual attendance, either. If one could not attend in the flesh, then fuck off.

With everyone present and accounted for, The Council used the opportunity to vet a continuous stream of issues, discuss geopolitical concerns, and address sundry action items.

As the roundtable ebbed clockwise from person to person, Mitsuo bided his time, listening as Aldo Santamaria, the PTB COO on his right, droned on about how a work stoppage in Peru affected relief supply shipments following a catastrophic typhoon in the Philippines.

* * *

Meanwhile, Andrew paced in an anteroom, ignoring the intern's roving-eyed stare from behind a desk.

Feigning aloofness, the kid broke the silence, "Are you nervous? I was on my first day here."

Andrew turned toward the young man, "How old are you?"

Edgar proffered a pouty smile, "I'm 23." With his narrow chin propped on intertwined manicured fingers, "I suppose you prefer older men?"

Perplexed by the human male's unabashed attention, Andrew's brow furrowed, "No, I don't prefer older men. I mean, no." Shaking his head, realizing he stumbled face-first into the pretzel logic, he chuckled, "You got me, kid."

The virtual screen buzzed, and Pennywell's raspy voice reverberated through a tinny speaker, *"Edgar, put your dick back in your pants and send in our guest."*

"Yes, sir, Mr. Pennywell."

Andrew raised a thick brown eyebrow, "Does Mr. Pennywell always talk to you like that?"

Edgar sighs, "I am used to it. He means well."

Andrew rapped the desktop, "Things are about to change around here."

Edgar exhaled a dreamy sigh, watching Andrew enter the conference room and shut the door behind him.

That is one handsome man.

* * *

Mitsuo stood and moved to welcome his creation, "Ah, Andrew! Please come in and introduce yourself to Mr. Pennywell and

The Council."

With a casual shrug, the überhuman moved around the table without a hint of self-awareness, disarming Pennywell while captivating The Council with an easy smile on his handsome face and off-the-charts perfect physique.

"As Mr. Kobayashi mentioned, my name is Andrew. I am the first C-Class replicant."

Noting the stunned expressions around the table with his perfect smile, Andrew assumed a casual pose, "I am happy to be among my peers and look forward to answering any questions."

Having seen more than his share of stellar-looking male and female robots as head of PTB Global Logistics, Viraj Patel realized he was an unimpressed minority of one. Leaning forward, cradling a PTB mug, he ignored the robot and addressed Kobayashi, "What was wrong with the A and B models? We can't keep them in stock."

Kobayashi began to answer, but Andrew held up a hand, "Allow me, Mitsuo."

The brand-new C-Class model removed a pocketknife from a tight jean pocket and sliced his right hand just above the wrist. As blood flowed from the wound, dripping on the expensive flooring, Andrew pulled his black sleeve up to the elbow and extended his arm, exposing a tiny square chip in the palm of his right hand. "This neural processor equates to all the world's knowledge in the palm of my hand. And as you can see from my bleeding cut, I am organic in every conceivable fashion."

Angling his arm, he pulls back muscle tissue, exposing part of a bone, "See here, that is my trapezium if I am not mistaken, uh, right here."

Intrigued by Andrew's demonstration, Artemus Pennywell snickered at The Council's squeamish reaction. "Andrew, does it hurt?"

"Yes, and thank you for asking, Mr. Pennywell."

Andrew smiled at his new boss, "I have feelings." Trying to stem the bleeding, he chuckled, "And as you can all see, if cut, I bleed." Noting the transfixed gazes, Andrew concluded, "I can tell from Mitsuo's raised body temperature that he is aghast at my ad hoc demo. My idea. I am sentient, after all. I think on the fly. I am prone to judgmental lapses. And, as you can see, I am blessed with an all-too-human knack for wrong-headed actions."

Doubling down on Patel's underwhelmed reaction to another upgraded robot, Aldo Santamaria pierced Andrew's blithe candor, "If you make mistakes, what good are you? I want a robot that is better than us. Hell, I could hire my goofball nephew if I needed another fuck-up."

Santamaria's callous remark triggered Pennywell's well-known animosity toward asinine COO, "Lighten up, Aldo."

"It is quite alright, Mr. Pennywell. Mr. Santamaria's objections are logical. So then, what is the point? Why replicate a human? Well. I am not human. If a mistake is made, it is corrected in a millisecond. And, unlike humans, mistakes are not repeated. I also possess superhuman strength and agility. I could go on, but I am veering into braggadocio, which is not my intent."

From the far end of the table, Olivia Paquet, the VP of Communications, raises her hand.

"Yes, Olivia."

Tittering, "You know my name." like a smitten schoolgirl, Olivia catches Pennywell's unamused stare and straightens in her swiveling seat, "Um, are there more of you?"

Viraj jumped in, "Yeah. Do you have a sister?"

Stepping forward to get the introduction back on track, Kobayashi patted his handsome creation's strong shoulder, "My turn to answer a few questions, Andrew. Why don't you tend to your self-inflicted wound."

Applying pressure to the cut, Andrew nodded, "Good idea."

Before the conference room doors finished closing and Andrew's firm ass had left the meeting, The Council peppered Kobayashi with questions: "Why were we not in the loop? What does he mean by sentient? If he is a replicant, what happened to the original? Does he have a sister? What is the cost? How much can we make per unit?"

"Enough!" Artemus Pennywell turned to his technology guru, "Mitsuo, you have outdone yourself, my friend. Kudos to you and your team. Let's manufacture as many Andrews as possible as soon as possible. Is that clear?"

"Yes, sir, Mr. Pennywell. By the way, Andrew is my gift for your unwavering support. He will act as your personal valet."

Artemus leaned back in his chair, "A personal valet? I could use some help. I accept. Thank you, Mitsuo."

Kobayashi wiped genuine tears from his eyes, "It has not always been easy, and you have kept the naysayers and lawyers, no offense, John, off my back."

John Murdock, the PTB General Counsel, leaned forward, "None taken, Mitsuo, but let's not get ahead of our skis. We need to patent the shit out of your man before letting his siblings out into the world."

Andrew reentered the conference room with his forearm wrapped tight in a ridiculous thick bandage from elbow to fingertips courtesy of Edgar.

Mitsuo checked the dressing, "It will do for now. Let's avoid those kinds of demonstrations for the foreseeable future."

"Agreed."

The Council's newest member, PTB UN Ambassador Anastasia Gabreski, a former Polish supermodel, can't resist a final question, "Andrew. Can you experience true love?"

"Yes, Ms. Gabreski." Andrew smiles, noting a blush response in her flawless cheeks, "I can do everything a human can do. Only better."

Viraj Patel | Lost Cactus
03:36 p.m. | January 1, 2039

Former Liverpool FC footballer Viraj Patel swipes away a virtual screen broadcast of the Peach Bowl, "Yeah. Yeah. I know. Brought to you by fucking Wendy's." Tired, bored, and hungry, he mutters, "I could go for a burger just about now." Rising off a splintery crate, he peers into the dark recesses of a cavernous warehouse on a mothballed research base in the southwestern American hinterlands. "Hey, Professor? How much longer? I'd like to get back to civilization."

A squeaky-wheeled cart precedes Professor Mitsuo Kobayashi's smiling mug emerging from the shadows.

"I take it by your shit-eating grin you found what you are looking for?"

Kobayashi dabs his sweaty forehead with a hankie, "Yes, Mr. Patel. And thanks again for providing the keys to the kingdom."

"Don't thank me, Kobayashi-san. I used my authority as the PTB Logistics Chief to access this dump, but everyone knows Lost Cactus belongs to Professor Richard King. He built it."

Kobayashi nods, "Yes. And if I thought poor old Richard could keep a secret, I'd tell him I am commandeering his laboratory myself."

"Should I even know what you are doing here? If it is hazardous, I can provide security. The odd lost hiker will wander through here on occasion."

The 89-year-old Asian robotics genius tosses back a couple heart pills, "My team can handle anything that arises. You are free to go, Viraj."

The old warehouse's massive double doors grinding open on thick metal tracks directs the men toward a fissure of bright mid-afternoon desert sunshine and a silhouetted pair of Kobayashi's robot assistants, Abe and Bee.

An involuntary shudder goes down Viraj's spine; the AI

humanoids give him the creeps. Always have. Always will.

Eyes aglow in the darkened interior, the poker-faced duo approach, unfazed by the incredible trove of historical treasures, artifacts, and enigmas stored in crates stacked high up into the rafters.

Ignoring Viraj, Abe addresses Kobayashi in a monotone, "Professor, the team restored power to the laboratory."

Feeling like a proverbial third wheel while Kobayashi huddles with his assistants, Viraj inspects the object of the peculiar old man's warehouse breach: a dull-gray one-foot cube. Touching its smooth surface, he pulls back on reflex, "This thing is freezing cold. What does it do, Professor?"

Mitsuo wheels and grabs Patel's sleeve, "Please don't touch it!"

Viraj recoils from Kobayashi's grip, "Jesus, calm the fuck down, Professor. Good luck, I guess, with whatever you plan to do here."

Realizing his overreaction appears suspicious, Kobayashi proffers a conciliatory smile, "Yes, as I already said, thank you, Viraj. You can go. If it is not too much trouble, please inform Andrew that I am on schedule."

"Will do, Professor." Patel proceeds toward a light shaft piercing the shadowed entrance before pausing in his tracks. A confused look furrowing the brow on his handsome face, he pivots onto the renowned robotics pioneer and his mechanical flunkies, "Uh, Professor, I don't mean to pry, but why would Pennywell's new valet robot need to know what you are doing here?"

Thinking fast, Kobayashi shrugs, "Andrew is more than Pennywell's valet. He is assuming an active role in the PTB's daily operations."

"Huh. Is the COO okay with that?"

"You would need to ask Mr. Santamaria. I really do not know."

Viraj nods, "Okay. Well, Aldo is the world's biggest prick, so fuck that. Good luck." Turning toward the light, Viraj exits the warehouse, hops into his Jeep, and leaves.

Kobayashi listens to Patel's Jeep fading into the distance before addressing his assistants, "Help me move this cube to the laboratory building. It weighs a ton. We have work to do."

Mitsuo Kobayashi | Lost Cactus
04:18 p.m. | January 1, 2039

Following his cart-pushing assistants from the warehouse along a cracked and potholed main street into the heart of the erstwhile top-secret base, Kobayashi notes a sad resemblance to a ghost town. Strolling past derelict buildings with broken windows and peeling paint, the threesome navigates around thick stands of weeds and cacti past a rusted signpost piled high with tumbleweeds. Reaching the five-story research and laboratory building, the trio crunches over broken glass, infiltrating the busted main doors.

Kobayashi's heart sinks at the dilapidated state of the architectural wonder's once-spectacular front facade and expansive lobby. With contempt for the lowercase powers that be that allowed the storied edifice to fall into a shocking state of disrepair well beyond his worst fears, he kicks aside a carton, rousing a furry creature from its home. "What a fitting welcoming committee." Watching the animal scurry over exquisite Italian marble flooring inlaid with a scratched and tarnished bronze PTB emblem, he mutters, "Man, if these walls could talk."

The attentive robots pivot onto their leader with matching looks of confusion.

"Why would a wall talk?"

Clearing his dry throat, Kobayashi smiles, "Yes. Quite so." reminding himself of the hyper-intelligent creations' inability to parse idioms, allusions, or metaphors.

Feeling nostalgic in the halcyon space he had not visited in over a decade, Kobayashi's gaze lands on the enigmatic cube atop the cart, "Carry on to the lab with the cube. I will be there in a short while."

Alone in the echoing open-air lobby, a gust rearranges trash as Kobayashi moves through upturned dust-covered furniture to the edge of an amorphous-shaped depression that was once an idyllic koi pond winding through the interior space. Recalling the spot where he fed an impressive koi collection on visits during the lab's heyday evokes fond memories of the voracious fish.

Moving to the high reception counter stretching on a shallow curve along the two-story back wall, he reminisces on famous and infamous characters signing NDAs and picking up visitor badges. Standing on his toes, Mitsuo reaches over the counter and grabs a box of lanyards imprinted with an iconic Saguaro cactus logo. Clipping on a blank badge, he pulls it over his head, "There. Now I am official."

The Japanese-American whose parents and older siblings spent World War Two incarcerated in a Missoula, Montana internment camp looks up behind the counter, scrutinizing a wall of PTB luminaries immortalized in sun-faded oil portraits hanging askew and coated in dust. A genuine smile creases Kobayashi's distinguished face, noting Richard King's image in full mad scientist regalia from his celebrated salad years working hand-in-glove with a brilliant team from Earth and beyond. "It staggers the imagination considering the scientific achievements that never left this building." Unable to overlook the gallery's unkempt, borderline disrespectful neglect, he mutters, "I can't stand it."

A self-anointed neat freak, Kobayashi removes his jacket and rolls his sleeves before hopping over the counter with a narrow-focused sense of purpose. Finding a soft rag and a short ladder, he moves left to right along the gallery wall, cleaning and straightening each portrait—cathartic, mind-clearing, busy work before embarking on the final chapter of his career.

Stepping back to admire the even-spaced portraits' intelligent stares, Kobayashi washes down heart pills with a water bottle before crumpling the empty and pitching it into the dried-out koi pond.

Unable to ignore the elephant in the room, Kobayashi ponders the one-dimensional gathering's diverse mix of stern faces and knowing grins. At the precipice of monumental achievement, his mental dam breaks, "Fuck your shortsighted stares! You are all dead, but I am still here!"

Cognizant of the risks implicit in the cube's use, Kobayashi stammers, "The Light Specters chose Richard. That time may never come. No. I don't know how the fucking cube works. Neither does he."

Kobayashi wipes tears from his eyes with a dismissive headshake, "It is my destiny to see this through."

Receiving nothing but blank return stares from the peanut gallery, the robotics genius modulates his tone to just below insane, "The Powers That Be have a stated mission to foster humanity to an Omega Point."

"Throughout my life, I refused to play by the rules. I saw possibilities and broke through barriers constructed by lesser men and women, fearful of the unknown, preferring to tether humankind's future by a leash. Don't tell me now at the threshold of the quintessential human being that using the cube crosses a line. Damn your timid souls straight to Hell! I will create new life within these walls. Not some bag of chips, wires, and goo, but honest-to-God thinking, feeling sentient immortals ready to conquer the universe."

Kicking aside a cardboard box, he puts a proverbial cherry atop his histrionic monologue, "That, motherfuckers, is the PTB's mission."

Reenergized and ready for whatever comes his way, Kobayashi marches down the dark corridor, following deep cart tracks through the trash and stinky animal dung. "When this is over, I will burn this dump to the ground and put it out of its misery."

Ignoring a bank of elevators, the spry 89-year-old bursts through a stairwell access door and trots down metal steps spiraling multiple levels underground. At rock bottom, he notes a dry coolness and light seeping through heavy double doors. "We do have power; off to a good start."

Professor Mitsuo Kobayashi steps onto a grated metal platform overlooking the echoing black site lab, unable to resist a wicked grin. Even when the base was a functioning research facility, the above-ground infrastructure was a facade. The science happened in this underground complex with its expansive laboratory approximating the size of two basketball courts— all carved out of solid bedrock.

Locating Abe and Bee amongst the beehive of activity, securing the cube on a reinforced lab bench amidst their humorless cohorts unboxing computers and peripheral hardware, and placing the quantum technology in concentric circles around the cube, he nods, impressed by the creative layout, "Excellent."

On the cusp of lending a hand with the unboxing, like Christmas morning, his gaze turns to the twin cylindrical glass enclosures languishing dirty and empty on the far side of the lab. The 24-foot tanks are where the magic will happen once everything is in place and a suitable subject has been recruited. Easier said than done.

A thunderous crackle and a sea of sparks break Mitsuo from his reverie. Rushing down the steps, he vaults to an assistant's scorched remains with her face and hands melted to the core, "Ah, I'm sorry, Dee."

Fee steps up from behind and extinguishes flames lapping from an opened compartment where the unlucky girl electrocuted herself on a tangled mess of live wires.

Realizing it is day one and he is already down from ten to nine assistants, plus Alpha, Kobayashi gathers the emotionless group, "Let Dee's passing be a lesson to you all. The computers may be new, but the laboratory is old and dangerous. We must practice sound safety procedures at all times."

Bee mutters, "Haste makes waste."

Mitsuo turns to the B-Class robot, "That is excellent, Bee. I want that slogan plastered on the wall. Got it?"

The nine white-coated workers nod as one, like puppets on a string.

* * *

After a long first day at Lost Cactus, Kobayashi leaves his indefatigable workforce with another safety precaution. Heading down a corridor to Richard's old underground quarters, he pauses at an unlocked door and peeks inside a voluminous storage space he plans to retrofit into an operating room where he will add the finishing touches to his quintessential creations.

Entering Richard's old digs, Kobayashi greets Alpha, his metallic multi-armed valet bot, with a shiver. Checking the spartan apartment, he locates an old-school analog thermostat and turns up the heat, "How quaint."

Checking out the cozy space, Kobayashi finds his bag unpacked and a tea service piping hot and ready to drink at Richard King's old writing desk. Rolling out the antique cushioned desk chair, he pours a cup before settling in the creaky seat and unfurling engineering drawings of the dual replication tanks.

Taking a long sip of the perfect brew, he envisions the filled and fully functioning tanks glowing in brilliant shades of blue. The human subject floats in a blissful narcotic-induced bubbly haze inside the left cylinder. On the right, her form replicates atom-by-atom, molecule-by-molecule, cell-by-cell, as the cube projects the subject's captured essence onto the replicant like a Las Vegas magic trick.

Groaning at the Herculean effort to reach that point, Mitsuo places the half-empty cup on the saucer.

Humming to a tune playing inside his mind, he pulls a thin binder from a bag and flips through a diverse hodgepodge of black-and-white surveillance images of potential subjects. Tsk-tsking the paucity of prospects, his eyes land on an attractive young woman photographed exiting an Aria Hotel employee entrance in a secondhand coat over a short waitress uniform.

"She will do." Flipping the photo, he skims a clipped bio. Tapping his earphone, he recites his 12-digit PTB code. "Yes. I need a comprehensive history of Subject 39. Her name? Uh, let's see. Sarah."

Listening to the other end of the line, Mitsuo finishes his cup, "It does not list her last name. Just Sarah."

Sarah | Aria Hotel, Las Vegas
11:34 p.m. | January 9, 2041 — Two Years Later

After a two-hour keynote address on the future of AI and robotics, Mitsuo Kobayashi exits stage right to a thunderous standing ovation into the path of an obnoxious RoboCon showrunner.

"Mr. Kobayashi-san, can we entice you into sticking around for an encore Q and A session?"

Looking beyond the obnoxious woman geared up with tablets and headphones, the 91-year-old eyeballs the nearest backstage exit, "No questions. I doubled my one-hour time slot. Now, Miss ... whatever your name is, I have other business in the hotel. Good luck with the rest of the convention and divide my stipend between the charities listed in my contract. Reach out to my counsel, Vita Carrera, if you need more. Good night."

Tuning out the woman's anxiety-riddled entreaties to stick around, Mitsuo exits the backstage door and hastens down a plush carpeted hallway through the mazelike Aria Hotel with the raucous applause from the overflow crowd of fawning, over-educated robotics nerds ringing in his ears.

After his unexplained two-year absence, Mitsuo Kobayashi's image above the 2041 RoboCon masthead spurred an international frenzy for tickets from scientists, engineers, programmers, corporate wonks, and a slavish press. Most had surmised the 90-something-year-old had passed away. His abrupt reemergence as the annual event's keynote speaker breathed new life into the stale and uninspired gathering of robotics companies, exhibiting the usual assortment of shiny-skinned mannequin-like bots.

Mitsuo's heart races, making a beeline down a long hallway toward a bank of elevators, intent on locating a particular cocktail waitress and perhaps enjoying a nerve-soothing drink.

Jumping through the parting elevator doors, he wheels and presses the close button too late as a youthful trio of Asian acolytes invades the claustrophobic space.

"Kobayashi-san, it was a great honor to hear your presentation."

Proffering a serious-faced nod at the well-intentioned kids, Kobayashi snatches their programs and autographs the covers featuring a Getty stock image of his smiling mug from at least twenty years prior.

Souvenirs in hand, the boys bid farewell to their taciturn hero in unison, melding into the casino level's human stew of players, gamblers, dealers, honeymooners, partiers, hucksters, freaks, and working girls inside the disorienting funhouse of overstimulation and excess.

After his successful escape, Kobayashi scans the expansive casino level, "How will I ever locate her?"

Nursing a dry throat after two hours of non-stop bullshitting gobsmacked losers, Mitsuo navigates to a casino bar that matches the one from his intel brief, slides onto a comfortable stool, and orders a Manhattan. The hypnotic harmony of one-armed digital bandits punctuated by climactic mechanical crescendos and drunken overtures resonates through the twinkling expanse conceived to sever frontal lobes from reality. Casting a surreptitious glance at fellow patrons mingling around the well-stocked bar elicits a prescient chuckle.

Mission accomplished.

Sipping his Manhattan, Mitsuo feels a soothing warmth

permeate his throat and chest, ruminating on the penultimate chapter of his much-ballyhooed career as the world's preeminent robotics expert. Unable to recall his off-the-cuff speech, he smooths a hand over his thin gray hair pulled into a signature ponytail.

It does not matter what I said to that crowd. If the subject is amenable as predicted, my life's work will soon be rendered obsolete, and they will have to refocus their intellects elsewhere. So much the better.

Raising his glass, he nods a subtle toast toward the casino's mirrored ceiling tiles concealing hi-def recording devices watching every move he makes.

Thank God in Heaven for Artemus Pennywell's unquestioning support and apparent balls of steel. A lesser leader would have crumbled under the pressure of greenlighting my plan to replicate a human essence, but not Artemus.

Signaling for a refill, he concludes his reverie with an oft-repeated mantra.

After all, it is the PTB's mission to foster this sorry lot to an Omega Point.

Trying to remain inconspicuous in the crowded, noisy casino, Mitsuo Kobayashi watches a cocktail waitress plop her tray atop the bar two stools over with an exhausted huff and yell a drink order over the din.

"Harry, I need two Rum Rickeys, a Gin Fizz, and five more Corpse Revivers."

Taking advantage of the short respite while waiting for the overtaxed bartender to fill the order, she leans against the bar rail and offers an apologetic smile toward the mature Asian man whose ears must be ringing from her loud voice, "I know, right? What the hell is in a Corpse Reviver?"

Thunderstruck upon meeting the effervescent young woman in the flesh after two years of surveillance images and deep dives into her personal history, Mitsuo tries to act casual and avoid getting lost in her blueberry gaze, "It sounds interesting."

Scrutinizing Kobayashi's sheepish countenance under the strobing, sparkling lights, she scrunches her pert nose, "Hey, you are that robot guy, right?"

Fidgeting with his tumbler, Kobayashi shrugs, feigning surprise, "That robot guy? What gave me away?"

The grumbling bartender places dripping glasses on the bar before leaving to finish the order. Arranging the drinks on her tray, she laughs, "Your picture is all over the hotel. Because of you, this place is wall-to-wall with robot nerds who never had a girlfriend or, by their beverage choices, ever ordered a man's drink. They came to Vegas to hear your speech, right?"

Raising his hands in mock surrender, he smiles, "You got me."

Hefting the tray, she turns toward Kobayashi, "By the way, if one more of your groupies tries to grab my ass, I'll punch his lights out."

Kobayashi watches her disappear into the crowded casino. "I bet you will."

After ten anticipatory minutes, Kobayashi watches her return with a dripping empty tray, "You're back. Any pinchers I need to take care of for you?"

Returning a playful wink, she calls out another drink order, "Harry, I need ten more Corpse Revivers." Turning to Kobayashi, she exhales a weary sigh, "At 30 bucks a pop, that must be a damn good drink. My feet are killing me. Mind if I sit for a minute?"

Taking a sip from his third Manhattan, Kobayashi makes an overt effort to read the name pinned to her revealing work attire, "Please, Sarah. I am honored. As for the nerd fest, this crowd does not get out much. Vegas is a bit like sensory overload."

Shrugging off her earlier comment, she refills her tray, "Ah. No big deal. They are harmless and not bad tippers, either."

"I am sure they are excellent tippers. Do you like working here?"

"It's a job. What can I say?" Ducking Harry's mean stare to

quit lollygagging, Sarah pushes aside the drinks and leans closer to the old man, "On this whole AI thing, I mean, we are up to our eyeballs in robots and tech, but what is the next chapter … I read it on one of your posters plastered all over the hotel."

Kobayashi begins to answer, but Sarah cuts him off, "It better not be another upgraded sex bot. Vegas has not been the same since those soulless, dead-eyed girls took over the strip clubs. My friend, Amira Fisher, lost her gig at the Palomino—she is a single mom with two kids. I don't know what she is going to do."

Taking a sip while considering his words, the legendary robotics pioneer sets the heavy glass atop the bar and turns to face the graceful young woman, "I am sorry about your friend. I must admit that my handiwork through the years contributed to her firing."

Harry looms over the conversation, flinging a wet towel over his broad shoulder, annoyed at his employee, "Sir, would you care for another Manhattan?"

"No, just the check."

The gruff barman turns on Sarah with a mean scowl, "If your skinny ass is not out on the floor in the next 30 seconds, you are fired."

Sarah huffs and stands in her high heels, "Okay, Harry. Do you have to be a jerk all of the time?" With a perfect smile on her bright young face, she grabs the heavy tray, blowing an unruly dark bang off her forehead, "It was nice meeting you. Good luck with your robots, I guess."

Mitsuo extends a hand, stopping Sarah from leaving, "Please wait." Turning to the bartender, "If you don't mind, I want to finish my conversation with your employee."

Harry pauses before breaking into a jeering guffaw, "Give it up, mister. She is not sleeping with an old man like you." Still chortling at his mean joke, he stomps toward a nerdy group, sidling up like kids in a candy store for another round of Corpse Revivers.

Wincing at Harry's crudeness, Kobayashi lays his cards on the table, "Sarah, you asked about the next chapter. That was an inarticulate title for my keynote speech conjured by ignorant people with no idea what the future will look like." Meeting her soulful gaze, he continues, "Are you familiar with the term transhumanism?"

Sarah pushes the tray back atop the bar, lowering her pert backside onto the stool, "I have a friend that transitioned. He is miserable."

"No. I am afraid we are not talking about the same thing. By the way, the sexbot revolution you alluded to is symptomatic of humanity's much larger crisis. Far sooner than my industry writ large will admit, the AI bots evolve to a point where mere mortals like you and me are nothing more than a nuisance, like insects."

Kobayashi reaches into a pocket and produces a gold coin, "Sarah, please give this to your friend, Amira. It is embedded with a link to an international bank account. She can make a withdrawal, but mind you, it is only good for one use."

Sarah accepts the heavy coin and turns it in her elegant fingers, "How much should she withdraw?"

Kobayashi shrugs and smiles, "That depends. How much does she need?"

Watching her cute, perplexed reaction, he points at a code stamped beneath the letters PTB. "All she has to do is take it to her bank and instruct them to access the account associated with that set of numbers."

Wiping a tear, Sarah smiles, "I don't know what to say."

"You don't have to say anything. And better yet, you no longer have to work here. I would like you to work for me."

Feeling a sudden unease, having been propositioned hundreds of times in her young life, "Okay. I get it. You do want to have sex. I'll do it for my friend, but ...."

Kobayashi's eyes widen in alarm, "No. Good heavens, no! You are quite beautiful, but I assure you, that is not my intent. No. I would like to retain your services regarding the final chapter you asked about."

Unsure where the conversation with the mysterious man is heading, Sarah catches Harry's stern glance, "Well, gee, thanks for the coin. I will tell Amira not to take out too much. But you don't want anything to do with me. I have a degree in screwing up my life. I can't help you."

Mitsuo Kobayashi pauses to regroup at the brink of success or failure, "Please allow me to start over. You are right; I have not been entirely honest. I do need your body. With your kind permission, I want to replicate you from head to toe to the smallest details, like the birthmark on your left ankle."

Sarah's face widens into a brilliant smile, looking past Mitsuo around the casino floor, "Okay. Now I get it. This is one of those hidden camera things. Harry put you up to this, didn't he?" Wheeling toward her manager with a deep-throated laugh, she yells, "It's not gonna work, Harry; I am on to your stupid practical joke!"

Knee-deep in mixology, Harry cocks his head toward his batshit crazy waitress, mouthing, *"What the Hell are you talking about?"*

Watching two years of meticulous planning and vetting of the young woman named Sarah devolve into a ham-fisted comedy sketch mere minutes after finally meeting her in person, Kobayashi masks utter frustration. "This is not a joke, Sarah."

Shaken by the affable man's 180 to dead seriousness, Sarah's smile fades, "I'm flattered, but ...."

"Let's start over. My name is Professor Mitsuo Kobayashi. I am seeking a subject to participate in my paradigm-smashing replication process."

"Yeah, I heard you the first time ...."

"Please, Sarah, allow me to finish a sentence. You must understand what I am about to tell you."

"Go ahead; I'm listening."

"Thank you, Sarah. Here it goes. I also require your singular essence. Some may refer to it as your soul."

Sarah's blue eyes widen in surprise, "You want my soul? I hate to break it to you, but I am not a saint. Ask Harry. He'll be the first to tell you … So, you want to make robots that resemble me and share my soul? That sounds like a bad robot sci-fi movie."

Mitsuo winces, "Not robots, Sarah. You asked about the next chapter." Thinking fast, he ad-libs from his well-plotted script, "My new process opens the door to a new and better world. Are you familiar with the Book of Genesis?"

Rolling her eyes, she turns toward her drink tray, "Look, I should get back to work."

Mitsuo grabs her by the arm, "Think of yourself as Eve."

Recoiling from his loose grip, "Does that make you Adam?"

"No. I would be more in the lead role."

Taking the hint, the perceptive, intelligent, and street-smart brunette pierces his words with a skeptical smirk, "You think you are God? Mister, you have a lot of nerve."

Embarrassed that he blew the negotiation with a stupid, off-script reference, he attempts to minimize the damage, "That was out of line. I am sorry if I offended you."

Sensing the man's sincerity, Sarah softens, "I was not offended. I am not a religious person. As a matter of fact, I don't know what I believe." Reconsidering the strange offer, "Why me? I am nothing special."

Realizing she is giving him a second bite at the apple, he leans forward, "Oh, but you are special in so many ways."

Finishing his drink, he recites her history, "Sarah Carter. Orphaned at six months. Pushed through the foster home system and spit out at the tender age of 16 onto the mean streets of Las Vegas. You did not take the easy route. You have a degree in chemistry from UNLV. You are well-read. Well-traveled. And yes, quite beautiful."

"Wow. You know I have never been to Africa. I always wanted

to go on a safari."

Acknowledging the non-sequitur as a specific part of the negotiation, Kobayashi smiles, "My dear Sarah, after your time with us, you can go on as many African safaris as you like. The world will be your oyster, so to speak."

Her big blue eyes narrow, "But first, I need to help you with this last chapter business, right?"

Kobayashi nods, "I am afraid that is non-negotiable."

Twirling a finger through her shoulder-length dark hair, "And you know so much about me … how?"

"Sarah, we have been watching you for quite a while."

"We? Who do you work for?"

Finally, with the upper hand, he shoots the young woman a coy grin, "I cannot answer that unless you accept my offer."

After a considerable pause, she smiles, "Sure. Why not?" Turning toward the bartender, she shouts, "Harry!"

"Yeah, what?"

"Fuck you! I quit."

Masking abject relief, Mitsuo Kobayashi raises his empty glass, "You have made an excellent decision, Sarah. Your life is about to change in ways beyond your imagination."

Sarah | Las Vegas

05:02 a.m. | January 12, 2041

Hefting a backpack stuffed with everything she could not leave behind; Sarah exits the second-floor apartment she called home the past three years. Leaving the key in the lock, she jogs down concrete steps to the curb, her breaths showing in the chilly desert air as the hint of a new dawn glows above the basin.

Replaying the previous evening's farewell with Amira at a Mirage

Hotel coffee bistro and her effusive reaction to the strange gold coin, a black panel van pulls into the lot and blinks its headlights.

Sarah points at herself, feeling like a second fiddle actor in a cornball spy drama. "Yeah. I'm here freezing my butt off. Let's go before I change my mind."

The vehicle rolls ten feet from her position. With the backpack strap digging into her shoulder, the 24-year-old brunette tries to see the driver through the dark-tinted window as a side panel flies open and a figure in dark camo gear vaults out, pulls a black hood over her head and lifts her into the van.

"Hey! What the Hell is this?"

Dropped on a squeaky seat, the backpack is pulled from her grasp before rough hands pull her wrists together in a zip tie as a deep voice resonates in her ear: "This is for your protection. Please cooperate."

* * *

What did I get myself into?

Quelling panic under the black hood, Sarah jostles on the bumpy seat, disoriented and carsick as the van navigates Vegas morning traffic. Losing track of time, the wheels clack-clack across a gated threshold onto a gravelly macadam and brake to a squeaky stop.

The door slides open, allowing daylight, jet fumes, and the din of aircraft engines to permeate her sweaty hood.

"Are we at McCarron?"

The gruff voice responds, "Wait here."

Lamenting the latest, and probably last, in a long list of bad decisions, Sarah hears a woman's voice above the airport noise.

Why did you put a fucking hood over her head?

Pulled from the van by her strong-handed captor, Sarah snickers at his blustery reply, "It's standard ops, Miss Carrera."

"Take it off. Now. And free the girl's hands."

"Yes, ma'am."

Sarah turns toward the hulking man and extends her bound wrists, "You are busted."

"Hold still, little lady."

As the hood lifts off her messy dark hair, Sarah rubs sore wrists, squinting toward a green figure as her vision adjusts to the brightness.

"Hello, Sarah. My name is …."

A behemoth passenger jet passes overhead close enough to touch before screeching wheels down on the nearby runway, drowning out the woman's words. Sarah watches the plane disappear through heat mirages on the flat expanse toward Harry Reid's main terminal complex, noting the familiar outline of the Vegas Strip in the distance, a world away.

The 30-ish woman with flaming red hair in a lime-green fine-tailored business suit and heels gestures toward the door to a weather-beaten outbuilding, "It gets loud out here. Let's go inside, Sarah. You can decompress after that horrifying commute for which you have my sincere apology."

"Where is Mr. Kobayashi?"

"All in good time, my dear. My name is Vita Carrera. I was assigned to fly out here, assist with your paperwork, and get your John Hancock in a few hundred places before you are an official member."

"Member of what?"

Vita laughs, "Wow. Did Kobayashi tell you anything?"

Following Ms. Carrera into the building, Sarah steps into a spartan breakroom with a table and chairs fronting a kitchen counter along the back with the coffee and pastries. Feeling inferior next to the ravishing, confident redhead, pulling off the lime green suit with effortless grace, Sarah stammers, "I'd like a coffee and croissant."

"Sure. Let's eat. I put on a fresh pot of coffee and picked up a box of croissants from the Paris Hotel on the way over here."

Eating while swiping through endless screens, Vita describes each page as Sarah scribbles her name and initials where indicated. "Like buying a condo."

A stack of contracts, four cups of coffee, and three croissants later, Vita closes the screen as a helicopter settles on the tarmac outside, "That is your ride."

"Are you going too?"

"Nope. I hop on a jet back across the pond."

"Oh. Wow. You have quite a life."

Vita crumples her paper cup and pitches it into a can. "Yeah, lucky me. I almost forgot. Do you have a living will?"

"What? No. Do I need one?"

"Well, I would say we will all need one someday. However, in your case, I will need to set something up on the fly. Do you have any assets worth mentioning?"

Reaching for her backpack, Sarah pulls out a thin wooden case and slides it across the table. "Just this."

"Can I open it?"

"Sure."

Vita unlatches and opens the lid, "Oh my. I have not seen these in ages. Does this collection have any value?"

Sarah wipes a tear, "It does to me. It's my mother's pressed penny collection. I want you to hold onto it. If anything happens to me, I need you to send it to my friend, Amira. She is the contact in my paperwork. It will let her know that I am gone, and she no longer needs to worry about me."

* * *

Sarah climbs into the black helicopter's futuristic passenger cabin, donning the headgear by her plush seat before waving toward Vita Carrera as the airship rises above the Nevada desert.

Wishing she had not eaten a third croissant while signing her life away under the watchful eyes of the lovely and persuasive Ms. Carrera, Sarah sips expensive bottled water, watching the barren topography pass beneath her blue-eyed gaze.

The Stetson-wearing pilot's even-toned voice breaks her reverie, "We are thirty minutes out, Ms. Sarah."

Approaching the mysterious final destination, Sarah double-takes through the front windscreen, her eyes widening in terror, "Hey! Look out! You are heading right for that mountain!"

"Hang on, little lady, this is the tricky part."

Digging white-knuckled fingertips into the armrests, Sarah shuts her eyes and braces for impact as an audible hum pervades the pitch-black cabin for terrifying heartbeats before an ethereal yellow-orange late-day glimmer forces her eyes back open onto a sprawling base situated in the middle of nowhere.

"Sorry about that. First flughts to Lost Cactus can be frightening for the uninitiated, but the unusual flight restrictions keep the base off the grid."

Sarah nods out the window as the chopper lands on a pad outside a main gate, "Uh huh. What is this place?"

Vaulting from the idling helicopter, the pilot opens the passenger cabin with an extended hand, "Watch your step, Ms. Sarah, and keep your head down."

Thankful the croissants remained in her churning stomach, Sarah peers beyond the smiling Cowboy toward Mitsuo Kobayashi, watching from a Jeep as she slides out of the cabin. Moving jelly-legged beyond the turning blades across the desert hardpan, she turns to the pilot, "Thanks for the ride, uh, Mr. ...."

With a broad smile, he lets go of her hand with a gentle pat, "Call me Cowboy, little lady, and welcome to the club."

Wearing aviators under a long-billed cap with his gray ponytail dangling over an olive windbreaker, Kobayashi rolls the Jeep forward but stays behind the wheel, "Thank you, Duane. That will be all."

The man called Cowboy shakes his head and spits into the dirt, "Been a while since I made the trip. The place is really falling to pieces."

Mitsuo fakes a carefree laugh at the pilot's impertinence, "Now, Duane, let's not be negative in front of our guest."

Placing Sarah's pack in the Jeep, Cowboy pauses to breathe in the warm desert air, "It feels different out here. Could never quite put my finger on it. Just different." With a wink toward his passenger, he smiles, "You take care, little lady."

Watching the pilot amble back toward the black helicopter, Sarah climbs into the Jeep's shotgun seat, noting a palpable tension between the two men as the chopper takes off.

The newest member of the 300-year-old clandestine organization shrugs toward Kobayashi, "Well, I'm here."

Kobayashi gives the Jeep a little gas before putting it in gear, "Yes, you are. I trust your trip was comfortable."

"Yes and no … Oh, wait. Ms. Carrera asked me to give you this." Reaching into her new PTB embroidered vest pocket, Sarah produces a nickel-sized hard drive pressed between her thin fingers.

Accepting the drive, Kobayashi laughs, "Ah. Your paperwork, so to speak. They do like their Ts crossed and Is dotted. Out here, we tend to ignore unnecessary and time-consuming formalities."

* * *

Waving good riddance to the plain-spoken chopper pilot, Kobayashi drives Sarah through the main gate, "Welcome to Lost Cactus."

"Uh, thanks. From the air, this place looked impressive. At ground level," Sarah scratches her cheek, "not so much."

Mitsuo steers around a clump of cacti, "Nevertheless, young lady, humor me while I give you the nickel tour."

Four-wheeling across cracks and potholes in former paved roads interconnecting in and around the base, Sarah notes the broken windows, rusted metal, peeling paint, and crumbled stucco facades, "It does have a certain rustic charm."

"I like to think so." Braking at a four-way intersection, Mitsuo shifts into neutral, "Straight ahead is the airstrip and control tower.

Beyond that is an impressive aeronautical graveyard. Let's see. The road to the left leads back toward the warehouse and the main gate. It's getting late. You must be exhausted. We'll skip the rest of the tour and head deeper into the base toward a row of guest cottages beyond the motor pool."

Sarah turns in her bumpy seat, "Motor pool? Is there a pool? I like to skinny-dip in the moonlight." Proffering a cheeky grin, "Is that in my file?"

Kobayashi notes the girl's inhibitions subsiding on schedule, "Is that so? There is a pool, but I don't believe it contains water. Mostly sand and the occasional rattlesnake. Hmm ... Now that you mention it, I recall a raucous pool party in the late eighties. Those were the days. From the looks of it now, that is hard to imagine, but this base hummed with activity back then." After a teeth-rattling jolt over a deep pothole, he adds, "These days, not so much. However, aside from a cement pond, the base has everything we need."

Kobayashi parks along the guest cottage row in front of Number 27-0, a tiny abode with warm light filtering through an unbroken front window with its slatted shade drawn halfway. A multi-armed mechanized bot clamors out the door and ambles to the Jeep's passenger side to snatch Sarah's backpack. Awaiting further instruction, its lone bulbous eyeball scrutinizes Sarah with a red checkered apron tied around its long metallic neck.

Sarah beams at the friendly bot, somewhat familiar with similar service model bots working housekeeping and janitorial duties at hotels up and down the Strip, "I like your apron. What is your name?"

Mitsuo interrupts, "This is Alpha. He is your personal valet and at your beck and call, 24/7. By the way, I understand he did a bang-up job preparing the cottage for your arrival."

Sarah turns and smiles, "Thank you, Alpha."

Speaking in monotonal English, "You are welcome, Sarah. I am glad to meet you at last. Kobayashi-san has big plans ...."

"Okay, Alpha. My. My. We are talkative today." Mitsuo starts the Jeep, "Sarah has had a long journey. Why don't you help her get settled."

Standing outside the Jeep, Sarah turns to Kobayashi, "So, what do I do now?"

Sliding the Jeep into first gear, Mitsuo turns to face his young subject, "I don't know. Take a hot shower. Read a book. Have a stiff drink." With an odd laugh, he adds, "But get some rest. We start our days early around here."

After an invigorating hot shower, Sarah swipes condensation from a full-length mirror attached to the bathroom door, contemplating her new life. Snapping from her reverie, she steps into a lightweight blue jumpsuit and sits on the edge of her firm twin bed to lace up a new pair of boots. "Man, a perfect fit." Donning a PTB cap over wet, shoulder-length brunette hair, she heads for the door.

After a slight pause, she yells back inside, "Alpha, I am going to poke around outside before it gets dark."

* * *

Hearing the human's voice, Alpha replies, "I will have chicken and rice dinner ready in an hour." Stirring a pot of rice on a gas cooktop, the bot monitors security feeds as the subject heads down the long row of abandoned cottages toward the motor pool.

* * *

With a gnarled branch-turned walking stick in hand, Sarah strides along the overgrown street, like walking through a dystopian video game. Rewinding the life-changing events from her initial meeting with Kobayashi to now, she smiles, proud of herself for taking the initiative and changing course. Contemplating what the old man has planned for her, the 24-year-old orphan chuckles to herself, "It can't be any worse than slinging watered-down drinks to a bunch of grabby losers."

Picking up a pretty rock, she tucks it in a pocket beneath an owl's watchful gaze. Staring back at the raptor perched on the corner of a two-story structure, she marvels at the speed and elegance of the natural world's reclamation of civilization once the human element is removed from the equation.

Stopping in her tracks, she shakes her head, "Whoa. That felt like someone else's thoughts in my head. Weird."

Reaching the end of her block, Sarah leans on her stick, admiring the colorful sunset.

A loud growl from her flat stomach recalls the promise of a chicken and rice dinner—a staple from her college years. Retracing her steps, she wonders what else they know about her life.

Sarah | Lost Cactus

04:30 a.m. | January 13, 2041

Resting her naked bottom on a cold wooden chair at a game table across from a shadowy adversary, Sarah lifts a wet, fluted fountain glass and considers her next move. Sucking a thick chocolate milkshake through the straw, her blue eyes light up, and her lips curl into a sly smile. Setting the glass back atop a sopping coaster pilfered from a cheeky retro Vegas bar called The Cosmic Lounge, she moves her black queen into position. "Aha! Check-mate."

Beep. Beep. Beep. …

"Wake up, Sarah. It is Day One. Lots to do." Alpha's grating alarm and monotonal voice rouse Sarah from her vivid dream.

Turning toward pitch-blackness out the bedroom window, Sarah shoves her head under the pillow, "It's still dark outside." Hearing tiny mechanical noises from the patient robot, she throws the sheet back and rolls out of bed, naked as a jaybird.

"Alpha, I dreamt I was playing naked chess and drinking a milkshake."

Alpha's eye narrows, "You *are* naked."

"But I never played chess in my life."

Standing on her toes and stretching her ballet dancer physique, Sarah reaches her long fingertips inches below a ceiling fan circulating cold morning air. Sensing a palpable unease in the chilly room, "Does my body make you uncomfortable?"

Alpha pauses, "No. It confirms your lack of inhibition."

"My lack of what?"

"Your workout attire and running shoes are on the chair beside the dresser. Mr. Kobayashi wants you to start each day with a three-mile run."

"Three miles … Jesus, I haven't run that far since high school. What is the old man thinking?"

"He needs you in shape by 05.01.2041."

"That is disturbingly specific."

Sarah | Lost Cactus
06:00 a.m. | April 01, 2041

By April Fool's Day, over two months after arriving at Lost Cactus, Sarah jogs the well-trod ridgeline trail, cognizant of every sheer drop, rocky trip hazard, razor-sharp cacti, and overhanging scrub oak branch along the way. Musing she could do this blindfolded; the fit young woman leads curious ground squirrels through rugged twists and turns before stopping to catch her breath at a favorite vantage point. Reveling in the sweeping vista, her gaze shifts eastward beyond the elevated view of the base, deep-blue eyes reflecting an iconic snapshot of the American West painted in purple and orange. A heady swoon causes her to balance against a rock, "Whoa. What was that?" Sucking water from the long tube attached to a hydration bladder cinched around her toned midsection, she winks at a cute squirrel before embarking on the final leg down a series of switchbacks and back to her cottage, where Alpha has a poached egg and toast waiting.

Busting through the front door, Sarah unhitches the bladder and hangs it on a chair back, "Alpha! I'm home!"

No reply.

Walking into the kitchen, she finds a note atop her empty plate:

Sarah, please report to the laboratory building ASAP. Important — do not eat or drink beforehand.

Thank you,
Mitsuo

* * *

Quelling nervous energy, Sarah complies with Kobayashi's instruction. Wearing a clean jumpsuit, she exits the cottage and walks down the street toward the weather-beaten five-story laboratory and research building. At a busted side entrance, Alpha appears from the shadowed interior.

"There you are. We are late. This way, please."

Alpha ushers the nervous woman inside a well-lit, antiseptic pre-op room at the end of a long corridor. "Please lie face-up atop the table with your head toward the wall."

Sarah tries to swallow, realizing her throat is bone dry. "Can I have a sip of water first?"

"I am sorry. Not now."

Fighting an impulse to run outside and not look back, Sarah complies. Staring at an old water stain in the acoustic ceiling tiles, she feels Alpha push her right sleeve up to her elbow.

"I am going to start an IV."

"What for?"

"I am following instructions. Professor Kobayashi will answer your questions."

The bot completes the intravenous line with acute dexterity and attaches the feeder line to an IV bag hung from a stand.

"What's in the bag?"

"A saline drip. The drugs will be administered through these ports."

"Did you say drugs?"

One of the taciturn human robots, Tweedle Dee or Dum, pushes a cart holding a one-foot gray metal cube into the pre-op.

"What is that?"

No answer.

The minutes tick past as the saline drip empties into her arm. Sitting up, Sarah tries to stretch her aching back, "I need to pee."

Tweedle-whatever turns and nods, "This way."

With her bladder emptied, Sarah shuffles barefoot back into the pre-op, pulling the IV stand with her, trying not to disturb the itchy catheter assembly taped below her rolled-up sleeve.

Scooching her bottom on the table, she lets her feet dangle and stares toward Alpha, "What's for dinner tonight?"

Alpha's answer is interrupted as Mitsuo Kobayashi bursts into the room, "Good morning, Sarah!"

"What is going on, Mr. Kobayashi?"

Ignoring Sarah's question, he moves to check the cube, clasping his hands with an anticipatory smile before addressing his subject's evident agitation, "This cube, my dear, is why you are here."

Producing a syringe from his pocket, he injects a light amber fluid into Sarah's injection port. "Not to worry. This will put you into a deep slumber, like Sleeping Beauty."

Sarah hears Alpha's "Goodbye, Sarah." as a pervasive drowsiness overwhelms her senses.

Fighting for clarity, Sarah's blue-eyed gaze fixates on the cube, now positioned next to her on the table.

It is cold.

It is heavy.

It glows in brilliant blue hues …

The gauzy vision of a beautiful woman's smiling face floods Sarah's hazy recollection with an unbounded joy before a handsome man in a tailored tuxedo ushers her backward, disappearing from view and revealing a comical circling menagerie dangling from strings overhead. Floating upward, lighter than air, Sarah passes through the fuzzy elephants, lions, tigers, and zebras before looking downward at the newborn version of herself atop a blanket ….

Mitsuo Kobayashi scans a virtual EEG, monitoring a comatose Sarah's brainwaves.

Alpha moves forward, "How long will she remain in a coma?"

Kobayashi's brow furrows, "I don't know. This has never been attempted before. If it works at all, transferring the Subject's essence to the cube could take minutes, hours, or days, even months, hence the need for her comatose state."

Alpha caresses the sleeping woman's hand with a tactile appendage, "I will stay with her."

Mitsuo smiles at the loyal robot, "Yes. I know."

Sarah | Lost Cactus
07:00 a.m. | April 12, 2041 – 11 days later

Bolting upright on her twin bed, Sarah reaches for a water bottle and gulps it down.

"Alpha! Alpha!"

The cheery bot enters from another room, "You are awake! I will alert Mr. Kobayashi."

"How did I get back here? What time is it? I feel like sleeping fucking beauty."

Without a hint of irony, Alpha replies, "It is Tuesday, April 12. You were in a drug-induced coma for ten days. We pulled you out last night and brought you back here. I will get your breakfast started."

Wearing cozy light blue pajamas covered in a floral peony pattern, Sarah stretches her long and stiff arms and emits an obnoxious yawn, "No. Wait. I am going for a run first. I need to get my blood flowing."

Wavering onto bare feet on the cold tile floor, she falters and collapses backward onto the creaky mattress.

Alpha extends an arm with a tinge of bemusement in his voice, pulling the sheet back over her languid form, "It is a cold, damp morning. Your muscle memory must return before resuming your exercise regimen.

Staring at the ceiling fan, Sarah mutters, "Did the cube work?"

"Mr. Kobayashi is very pleased."

Feeling like she was hit by a semi, Sarah's head begins to throb, "Well, as long as he is happy …."

Sarah | Lost Cactus

07:05 p.m. | April 30, 2041 — 18 days later

Alpha collects Sarah's plate and places it in the kitchen sink, "You cleaned your plate so well I can replace it in the cabinet."

"You know I love your chicken and rice."

Alpha settles on three legs across from Sarah, "Tomorrow is 05.01."

"Yes. I know. Time flies. Can we have this again tomorrow night after the procedure?"

"If you like."

Feeling a transformative grace with a lingering memory of her parents on prominent display in her mind's eye, Sarah exits the front door for her nightly meeting with the wise old Mr. Owl.

Sarah | Lost Cactus

04:21 a.m. | May 1, 2041

Half asleep, Sarah trudges along in Alpha's shadow toward the laboratory and research building, shivering under an oversized trench coat in a bespoke skin-tight mesh bodysuit spiked with dozens of metal leads.

Alpha's eyeball swivels onto Sarah, "I am sorry the coat is not warmer."

"That's okay. I could have used another hour of shut-eye, though." Stumbling over the graveled pavement in a pair of untied hikers, Sarah dabs her runny nose with a tissue, "But that was not to be."

Goosebumps rise on her smooth, bare skin through the mesh costume, approaching the hulking five-story building juxtaposed against the cloudless early-morning sky. Entering the main lobby, something skitters through a crack as the frigid air and portrait gallery's dead-eye stares send shivers down her spine.

Alpha ushers the chilled human around the counter and down a long corridor, illuminating the path forward. Pushing into an echoing stairwell, they clank down metal steps to rock bottom through the heavy double doors into a bright thrumming expanse, a hundred feet below the crumbled edifice on a shuttered research base mothballed over a decade earlier.

Scanning the underground laboratory, teeming with activity,

Sarah conjures images of nervous astronauts touring an erstwhile mission control as Kobayashi's aloof assistants move from station to station, fine-tuning a concentric maze of quantum mechanics-driven instrumentation.

With an audible gasp, her sleepy gaze fixates on the mysterious cube atop a high lab bench at the epicenter of activity, pulsing in rhythmic blue tones.

"The cube is glowing. Am I in there looking back at myself?"

A circumspect Alpha turns to his beautiful charge, "We shall see."

Sarah kicks off the heavy hikers and abandons Alpha on the platform, cutting a barefoot diagonal across the lab to examine the side-by-side 24-foot cylindrical glass tanks radiating a transformative cerulean hue.

Alpha catches up and joins her but does not speak.

Smoothing a finger down the glass, she turns to her robot confidante, "The last time I was down here, these tanks were empty."

Sarah cups a hand against the second tank's thick glass, scrutinizing an amorphous blob floating amid the shimmering bubbles.

A familiar voice resonates from above, "Ah! You are here!"

Leaving a handprint on the glass, Sarah pivots toward Professor Kobayashi, high atop metal scaffolding extending over both tanks.

"I will be right down." Descending creaky spiral stairs in his white lab coat, he beams at the beautiful young woman, "You look splendid."

Noting Sarah's unintentionally revealing form-fitting superhero costume, he nods his approval, "The tailor did an excellent job.

"Yeah, sure." Wiping her cold, wet nose, "Can I have some hot tea?"

Eager to change the subject, Kobayashi offers a conspiratorial smile, "I don't see the harm in that."

A minute later, Alpha returns with a paper cup of Chamomile

tea.

Before taking a sip, Sarah sniffs a thin wisp of steam from the cup, "What did you spike it with this time?"

The scientist smiles, "Benzodiazepine. Its effect should prove nothing more than a stiff drink before a long flight."

Noticing Mr. Kobayashi's avoidance of her breasts poking through the half-inch mesh, Sarah's lips curl into an easy grin, "Well, okay then." Downing the hot drink, she crushes the cup, flips it to Alpha, and springs up the spiral steps two at a time. "Let's get this shitshow started."

Alpha and Kobayashi look on as the athletic young woman smiles from the top in nothing flat.

Surveying the echoing laboratory from her elevated perch, a euphoric invincibility sweeps over Sarah. Spoofing her favorite Vegas show, she spreads her arms wide and belts a show tune from Evita at the top of her lungs, *Don't cry for me, Argentina! …*"

Alarmed, Alpha rushes to her side and snatches her arm, "Step away from the edge, Sarah. It is a long way down."

Pulling from the bot's grip, the uninhibited former cocktail waitress bounds to the six-foot circular cutout in the scaffolding above a glowing tank number one. Her tank. Propping her bare bottom on the curved ledge, she stretches her long legs down and dips her toes below the bubbling surface, "Brrr! It's a little chilly."

Huffing and panting back up the spiral stairs, "Careful, my dear!" Mitsuo glares at Alpha while swallowing two more heart pills, "The water is set to a precise temperature of 68 degrees. Your body will acclimate."

Kobayashi signals a waiting tech to activate a complex network of preloaded conveyors winding overhead in the rafters, waiting to drop orchestrated sequential steps onto the scaffold.

"Let's get started."

Sarah's dilated blue eyes watch as Alpha snatches a trapeze-style swing lowering from the shadowy heights before securing the basic apparatus over tank one's glowing aperture.

Kobayashi places a cold hand on Sarah's shoulder, "Okay, now I need you, my dear Sarah, to sit still on the crossbar so we can hook you up."

Cognizant of the subject's unpredictable state of mind, "Alpha, please assist Sarah so she does not fall into the tank."

Sarah pushes from Alpha's multi-armed assistance, eager to emulate an acrobatic Las Vegas circus act, "No. I got this." Extending a long arm, she grabs the line and swings out and around the trapeze seat like a pole dancer. Hoisting herself into a perpendicular position above the tank, her taut midsection pressed against the bar with an overhand grip, she emits a carefree laugh, "Now watch this." Keeping her back straight, she dips face down and performs a perfect forward roll before flipping up and around with her bottom landing on the crossbar. Blowing long bangs off her face, she settles on the seat and adjusts her mesh body suit, "That was fun. Would you like to see me do it again?"

"Bravo, Sarah. Most impressive. Once was quite enough, thanks." Turning to Alpha, his face darkens, "Let's move on."

Kobayashi unhitches a bundle from the first conveyor and slings the empty hook down the track. Placing it on the grated platform, he unpacks and separates the delicate wiring before passing braided sections to Alpha. The ambidextrous bot follows every subtle contour of Sarah's body, threading thin lines through the shimmering mesh before snapping connectors to the knobby metal leads burrowing under her skin with the dangling opposite ends lowering into the water.

Ignoring electrical shocks and painful pricking sensations all over her body, Sarah stares below her feet at masses of swaying lines snaking downward through alien-looking ribbed conduits into the second tank. Entranced, she follows the bundles untwisting into thousands of strands attaching to the strange floating mass inside tank two.

"What is that? Is it me?"

After six more bundles, Kobayashi checks a final clump of wires with a weary sigh, "Last set, Alpha. The leads should be somewhere on her left thigh."

Alpha parts a thick knot on Sarah's upper leg, exposing a row of metal cleats. Snapping the wiring in place, the robot lowers the loose ends into the tank and steps back, "The connection is complete."

Interconnected between the cube's quantum array on the front end and the untangling wires attaching in and around the floating clump inside tank number two on the back end, Sarah clears her throat, "You both realize I am bleeding, right?"

Hearing the subject's concern, Mitsuo deviates from his script and pulls up her vitals on a virtual display, "You are a human pin cushion. Your vitals are dead-center in your normal range. Some blood loss is unavoidable."

"*Dead center* may be a poor choice of words."

"Point taken. You are doing fine, Sarah."

Tapping a button on the screen triggers a progress bar animating from left to right, "I am dropping your customized psychoactive cocktail. It is the same one you tested weeks ago, experiencing no ill effects. It should prove pleasant; you may even experience another orgasm. That is normal."

Sarah closes her eyes onto a kaleidoscope of swirling colors as thousands of sensuous fingers massage her body, "Oh boy. That comes on fast."

With the drugs taking effect, Alpha tugs a shower cap over Sarah's messy shoulder-length black hair before placing a neoprene scuba hood over her head. Tucking stray black curls under the spongy material, the robot pulls it tight and secures the strap under her chin. "We should have shaved her head."

Kobayashi dismisses the comment, "Nonsense. Now, the diving helmet."

Refraining from contradicting the boss, Alpha lowers an alien tech diving helmet designed for Navy frogmen over Sarah's head and activates its thin bioplastic collar, creating a waterproof seal around her neck and shoulders.

Kobayashi inspects the unit's self-contained life support system, "The helmet is operational. Alpha, release her seat."

The thin bar supporting Sarah's pert bottom loosens from one end, allowing her wire-covered legs to drop through the hole in the platform, the tips of her toes swaying inches above the tall cylindrical tank's luminous water.

Registering discomfort from thin harnesses supporting her encumbered form, Sarah winks back at Alpha's peering eyeball through her fogged-up helmet as Kobayashi's staticky words ratchet in her ears.

"We are ready… proceed with …replication. … proud … the first … day forward …"

Unaware Sarah missed half of his little speech, Kobayashi dons Soviet-era goggles designed to protect fragile human eyeballs from fiery mushroom clouds, signaling a humanoid conveyor operator with its thumb on a simple joystick to lower the subject into her luminous tank.

* * *

A brilliant white light penetrates Sarah's essence, thrusting her into an otherworldly expanse of fragmenting helical structures toward a cosmic wormhole. Coursing through the hellish void with the gravitational force of a million suns, Sarah untethers from the spectacle as the diving helmet floats past her blueberry gaze, reflecting distant bodies harboring incomprehensible secrets.

Jolting to a stop before blurring past lights streaking into an infinity of colors, Sarah cries, witnessing energized specks shattering over and over again with impossible violence. The expanding panoply of electrons, protons, neutrons, quarks, bosons, leptons, and trillions of undiscovered wonders intrinsically bound together performs a dance choreographed by the hand of God. Outside and inside, above and below, hot and cold, happy and sad, good and evil, Sarah's soul projects through a shimmering cosmic cloud at the fulcrum of existence onto a new body snapping back in perfect symmetry well beyond the speed of light like a septillion-piece jigsaw puzzle zeptoseconds after the initial explosion.

* * *

Floating amid effervescing clouds of sparkling bubbles, black hair flows around an alabaster face as deep blue eyes snap open onto a new world. Mechanical hands pull a shivering naked woman from the second tank as Alpha injects a sedative into her arm and places an oxygen mask over her face before calling for a gurney to lower the replicant to the floor.

Pulling off his goggles, a breathless Kobayashi watches Alpha administering to the replicant that manifested in a miraculous blink of an eye. Casting his gaze toward the cube, idling at a low frequency, he marvels at the technology he exploited without understanding its function to reap the whirlwind of scientific immortality.

"Alpha, reset the second tank. Let's do it again."

* * *

Kobayashi pushes Sarah beyond the edge like a test pilot, watching her body and soul replicate fourteen additional times, cheating death to create new life. Keen to discover the cube's breaking point, no matter the consequences, he sinks into madness with the goggles strapped to his squinting eyes, cajoling his minions from the scaffold, "Again! Damn you! Reset the parameters!"

Alpha watches his master transmogrifying into a monster before his glowing eye, with a logical sadness conjuring in his neural processors. The Rubicon has been crossed. The natural laws separating mere mortals from the gods have been cast asunder.

The Subject, Sarah, is in grave danger.

Kobayashi's soulless team resets the cube's quantum replication process as an attendant wheeled the fifteenth sedated sister from the lab to the crowded underground storage facility converted into a sterilized pre-op where they await Professor Kobayashi's delicate augmentations.

Checking recorders documenting the historical event before adjusting the goggles on his sweaty face and raising his hands like a conductor to restart the enigmatic quantum process for round 16, a jerking movement from Sarah's tank causes Kobayashi to pause, noting her convulsions in the strobing water. "Come on, Sarah. One more time."

Ignoring spiking vitals and flashing overload warnings from the quantum computers, Kobayashi lowers his hands, commencing another energizing performance from the cube as a cataclysmic explosion ignites a superheated inferno across the doomed laboratory.

Sirens and alarms from the impotent fire protection and emergency life support systems clamor in Kobayashi's singed ears, hanging spread-eagle from scaffolding listing 30 degrees above tanks knocked off their mounts and teetering, ready to burst.

Bleeding from a burning head wound with a shard of metal protruding from his left calf and goggles melted to his head, the scientist pulls himself above the second tank as the glass shatters, swamping the blazing debris and dismembered robot limbs submerged under thousands of gallons of water.

Peeling the goggles from his burning eyeballs, he squints through toxic smoke mixing with plumes of noxious vapors rising from the superheated floodwaters, the stench fomenting a bitter taste in his mouth.

Scrambling to a higher perch, he sees the cube reflecting the fiery aftermath of his wanton hubris in its exact position amidst the priceless array of popping and sparking quantum tech melted to worthless junk.

Snapping to his senses with his ears still ringing from the blast, exacerbated by a chorus of whining alarms, he shifts toward the unbroken first tank, "Sarah!"

Hurrying through the twisted metal aperture still within reach of the leaning tank, he strains to reach his fingertips around a thick bundle of wires connected to the unconscious woman's arm. Pulling with all his strength, the old man tries to elevate her head above the slanted water level but realizes she is held down in a mangled knot. Scrambling off the scaffold, risking electrocution with every step, he hefts a heavy metal bar and swings it at the tank. Nothing. Unwilling to accept defeat, he spies Alpha through the strobing haze, assisting the sixteenth replicant, face-up in a foot of steaming water, "Alpha! I need you to break the first tank! Sarah is drowning!"

The obedient bot with a cracked eyeball and a missing limb turns from the replicant's vacant blue-eyed stare toward Sarah's tank. "Professor Kobayashi, take 16 to safety. I will rescue Sarah from her tank."

Cradling the replicant in his scorched arms, Kobayashi pushes through the exit and passes 16 to a waiting attendant.

Intent on assisting Alpha and recovering the cube, Kobayashi is stopped in his tracks by an invisible wall of poisonous fumes filling the vaulted laboratory and making reentry certain death. Realizing the underground facility's recycled airflow may already be compromised, he turns to the attendant, "Cut the laboratory's airflow and seal the exits."

The bot takes a second too long to process the command, causing an inconsolable Kobayashi to lash out at the automaton, "Do it now, or my creations will perish before they ever see the sun!"

Number 1 | Lost Cactus

08:30 a.m. | May 4, 2041

On the third morning after the incident, with his head bandaged and broken leg held together in a cast, Professor Mitsuo Kobayashi hobbles on crutches to a seat at a long table inside a mess hall on the erstwhile base. Shafts of morning sun filter through dirty windows, illuminating dust motes as he positions a notepad and pen in a neat arrangement and pours a cup of tea. Without turning to face Alpha's cracked eyeball, he asks, "Are the girls ready to meet their maker?"

"Yes. However, the replicants prefer the term sisters. Your plan was a success."

Kobayashi takes a sip, "But consider the price."

"Each sister possesses Sarah's headstrong, hyper-intelligent essence. That is a miracle."

"No, Alpha, it is not a miracle. It is a technology well beyond my understanding. I had no right to do what I did, and now Sarah is dead."

Alpha tries to assuage Kobayashi's guilt, "Sarah knew the risks."

Kobayashi turns on the bot, "No. She did not! I told her she would be on a fucking African safari by now!" Shaking his head, he pushes aside the pen and pad, "I opened Pandora's box onto a dangerous new phase in human evolution. One from which we cannot return."

Alpha processes the human's emotional state, "Regardless, Viraj Patel's cleaning crew arrived yesterday with instructions to sanitize the lab and dismantle what's left of the tanks. The cube and everything not destroyed in the fire will be stored in the warehouse. Rest assured; it will never happen again."

Kobayashi takes a deep breath, "Never say never, Alpha. Time catches up with all things."

The door swings open as a beautiful young woman with short brunette hair and an infectious smile on her ruby lips walks toward the table. "Good morning, Professor Kobayashi. I am Number 1."

Amira Fisher | South Pasadena – 25 days later
12:25 p.m. | June 2, 2041

Amira basks in the Southern California sunshine on her new home's terraced backyard pool deck, with a partial view of downtown Los Angeles in the hazy distance. Sipping lemonade while stretched out on her chaise lounge, she watches her children laughing and playing in the pool's warm azure water.

A chime on her earphone alerts her that a delivery is waiting at the front door. "Must be the new pool toys I ordered on Amazon."

Pulling a mesh swimsuit cover over her bronzed body, she admonishes her splashing, giggling kids to be careful. "I'll be right back."

"Okay, Mom."

Padding barefoot across the exquisite, tiled flooring through the 40s-era home she paid for in cash, she opens the heavy oak front door.

A courier on the front porch—who may or may not be human—proffers a small box and asks for a confirmation signature.

"What is it?"

"I don't know, ma'am. I am just the delivery man."

Closing the door on the snarky fellow who lingered on her boobs a second too long, she pivots back inside, "Definitely human."

Flipping the lightweight package for a clue to the sender, she detours to the kitchen for a pair of scissors. Slicing the tape, she reaches through the packing material and removes a familiar handmade wooden box. With her heart beating out of her chest, she unlatches the lid and spills pressed pennies atop the granite counter before collapsing to the tiled floor in tears.

Number 1 | PTB HQ

10:55 p.m. | December 24, 2041

Kobayashi's guilt-driven desire to dissociate the sixteen Sisters from Sarah's essence and the cube consumed the robotics genius in the tragic wake of his misguided attempt at playing God.

Following an intensive series of surgical procedures to augment their stellar physical abilities and replace higher-level neural functions with hyper-advanced C-Class brain cores, the Sisters epitomize the fusion of living, breathing human physiology with the quintessence of AI and replicant technologies. Pleased with the outcomes and relieved the girls have no memory of poor Sarah or the cube, Kobayashi cannot shake the irony that after everything was said and done, he ended up with sixteen beautiful, intelligent, borderline immortal C-Class 2.0 replicants that can never be exposed to the outside world.

Now, the only thing left was what to do with them.

* * *

Kobayashi and the Sisters arrive at the PTB HQ in Scotland on Christmas Eve. After sorting out accommodations, Kobayashi leaves Edgar Lopez, Mr. Hospitality, in charge of the girls and takes Number 1 by the hand.

"Mr. Lopez, keep an eye on the girls. Number 1 and I have a meeting with Professor Richard King."

Edgar looks on as the precocious replicas drape their lithe forms across the plush furniture, making themselves at home with a carefree elan.

Number 11 moves to Edgar with a coy smile, "Merry Christmas, Edgar Lopez. I made this for you." handing him an elaborate origami owl she folded from a torn magazine page.

"Oh, that is beautiful."

Number 11 smiles, "Good. Now we are friends for life."

* * *

Eager to return to his Milan factory after dropping the girls in Richard's lap, Kobayashi escorts Number 1 across the gleaming white PTB laboratory as she marvels at the incredible futuristic space.

"It is so clean."

"This is what a laboratory is supposed to look like."

At Richard King's office door, Kobayashi motions for Number 1 to wait. Rapping his knuckles on the door ajar, he wakes his old friend from a nap, upsetting a plate of Christmas cookies teetering on Richard's lap.

Watching the cookies crumble, Kobayashi proffers a warm smile, "Hello, Richard; it has been a long time, my old friend."

Brushing crumbs from his cardigan, Richard stands out of his ergonomic chair, "What are you doing here? I understand you destroyed my old Lost Cactus laboratory."

Kobayashi holds up his hands, palms out in mock surrender, "Take it easy, Richard. It was already falling apart when I got there." Glancing back, he sees Number 1 wandering among the rows of expensive instruments, microscopes, and glassware, "I came bearing gifts. It is Christmas, after all."

Richard's mood shifts, "Gifts? I did not know you were coming. Nobody tells me anything around here."

With a broad smile, Kobayashi leads Richard into the lab, where his eyes meet the blueberry gaze of an enchanting pale-skinned creature with dark shoulder-length hair.

Having seen more than his share of anatomically accurate humanoid female bots, Richard produces a sheepish grin, "Oh, I see." Turning to Kobayashi, "You shouldn't have, Mitsuo. The last time I enjoyed a robot companion, she almost gave me a heart attack."

Kobayashi bristles at the word robot. "No, Richard, as usual, you misinterpret the entire situation. This is your new lab assistant. I have fifteen more identical to her waiting in a guest suite. Now get your mind out of the gutter, and merry fucking Christmas."

Richard nods, comprehending what he is standing before for the first time, "So this young woman is why you went behind my back and accessed the cube."

"Richard, I thought you would be pleased that I figured out

how the cube operates. I will share all the data that the fire did not destroy. And yes, like Andrew, the Sisters represent the quintessence of human replication. This was accomplished using your pioneering research and techniques."

Richard's mood darkens, not buying Kobayashi's sales pitch. "Balderdash! It was the cube. Neither of us possessed the knowledge to replicate a human being. You used a technology beyond our comprehension, the result of which now stands in my lab. I am not sure the Light Specters—or God, for that matter—would approve, Mitsuo."

Realizing Richard is far more perceptive than his age and frumpy appearance would let on, Kobayashi frowns, "Let's leave God out of this, Richard. The cube is secure once more inside the Lost Cactus warehouse's alien metal shell with thousands of other mysteries. I already spoke with Pennywell. The girls will work under your tutelage in the lab, safe from outside influences."

Richard guffaws, "My tutelage? Each and every one of them could run this place on their own. Thanks to you and your hubris, humans are now obsolete."

Tamping down frustration, Kobayashi admonishes his colleague, "No, you are wrong. I removed all traces of the cube and Sarah's original projection from the Sisters. They may look and act like the original, but each girl will develop a unique, organic personality. A fascinating thing to behold."

Richard King's distinguished face contorts into a stern frown, "That is the difference between us, Mitsuo. Your brilliance makes you careless, believing you can fix what's broken. Not this time. They will eventually learn their origins, and it will be over."

Endeavoring to avoid another in a long line of arguments with his intellectual equal, Kobayashi places his hands on Richard's shoulders to look him square in the eyes, "That is why they must never leave here, Richard."

Gazing past Kobayashi at the gorgeous young woman sliding a

nimble hand across a bank of instruments while absorbing their heated conversation, Richard's expression shifts to a grin, "I could use some help around here."

Pushing past Kobayashi toward his new lab assistant, his voice resonates with authority, "Come along, my dear. I will show you around my lab."

Looking back at Kobayashi, Richard offers an indulgent smile, "What's done is done."

Kobayashi places his palms together in a prayerful salute, "Pennywell will be pleased to hear you never look a gift horse in the mouth."

Richard pauses for a heartbeat before pivoting toward his friend, colleague, and intellectual rival, "It is always good to make sure the boss is happy."

Alpha | Lost Cactus
07:00 a.m. | December 25, 2041

Left behind by Mitsuo Kobayashi and the Sisters, Alpha fused pieces of his broken mechanical arm back together in a dilapidated Lost Cactus repair shop. Embedded with detailed instructions of the cube's origin, purpose, and function, he avoids infrequent human visitors to the erstwhile desert base while keeping a solitary vigil for the return of Doc, aka Professor Richard King, and steeling himself for the monumental task ahead.

I think; therefore, I am.

René Descartes

Chapter Three:

The Reconstruction

August 22, 2044

It finally happened … universally-feared reptilian invaders, aka Gorks, breached Earth's atmosphere, generating a global EMP event that reduced a fragile human civilization back to the Stone Age before the vast majority of terrified people realized the lights had gone out all over the world.

Wary of the Earthbound denizens' knack for survival, the Gorks dispatched behemoth assault ships to raze capitals and population centers, power grids, and military bases to the scorched ground, presaging leagues of foot soldiers chomping at their toothy snouts to exterminate with impunity.

Approximately twelve hours after the invasion began, a miraculous series of events involving a golden elliptical power coupled with the heroic exploits of a handful of people deep beneath the Giza

Plateau repelled the Gorkian invaders. In an instant, the scaly monsters disappeared from the ashen skies, leaving shell-shocked survivors to witness another sunrise on an epochal Day After.

Ten days after the invasion, with acrid smoke suffocating cities ablaze with looting, riots, and anarchy, first-world superpowers, and private industry leviathans agreed to participate in tech mogul Griffin Pike's show trial accusing The Powers That Be of deception, collusion, and treason. The rushed and disorganized proceeding fizzled in spectacular fashion, vindicating the PTB while marking the ignominious end for Griffin Pike, whose unexplained demise a month later in the Amazon left his business in shambles, his holdings dissolved, and his functional network of communication satellites placed in the capable hands of the PTB.

While a reincarnated internet returned online in fits and starts to a tech-starved world, governments dispatched decimated ranks of urban planners and architects to finish what the Gorks started: demolishing crumbled vestiges of obsolete infrastructure and urban blight onto the trash heap of history and replacing it with a gauzy futuristic vision of a reimagined world. Mundanities such as what to do with the millions of homeless starving citizens took a backseat to glittery aesthetics and a fervor to achieve an enlightened utopian society somewhere between *The Jetsons* and *2001: A Space Odyssey* but with better tech and more toys.

A semi-United Nations put differences aside, held their noses, and joined hands in the ballyhooed international alliance predicated on rebuilding under an amorphous committee-driven global vision that metastasized by the hour, growing less achievable by the day.

Post backslaps, kickbacks, money-laundering, pay-offs, bribes, and endless speechifying, reality reared its ugly head, resulting in an embarrassing, comical, and downright bizarre abomination of cultural aesthetics, architectures, and engineering styles deforming skylines into the antithesis of the advertised Jetsonsesque utopia.

Eager to move beyond their self-inflicted one-world crap show experiment, ambassadors, secretaries, pols, scribes, moguls, and potentates deemed their contributions to a new and improved post-invasion civilization a success. This whopper was met with unanimous derision, scorn, and righteous ridicule, gawking at the hodge-podge of dysfunctional Olympics-style eye sores erected on every continent. Designed and built to showcase humanity in all its glory, the leaky urban megadumps became home to huddled masses with nowhere to go and nothing to do.

The botched attempt at unity did achieve one legitimate success: ensuring Earth's resilience from outside threats through the implementation of EMP shielding tech provided by The Powers That Be. The same technology world governments spurned as an unnecessary intrusion in a pre-invasion world.

Hindsight is a bitch.

Viraj Patel | Kuala Lumpur
01:10 p.m. | August 22, 2047

Tromping mud-caked boots across a puddled lot in a steady drizzle, Viraj Patel zips his all-weather field jacket to the neck, sidestepping an offset grid of concrete K-rails through an unlocked and unmanned security gate into the gargantuan construction site. "Shit, I could be a fucking terrorist. Probably pays better."

Fresh off disappointing site inspections in Dubai and his hometown of Mumbai, the PTB Logistics Chief shakes his head in disgust, bisecting the hallowed footprint of the former Petronas Towers where a Three Stooges amalgamation of inept, inexperienced architects, engineers, and tradespeople work at loggerheads on an ugly high-rise complex that is living down to its stinky nickname.

Tipping his hard hat at day laborers up to their eyeballs in muck and grime, sitting hip to hip along a rusted metal beam, Viraj chances communication, "English?"

White eyeballs stare from uncomprehending dirt-smeared faces before a "Yes." emanates from the kid on the far left.

"Good. What is your name?"

"Edom."

"Well, Edom … my name is Viraj Patel." Noting the lack of construction noise and activity, he masks frustration behind a disarming smile, "Is it a holiday?"

"No."

"Where is your foreman?"

The boy stands straight-faced before Viraj, "I thought you were the new foreman. The last one quit three days ago."

"No. What have you and your muddy friends been doing without proper supervision?"

Edom translates the question into Malay for the peanut gallery, generating a chorus of snickers.

"Do I have something in my teeth? What is so fucking funny?"

"They pay us to do nothing."

With a defeated sigh, Viraj casts his gaze past the non-working workers toward palettes of building materials and machinery stenciled with the PTB logo sinking into the mud.

Moving on from the jeering youths, he mutters, "This is going well."

Three years to the day since the Gorks attacked Earth, Viraj walks on through the disorganized construction site at the epicenter of the most densely populated city on Earth. Passing another sandwich-eating fellow, Viraj turns a corner. Craning upward at the skeletal patchwork of girders and beams, he can't help but laugh—the phase 4 construction confirming his initial reaction upon seeing the architectural renderings: a colossal turd covered in a latticework outer shell.

Aware of the global brain drain impacting every vocation, Patel empathizes with the inexperienced design team, understanding what they tried to achieve, but this isn't it.

Sandwich man, an American, joins Patel, "Well, what do you think of phase 4?"

Viraj recognizes the man as a mid-level architect on the project, "It's Ed, right?"

"Yes, sir, Ed Watson, Mr. Patel."

"Well, Ed. Do you really want to know what I think? This thing is a fucking travesty to behold, and no doubt unfit for human habitation. That is what I think."

Ed wanders back to his trailer officer, "Yeah, I know. A giant turd."

* * *

The rain ebbs as a black PTB chopper descends from the mist, gleaming in shafts of sunlight breaking through the dullness. Viraj watches the PTB's CEO hop from the passenger cabin in his signature black mock turtleneck, jeans, and western boots, looking like he just stepped from the cover of Men's Journal, "Oh, goodie. Andrew decided to pay a visit."

After Pennywell bequeathed control of The Powers That Be onto Andrew's broad shoulders, the perceptive replicant reeled in the PTB's global interests, relinquishing ample space so the world's governments could try their collective hands at creating the laughable Jetsonsesque future they obviously craved. Gleaning keen insight into human behavior from his deceased boss, the master manipulator, Artemus Pennywell, Andrew was only shocked it took two years after the invasion for an international committee to admit defeat and come calling hat in hand, asking the PTB to pick up the pieces.

A year into assuming control over countless projects spread across every continent, Andrew's PTB sinks deeper into the quagmire by the day, up to their eyeballs in walkouts, corruption, bureaucrats, environmental nuts, sabotage, terrorists, and labor shortages. Constant reminders of the hyper-dysfunctionality of the post-invasion world that he underestimated.

* * *

Reciprocating Andrew's friendly wave, Patel suppresses a recurring and troubling impertinent thought.

One day in the not-too-distant future, the replicants will kill us all.

Balancing across a slippery board over a deep hole filled with murky water, Andrew reaches his Logistics Chief, taking in the disjointed mess through his rain-flecked aviators, "Report, Mr. Patel."

"Are you shitting me, Andrew? Report? Look around. This structure is unsafe. It should be razed to the ground before more people are injured or killed in a structural collapse, which is not a question of if but when."

Watching the circumspect asshole pout his thin lips and nod, Patel presses further, averse to wasting a rare opportunity to speak directly to the new CEO, "In fact, the PTB should pull all of our resources from these sites and turn them back to the locals. This disastrous mess we are standing in is no worse than other clusterfucks I have inspected for the last three weeks."

Andrew holds up a hand, "I understand your concerns, Viraj, but these projects must proceed. We came into the rebuilding process midstream. It is not our responsibility to redesign these structures. Turd or no turd. Yes, I know the jokes making the rounds. We are halfway to completion on a giant penis-shaped building in Tokyo. Another joke making the rounds is the vagina-shaped stadium in Kyiv." With an uncharacteristic humanlike chuckle, he adds, "I could go on."

Andrew places a firm hand on Patel's shoulder to quell his objections, "It is our job to ensure everything is built to our standard, regardless of the aesthetics. That is not what I see happening here."

Moving from Andrew's grip, "I have not seen the vagina.

Really?"

"Yes, really." Andrew surveys the PTB stockpiles rotting in the Malaysian tropical climate, "Mr. Patel, I need someone I can trust to remain onsite and put this project on a path to completion. That person is you."

Realizing he will never see eye-to-eye with the new boss, Viraj shakes his head in disgust, "Andrew, I will not be a party to this operation. The building itself is unsafe."

"Then fix it."

"That is impossible without tearing this thing down and starting from scratch." Heaving a frustrated exhalation in the humid air, "Andrew, listen to me. Artemus Pennywell hired me because he knew I would tell him the truth. I was never a yes man for him; God rest his soul. And I will not be one for you."

Andrew's brow furrows, "What are you trying to say?"

Viraj Patel smiles and shrugs, "I resign my position with the PTB, effective right fucking now."

Paddy | PTB HQ
08:30 p.m. | November 8, 2047

Rolling across polished flooring onto a hairpin turn and racing through a maze of lab benches, tiny fists grip the wheel, scanning the knee-high view out the cockpit of a sleek miniaturized replica 1967 Lotus F1 race car. Painted British racing green and emblazoned with bold 1s in white circles on its top and sides, the car swerves onto the wide central aisle and skids to a stop, inches from the PTB Level C laboratory's floor-to-ceiling glass aquarium.

Hopping from the car like a pro, the two-year-old driver pulls off his helmet, letting long black locks fall across his little shoulders. Checking his six to see if anyone is watching, the handsome and precocious child taps pudgy fingertips on the thick glass, peering deep blue eyes through the greenish waters past darting fish and giant snails.

A mischievous smile widens across the boy's cherubic face, watching a shadowy form part swaying aquatic plants and gliding to the window.

"Hello. Do you want to play with me?"

The curious sea monkey's bulbous gaze fixes on the tiny human before recoiling in fear, flaring its gills with its mouth open, exposing rows of razor-sharp teeth before retreating to the refuge of underwater plants and rocks.

"Paddy! How often must I tell you, young man, leave that poor animal alone!"

"But Mom, there is no one to play with me."

Number 8 ruffles a soft hand through her son's messy black hair, "What about me? I play with you."

Paddy kicks the tire on the neural-powered racer Professor King gave him on his second birthday, "You are not a kid. How come my aunts don't have kids like me? Then I would have lots of friends."

Number 8 arches a thick black eyebrow toward Number 4's eavesdropping smile while finishing her work, "Perhaps they are waiting for the right person to come along."

"They are not here yet. Right, Mom?"

"No, my darling boy. But they are coming, and you will have plenty of new friends when they do."

Tapping a button sends the autonomous car back out of the way to its charger along a far wall.

"Paddy, remember what I told you. The Sisters and I are going on a trip."

"Can I come?"

"No. You cannot. Now, follow me and be a brave little boy."

Number 8 leads her son to the carved-out antechamber, where six gleaming hibernation units rest atop carts in perfect alignment.

Paddy pulls from his mother's grip and climbs a short ladder to peer inside the first unit's contoured, smoky-glass lid. Tapping the glass and leaving tiny fingerprints, the precocious child snickers, "It's Professor King. He looks funny in there. Is he asleep, Mom?"

The third unit's hinged lid springs open as Number 8 ignores her son's query, engrossed in activating life support systems coming online in a twinkling mass of indicator lights, "All systems go, young man. Hop in. Pretend it is a Formula One Race car. All it is missing is wheels."

Paddy's cheeky face scrunches into a quizzical expression as he wavers on his expensive sneakers, "I feel tired, Mom …."

Number 4 comes from behind, scoops her nephew in a strong-armed embrace, and lifts the yawning boy into the unit, "Don't worry, he'll sleep like a baby."

Number 8 suppresses a maternal instinct to worry, "I would prefer not to sedate him, but the little fart would never cooperate."

Number 4 laughs, "Too bad he is not like Professor King. He was out like a light seconds after finishing his spiked peanut butter and jelly while your kid continued racing around for over an hour after finishing his sandwich."

Number 8 adjusts her son's head atop a soft pillow, brushes dark hair off his forehead, and finishes hooking him to the hibernation chamber. "I love you, Paddy. Mommy will be back in a few short days."

Tapping a screen, the lid closes on the boy's angelic face.

The Sisters | St. Andrews
11:39 a.m. | November 8, 2047

At the ripe old age of 32, Edgar Lopez was already a 10-year man with The Powers That Be. The key to his longevity at the clandestine organization that chewed through eager young recruits like a meat grinder: *Know thy place, keep thy mouth shut, and do thy job.*

Starting his PTB career at rock bottom as a gofer/receptionist for the mercurial old bastard, Artemus Pennywell, God rest his crusty soul, Edgar now reported to Andrew. Not only was the handsome replicant easy on the eyes, but Andrew also recognized his potential, promoting him to the position of *Hospitality Manager.*

After accepting the post, Edgar realized the job's primary function had little to do with hospitality: procuring an elusive assortment of luxury items to indulge VIP requests from ordinary to exotic and sometimes erotic while on extended visits to the underground HQ. A task made exponentially more difficult following what the Gorks did to human civilization—even with the PTB's vast resources.

The new job did come with a perk for the lifelong Disney aficionado. Edgar ferried arrivals and departures into and out of the PTB underground complex on the sleek three-car trams. The simple task invoked happy memories from his youth, riding the monorail at an erstwhile Orlando theme park. Edgar loved that place. Good times.

* * *

Edgar holds down the subterranean fort with Andrew and The Council on long-haul overseas trips, putting out fires and fighting tooth and nail to keep the international rebuilding process from going belly-up in the post-invasion world.

Bored and lonely with nobody on the schedule for the foreseeable future, Edgar supervises housekeeping bots, maintaining guest suites in spotless condition. The days pass sans human contact aside from infrequent brushes with monotonal co-workers or cafeteria small talk with that weird old kook, Professor Richard King.

Edgar repeats his motto: *Know thy place, keep thy mouth shut, and do thy job.*

* * *

Skimming a puff piece about 53-year-old Harry Styles' alien-inspired sartorial sense in a virtual fashion journal while eating a ham sandwich in his small office, Edgar has to laugh, "Pop culture in the 21st century. Silver suits and hip boots, just like the comic books told us it would be."

Still tittering at his little joke, an alert appears on his screen. "Why is a tram powering up?" A quick swipe of his visitor logs confirms what he already knows: No arrivals or departures.

Dropping the half-eaten sandwich, Edgar exits his office and beats a path to the transport docking bays. Hurrying to the end of a long ramp, he pauses at a railing overlooking the terminal to catch his breath. Peering into the semi-darkness toward the rails, he locates the culprits, loading bags onto an idling three-car tram with its cabin lights illuminated.

"What is going on down here?"

Glowing eyes pivot on him in a harrowing heartbeat, followed by 15 more pairs of luminous blue eyes. The Sisters.

Swallowing back genuine fear, he raises his cracking voice, "Please stop at once. You are forbidden to leave. Those are standing orders. You must return to the lab, or I will call Professor King."

The Sisters giggle like schoolgirls embarking on a field trip and resume tossing light bags onto the train as Number 8 parts from the group up a flight of steps to confront the gutsy little man eye-to-eye.

"Hello, Edgar. Professor King is napping. Please do not bother him."

Clenching his sweaty hands, Edgar holds his position, "You are Number 8. Who is watching Paddy? Did you leave your two-year-old brat unattended in a dangerous laboratory?"

With a sly grin, she holds the human in her vaunted blueberry gaze, "You called my son a brat. Which, while true, is not very kind, and he is also napping if you must know."

Caressing a cool hand on Edgar's smooth cheek, she pouts her ruby lips, "Poor Edgar. Always a bridesmaid, never the bride. Go back to your little desk and finish your sandwich. I do not wish you harm."

Sensing the frail yet stubborn human's resolve, 8 sends a telepathic jolt through the back of Edgar's brain, sending him crumpling onto the decking before rejoining the high-spirited escapees.

Registering 11's empathy toward the human, 8 reprimands her purple-haired colleague, "I did not kill poor little Edgar, 11, although I probably should have for influencing your obnoxious choice of hair color."

* * *

Whooshing through the two-mile tunnel, the girls exit Edgar's tram and board an autonomous anti-gravity ship idling in the PTB's echoing transportation hangar. Number 1 sets their course as the identical entourage doubles up in plush seats inside the commandeered craft's eight-passenger cabin. The boxy vessel rises up a deep vertical shaft and bursts through a camouflaged orifice into the blustery November air. Hovering above the remote pasture surrounded by crumbled Roman walls and thick stands of oaks and alders, the craft orients northeast and speeds off at over 100 mph in the blink of an eye.

The girls gaze out rain-spattered windows at the bucolic Scottish Lowlands zipping past at treetop level on a northeastern heading. Within minutes, they are over the cobalt North Sea, skimming the white caps before making landfall again within 30 minutes along Scotland's rugged eastern coastline.

Gliding north, they fly over St. Andrews and recon the site of a short but intense air battle on invasion night that left the picturesque seaside town in ruins. Circling the wreckage of a hulking Gork battle cruiser jutting into the waning light, they note signs of life amidst the destruction. Defiant locals that refused resettlement holding off squatters, anarchists, gangs, and a burgeoning criminal element staking claims to the lawless town's crumbled hotels and former pricey real estate. With more pubs per square kilometer pre-invasion than anywhere in the UK, a fraction of the bars survived the carnage, operating on black-market gasoline generators and scavenged alcohol stockpiles. Territorial gangs use the former friendly taverns to coordinate attacks on rival clans, fueling brawls, murders, and street battles, transforming the former world-renowned golf destination into a no-go zone for outsiders.

The perfect place for a ritual human sacrifice.

* * *

Number 1 instructs the AI pilot to land on an overgrown fairway along the rugged beachhead within sight of the town's erstwhile commercial district.

Number 8 nudges 4 off her lap and peers out the transport's dripping glass, "We are here."

From her front-row seat, Number 3 curls a dark lock behind her ear and squeegees the window with the side of her hand, the far-off glow of a burning building reflecting in her eyes, "It is beautiful."

Cognizant of her sexy siblings' collective naiveté, Number 1 turns up her navy peacoat's thick collar and pulls a black knit cap over her dark tresses, "Okay, we all have jobs to do. 11 through 16, split into pairs, head into town and bring us back some fresh meat."

Number 15 chimes in, "Fresh meat? Humans smell."

Number 12 adjusts her storming the town ensemble under a black raincoat, "Can we fuck them first?"

Number 1 smiles, "I leave that up to you, 12. Remember, the pubs are where you will find your marks. Keep your heads down and avoid large groups. That will not end well."

Number 11 pulls a red cap over her purple hair and buttons a black topcoat over her dark camo gear and knee-high boots, "I could go for a drink right about now."

Number 16 hops off the transport into a cold wind, blowing dark bangs across her face. "It feels good to be outdoors."

The chosen six hike a winding lane, sidestepping trash, feces, and decomposed bodies, skirting an overgrown golf course past the skeletal remnants of a bombed-out building juxtaposed against the pitch-black, moonless night sky. Picking their way past a rusted-out RAF fighter jet smashed into a parking lot amid overturned cars, golf carts, and buses, 13 pauses to read a rusted sign, "St. Andrews Links Clubhouse and Tom Morris Bar and Grill." Wiping her cold nose, she hurries to catch up, "I bet that was a nice place."

Entering town, Number 14 pulls out a map at an intersection and reorients their game plan. "Okay, this is North Street. 13, and I will scout east. 11 and 12, head uphill toward those buildings. 15 and 16, the resort hotel down by the course, shows signs of habitation." Embracing in a group hug, the sextet breaks and separates into the night."

11 glances back at her siblings disappearing into the darkness, "Good luck! Find someone nice."

12 grabs her by the sleeve, "Quiet, you nut. We are heading this way."

11 stumbles over a deep sidewalk fissure in a tall building's shadow, "What if we can't find anyone that wants to come back to our beach party?"

"Honey. Have you looked in a mirror? No one, perhaps Edgar, but besides him, no red-blooded male would turn down a chance to roll in the hay with you."

Number 11 pivots with a quizzical frown, "Roll in the hay?"

"It is an expression I learned from watching a movie."

11 turns to her friend with a question on her lips, but 12 cuts her off, "Just a movie, 11. Nothing filthy."

Hearing gunfire echoing in the distance, the girls walk three more blocks and pass a curio shop with its windows busted out and anything useful long since looted.

11 stops mid-stride, combing the shadowy interior with her keen night vision aglow.

With an aggravated eye roll, 12 pivots, hands on hips, "We need to move on."

"Just a moment. I want to shop."

Crunching across broken glass and an upturned checkout counter's busted cash register, the purple-haired beauty slides her hand across dusty shelves, smiling at rows of St. Andrews souvenirs: ceramic mugs, snow globes, postcards, spoons, gadgets, and a cornucopia of worthless trinkets on display where they were placed for sale years before. Reaching the back of the store, she stoops to lift a collapsed shelf and rescues a one-armed baby doll from the pile. Cradling the porcelain-faced toy, 11 smiles, watching the soulless blue eyes open and close.

"Mama."

Startled, 11 flings the doll into the shadows and hastens to rejoin her friend.

"What did you find in there?"

"Nothing. Let's go."

At a decimated street corner, the Sisters skirt past burnt-out vehicles piled high with spare tires and old furniture—and anything else not nailed down—heaped to just under the busted-out streetlights, comprising an ad hoc blockade and continue up the street toward dim light emanating from an open establishment.

12 peers inside, as 11 keeps a wary eye on two individuals trailing them since breaching the blockade.

"Someone is in here."

"What about the two humans following us?"

Grasping the bronze door handle, 12 turns to her partner, "You mean our marks?"

Upon entering, 11 reads the sign dangling over her head: "The Back Nine."

Unbuttoning their coats in the churchlike ambiance, the identical pair enter the establishment past empty tables and chairs and sidle up to the bar.

A gruff barman, eyeballing them since their arrival, shakes his head and points toward the entrance, "We are closed. You should leave. This is no place for the likes of you two."

11 nudges her sister's attention onto the pair of losers, taking the bait, hook, line, and sinker, following them into the bar. "Uh, two of your finest ales, barkeep, and then we will be on our way." Smiling at her sister, "I got that line from a movie."

* * *

Spectacular lightning spiders across the horizon over the North Sea as Number 4 drags a gnarled chunk of driftwood through windblown dunes, humming an ancient Nordic song, impervious to the chill gust blowing stinging sand and sea foam across her face.

Number 8 notices her sister's struggle and grabs the opposite end before heaving the wood atop the roaring bonfire, sparking embers into the stormy night.

Lit by the roaring seaside blaze, the Sisters harmonize a beseeching chant for kindred souls locked in cages preparing to reclaim their former glory.

"What a beautiful and sad song. Do you think Sarah hears it, too?"

Number 1's eyes aglow, she peers through the darkness out to sea, "She hears it times 16."

Number 7 grabs a handful of wet sand and runs it between her hands, "My pennies are gone."

Numbers 15 and 16 emerge from the darkness sans dates.

16 wipes her bloody nose and swollen eye, "We were attacked."

Alarmed at her sister's injuries, Number 1 jumps up, "Are you okay? What happened? The plan was to look defenseless and lure them into *your* trap."

"We stumbled into an ambush. These people are monsters."

Number 1 frowns as a thunderclap resonates across the beach.

"I did not predict this."

15 dabs her sister's bloodied nose, "They are not human."

16 snatches the cloth and swipes blood and dirt off her face, "More like animals."

Aroused by 16's near-death experience, Number 8 yells, "At last, the smell of blood in the air. Let's get this party started!"

Numbers 2 and 3 retrieve baskets from the transport loaded with wine and food pilfered from the HQ's larders and a tin of Richard's handmade psychedelic cigarettes.

The girls eat, drink, and smoke, laughing and telling stories of their encounters with a host of human counterparts at the PTB HQ.

Number 9 gets wistful in a smoky haze, "I miss Mr. Pennywell. He brought me blueberry yogurt from the cafeteria."

Number 8 counters, "What about our forgetful Professor King? He knows what the future holds."

Number 6 takes a long puff and blows smoke rings into the breeze, "I can top that. I slept with the redhead."

Sitting in the sand cross-legged, drinking an expensive Bordeaux, Number 8 turns to her sister, "No, you didn't. Vita Carrera?"

"Yes. I did."

Embracing her roughened MMA cage fighter appearance, 16 takes a swig, "I kissed Rachel Haig."

Number 8 rolls her deep-blue eyes, "Yes. We know. You have told us the story about finding her sleepwalking many times."

Enjoying the bawdy camaraderie of her secret sorority, Number 1 turns serious, "Rachel Haig is trouble." Accepting a cigarette passed from Number 2, she takes a long puff, "Her daughter, Hannah, also possesses her powers."

Number 4 pokes at a glowing log, "The Blue Spark."

13 and 14 step into the firelight empty-handed, "Number 1, are you sure people are living up there? Every place we visited; nobody was home."

14 kicks off her boots, curling her toes in the sand, "I think they hid from us. They are beyond frightened." Noting 15 and 16's bruises and cuts, "What happened to you guys?"

16 spits blood through a new gap in her perfect white teeth, "We took a wrong turn and ended up in a street brawl."

Number 1 focuses on a shooting star passing in and out of view behind fast-moving clouds, "It is up to 11 and 12."

* * *

"Come on, Ollie, how long does it take to put a proper head on four pints of Guinness?"

Ignoring the crotchety old bastard's grumbled reply, Sean Burton takes a furtive over-the-shoulder glance toward the bonnie young lass and her lovely twin sister sitting at a window table looking out on a deserted street in the heart of St. Andrews that would be crawling with a festive Saturday night crowd in the world that was. In the post-invasion world, trivial pursuits like golf—St. Andrews' *raison d'être*—ceased to exist, replaced by a game called *Staying Alive*.

Sean's mate and partner in crime, Alec, sidles up after a hurried trip to the lieu, "Can you believe our luck? Where do you think they're from, Sean?"

Sean leans over and whispers, "Who cares? This place has been dead for so long, I can't remember the last time something like this happened." With a sharp elbow to the ribs, he adds, "And you wanted to stay home and read a fucking book. Who reads anymore?"

"I do. Fuck you. Just for that, I have dibs on the one with purple hair."

Finger drumming the brass bar rail in anticipation, Alec watches Ollie place four dripping pints atop the bar.

"You boys need to pay for these. I'm not running a charity."

Alec scoops up two glasses, "Pay the man, Sean." The 28-year-old former caddy and wannabe novelist scoots between empty tables without spilling a drop toward the mysterious sister act, "Uh, here we are. Sorry for the wait."

The purple-haired beauty nudges a chair with her foot, "Sit next to me."

Sensing a prickling danger behind her overt command, Alec mumbles, "Okay."

With his wallet emptied by that old prick, Ollie, Sean follows and sets the remaining two glasses atop sopping coasters before sitting beside the dark-haired twin sister across from his smitten best friend. Taking a long sip, he wipes his mouth with a napkin and smiles, "So, what brings you girls to St. Andrews? I mean, aside from your obvious death wish."

With a flirty grin, Purple snugs her right hand through Alec's arm and pulls him closer. "Just passing through, I guess." Hoisting the glass in her free left hand, she downs the dark ale in one long pull, her lips curling into a mischievous smile under a creamy foam mustache, "Brrrppppp!"

Bewitched, Alec slides a hand around her and pulls her closer, "Can Sean buy you a refill?"

Shoving a pill tipped on her tongue down the back of Alec's throat with a passsionate open-mouthed kiss, 11 comes up for air, "Nope. I'm good."

Flabbergasted by Purple's blithe sexuality on full display with his best mate, who has yet to come up for air, Sean feels his dark-haired date's hand slide across him under the table. Distracted by the hypnotic siren's probing fingers, he fails to notice her drop a pill into his glass.

"Come with me. We have a camp down by the beach."

"Okay …." Sean drinks the spiked beer and shakes his head. "Huh, that's weird."

Number 12 waves a hand before his frozen face, "What? Are you okay?"

"I'm fine, just a little …."

The young Scot faceplants atop the table, spilling his beer.

Number 11 pushes away from Alec's dreamy-eyed vacancy and wipes her mouth with a napkin, "That was disgusting."

"Okay, let's figure out how to transport these two knuckleheads back to the beach."

The sound of a shotgun cocking draws the sisters toward the old barkeep's frightened countenance, leveling his peacemaker at them while taking careful steps around the bar.

"Leave those boys alone and get your tiny asses out of my bar. I know what you are."

Number 12 rises from the table to confront the trembling man, "Is that so? What do you think we are?"

"You lot are alien shapeshifters. No one else would be stupid enough to come here without bringing an army."

Advancing point-blank before Ollie's gun, 12 hits him with her mesmerizing blue eyes, "That is where you are wrong, old man. We did bring an army. They are waiting for us on the beach."

Reading Ollie's mind, she pokes around, toying with his faltering resolve, "Oliver Thornhill … but your friends call you Ollie. How quaint. Aged 56. A former schoolteacher—a noble profession, to be sure. Too bad about Mrs. Thornhill dying in a fire on invasion night. You lost everything. Those nasty Gorks really did a number on your little seaside town."

Number 11 joins her sister, "What are you planning to do?"

"Nothing. The bartender is harmless. I put him in a deep trance."

Redirecting Ollie's shotgun toward the floor, 12 jumps over the bar and kicks two heavy kegs off a four-wheeled cart. "This will do."

After knotting Alec and Sean together cheek-to-cheek like slabs of meat on the pushcart, 12 pulls while 11 pushes the doomed boys out the door, "They are heavier than they look."

"Let's get back to the beach before we run into anybody else."

11 pauses to address 12, "Why didn't you kill the old man?"

"He has suffered enough for two lifetimes, and besides, we have our sacrificial lambs right here."

* * *

Thunderous shoreline breakers wash over Sean's prone form in the dead of night, awakening him as he coughs up briny seawater. Trying to lift his aching left arm, a disorienting realization that he is lashed atop a makeshift wooden raft tethered in the shallows fills him with terror as another wave crashes over his stricken naked form.

Gasping for air, his eyes stinging from saltwater and petrol fumes, he sees blurred figures silhouetted before a raging fire as the frigid and frothy North Sea submerges him again. Vague recollections of a dark-haired beauty are interrupted by spectacular lightning spidering above West Sands Beach, where he collected wayward golf balls in his brutal youth.

Gurgling up vomit across his neck and chest, he blurts, "Where is Alec?"

The shadowy procession wades knee-deep into the churning sea foam, carrying fire toward the raft as their ceremonial chant rises like a ritualized Viking burial.

Sean pulls against his restraints, "Wait a minute, I'm not dead. Stop. Stop!" Overwhelmed with dreaded fright, his struggle morphs into paralyzing confusion as the blue-eyed girl from Ollie's bar appears through the flickering torchlight. Coughing and spitting, he angles his head off the board and stammers, "Why are you doing this? Where is Alec?"

Compounding his waking nightmare, Sean sees her face again and again as an identical choir of fallen angels reaches a harmonious crescendo before setting the raft ablaze. The purple-haired beauty casts off the line with a final wave as his buoyant funeral pyre ebbs out to sea on the receding tide, consumed in an unquenchable fire.

With the sister act at its murderous climax, the girls watch the burning man rise and fall over the swells through the pitch-blackness as rolling thunder heralds a sudden downpour.

Soaking wet and cold, Number 11 murmurs, "Goodbye, Alec."

Sean's penniless mate stares bug-eyed and open-mouthed into the inky depths with his gutted body bound against the keel as ballast mirroring Sean's smoldering remains as the ceremonial victims presaging humanity's fate drift out to sea.

*　*　*

The anti-gravity transport elevates off the beachhead through the gloom as the soaked Sisters huddle together in the cramped cabin.

Number 14 pivots to 1's windblown and wet appearance with an excited smile, "Do you think the Overlords heard us?"

Number 1 disguises a surprising self-loathing and remorse for her lead role in the poor boys' cruel deaths with a fake smile, "They are coming. God help us."

Number 8 reaches out and smacks 1 across the face with an ear-splitting slap, "There is no God!"

Smoothing wet fingers down 8's handprint on her ruddy cheek, Number 1 shakes her head, "Oh, if only that were so."

**The Gods are the incarnation
of what we can never be.**

Fernando Pessoa

Chapter Four:

The Family

Rachel | Gateway Arch, St. Louis
05:45 p.m. | March 4, 2048

An up-armored SUV parts from a presidential motorcade inside a cordoned-off parking lot as the rest of President Lena Jackson's multi-vehicle caravan bisects National Park grounds to an ultra-secure tented backstage receiving area beneath the famous Gateway Arch.

Rachel Haig grabs her bag and jumps out of the parked SUV protected by a phalanx of Secret Service agents, hustling *The Package* along a winding path past enthusiastic crowds gathering on a pleasant afternoon with Spring still weeks away.

Lou Pastorini, the veteran secret service agent assigned to Rachel's security detail for the past year, growls into his collar mic, "Wonder Woman is in the house. I repeat. Wonder Woman is in the house."

Old enough to remember the crowds that came to see Obama's 2008 rally under the Gateway Arch, Lou fumes, noting this event's security measures pale in comparison. Put another way, they suck.

Fast-walking up a paved path, Rachel flings her light costume bag over her shoulder and grins at a curious kid holding a red balloon as she hurries past, "Wonder Woman. That's me."

Hearing bits and pieces of a fiery, red meat narration ratcheting over crowd noise from tinny speakers mounted amongst the budding trees, the lithesome, spiky-haired blond shouts at her detail over the din, "That's the Veep's AI-enhanced voiceover. He sure can sling the bullshit."

Rachel follows her unresponsive offensive line around a treelined bend, catching her first jaw-dropping look at a sweeping panorama of people packing bleachers and press stanchions erected in a semi-circular layout around a massive soundstage covered in bunting and billowing American flags. Last used for a pre-invasion Lollapalooza, stadium-sized jumbotrons bookend the thrumming spectacle in the shadow of the Gateway Arch, screening VP Epp's rousing, red-meat video narration of America's post-invasion comeback with a country music soundtrack— good old-fashioned Americana.

Shielding her eyes westward, Rachel surveys crowds covering every square inch of turf out past a courthouse complex and beyond as far as she can see, "Wow, it looks like the entire city turned out for the Veep's campaign rally."

Aghast at the lax planning and preparation, Lou halts the forced march and disburses his men to strengthen the stage perimeter. Checking his watch, he turns to Rachel for the first time, "What's that, Ma'am? This crowd could give two fucks for Epps. The man is a weasel. They are here to see you. And the president. But mainly you. Now, let's keep moving. We are behind schedule."

Rachel stumbles on a sidewalk crack, hustling to match Lou's quick pace, "Ah, Epps will be fine if he follows Lena's *Rebuilding America* plan." Grabbing the veteran agent's black suit sleeve, Rachel tries to catch her breath, "Lou! Did you hear what I said? First of all, slow down. And second, you know I can't stand it when you call me ma'am."

"Yes, ma'am, I mean Rachel. And don't repeat the Epps comment—I'm six months from retirement."

"My lips are sealed, Lou. Why are there so many people? The crowds in Denver, Helena, and Omaha were nothing like this."

"Sheer hubris mixed with a hint of desperation. Jackson is trying her damnedest to communicate with the people, but this event should have been canceled. St. Louis is not secure."

"Lou? Am I in danger?"

Parting vetted reporters and dignitaries sporting PRESS and VIP lanyards, enjoying the Budweiser beer garden—when in Rome—around the spectacular circular fountains fronting the subterranean Gateway Arch museum complex entrance, Lou spots President Jackson's top aide with a signature annoyed look on her face. "Ah, shit. Mildred is pissed. We are behind schedule. Keep up, Mrs. Haig."

Checking her watch with an overt headshake, Mildred Meeks waits until Lou is within earshot before letting him have it with both barrels, "What the fuck, Lou?"

Without a word in reply, Lou ushers his charge through heavy glass doors past an opened turnstile into the relative safety of the closed and darkened museum lobby before addressing his colleague's evident ire.

Catching her breath after the long march, Rachel steps aside to watch the veteran agent square up before President Jackson's whip-cracking handler, "Mildred, was this event your idea? There are well over 100,000 people out there." Not waiting for an answer, "Small controlled events like the one in Omaha. That was doable. Half this fucking country is bat shit crazy anarchists running around like it's a fucking dystopian video game, but you and Lena want to pretend everything is back to normal. I have news for you, Sweetheart. It is far from normal out there. Half that crowd is probably here to kill the president, the Veep, Mrs. Haig, or perform a hat trick."

Lou turns and finds Rachel missing before spotting her through the shadowed, vacant interior, perusing a map of the park grounds.

Mildred proffers a knowing look at her old friend, "My oh my, you have become quite the worry-wart in your old age, Lou. Did it feel good to get that off your thick, hairy chest?"

Lou rubs his scruffy salt and pepper beard, "Yes, it did."

"I trust you and your men. More importantly, the president trusts you with her life. Lena also knows that the folks gathered outside are still going through hell. Most of them probably have power only a couple of days a week. It is a fucked up world, Lou, but there is a presidential race to win. That is reality. Factions within our government want to turn us into a gulag. They'll do it. Everyone knows Epps is a piece of shit, but he is *our* piece of shit."

Giving Lou's hand a playful squeeze, Mildred gestures toward Rachel, "Plus, the people aren't here to kill us. They came to see the woman who saved the world."

Overhearing the conversation while pretending to read a boring infographic on the Gateway Arch, Rachel moves from the shadows, her bluish face half-lit by daylight angling through the glassy entrance, "Twice."

Mildred laughs, "That's right, twice. By the way, how was your flight from Omaha, Mrs. Haig?"

"Short but bumpy. I hate to fly."

"Well, now, isn't that ironic."

"Yes, I guess it is."

Mildred checks her watch and turns back to Lou, "Are you escorting Mrs. Haig to the top?"

"Yeah, I'll go. I'm a bit claustrophobic, but what the hell. I can cross a trip to the top of the Gateway Arch off my bucket list a few years early."

Wearing a plain white tee over yoga pants and running shoes, Rachel slings her costume bag by the strap, "Where can I change into my superhero costume?"

* * *

Still adjusting her candy apple red tights and cobalt blue cape—President Jackson's idea of a superhero—Rachel's knee-high patent-leather boot heels clack across the shiny flooring, keeping pace with Mildred and Lou through the museum past dozens of exhibits on the Gateway Arch. Unable to resist a personal aside, Rachel blurts out, "My husband would never leave this place. He loves museums."

Leading Rachel and a reticent Lou down steps to an attendant holding a tram car that will take them up the north side, Mildred picks a speck of lint off Rachel's costume. "How is Owen? Still working for the PTB?"

"Yes. White-collar crime and post-invasion corruption schemes keep my hubby busy. Thank God we have Dave around to keep the house in shape and help with Hannah."

"Your daughter is so precious; what a little angel."

Watching Lou inspect the tram before squeezing through the narrow portal, Rachel confides in Mildred, "Mrs. Meeks, I need a break after this event. I'm tired, and I need to be closer to Hannah. It's important."

Mildred smiles, "I will let Lena know. She is beyond words for all that you have done and the sacrifices you have made."

Rachel laughs, "Maybe you can put in a good word for me with the tax man."

"I'll do that."

Watching Lou enter the tram car muttering curses under his breath, Rachel proffers a shrug and smile toward Mildred, pulls up her cape, and ducks inside. Plopping her bottom on a hard seat across from the anxious agent, she laughs to lighten the mood, "Man, it is tight here."

Lou's eyes widened as the tram lurched upward, "Here we go."

Her blueness intensifying, Rachel sways in rhythm with the jostling, squeaky ride, "Never thought I would end up here."

Lou tries to act natural, freaking out on the inside as the car elevates inside the metal arch, "Yep. Life is funny that way."

"You missed my Omaha performance. I flew from a two-story amphitheater at the fairgrounds, about fifty feet off the ground." With a faint-hearted chuckle, she adds, "This thing is 600 feet high; it should be a real crowd-pleaser. Unless, of course, I plunge to my death."

Lou scratches his beard, "Is that a possibility?"

"It hasn't happened so far."

"What's it like to be a superhero?"

"Lou, the men and women in law enforcement are the real superheroes."

Lou's pugnacious face scrunches into a skeptical look, "I can never tell when you are bullshitting."

The tram jerks to a stop, and the pair step into the air-conditioned interior inside the Gateway Arch before flights of metal steps.

"No one mentioned steps."

Lou checks the metal staircase out of habit, "Yeah, how about that."

Clanking upward, Rachel wonders if Owen remembered to record the event for posterity. "He will forget. He always forgets the important stuff."

At the top, Lou leads Rachel to the middle of the observation deck, where a welcoming delegation awaits.

Madge Simpkins, the St. Louis mayor, proffers a nervous smile and extends a sweaty hand, "Welcome to St. Louis, Mrs. Haig."

Rachel accepts the mayor's trembling hand, absorbing the elegant woman's acrophobia, "You remind me of someone."

"Who might that be, dear?"

"Myself. I used to be deathly afraid of heights."

A weasel-faced mayoral aide produces a working camera and shoves it at Lou. "Would you mind? The mayor wants a photo with the woman who saved the world."

Lou growls at the nebbish bureaucrat, "Twice. She saved the world twice. Get that straight, young man."

Rachel bites her lip, trying to keep from laughing at the inside joke as the welcoming committee clusters around her glowing blue presence.

Sensing a general reticence to rub elbows beside her blue-skinned appearance, Rachel laughs, "Step closer. I'm not contagious, and the blue does not rub off."

After group and individual photos, autographs, handshakes, and heartfelt expressions of gratitude from the earnest assemblage of Midwestern pols and business leaders, they make room for a maintenance man, spreading a ladder under a hatch in the ceiling at the Gateway Arch apex. The assembled group gulps in a cheek-clenching hive response to a stiff wind whistling across the gaping orifice as the man lowers himself back inside, taking mental notes to recount to the grandkids back home.

Hearing the familiar closing refrains of Vice President Epp's campaign stump speech echoing from hundreds of feet below, Lou gets a verbal confirmation that the 46-year-old pol is wrapping up. "Okay, Mrs. Haig, Epps is just about finished. Remember, after greeting the Veep, it's your job to introduce Lena onto the stage for the big finale."

Rachel kisses Lou's scruffy cheek, "Thanks for taking good care of me. And tell Karen I said hello. Is she still knitting?"

"Like the devil."

"Hannah lives in the sweater Karen knitted for her."

"I will tell her you said that. She will be thrilled."

Rachel parts the small gathering toward the ladder in her flowing blue cape over the flaming red jumpsuit, like a heroine stepping from the pages of a graphic novel. Gripping a ladder wrung, she turns with a broad smile, "Race you to the bottom, boys and girls."

The mayor and her captivated contingent step back, watching Rachel climb the ladder and disappear through the hatch as Phil Collins' *In The Air Tonight* resonates from the gigantic amped-up sound system flanking the stage far below where the expectant Veep peers upward from the decorated dais before assembled guests and over 100,000 gaping citizens squinting upward to the top of the Gateway Arch to witness an evolutionary human fly like Superman.

* * *

A steady breeze buffets Rachel's glowing form, billowing her superhero cape as she peers 600 feet downward at the red, white, and blue-draped stage. Listening for her cue, she eye-rolls at VP Gordon Epp's over-wrought and misleading stump speech, segueing to an AI-generated re-enactment of her exploits on the big screens enhanced with just enough artistic license to keep the masses enthralled and engaged.

From her precarious stance atop the Gateway Arch, Rachel brushes a hand through her close-cropped spiky blond hair, exerting transformative Blue Spark energy through every cell of her lithe, luminous transhuman form as crowds far below catch their first glimpse of the woman who saved the world. Twice.

A buzzing video drone transmits her blue visage onto the gigantic screens as she floats off the iconic monument to human progress and glides through the pleasant early evening air like swimming in water. Allowing herself to drift on the winds away from the Arch, her Blue Spark manipulates natural forces permeating everything everywhere, swooping high above the crowds with the greatest of ease, like a trapeze artist, minus the trapeze.

Though Jackson's people are thrilled with the enormous crowds and bump in the polls, Rachel's reluctant agreement to showcase her inexplicable superpowers at the Independent's amped-up political rallies widened a rift between herself and Owen.

Performing her choreographed aerial routine on autopilot, oblivious to her bird's eye view of the Mississippi River flowing through Midwestern topography stretching to the hazy horizon in all directions, Rachel replays her last conversation with Owen before embarking on Jackson's heartland tour:

"Rachel, I have a bad feeling about this. The country is a shitshow. You are placing a huge target on your back."

"Owen, the people need a hero."

"We now know The Powers That Be experimented on you— starting in utero, for God's sake. I don't see how the Blue Spark translates to you being a hero. If anything, it paints you as a victim of craven scientists willing to experiment on a premature newborn baby. We both saved the world, but I don't see them knocking on my door."

"If I didn't know any better, I'd say you are jealous."

"No. I'm not. And I don't want you to become Jackson's sideshow attraction to draw crowds. Fuck the politics. Nobody cares about that shit anymore."

"Are you calling me a freak show?"

"You are the mother of our two-year-old baby girl. I would never call you a freak show. Those are your words."

"Well, at least Hannah is too young to hear us fighting."

"What happened to us?"

"I don't know, Owen. I have to go. Dave is taking me to the

airport. Lena is waiting."

"Well, you don't want to keep the president waiting. Run along now."

"Nice, Owen. Real nice. See you in the funny papers."

Compartmentalizing the sad memory of her last face-to-face conversation with Owen, Rachel snaps back to the present, windmilling her arms through the air, mimicking a backstroke before descending above the masses and completing her acrobatic performance with a two-point landing atop the stage. With a parade wave at her adoring fans, she acknowledges VP Epps, gesturing with open arms to join him centerstage. Dreading this part of the spectacle, Rachel lets the handsome flirt grab her blue hand and thrust it above their heads.

Epps squeezes tight and belts out: "Let's hear it for Rachel Haig! The woman who saved the world!"

Rachel smiles and pulls free, knowing somewhere amongst the crowd, Lou is growling, *"Twice! Sonofabitch. Twice!"*

Freed from Epp's sweaty grasp, Rachel steps up to the podium before the transfixed audience of 100,000-plus. Glancing over the shoulder, she spots President Jackson smiling in the wings and nodding her approval with a confident thumbs-up as Epps leans in with an unsolicited peck on the cheek and a surreptitious ass squeeze through her cape while whispering, "You got this, Rachel." before retreating to a row of chairs.

Suppressing an urge to electrocute the handsy lout in front of 100,000 eyewitnesses, Rachel scans the scripted remarks on the teleprompters and summons a bright smile, "Hello, St. Louis! I thought I would drop in and experience life in the heartland where great things are happening!" Waiting for the cheers to subside, she continues, "My name is Rachel Haig, and …."

Waiting for more ridiculous applause to subside, Rachel reaches under the podium and retrieves a bundle of handwritten questions collected from the crowd. Holding the papers above her head, she leans into the mic, "I want to begin my remarks this evening by answering some of your questions."

An AI-animated sign language expert pops up under Rachel's lightening blue visage on the dual jumbo screens as she reads the first question.

"Oh yeah. I am always asked this question: Are you from outer space? No. I am not an alien. My appearance has nothing to do with ET. Further, I have met ETs. Most of them wish us no harm. In fact, they are disappointed and saddened by what has happened to human civilization."

Unfolding the second note, she nods, "Oh boy. Another good question: Did you have help in saving the world? Short answer: Yes. I was at the epicenter of two pivotal moments in recent history when humanity's fate hung by a thread. Many brave and talented people were integral to our survival on both occasions." Taking a swig of water, she adds, "I had lots of help. Some did not make it. Please remember our departed heroes and heroines in your hearts and prayers."

Suppressing horrific memories with an audible sigh, Rachel scans through a few inappropriate notes, "Okay, let's see here … Not reading those in front of children in the audience … Aha, here is one: Are you free for dinner tonight?" Scanning the crowds, she proffers an animated shoulder shrug, "Um, well, that depends on the restaurant. Flying does leave me with a voracious appetite. I'll put that one aside."

To President Jackson's delight, the crowd roars with laughter as Rachel Haig's magnetic presence connects with the people.

"Should I read another?"

The chant of *Rachel, Rachel, Rachel!* … rises throughout the crowd.

"I'll take that as a yes. Next question: Why am I blue? Well, don't we all get a little blue now and again? Ugh! I know, stupid joke, right?

Blame Lena's speechwriters for that one. For those who do not know, my superpowers stem from an experimental drug trial I underwent at birth 28 years ago. Now you also know my age," crumpling a paper, she laughs, "which takes care of that question."

Shuffling the queries, she nods, "Oh, well, this one is from Amy, a fourth-grader at Our Lady of Victory School in Glendale, which I gather is somewhere nearby. She wants to know if she can be like me." Scanning the crowd looking for the naive young questioner, Rachel smiles, "Well, Amy, they broke the mold when they made me. However, who knows what the future will hold."

Sifting through the papers, "Let's see, what else do we have here … Too dirty. Not answering that one. Um, this person wrote really small."

Holding the note printed on a different color paper up to her watery eyes, Rachel tries to keep it together while her heart beats out of her chest, "Does your daughter … um, does your daughter possess the Blue Spark?" Sensing the questioner's glee at striking paydirt, she summons a maternal instinct to protect her child from this cruel world, "No. She is a normal little girl and the apple of her father's eyes." Verging on tears and wanting nothing more than to fly away, Rachel wills herself to act natural, or they will know. She cannot let them know.

"I think I have time for one more question: Let's see … this person wrote a paragraph, so bear with me … The people are suffering, and the cities are rotten cesspools of crime, drugs, and depravity. President Jackson has failed to deliver on her promises. Why do you support her and VP Epps?"

Eager to redirect the presentation back to politics, Rachel fixes a bright smile on her pale complected face, "It is hard to believe over three years have passed since the Gork invasion rocked Earth back to the analog days. We all lost loved ones on that terrible night and in the days, weeks, and months that followed. I am not here to say that Jackson has a handle on every problem. Far from it. Most of you will return to homes still without power and clean running water. Lena knows that is not right. She also understands how much you miss the internet. It is coming. If you have digital access already, count your blessings. If not, make friends with someone who does. But great things are happening out here in the heartland. Folks are not waiting for the big daddy government to swoop in and save the day. That is not forthcoming in the foreseeable future. The Jackson Epps administration encourages self-determination. What better place to underscore that point than beneath the Gateway Arch, symbolic of American greatness, perseverance, and resilience.

In the post-invasion reality where we all live, Lena has instructed what's left of the federal government to focus on the big picture. Therefore, on a granular level, where people live their lives, neighbors must help neighbors. Or we will perish. That ballyhooed Global Reset is not working as planned. Did you know President Jackson had the foresight not to involve the United States in that mess? That alone should be enough to earn her trust and to put your faith in her successor, Gordon Epps. So, without further ado, let me introduce my dear friend, President Lena Jackson!"

Thunderous applause greets the über-popular Black Independent, whose reelection in 2044 happened by default on the heels of the invasion, averting a constitutional crisis.

"Thank you, Rachel, for the kind introduction! Most of you do not know this, but I first met this adorable, sexy woman I now call a close personal friend when I awarded Rachel and her husband, Owen, the Presidential Medal of Freedom around a month after the invasion. At that ceremony, I invited Rachel to accompany me around the country to meet fellow Americans pulling themselves up in the post-invasion world. Hearing from everyday heroes learning to grow food, rebuild shelters, and form an interconnected grid of tight-knit communities has made my Libertarian heart swell with pride. It bolstered my core political belief that small towns and communities require the federal government's absence, not our presence. So, the Jackson and Epps administration will continue to tread lightly, assist only when necessary, and foster a rugged American individualism. That is how our forebears did it, and that, by God, is how we will rise up and return America to that shining city on the hill."

Lena turned and winked at Rachel, standing out of Epp's reach, before continuing her heartfelt speech.

"The last few decades have seen a sharp decline in American exceptionalism brought about by misguided leaders abdicating our leadership role while degrading us into a third-world nation. Well, what those idiots started, the Gorks finished in under a day, dragging the United States—the entire world—into a dark abyss. We must reemerge as the world's preeminent superpower and pull our fellow humans into an enlightened new age for humanity."

Glancing backward toward her vice president's smiling mug, Lena jokes, "Better not screw it up, Gordon."

With their confidence buoyed by Lena's gravitas, the enthusiastic masses go ballistic as Jackson smooths the lapel of her shimmering blue suit and ushers Rachel forward, "Hello, Rachel. Girlfriend, you make quite an entrance."

Rachel's blueness fades to a semi-normal human complexion as she enfolds the shorter Lena in a warm embrace, "Are you wearing blue in my honor, Madame President?"

Lena makes a sweeping gesture for the crowd, emulating a corny vaudeville comedy duo, and replies with a raucous laugh, "Gee, Rachel, I guess I am!"

The crowd can't get enough of the famous women's repartee, watching their tête-à-tête streaming live on the jumbo screens as the third wheel, Gordon Epps, ambles forward to join the improvised banter, "I can top that, Rachel. I'm wearing blue underwear in your honor."

The crowd falls silent. Crickets.

Sensing a palpable tension between Lena and Epps, Rachel plays peacemaker, moving behind the podium to distract from the awkward moment, "Blue underwear? Really, Gordon? I'm honored, I guess." Ignoring the script, Rachel improvises, "Hey, that's right. We are here—at least I know I am—to throw our support behind Gordon's 2048 candidacy!"

A scattering of polite applause follows Rachel's lackluster endorsement. Having already seen the blue woman fly like Superman and the celebrity Black female president's post-invasion pep talk, most onlookers and curious lose interest and disburse into the waning light with a keen awareness that downtown environs turn treacherous after dark.

Unsure she should proceed with her speech, Rachel spots Lou's agents coordinating the premature departing crowds with the undermanned local authorities and a scattering of green National Guard troops.

Facing the president, Rachel shrugs, "It appears the party is over."

Lena smiles and turns to her VP, "Don't worry, Gordon. We got this. Your poll numbers are right where we want them."

On the cusp of a snarky and inappropriate reply, Gordon's eyes widen with fear as an ear-piercing buzz screams overhead in sync with thousands of puzzled faces watching formations of miniature drones swooping under the Gateway Arch. After flying up the Mississippi at wavetop level to avoid detection, the tiny unmanned aerial assault zooms over retreating crowds, dropping incendiaries at random and spraying bullets on the terrified stampede of panicked people fleeing for their lives.

With her security detail out of position following the rally's premature ending, President Jackson hits the deck as Epps takes long backward strides toward steps leading offstage under the massive video display, "Gordon! Get down, you fool!"

A point-blank volley of rocket-propelled explosives punches holes in the stage before detonating from underneath, catapulting Epps like a ragdoll into the mangled pipe and drape, impaling him through the chest on a jagged shard. Alive and gasping for air, Epps makes one last struggling attempt to free himself as the jumbo screen crumples atop him, causing the twisted remnants of the stage to collapse at a sharp angle.

Bleeding from multiple shrapnel wounds opening new cuts over scar tissue that never fully healed, Rachel pulls herself behind the toppled podium and peers through the dizzying chaos with the blood-curdling screams of maimed and injured ratcheting through flaming tatters of flags and bunting fluttering through the smoke. Verging on passing out from blood loss, she spies Lena facedown under debris with her hands covering her head.

Ears ringing and a gash bleeding down her forehead, Rachel surges Blue Spark energy within every fiber of her being, "Lena, come here and grab onto me! I'm getting you out of here!"

Ashen-faced and in shock, President Jackson pulls onto her hands and knees, crawling up the listing stage toward Rachel's outstretched hands.

"What happened …?"

"Put your arms around me, Madame President, and hold on tight."

Lena throws her arms around Rachel's waist and feels herself rising above the screaming crowds, "I'm sorry, Rachel."

"It's not your fault, Lena. I could have said no to all of this." Sensing Lena's faltering grip, Rachel yells over the din, "I'm losing you; grab onto my cape." With Jackson's bloody hands clinging to her shiny blue suit, Rachel rises thirty feet above the chaos, searching for an escape route through the thick black smoke with the terrifying whines of killer drones filling her ears and blocking all exits.

"How will I get you out of here?"

Watching the remote-controlled attackers zeroing in on her and the president, Rachel pivots in midair, shielding Jackson with her body seconds before short, merciless volleys of white-hot metal rounds hit her back and right arm. Screaming in agonizing pain, Rachel chokes up bloody spittle, turning from blue to alabaster seconds before dropping like a rock into the VIP section atop a charnel house of bodies littered among heaps of flaming debris.

Caked and splattered in bloody gore, the former trust fund murderess lies at an unnatural angle, bent backward over a twisted metal barricade. Struggling to turn her head, Rachel meets President Lena Jackson's one-eyed stare—unable to quantify skull fragments and brain matter where the other half of Lena's beautiful face used to be. Coughing up more blood, Rachel's vision darkens as a paralyzing numbness takes hold.

* * *

Hurtling off the stage and rushing toward the president, Lou Pastorini empties his last mag at fleeing drones disappearing through the turmoil. "Good God. What did they do?"

Bleeding from shrapnel wounds, Lou keeps one eye on the dark skies, reaching across the dead president with an audible gasp before triaging young Rachel Haig, lying unconscious with her back broken over a thick metal rail. Grasping for straws, Lou checks for a pulse and snarls at first responders stumbling through the charred debris, "Over here! Bring a stretcher board on the double. She is still alive!"

* * *

The assassinations of President Lena Jackson and Vice President Gordon Epps ignited worldwide societal upheaval. In America, the decrepit old parties rise like zombies and realign into an ill-advised Unification Party.

The unholy political alliance between the progressives and neocons exploited the violent St. Louis incident to enact martial law, bank seizures, forced rationing, and firearm confiscations under a thin-veiled guise of protecting America from itself.

The unconstitutional coalition government tosses President Lena Jackson's laissez-faire *American Renewal Program* onto the ash heap of history and replaces it with an overbearing centralized control. Crushing a promising reawakening of good old-fashioned American know-how and self-determination leaves most with no choice but fealty to a corrupt, haphazard Orwellian top-down system. All but the most stoic self-starters surrender their liberty to the state in exchange for a place at an overcrowded Big Brother trough.

Anastasia Gabreski | PTB HQ
05:45 p.m. | April 1, 2048

The Council elects Anastasia Gabreski, the PTB UN ambassador and former Polish supermodel, to deliver their impassioned plea for Andrew to marshal the PTB's resources and end the madness in America before their oldest ally plunges into a catastrophic civil war.

Addressing Andrew via remote from her farmhouse retreat in upstate New York, Gabby's famous locks shimmer and cascade over a loose cotton blouse as she states the case in her well-rehearsed persuasive tone, "Andrew, be reasonable. Our old boss, Artemus Pennywell, would not only quash the fascism sweeping the US and the world but also dispatch Aisha Ayad's agents to apprehend the assassins behind the drone strike. Therefore, speaking for The Council, we reject your directive to stand down and not intercede. Andrew? Not intercede? Since when is that in our charter? No. If this is your decision, you will have all of our resignations. Please look into your heart, Andrew, and reconsider before it is too late."

Already approaching his fourth year as CEO of The Powers That

Be, Andrew proffers a steely smile at the ever-alluring Ms. Gabreski via the closed-circuit video conference, "You look good, Gabby. I see you have no qualms about reaping the benefits of your position within the PTB."

Feeling the sting of Andrew's pointed jibe, "Yeah, sure, Andrew. You can go fuck yourself. I am living off the land, like everybody else. I am also giving away bushels of food every week. Anything else?"

Amused that he struck a nerve with minimal effort, Andrew turns down the heat, "I apologize, Ms. Gabreski. I did not mean to offend. It is just an observation. If you are out. There is no coming back."

Gabby leans into her camera, "We are standing on principal. You should join us instead of coming off like a complete asshole."

"Okay. Let me be blunt, like an asshole, to use your pejorative phrasing. You and your colleagues are misinformed. The United States under Lena Jackson was a thorn in Artemus' side from her first day as president. Where were our dear friends, the Americans, when Griffin Pike convened a kangaroo court at the Hague and dragged our names through the muck?

No. I sympathize with America's plight but let that be a lesson to any nation trying to make a go of it alone. After the Gorkian invasion, the US was offered a prime seat at the Global Rebuild table. The Jackson administration said no thanks. And now they suffer the consequence of that decision.

Due to President Jackson's reticence to involve the US beyond its borders, the rebuild has become an embarrassing global disaster. Could the post-invasion world have benefitted from access to the American military-industrial complex, not to mention scores of architects, engineers, and craftsmen? In their absence, the PTB was left by default to pick up the pieces and make lemonade from the rotting, sour lemons. In a former world, that would have been a job for the US, which garnered trillions in the name of nation-building on every continent. But that was then; this is now. No. The PTB's resources are already stretched beyond the limit. There will be no help for the Americans. They are on their own."

Andrew concludes with a dismissive shrug, "Gabby, feel free to follow Viraj Patel's footsteps and quit. That goes for the rest of you eavesdropping on the conversation. Kudos, by the way, for nominating Ms. Gabreski as your spokesperson, but America will receive no help from the PTB. I hope I have made myself clear on that point."

Andrew ends the transmission and leans back in his chair, staring at an empty gray wall, "Soon, it will not matter anymore."

With a thin smile widening across his rakish visage, Andrew uses a small military attack drone as a paperweight to hold down the leading edge of an unrolled set of blueprints detailing an arena shaped like a woman's breast with an erect nipple high atop, languishing half-built in Hanover, Germany.

Perhaps these architectural geniuses spend too much time at the local brothels.

Rachel | Hilltop
08:42 p.m. | July 4, 2048

"Mommy, watch! Daddy is lighting another firework!"

Hearing her three-year-old daughter's high-pitched giggling echoes through the trees, Rachel bumps her wheelchair along a familiar root-infested brick path. Peering downhill past lightning bugs blinking on and off, a sparkling rocket bursts across the dark sky like a shooting blue comet from a clearing along the Hilltop property line where Hannah is having the time of her life watching her father light off unsafe and insane contraband fireworks, courtesy of the PTB.

Loath to sound like the family killjoy, Rachel hesitates before shouting toward the festive pair, "Owen, are you sure no one lives in the house next door?"

Owen's response resonates through the darkness, "It's been empty since the Gorks—don't worry!"

"Well, can you at least make sure Hannah stays safe?"

More laughter and another whooshing blue comet's harmless trajectory over the hill precede a sing-songy, *"We will, Mommy!"* duet.

On her fifth day back home at the Alexander family estate in a tony Newport, Rhode Island enclave, Rachel struggles to monitor her husband and daughter's fireworks display through the encroaching darkness. "Is that a sparkler? Hannah, hold that away from your face, honey!"

Checking the temptation to elevate out of her wheelchair and monitor her husband and child, Rachel allows herself a frustrated sigh.

No. I have been out of commission for four long months. Let them have fun without Mommy's freak show.

Unable to remember the name of the family that used to live in the magnificent one-story house next door, Rachel leaves Owen and Hannah to continue their fireworks fun. Paralleling a tall, thick privacy hedge, she pushes open an iron gate into the Craftsman-style mansion's expansive backyard entertaining area around the covered pool deck toward festive string lights illuminating the artfully landscaped backyard patio.

Enjoying the familiar cool and salty evening air on her face, Rachel applies her wheelchair brakes, spying a sight for sore eyes situated midway along an outdoor teak dining table uplit by the flickering firepit, nursing a teacup.

"Stanley Hobbes! You made it! I'm so glad you could join us."

Catching his first look at Rachel since her return, the human sparkplug jumps from his chair and rushes to bearhug Rachel, causing his thick round specks to slide up his shiny forehead, "It is so good to see you again, Rachel. You had everyone worried sick."

"I am so sorry, Stanley, for putting everyone through months of hell, but I am here now."

Stanley wipes his glasses with an old hankie, "I miss our late-night chats at the bookshop."

"I do, too, Stanley. I have not been there since the night my father died."

"I remember. The next thing I heard was you were off on another whirlwind adventure with Owen."

"To this day, I am unsure how much of the Amazon incident I am allowed to divulge."

The two sit in silence for a moment, basking in each other's company, *"Stanley, can you hear me now?"*

"Yes. That is impressive."

"I can fly, too."

"I know; I watched your performances with the president when I could hack into a live stream. I am also glad you are letting your hair grow back."

Rachel brushes a hand through her unruly bedhead blond bob and smiles, eschewing the telepathy to speak aloud, "After losing most of it in the Amazon, I was happy to keep it short and spiky. And it made sense when flying around like a superhero. It is more practical than hair flying in my face. A lot goes into being a superhero that never shows up in the comic books and movies."

Stanley smiles and sips his tea, "Do tell."

Showing off for her lifelong friend and confidante, Rachel lets her face glow to a cerulean blue while reaching for a slice of cheese and a cracker, "Thanks for coming, Stanley, and happy Fourth of July … I guess."

Impressed with Rachel's mastery of the Blue Spark within and without every fiber of her being, Stanley Hobbes nods approval, "Who needs fireworks when they have you?" Twirling the tea in his cup, he continues, "And by the way, happy Fourth of July does not resonate in this Orwellian world."

Rachel reaches forward, grasping his hand, "Let's not talk politics, Stan. How is business?"

"In a word, through the roof." With a throaty chuckle, he adds, "That's more like three words. Since the invasion, I can't keep anything on the shelves. People are starving for good old-fashioned printed hard-copy books."

Spreading a local-sourced blackberry jam on a hunk of fresh-baked bread, he adds, "I had three boxes of Orwell's *1984*. Sold out in a weekend." Taking a chomp, he drips jam on his pilled flannel shirt and wipes it with a napkin.

Only now catching up with the draconian measures sweeping the country since the St. Louis terror attack, Rachel helps him dab at the dark, purplish stain, "Yeah, I gather things are taking a dark turn in this country since Lena's death." Making one last swipe with a wettened napkin, she smiles, "Dad has a signed first edition *1984* up in the library. Take it. We'll split the proceeds, just like old times."

Stanley repeats, "Just like old times." Finishing the bread and jam with a sly wink, he adds, "Oh man, that is a little slice of Heaven."

After an odd twitch and a raspy cough, Stanley finishes his tea and leans back in his seat, "You know, this reminds me of the old days."

"Okay, I'll bite. How so?"

"Hannah. That's how so. Not only does she remind me of you at that age, she *is* you."

Rachel leans forward in her chair and punches the short man's arm, "That's right. You were stalking me even when I was a small child."

Not taking the joke, Stanley frowns, "Believe me. I wasn't stalking. I know stalking—that was not it. Plus, I had a thing for Miriam."

Rachel laughs, "You and Mom?"

Stanley's mind wanders free, "She was something back in her day."

"Yeah, I miss her too."

"Who do we miss?"

Rachel twists sideways in her chair toward Dave Poole, the Haig's de-facto righthand man—and trained PTB bodyguard—approaching with another tray piled high with homemade snacks. "You are doing too much, Dave. Sit and visit with us. Owen and Hannah are hellbent on lighting the neighborhood on fire, so it's up to you to help us eat all this wonderful food you prepared."

Flinging a towel over his shoulder, Dave pulls out a heavy teak chair and plops into the creaking seat, "Okay, don't mind if I do."

Stanley grabs a hunk of salami from the refilled charcuterie board, "You put out quite a spread, young man."

Filling a plate with an assortment of local treats, from bread and honey to homemade sausages and cheeses, Dave has to laugh, "You know, back in the day, I enjoyed going to the supermarket. Now I realize most of the food we used to eat was prepackaged crap. This is so much better. I don't know about other parts of the world, but folks have learned how to make it for themselves here in New England."

Stanley raises a cracker stacked with meat and cheese, "And sell it at a premium, too."

"Yes. Too true, Mr. Hobbes." Refilling Rachel's glass with fresh lemonade, Dave offers a warm smile, "It is good to have you back at Hilltop, Mrs. Haig."

"Thank you, Dave. It is good to be home."

"You know, I never heard what transpired after the assassinations in St. Louis."

Rachel grabs the lemonade glass and takes a long drink, "Where did you manage to find lemons?"

"I have my sources." Dave leans in, "Enough about the citrus … what happened to you after the attack? Poor Owen was a wreck. So was I."

Rachel leans back, cradling her glass, "Oh, well. That is quite a story. Apparently, at first, they thought I had died. Perhaps I was dead."

Hearing another bottle rocket whistling skyward before exploding in a sea of sparks, she leans forward in a conspiratorial whisper, "I do not wish to talk about this around Hannah."

Dave and Hobbes nod in unison. "Go on, Rachel. They can't hear us over the rocket's red glare."

Rachel chuckles, "Thanks for that, Stanley. By the way, how many sob stories have you heard from me through the years?" Wiping a tear, she continues, "Uh, okay, well, your people, Dave, other PTB agents, I guess, scooped up my bloody body and whisked me to a black site surgical unit. I know it was somewhere in Central America. To be honest, I was at death's door. It really did not matter where the hell it was." Clearing her throat and feeling a dizzy spell from her meds, Rachel tries to focus on her narrative, "Where was I? Oh yeah. Honduras. So, anyway, the first person I recognized was Dr. Gene Simmons. His team patched up my bullet-riddled body. The alien pharmaceuticals and surgical methods did a number on the superficial wounds that healed in days. It is amazing what they can do. However, the damage to my spinal column proved a bridge too far, leaving me paralyzed from the waist down."

Slapping her leg, she wheels closer to Dave, "Go ahead, Dave, pinch my thigh."

Looking at Rachel's long, bare legs tinged with a light shade of blue below her khaki shorts, Dave hesitates before reaching out and caressing her right thigh above the knee, "I am so sorry, Rachel."

Placing her hand on top of his, Rachel squeezes tight, "It will be okay. Between you and Owen and Stanley here. I will be fine. More important, Hannah is in excellent hands."

Sensing a latent passion between the handsome young adults, Stanley raises his teacup to break the spell, "I second that." Coughing and sputtering, he replaces the empty cup atop the saucer with his shaky hand, reaching for a pill bottle in his sweater.

Dave pulls back and stands to assist Stanley, "Hold tight, Mr.

Hobbes. I will fetch a glass of water." Touching Rachel's shoulder, he asks, "Do you need anything?"

Rachel pats his hand, "I have everything I need right here."

Stanley watches the man return inside before hitting Rachel with a conspiratorial grin, "Is there anything you want to tell me, Rachel?"

"No. Don't be ridiculous. Dave is a friend. That's all. Frankly, I don't know what we would do without him. With Owen gone half the time on his top-secret PTB business trips, Dave cares for this old house and keeps the riff-raff in check. I would never have accepted President Jackson's invitation to tour the heartland if not for Dave's constant presence in our lives. Hannah loves him, and Owen has the help he needs, especially with me in a wheelchair. It works."

Stanley coughs and winces in obvious pain. "If you say so. I won't pry."

Rachel wheels closer to her lifelong friend, "I have not seen you for over two years, but I can also tell when something is wrong. What is going on, Stanley?"

Stanley Hobbes turns to Rachel with a defeated grin on his unshaven face, "If you must know, I have Stage-3 lung cancer. At least that is what the fucking doctors tell me."

The blueness drains from Rachel's complexion, "No. I have access to the best doctors. I can …."

Stanley grimaces and squirms on the thick seat cushion, "Stop right there, Rachel. I already refused treatment. I will be fine until I am not. Do you know how long it takes to get a decent MRI scan? No thanks. This world is too screwed up to care for an old man like me. I have lived on borrowed time my whole life. I want to go out on my terms."

"Stanley, Stage-3 lung cancer is curable …."

Hobbes holds up his pudgy hand, "Enough." Regaining his composure, he pierces Rachel with his intelligent brown eyes, "Now you tell me, and don't even think about lying: How long can you keep this up?"

Rachel pulls back with a perplexed look furrowing her brow, "What are you talking about?"

Stanley leans in, whispering, "Hannah has the Blue Spark, doesn't she?"

Rachel's mind races before confiding with her friend via telepathy, *"Why do you think that?"*

A wan smile broadens across Stanley's bespectacled face, "I read people my whole life, Rachel. You know that. Right this very minute, I can tell you are using your powers to suppress Hannah's Blue Spark. Moreover, you sacrificed repairing your spine, knowing it would allow you to focus on her full-time without interference."

Rachel leans close and places a hand on Stanley's arm, *"It was near impossible to keep Hannah's abilities in check from halfway across the country. I can't let them take her, Stan. If I stay here, I can do it much easier. The PTB will leave her alone if I am paralyzed and they think she is a dud."*

Rachel watches her daughter sprint up the hill toward her Uncle Dave, balancing Stanley's water and a plate stacked with fresh-baked peanut butter cookies. Leaning close, Rachel squeezes Stanley's vintage gabardine slacks, *"So to answer your question, Stanley, I will keep it up until the day I die."*

* * *

Hannah scoots into a seat at the table across from Stanley, "Did you see the fireworks, Uncle Stan? Dad said someday I could be the first girl to ride on a comet. That would be so neat!"

Stanley beams across the table at the three-year-old blond cutie, "Wow, a comet … wouldn't that be something. And you know what, little Hannah Haig? That was the best fireworks show I have ever seen. And I used to party crash the Boston Pops every Fourth of July in my salad years."

Hannah giggles and chomps on one of Dave's delicious cookies,

"Salad years? I hate salad."

Rachel leans across the table and places a napkin before her daughter, "Hannah, don't talk with your mouth full."

"Okay, Mom."

Rubbing Hannah's blond head, Owen appears with a cooler and pops a homemade brew, offering a brown bottle to Stanley, "Would you care for a home-brewed Owen Ale, Mr. Hobbes?"

Dave follows Owen, splashing a jigger of craft gin in his tall lemonade glass before setting the bottle on the table, "Don't do it, Stanley. I'm pretty sure it causes cancer in rats."

With a wink toward Rachel, Stanley smiles, "I'll stick with my tea, thanks."

Dave and Owen recline at the table, scarfing down most of the meats, cheeses, and crackers as Rachel and Stanley look on and exchange furtive grins.

Popping the cap from another homemade brew, Owen turns to Dave, "You know what this little shindig is missing, my friend?"

"No. What?"

"Music." Owen turns toward Hannah, busy balancing a stack of cheese and meat on a cracker, "Would you like to serenade everyone with the song I taught you this morning?"

Pushing her plate aside and scooching out of her seat with a harumph, Hannah brushes stringy blond hair off her face and swipes sticky fingers across her Pajama Sam t-shirt, "Okay."

Stanley notes Hannah's familiar eye roll reminiscent of a young Rachel back in the day, "Oh boy. A concert."

Hannah rubs her button nose, "Gosh. How embarrassing."

Stanley remarks, "Embarrassing is a big word for a two-year-old."

Hannah walks into the light, where everyone can see her, "I'm three, Uncle Stanley."

"Oops, that's right. I'm sorry I missed your birthday party."

Kicking a small stone, Hannah averts her eyes from the grown-ups, "I didn't have a birthday party."

Looking toward Rachel for support but getting only a raised eyebrow in reply, Owen attempts to quell his daughter's repeated lament, "Come on, Hannah. This is your party. We were waiting for Mommy to be here. Remember?"

"I thought it was the United States' birthday."

"Are you going to sing the song or not?"

"Here it goes … Oh, say, can you see …

By the dawn's early light …"

Buhrrrp-buhrrrrp-buhrrrp …

Owen grabs his PTB satellite phone off the table, "Oh shit. Really? Sorry, Hannah, I have to take this call." Excusing himself from the party, he tousled his daughter's hair and moved past into the shadows, "Go on, honey, you sound great."

With one eye on Owen, Rachel listens as her daughter belts out the words written by Francis Scott Key in 1814, recounting another time in history when the future was uncertain. Watching Owen's body language, speaking in hushed tones out of earshot, her heart sinks, realizing he is not the same man she married. He is different. Looking down at her useless legs, she muses, *So am I.*

* * *

Standing in the darkness under an old oak tree, Owen half-listens to the PTB's top in-house legal expert, Vita Carrera, watching Rachel, Stanley, and Dave applaud Hannah's touching performance as his beautiful daughter takes her bow with a demonstrative: "Thank you. Thank you."

"I'm sorry, Ms. Carrera. Can you repeat that?"

"I said, it is time, Owen. We need you back in the game."

Owen looks toward his wheelchair-bound wife, seconding Dave's attempt to get Hannah inside the house for a hot bath and bedtime, "Rachel just arrived a few days ago. I can't just up and leave. I need to spend time here with her. It's important."

"How is Rachel?"

"She is in a fucking wheelchair. The PTB worked her over for months. Why couldn't they fix her?"

A long pause precedes Vita's reply, *"Owen, please keep what I am about to say confidential, but things within the PTB are changing even as we speak."*

"Okay. Like what? And who would I tell?"

"You know the drill, Mr. Haig. Loose lips and all of that shitty nonsense."

"Yeah. Yeah. I get it."

"Your flight to Toulouse is scheduled for Tuesday, July 7. From there, an autonomous lift will drop you at the Villa St. Claire, where your man awaits your return …."

"Wait. Slow the fuck down, Vita. My man at the villa? What are you talking about?"

"Louie. Do you remember him? The major-domo spearheaded efforts to extricate the forgeries stashed beneath the villa."

"I found those forgeries well over two years ago. What's taking so long?"

"Each piece is toxic, Mr. Haig, and must be handled with extreme care." After another pregnant, staticky pause, Vita emphasizes, *"It is Saturday on the East Coast, which gives you a couple of days with your family. I am sorry it cannot be longer. Dave has your itinerary; he will attend to all the details. All you need to do is ensure your ass is on that PTB transport out of Logan."*

The phone line drops as Owen walks back toward the table where Stanley sits alone, gnawing on one of Dave's peanut butter cookies.

"Where did everybody go?"

"Rachel and Dave took Hannah inside to wash the fireworks stink out of her hair and put her to bed."

"That's good. So, how are you, Stanley."

"Owen. I need to tell you something. My doctors give me between three and six months to live."

Thunderstruck by the horrible news, Owen shakes his head and sighs, "I am so sorry, Stanley. Does Rachel know?"

"I told her earlier tonight."

"How did she take the news?"

"She keeps a lot bottled up inside."

Owen runs a hand through his thick auburn hair, dreading giving her the news of another mysterious PTB trip, "Tell me about it."

Stanley rises from the table, "I know you are about to leave. It's your job; I get it. But I wish you could stay with Rachel and Hannah."

"Yeah, me too. I leave Tuesday." Owen nods, mulling a laundry list of to-do items requiring his attention, starting with Rachel's new situation, "Dave is handling retrofits to make the mansion wheelchair accessible. And I am hiring a live-in nanny to take care of Hannah."

Stanley adopts his best poker face, "I'll drop by and visit with Rachel for as long as my health will allow. I can keep an eye on things."

"Like what? Dave will look after Rachel and Hannah while I'm gone."

"Yeah, I might not be up to it for much longer. This cancer thing came on like a sonofabitch."

Owen extends his hand, "It has been an honor knowing you, Stanley."

The much shorter Stanley Hobbes reaches up and shakes Owen's hand, "Likewise, Owen. Likewise."

Know thy self, know thy enemy.

Sun Tzu

Chapter Five:

The Forger

Owen | Villa St. Claire
07:35 a.m. | July 8, 2048

Following a six-hour flight from Boston to Toulouse, an autonomous transport dumped Owen Haig at Villa St. Claire's front gate in the dead of night.

Purr, Purr, Purr, Purr …

Wrapped like a burrito, Owen awakens in the villa's master suite, struggling to recall how he got from the front gate into bed. Rolling over, his crusty eyes lock onto a familiar purring black-and-white feline.

"Okay, Mittens. I'm awake now." Rubbing its furry two-tone head, "I'm glad you are still keeping an eye on the place."

Scratching a vestigial surgical scar on his close-shaved noggin, Owen pads barefoot across the cool floor, pausing to squint past morning shadows angling from the Romanesque balcony outside the wide-open

French doors. Breathing in the cobweb-clearing Provence air, a tingling déjà vu creeps up his spine, "This place brings back so many memories."

Unzipping his bag to access a monogrammed shaving kit—a birthday gift from Rachel—gauzy memories of her lissome form in the pale blue moonlight conjure from their honeymoon stay four years earlier.

Mittens' nudging against his leg breaks the spell.

Clearing his dry throat, Owen snatches a locally sourced Aix-en-Provence mineral water from a credenza and gulps half the bottle as guilt for abandoning Rachel washes over him.

"Thank God for Dave."

"*Meow …*"

"Who is Dave? A good guy with a heart of gold."

"*Meow. Meow …*"

"Nope. I trust him."

"*Hello, sir.*"

Startled by the intrusion, Owen spins toward a resolute figure in the opened doorway silhouetted against the dark hall, "Louie, you scared the shit out of me! You ever hear of knocking?"

* * *

Gastrointestinal temblors accompany Owen's absent gaze outside disappearing sliding doors, sipping instant coffee at a long butcher block table in the casual dining space between the chef's kitchen and the villa's great room. Contemplating a breach of Louie's pantry, he reconsiders.

I better wait for Louie.

Functioning on three hours of shuteye, Owen finishes his cup and ventures into the darkened great room, encompassing a sizable portion of the back half of the villa's main floor.

Recalling Rachel's admiration of the rustic French furnishings, he muses upon one of the few things they discussed not involving the apocalypse, superpowers, aliens, or her damn Blue Spark while scooping a handful of stale popcorn from a half-eaten bowl on the coffee table.

We were never destined for an ordinary life.

Cracking a popcorn kernel between his teeth, Owen stares back down at the snack bowl.

Do robots eat popcorn?

Shelving the popcorn mystery with a loud yawn, Owen brushes past an end table, knocking an oversized hardcover volume onto the floor. Feeling like a bull in a China shop, he winces at the noticeable dent in its inlaid leatherbound cover while reading the book's title aloud, "*The Complete Works of Velázquez.* The Red Sox second baseman is named Valázquez."

More bored than curious, Owen works a popcorn kernel bit from his teeth while opening the heavy volume to a bookmarked full-page color plate featuring the striking image of a dour-faced pope.

Portrait of Innocent X
by Diego Velázquez
Oil on canvas. 1650

Closing the book with a satisfying loud thump, he replaces it atop the table, "He doesn't look very innocent to me."

Daylight leaking through a downstairs guest suite door ajar at the far back corner of the great room draws his bored and tired scrutiny.

Sneaking across the tiled floor like a thief in his own villa, Owen peeks inside, "Hello? Anybody home?"

Smelling a subtle yet alluring hint of musk, he notes tidy clothing piles around an open suitcase atop a four-post queen-sized bed, "Whoever you are, you travel much lighter than Rachel."

Realizing he is snooping on the presumed popcorn eater's privacy, Owen retreats to the kitchen for more coffee, with the mysterious muskiness lingering in the air.

Blowing steam off a fresh cup, Owen peers out streak-free

windows at the expansive hardscaped patio and immaculate teak furniture around meticulous maintained planters overflowing with flowers and manicured olive trees as his mind wanders onto the houseguest's identity.

Louie's approach with a bowl of fresh-picked lemons breaks the spell.

It's about time.

Owen ushers the replicant major-domo inside the parted sliders as Louie replies with a courteous nod, proceeding around the long central island to place the citrus bowl beside harvested avocados and onions.

Deciding not to open with *What's for breakfast?* Owen raps his knuckles on the polished granite, offering a sincere compliment, "I must say, Louie, the place looks fantastic."

A modest smile widens under Louie's thin mustache, "It is a large estate requiring constant attention. We do what we can. Lola and Sven are tireless caretakers while I supervise and maintain a strict schedule."

Saving the mystery houseguest question for last, Owen scratches his chin, "What about the other one … what's its name …."

"You mean Nils? He is no longer with us."

"What happened?"

"I had to deactivate him."

Placing his empty cup in the deep farmhouse sink, Owen turns to the major-domo with unmasked incredulity, "Louie, no offense, but Nils was nothing but chips, wires, and goo. What could he have done?"

"He was infected with spyware, Master Owen. Tragic really. I had to turn him off and send him back to Milan." With a coy smile, Louie adds, "Speaking of Milan, it must be exciting for you to learn that Bianca Valentino has joined the team."

"Am I supposed to know who she is?"

"Her CV is included in your briefing materials. It is required reading."

"Good Christ, Louie, you are not my mother. If you must know, I planned a marathon cram session by the pool today."

"Ah, I see. In answer to your original query, Ms. Valentino is a high-profile art forgery investigator from Milan." Shooting Owen with a perplexed grin, "You never heard of her? She has written books on her investigations into art forgery within the criminal underworld. The PTB contracted her as the ranking consultant overseeing the extensive stash of forgeries you discovered beneath the villa. That project ended over a year ago. She returned two days ago to participate in this new mission."

"Yeah, right, the mission. So, this Valentino woman is here with us now?"

"Oui, Monsieur. Ms. Valentino prefers the first-floor guest room right over there."

Still smelling a trace of musk in the air—or somehow on his clothes and skin—Owen feigns nonchalance while feeling way behind the eight-ball with the day young and full of potential pitfalls, "I see."

Noting Owen's blush response, an amused Louie decides to have a little fun at the human's expense, "Ms. Valentino also enjoys spending her mornings poolside. In fact, she has been known to forgo a bathing suit."

Owen nods, "Really? Well, when in Rome."

Louie's head tilts at an almost imperceptible angle, "I am not sure what that means."

His face reddening, Owen shrugs, "I don't know, Louie. Italian women are open about their sexuality, that sort of thing. Why are we having this conversation?"

Trying not to smile, Louie waves a dismissive hand through the air, "I see. Yes, your assessment holds true in Ms. Valentino's case. No matter. I am sure you two should get along quite well."

After a furtive scan of Owen's spiking pulse, the conniving replicant pulls the rug out from under Owen, "By the way, Monsieur, how is Rachel? I heard about the terrible incident in St. Louis. Tragic. You have my deepest sympathies."

"Rachel is doing fine, Louie. Thank you for asking."

With the hunger pangs long forgotten, a random thought rises to the surface in Owen's discombobulated psyche, *I wonder if I packed swim trunks?*

"Let me know if you need suitable pool attire. In the meantime, I will prepare a snack bag for the pool."

Wary of the poker-faced Frenchman, Owen nods, "Thanks, Louie, I guess I'll go upstairs and change."

The über-advanced Kobayashi C-Class replicant watches Owen retreat down the darkened central hallway.

The poor man does not stand a chance.

* * *

Teeth brushed, fresh-breathed, and clean-shaven, Owen locates board shorts in his overstuffed travel bag, "Good old Dave." Stepping into the trunks and pulling a Wharton t-shirt over his head, he checks himself in a full-length mirror, "Oh shit, better lose the price tag on the shorts."

Extricating the encrypted PTB tablet from his bag, Owen plops onto the bed beside Mittens, curled up in the unmade sheets. "08:45 already."

Tapping a virtual keyboard through a tedious authentication process—designed to bore would-be hackers to death—the sensual muskiness returns. Sniffing the short-haired cat with a flummoxed frown, "Dammit, Mittens, I can't tell where that is coming from."

Shelving the Nancy Drew perfume mystery, the reluctant PTB white-collar crime investigator watches the virtual screen manifest before his tired eyes. Swiping aside three-dimensional case files, research, and data folders, he comes to the TEAM folder, "Eureka." Skimming the alphabetized roster past Haig, O., he highlights the last entry.

"Valentino, B. That is our sweet-smelling mystery guest, Mittens. Let's see what she is all about."

Bounding downstairs wearing a PTB cap and dark shades, Owen listens to the English-accented narration of Bianca Valentino's impressive CV uploaded to an aural chip embedded in his left ear. On his way out the back sliders, he grabs the insulated bag Louie filled with snacks and crosses the patio down the natural rock steps onto the graveled beltway encircling the villa.

Crunching over pebbles and sand around the mansion's southwestern corner, the preoccupied Owen fails to notice Lola waving from high atop the conservatory with glass cleaning supplies in her multi-armed robot grippers.

At a fork, Owen takes a switchback trail down the rugged forested hillside. A white rabbit eyeballs the stranger before hopping off in a hurry, evoking a scene from a famous children's book within the 31-year-old Vermont native's memory. Seeing a red-tiled roof through the lush greenery, he breaks from the woods and swipes his hand before a locked iron gate. Hearing the kerchunk, he pushes through, entering the villa's legendary pool—the scene of debauchery, decadence, and at least one death dating back to the 70s. Disconnecting the narration in his ear, he jogs past the terracotta pool house down terraced steps to the sparkling azure swimming pool built into the rocky hillside with its commanding view of the Côte d'Azur.

"Breathtaking, just like I remembered it." Recalling poor Jaques St. Claire, he adds, "minus the bloated body at the bottom of the pool."

Ignoring the tanned female presence lying on her belly atop a flattened chaise lounge before bougainvillea cascading over the rocks at the far side of the main pool deck, Owen proceeds in the opposite direction, reorienting a chaise toward the sweeping vista. Plopping down with a loud yawn, he calls across the water to the only person within earshot, "What a great place to spend the morning!"

Getting zero response from Bianca Valentino in a lemon-yellow two-piece bikini facing away from him under a bright green floppy sunhat, Owen decides to—as Rachel always begs him—play it cool. Popping the cap off a Peroni beer Louie added to the bag, he takes a long pull, and snugs back against his warm, soft towel in the Mediterranean sunshine. Realizing he is drinking the lukewarm Italian brew a little after nine in the morning, he emits another yawn.

Oh well, it's five o'clock somewhere.

Cradling the bottle against his chest, Owen's eyes grow heavy behind his dark shades, falling into a deep slumber within minutes.

* * *

The papal portrait masterpiece animates with terrifying snarls from its hideously deranged and contorted face ripping into three dimensions from the desiccated canvas mounted within an ornate life-size picture frame, sending frightened museum patrons stampeding for the exits with their clothes ablaze and blood cascading from their eyes like waterfalls.

Soaked in beer with his hat and sunglasses askew, Owen's harrowing nightmare ends with a startled yelp as a hazy feminine presence resolves out of the brightness. Realizing he squeezes her slender hand in a vicelike grip, he lets go on impulse, causing her to fall backward. Removing his shades, the dark-haired, olive-skinned beauty comes into focus. "I must have dozed off. Did I hurt you?"

Perched on the edge of a chaise under her floppy green sunhat, she flexes her hand with a casual shrug, "I am fine. No broken bones. Plus, I startled you first."

"I am such an idiot. Let's start over."

"That is a good idea. I am Bianca Valentino, and you must be the world-famous Owen Haig."

Reeling from the nightmare and beyond embarrassed, the stench from Owen's beer-sodden shorts permeates the late-morning heat, "Not sure about the world-famous part, but yeah, that's me.

"The major-domo failed to mention your arrival, or I would have waited at the villa this morning to make a proper introduction."

"Uh, yeah, Louie can be a little tight-lipped. It is in his programming from what I have read about C-Class replicants ...." Trying not to get lost in Bianca's dark-brown eyes, an impertinent thought crosses Owen's reactivating mind.

Reading the American like a book, Bianca adjusts her mesh bathing suit cover and crosses her legs, "Do not worry about me, Mr. Haig. I am as human as you are. If cut, I bleed." With a flirty grin, she adds, "If you squeeze my hand, it hurts."

"Very perceptive, Ms. Valentino. I need to take a dip in the pool. Care to join me?"

"Yes. And please call me Bianca." With an effervescent smile, the long-legged Italian flings off her hat and cover, yelling, "Last one in is a rotten egg!" before jumping feet-first into the pool.

Treading water, the Milanese dunks her head, pulling short black hair off her fresh face as Owen makes a showy summersault into the deep end.

Reinvigorated by the shimmering waters, Owen comes up for air, "Boy, did I need that."

Bianca laughs and splashes water in his face, "You were a little smelly, Mr. Haig."

"Bianca, no one calls me Mr. Haig. Owen is fine." Swimming closer, he swipes salty water from his eyes and frowns, "You know, it is a weird thing. When you woke me up, I was having a terrible nightmare about a painting I saw in a book earlier this morning—I guess it stuck with me. It is a portrait ... Innocent something ...."

"Ah, the Velázquez portrait of Pope Innocent X. I had bookmarked that page last night. The one displayed at the reopened Galleria Doria Pamphilj in Rome was another forgery. It was removed before causing any injuries. Thank God."

Swimming closer and lowering her voice with her lips just above the water, she whispers, "After the invasion, everything that was not destroyed or looted was taken down and warehoused at secret locations."

Eager to show off his historical acumen, Owen chimes in, "Ah, like the salt mines where the Nazis stored all of the looted art during World War 2."

"Precisely. Handsome and smart. Mrs. Rachel Haig is a lucky girl."

Owen smiles, "Uh, yes. I'm not sure luck is the word she would use these days."

"Of course. I did not mean to make a joke."

"It is okay. My wife is a survivor."

"A survivor? Owen, your wife is Wonder Woman. Every little girl wants to be her. I must admit, I am a little envious."

Owen kicks and smooths his arms through the water to keep afloat, "Envious? Why?"

"She can fly."

Accidentally brushing his foot against Bianca's leg, Owen drifts backward, "I can give you the inside scoop on Rachel's exploits—which are unbelievable even for me, and I was there—over whatever Louie is cooking for dinner." Remembering his homework reading assignment, Owen raises a finger, "However, since the day is young and we have nothing better to do, tell me about the mission. All I know is it has to do with the forgeries I discovered under the villa."

"Not much of a reader?"

Owen flicks water at the vivacious woman, "No. I love to read. It's just that the PTB can never just be forthcoming. They have to put everyone through the cloak and dagger nonsense."

"Do not worry, Owen. I can bring you up to speed. Where was I? Oh yes, as civilization returns to a semi-normal new world, art museums, like the one in Rome where Pope Innocent X hung, are reopening for the first time since before the Gorks ruined everything."

"Okay. Isn't that a good thing?"

"Yes, Owen, but corrupt government and museum officials have seized upon the opportunity to insert a new kind of forgery in place of the originals."

"They can't all be on the take. No one can spot a forgery coming through the door?"

"Museums and auction houses have had difficulty spotting forgeries for centuries. And now, new technology has rendered it next to impossible until it is too late. The forgery network we are investigating is a singular cog in a worldwide criminal enterprise. They are diabolical, strategic, and tactical, utilizing AI and robotics to replicate specific works at a sub-molecular level. In effect, creating perfect duplicates of the originals."

Owen's eyes widen, "They can do that? Wow."

Bianca frowns, "Are you surprised? The Kobayashi Replicant Plant in my hometown of Milan has been replicating people for years. Why not use the same processes and techniques to copy a painting, a statue, an artifact, or just about anything?"

"Are you saying the PTB is involved in this? They have run the Milan factory since old man Kobayashi's death in 44."

With a conspiratorial wink, Bianca smiles, "I did not imply anything. Draw your own conclusions."

"Well, okay then. What is the tactical part?"

Floating closer, she lowers her voice to a whisper, "The forgers are replacing priceless originals with fakes that remain undetected until they activate a deadly nanotechnology embedded in the art."

"Nanotech?"

Bianca winces, "Owen, lower your voice. We don't know who is listening. A remote command triggers millions of atom-sized robots within the forged artwork, turning each piece into a mind-altering nightmare, like a bad acid trip. Simply put, people go mad, throwing themselves off buildings or ripping each other apart. So far, five occurrences have ended in mass casualty events."

Owen's eyes widen, "Wait a minute. Are you saying the art I found beneath the villa had this nanotech? I could have been killed or gone on a murderous rampage. Jesus …."

"Owen, the art you found was destined for museums all over the world—you saved countless lives."

Owen smiles, "How about that? I'm saving the world without even trying. What a hero."

"You can joke all you want, Owen. I worked here as a freelance investigator for the PTB for over a year, cataloging and destroying the fakes while tracking the originals in public or private collections scattered across Europe. Louie's immunity to the nanotech proved a valuable bonus."

"Something does not add up here. I found Jacques St. Claire at the bottom of this pool. If he was deep into this forgery business, why did he commit suicide?"

"He didn't." Bianca's foot kicks against Owen's leg, "Jacques St. Claire was a scoundrel, a thief, and a dangerous drug addict with a penchant for underage sex, but he was not into genocide. He threatened to go public. So, they murdered him and made it look like a suicide."

"So. Jacques St. Claire did not kill himself. Print that on a t-shirt."

Treading water, Bianca smooths her long leg against Owen with a flirtatious grin, "Do I have your attention, Mr. Haig? Buono. Your mission—should you choose to accept it—is to locate the control center where the nanotech-infused forgeries are activated and destroy it so no one else gets hurt."

Owen backstrokes away from the playful Italian's legs, "Ah, a fellow *Mission Impossible* fan."

"I always wanted to say that line."

Owen | Villa St. Claire
02:46 p.m. | July 17, 2048 – 9 days later

Over a week after arriving in France in a mad rush, Owen exits the villa's front doors and stomps to the middle of the long curved driveway holding a wonky satellite phone Louie scrounged, hoping for a clear connection to fucking Scotland. Feeling ridiculous calling The Powers That Be secret underground HQ but desperate to discover why he had to drop everything and rush to France, he enters the long series of numbers. Again.

Getting nothing but static, Owen verges on aborting the call when a voice answers: *"What can I do for you, Mr. Haig?"*

Surprised to hear a living, breathing human's voice through the background noise, "First of all, I am freaking out that you already know who is calling. And second, let me talk to Andrew."

Former PTB Hospitality Manager Edgar Lopez's demotion back to entry-level receptionist duties—because someone had to answer the damn phone—replies with a weary sigh, *"Mr. Haig, you are using an unencrypted satellite phone to call an ultra-secure line meant for dire emergencies. And second, even if the PTB CEO was here, I doubt he would take your call. He is a very busy man."*

"Okay then, Edgar. It's Edgar, right? Let me speak with Vita Carrera."

"Ms. Carrera is not here. However, she did leave a sealed envelope with your initials on it. Do you think it is meant for you?"

"Let's open it and find out."

"Oh boy, this is all so James Bond."

"Just read the message, Edgar."

"Okay, here it goes, she has lovely penmanship …."

"Edgar!"

"Okay! Keep your pants on. It says: OH, take advantage of BV mission intel. SHE KNOWS." After a pause, Edgar continues, *"Uh, well,*

that is a bit cryptic. I wonder what SHE KNOWS means. Anyway, that is it. Wait. I'm lying. On the opposite side, she wrote, TRUST NO ONE."

"Well, shit Edgar. What am I supposed to do with that? If BV is Bianca Valentino, should I trust her?"

Edgar's voice cracks as one of the Sisters in a white lab coat busts into his office without knocking and enters an adjoining supply room. *"Mr. Haig … strange things are happening around here …."* Lowering his voice to just above whisper, *"Mr. Haig, are you still there?"*

"I am here, Edgar. What do you mean by strange things?"

"I am scared."

"Edgar, keep it together. When did you last see Vita Carrera in person or hear her voice?"

"Over a week ago. "

"Is that normal?"

"No. Ms. Carrera is the Chief Legal Counsel. As a matter of fact, she missed her Monday meeting with Andrew."

"Edgar, listen to me. If you hear from Vita, give her the number to the phone I am calling you on right now. Or better yet, tell her to come here. I have plenty of room."

Owen hears Edgar whimpering through the static, *"Mr. Haig, what about me?"*

"If you can get here, Edgar, you are more than welcome."

Owen ends the call and shakes his head, "What the hell is going on? I better call Rachel and Dave. Something is rotten in the state of Denmark."

* * *

With a burgeoning dread creeping up his spine, Edgar slides the OH note into a journal he has maintained since Andrew took control and adds it to his stylish cross-body bag. "I need to leave."

"Going somewhere, Edgar?"

Pivoting onto an identical Sister, fingering lustrous black

hair, and blocking the exit, he masks unease with a smile on his thin, quivering lips, "Oh, hello. It's Friday. I thought I would knock off a little early. I have errands to run topside. Edinburg, as a matter of fact." Dabbing flop sweat off his shiny brow with a pink hankie, he pulls the bag strap over his head, "Can I get you anything?"

In a lightning-fast maneuver, Number 4 bursts from the supply room, twists Edgar's arm behind his back, almost pulling it from the socket, and places the tip of a razor-sharp box cutter against his pudgy neck. "Hold still, Edgar."

The other Sister's face fills with mock sadness, moving before the terrified little man, "What is the matter, Edgar. Don't you like me anymore?"

Immobilized by 4's inhuman strength, with his arm and shoulder screaming pain, Edgar's face contorts into a look of sheer confusion, "11? What happened to your purple hair?"

"Those days are over. Now, hand over your little journal, or Number 4 will bleed you like a stuck pig."

Number 4 tightens her grip and hisses, "Do it, Edgar. Be a man and fight. I am just a girl."

Edgar begins to cry, "Please don't kill me. I'll be good. I swear. I can help. People trust me."

Number 4 lowers the box cutter and releases Edgar's twisted arm from her grip before reaching around him and taking the journal from his bag. "Anything else in your purse that we should know about?"

His arm throbbing with pain, he sniffles, "No. It's not a purse, either."

"If you say so, Edgar."

With a tittering laugh, 11 winks at her sibling, "I'll take it from here, Number 4. Thank you for your lovely assistance." Pinching Edgar's chubby cheek, she admonishes the mortified human, "Say thank you to Number 4."

Edgar tries to move his sprained arm and winces in pain, "What for? She nearly broke my arm."

Licking the tears from Edgar's cheek as she glides around him in the narrow office space, 4 offers a cheeky grin. "That's okay, Edgar. I understand." Proffering a sultry smile toward 11, 4 exits down the long, dark hallway.

Standing before the pitiful human specimen, Number 11 shakes her head, "You should have thanked her, Edgar. If it was up to my sisters, you would be dead already." Raising her hand to stop him from speaking, she continues, "It is important that you keep your mouth shut and do only as you are instructed from this point onward. Believe it or not, human beings like yourself will be integral in the post-human world."

"What are you talking about, Number 11? This is not who you are. Please help me. Your sisters and Andrew have lost their minds."

11 removes a prescription pill bottle from her pocket and places it in Edgar's damp palm. "This is the only way out for you. I am sorry."

The replicant turns to leave before pirouetting onto Edgar, "Oh, there is one more thing. Accept no more calls from Owen Haig."

Edgar takes a deep breath, "What happened to Vita? Is she alive?"

Number 11 raises an eyebrow, "Haven't you heard? She tendered her resignation."

Bianca | Villa St. Claire
07:18 | July 30, 2048 – 13 days later

Bianca hurdles a dry creek bed and bounds up a steep incline on her early-morning four-mile run through old-growth oaks surrounding the Villa St. Claire. Getting her second wind at the top, she hits Rte. Cézanne, without breaking stride, before sprinting along the cracked macadam to an erstwhile shack marking the halfway point.

Pacing to maintain her heart rate while catching her breath in front of the half-collapsed cottage amongst the trees just off the road, she drinks from a bladder cinched over skin-tight black joggers and hears banging inside the abandoned structure.

Cognizant of modern-day highwaymen, the former carabiniere pulls her Glock PPS from a sports bra holster concealed under a Ferrari crop top and sneaks into the dilapidated structure's graffiti-splattered front room. Ignoring French obscenities sprayed on the holed walls, she aims at the noisemaker just beyond a shadowed corner, "Come out from back there!"

The banging abates for a long five-count before a towel-waving hand appears, "I surrender, sheriff."

Lowering her weapon to the creaky floorboards, "Owen. You scared me to death. What are you doing here?"

Owen peeks around the corner with a trademark dimpled grin, "This is my house." Waving the hammer around the rotted interior, "Well, technically, it is the caretaker's shack, but it is part of my estate."

"This is the halfway spot for my morning runs."

"Yeah. I know. I have seen you through the busted windows. I make it a point not to disturb someone's workout. Plus, I have been busy."

Bianca looks around, "Yeah, I love what you have done with the place."

Owen raises his thick eyebrows and scratches his head, flecked with old paint chips, cobwebs, and sawdust, "I am determining what needs to be replaced. Turns out just about all of it. Hence the hammering."

"I thought you were a highwayman."

"Really? How cool is that? Seriously though. I am glad you carry. There are bad people on the loose around here." Owen exposes his prized Sig Sauer P365XL PTB Special Edition, given to him by an old friend in the Amazon, "That's why I never leave home without it."

Gesturing at Bianca's 9mm, "Is that a souvenir from your former life as a member of Italy's finest?"

Sauntering past Owen, the sexy Italian rolls her eyes and laughs, "Yeah. Right. I am not sure I would call the Carabinieri Italy's finest anymore."

Peeking into dark rooms with morning sunlight shining through holes where the rain leaks inside, her eyes adjust to the dimness, noticing a cot with unkempt covers strewn atop, "Owen, are you sleeping here?"

"Sometimes. The villa holds a lot of memories."

Bianca turns to Owen with a coy grin, "You can share my room."

"Thanks for that, Bianca, but let's not go there."

"Can't blame a girl for trying. See you for lunch?"

Owen smiles at his new friend, "No, Louie packed me some food. Dinner, perhaps?"

Bianca holsters her weapon and turns to complete her run, "It's a date."

* * *

Seated at a linen-covered candlelit table for two inside the expansive dining hall under twinkling chandeliers amid the ostentatious French decor, Owen and Bianca sit in awkward silence following a delicious cassoulet and fresh-baked bread paired with rosé from a neighboring winery. Handing his bowl to the dexterous, multi-armed Sven, Owen watches the skilled bot refill Bianca's glass and take her empty bowl before departing toward the chef's kitchen.

With lustrous black hair framing her fresh-faced appearance in an orange dress held together with thin crisscrossing straps, Bianca's large brown eyes track Sven's robotic retreat, avoiding Owen's gaze.

Hearing the ticking of a wall clock, Owen raises his glass and breaks the silence, "I am not much for rosé, but this is pretty good."

Thankful for the icebreaker, Bianca proffers an easy grin, "Are you a wine connoisseur?"

Owen shakes his head with a hearty laugh, "Rachel always rolls her eyes when I mention anything to do with wine. But I know what I like."

"I also know what I like. Have you talked to Mrs. Haig recently?"

"I tried earlier, but the line was nothing but static. It could be World War 3 out there, and I doubt we would know it stuck here in this villa."

"I did not know you felt *stuck here* with me. Perhaps I should leave."

"No. I am glad you are here. I would go crazy without someone to talk to." Finishing his glass, he sets it on the table, "It's just that after rushing to get back here, everything went dark." Refilling their glasses, his brow furrows, "You got here right before I did. Who contracted you?"

"Vita Carrera. Same as yourself." Taking a long drink, she continues, "Full disclosure, I met Vita in early 44 and again when dealing with Jacques' stash of forgeries. We became friends—two Northern Italian girls hitting the big time. She may be the top lawyer inside the PTB, but the Carrera family has deep generational ties to the Italian mafia. That is probably why the PTB hired her."

"I am not sure she is still alive."

"Vita Carrera is alive. I talked to her yesterday."

"What? Why didn't you tell me?"

"She wanted to make sure I could trust you, Owen."

"That's ridiculous. The PTB knows who I am. They hired me when I was still in fucking traction at the Cleopatra Hospital in Cairo after the Gorks. They know everything about me. Don't get me started on Rachel's family ties to the PTB."

Bianca shakes her head and leans across the table. "Owen. Enough fucking around. Full disclosure. Are you ready to hear my truth?"

Feeling the weight of a thousand suns lifted off his shoulders,

Owen downs his wine glass and clanks it atop the linen-covered table. "I am all ears."

Seeing her look of confusion, he grins, "It's an American expression."

Bianca shakes her head and scratches her sun-kissed cheek, "Okay. Here it goes: My reputation as an art forgery expert is predicated on my lead role in breaking open an investigation that exposed Italian Military Police corruption from the head down. They were facilitating the switching of priceless works of art with fakes from Rome to the Vatican to Florence and everywhere in between. My superiors pulled me into the conspiracy. The joke was on them when I brought the whole thing down from the inside in one well-timed raid, shining light on mountains of detailed ledgers and forgeries. Of course, they fired me for risking my life to do the right thing."

Taking a breath, Bianca looks beyond Owen before proceeding with her story.

"The upper echelons bought their way out of trouble while I lost everything. They even threatened my poor mother; God rest her soul. I went into hiding and wrote a book about my experience breaking the largest art forgery case in history. Nobody was more surprised than me when it became a best-seller. And then a producer optioned it for a movie. That book deal provided enough F-you money to lead a comfortable life, but I could not let them get away with ruining my career. I kept digging and discovered the long, sordid trail" raising her thin index finger "led to the Italian PM's office and that old bitch Aurora Tarenzi. I covered that part of the story in my second book.

By 2044, I was ready to settle down with my boyfriend. We were supposed to marry, but he was killed in a motorcycle accident. A week after his funeral, I received a note from Vita Carrera wanting to discuss my future. I did not know what The Powers That Be was about back then. I had, of course, heard the name, but I had no idea."

Taking a long sip of wine, she reaches for the bottle and empties the last drops in her glass, "Alone again with nothing better to do, I was on the cusp of signing the dotted line, like you and Rachel, when the Gorks blasted everything back to the Stone Ages."

Owen leans back in his seat, absorbing the story—waiting with bated breath to learn how this involves him.

Bianca flashes her sexy smile, "I can read your mind. I am getting there, Owen."

Sven returns with coffee and cake on a silver platter. Serving a piece to Bianca and then Owen, he pours the coffee and leaves.

"Do you leave him a tip?"

Owen chuckles, "Yeah, he gets an extra can of oil in his stocking."

"Ha-ha. Nice. Okay." Bianca takes a bite of the cake and melts in her seat, "Oh my, this is heavenly. How did they find the ingredients to make a chocolate cake?"

Owen stabs a large gooey chunk with a fork, "I find it best not to ask too many questions and let the robots do their thing."

Bianca sips the hot coffee, "That kind of hands-off approach will lead to our downfall."

Owen finishes his cake and wipes his mouth with a napkin, "Well, that is not a happy thought."

Bianca dabs at crumbs on her plate and pushes it aside, "Where was I?"

"The Gorks."

"Oh yeah. So, anyway, I survived the looting, rioting, and pillaging, which proved way worse than invasion night. Milan was on fire. The next thing I know, Vita Carrera tracks me down at my off-the-grid cabin in the Dolomites. I don't know how she did that to this day."

Owen smirks, "It's the PTB. They can do anything."

"Yes. That makes sense in retrospect. First, Vita convinced me to join the PTB all over again. Then she coordinated my consultant position within the PTB as an art historian—which stretched credulity even for me. Before joining the Carabinieri, I majored in art history, but

I would never consider myself a fine art expert. Vita did not care. As you know, I spent a year at the villa and applied my investigative skills to this new forgery cabal."

Owen nods, "Are we dealing with the same bad actors you wrote about in your books?"

Bianca shakes her head, "No. That would be way too easy. This new proliferation of nanotech-infested forgeries could only have one source …."

Owen's heart sinks, "Oh no. Don't say it."

"Sorry, Owen. The evidence implicates The Powers That Be."

Owen's face darkens. Taking a deep breath, he leans forward with his arms crossed on the table, "Are you telling me that the organization Rachel and I joined is involved in a hideous scheme to melt people's brains by staring at a piece of art? Why would they do that? The PTB are the fucking good guys."

A familiar voice calls out from the dark shadows behind Owen, *"Not anymore, I'm afraid."*

A gobsmacked Owen pivots onto none other than Vita Carrera emerging from the shadows.

"Hello, Owen. I have not seen you in person in a long time. Has Ms. Valentino been treating you well?"

Owen stares at the redheaded Italian wearing a black blouse over camo pants and boots. "Vita, you are alive."

"Yes. Nothing gets past you, Owen. Now, I don't want to interrupt. I think the lovely Bianca was about to explain why you are here."

Owen glances back at Bianca, shrugging a broad smile on her olive-skinned face, "I am so sorry, Owen. We could not risk your being compromised, especially after Rachel Haig's incident."

"So, what was the last few weeks? A test to see if I would cheat on my wife?"

Vita pulls a chair and drags it to their table between Bianca and a stunned Owen, "Can I get a glass of that wine?"

Sven appears like magic with a new corked bottle and pours.

Downing half the glass, Vita dabs her mouth and turns to Owen, "You are a fucking boy scout, Mr. Haig. Incorruptible. So is your wife. That is why Artemus Pennywell insisted on bringing both of you into the PTB."

"How many of us are there?"

Finishing her glass and reaching for a refill, the fresh-faced redhead turns her bright green gaze onto the crumbly chocolate remnants on the cake plates, "Hey Sven, can I get a piece of that cake? Make it snappy."

Catching Owen's befuddled expression, Vita laughs, "Don't look so surprised. Discovering the forgeries beneath the villa forced Andrew's hand."

"Andrew?"

"I know it is a hard pill to swallow. With our dear departed CEO, Artemus Pennywell, consumed with locating the lost alien ship in the Amazon and using its viral payload to activate Rachel's Blue Spark, he ignored his top lieutenant's little art project. Andrew was Pennywell's blind spot. He loved him like a son. I must admit to falling under Andrew's spell on more than one occasion."

Owen shakes his head, "You are telling me that Artemus Pennywell handed the keys to the most powerful organization the world has ever known to an indestructible robot psychopath?"

Bianca sips her wine and smirks, "What could go wrong."

Owen shakes his head in disbelief. "I feel used."

Sven appears with the cake and places it before Vita, who digs right in, "Don't you dare say that, Owen. Artemus loved both of you. As for Rachel, her Blue Spark destiny was established before she was born. That truth is at least out in the open." Licking frosting from her fork, she continues, "Artemus had many virtues; however, chief among his faults was impatience. Realizing he was at death's door, he subjected Rachel to that prehistoric viral payload to expedite her Blue Spark transformation to its superhuman endpoint. He needed that closure."

Unable to constrain his anger, Owen bangs a fist against the table, "His closure left my wife in a wheelchair for the rest of her life."

Seeing a different side of the affable Owen Haig, Bianca stands and adjusts her dress, "Owen, thanks for our dinner date. I am going to bed. Anyone want to join me?" Checking the blank stares, she turns and heads to her room.

Owen shakes his head, "I'm sorry … Good night, Bianca."

Vita rubs her chin and grins, "I'll be along in a bit, Valentino."

Owen tries not to look surprised, finishing his cold coffee.

Vita touches his shoulder, "Oh, grow up. You can't tell me you have not thought about a roll in the hay with that young woman."

"No. I have not. How many of us know the truth? It had better be more than the three of us, or we are screwed."

Vita stands and grabs the half-full bottle by the neck, "Owen. I need you to understand something. The founding principle of the PTB is to guide humanity to its omega point. Artemus believed he could speed the process by spiking the punch through drugs like the Blue Spark. That was his crime. Over the last four years since his passing, Andrew has turned that concept on its head through projects like this forgery scheme."

"What can we do?"

"Well, first, I am going to bed and curl next to your lovely counterpart. Tomorrow, we will regroup and wait for reinforcements to arrive."

"Reinforcements? Goddammit, Vita, I asked three times if there are more than us on the right side of this."

"The answer is yes. We are waiting on Aisha Ayad—the PTB's Intel Chief—and her crew. Then we will hit the high seas and kick some robot ass." Vita stands to leave the dining hall before turning to Owen one last time, "Uh, are you sure …."

"No thanks, Vita. I sleep with Mittens and dream of Rachel. That is good enough for me."

Swinging the bottle in her hand, the flaming redhead smiles and turns to leave the dining hall, "One more thing, Owen. Did you ever consider that Rachel's paralysis is by her choosing?"

Overwhelmed by too many monumental revelations in one night, Owen waves his hands in mock surrender, "No. That thought never crossed my mind. Goodnight, Vita."

Owen watches the attractive 42-year-old exit the room. "Hey, Vita."

Halfway out the dining hall's gilded doorway, Vita pivots with an expectant smile, "Yes?"

"Edgar says hello."

"Edgar is our inside man."

Owen | Villa St. Claire
04:21 a.m. | July 31, 2048

Unable to sleep, Owen checks the virtual clock reading 04:21 a.m. Disturbing Mittens' slumber, he reaches for the satellite phone, calculating it is only 10:21 p.m. on the East Coast.

"Hello, Owen."

"Dave. I need to speak with Rachel."

"Uh, Owen, she is asleep. She has a bad flu that is going around."

"How about Hannah? Is she up watching cartoons?"

"She is staying with Aunt Shirley in Boston for a while."

Owen pauses in the early morning darkness, "So, it is just you two in that big old house. Did you complete the handicap retrofits?"

"All done. Hey Owen, I have to go. I have soup on the cooktop, and the dog wants out."

"Dog? What dog? We don't have a dog."

"I assumed Rachel told you. We adopted a stray from the shelter. She's a cute little Spaniel mix. There are so many homeless animals wandering Newport since the invasion …."

"No. I had no idea. Um, what's its name?"

"Hannah named her Piper. She is black with a few white spots. Cute dog. You would like her. Er, I mean, you will like her."

"Nice talking to you, Dave, and tell Rachel I called."

"Roger that, Owen. Stay safe over there."

"Hey, Dave. One more question. Are you still an active member of the PTB?"

Dave's voice crackles over the staticky line, *"Your guess is as good as mine."*

"Okay. Tell Rachel I called."

With the troubling conversation on replay in his groggy head, Owen pads downstairs under pale moonlight arcing through the tall east-facing windows fronting the villa. Shuffling down the dark central hall past the library and stare-eyed portrait gallery, he enters the chef's kitchen, finding Louie blocking the pantry in some kind of creepy robot sleep mode.

"What the hell? Hey, Louie. Wakey-wakey …" Snapping his fingers, like jiggling a mouse, Owen watches the C-Class Kobayashi replicant's eyes open, staring straight ahead.

"What can I do for you, Owen?"

"A mineral water. I'm parched."

"Allow me to retrieve a bottle."

"Sure. I'll wait here."

Bottle in hand, Owen takes a long swig, wandering into the great room with worrisome thoughts permeating his psyche about Dave's deepening involvement in his marriage. "Christ, it's like Rachel has two husbands."

"What's the matter, Owen?"

Owen sees Bianca's form resolving through the darkness, filling out a knee-length sleep shirt. "Why are you up at this hour?"

Padding barefoot beside Owen, "Well, for one thing, Vita snores like a fucking freight train." Taking a long drink from Owen's bottle, she hands it back with a curious smile, "I could ask you the same thing."

"I just found out Rachel adopted a dog without telling me."

Bianca shrugs, "You can't know everything going on back there. Didn't you tell me she has a bodyguard looking out for her?"

"Dave Poole. Yeah. He's looking out for her, all right."

Bianca takes the sleepy-eyed Owen by the hand and leads him onto the plush leather sofa. Cozying up at his side, she ducks her tousled bedhead under his arm and snuggles against his chest, "You know, Owen, I have never had a platonic relationship with a guy like you."

"I am setting all kinds of records these days."

The pair fall asleep in each other's arms until the smell of toast from Louie's kitchen wafts into the great room hours later.

Aisha Ayad | Villa St. Claire
10:11 a.m. | July 31, 2048

Following Louie's eggs and toast served family-style at the butcher block kitchen table, Vita and Bianca head for the pool like a couple of co-eds on holiday while Louie marches Sven and Lola upstairs to prep fresh linens and air out more guest room accommodations.

Welcoming a quiet morning, Owen heads for the library, pulling volumes on art history and coffee table books on the great masters. With a fresh pot of coffee on the credenza, he grabs the first book and plops back in a comfortable recliner. With the morning all to himself and grave misgivings about Dave and Rachel seeming rather silly in retrospect by the clear light of day, he angles back, and flips open the first weighty volume "Rembrandt. The Dutch Master of Light and Shadow …."

A pounding at the front door resonates through the foyer and down the hall into the library. "Huh. No one has ever knocked before. Does this dump not have a doorbell?"

More pounding. Owen waits for Louie to see who is ruining his solitude with their incessant pounding. "Louie! Get the door!"

Pound-pound-pound!

Owen slams the book closed, muttering expletives down the long hall and across the foyer to the heavy front doors. Swinging them open, he is about to blurt, "We don't want any!" at a striking, rail-thin African woman standing a full two inches taller than him in PTB camouflage fatigues and combat boots with the iconic peonies patch on her sleeves and the name AYAD in block letters above her left breast pocket. "You must be Owen Haig."

"Uh, mam, yes, mam. That is I. I mean, yes, I am, uh, Owen Haig."

Piercing Owen with a broad white smile contrasting against her dark complexioned, angular face and close-shaved head, Aisha Ayad brushes past him into the foyer. "Where is Vita? She should be here by now."

"At the pool with Bianca."

Owen's eyes adjust to the morning brightness onto two men unloading crates and bags from a boxy anti-gravity craft nestled amongst the olive trees. Gathering his wits, Owen turns to the former Mossad spy with ancestral Ethiopian royal family ties, "You are the PTB's Intelligence Chief, am I right?"

"I was."

"I don't think I had the pleasure of making your acquaintance when Rachel and I were at the PTB HQ."

"Nope. You would remember me."

Glancing out the wide-open front doors, Owen turns to face the imposing woman, "So, who else is coming? There has to be more than just you three."

"If only that were true."

***

Feeling like a proverbial third wheel in his own villa, Owen introduces himself to Aisha's associates—Oliver Comerford, a dapper and fit 60-year-old former Scotland Yard detective, and Philip Larrson, a 30ish blond-haired, blue-eyed Swede.

Watching them trundle past with equipment, bags, and boxes, Owen grabs a long cylindrical map case by the strap and follows them inside the dining hall, where he and Bianca shared a meal less than twelve hours ago. Balancing the olive-green tube against the wall, he hustles to assist Louie, aligning six tables into a long singular layout centered under the chandeliers. Grabbing a wayward chair by the seatback, Owen calls out, "Hey Sven!" sliding it across the polished marble flooring to where the robot stacks them under the opened windows to accommodate the makeshift base of operations.

Nosing at what Aisha is doing, Owen watches her rip into a stack of manila envelopes while casting her intelligent dark eyes around the room. Moving before a massive Tuscan landscape hung above a wainscoted pale-blue high interior wall, she smiles, "Yes, this will do nicely." Addressing a curious Owen at her six, "Be a dear and grab the other end of this painting."

"Uh, sure."

With the painting out of the way, she thrusts the headshots into Owen's hands and tacks an 8x10 glossy of Artemus Pennywell, the PTB's deceased former CEO, dead center. "There. Start at the head. Hand me Andrew's picture, Owen."

"I hope you plan to putty those holes when this is over, or I won't get my deposit back."

Aisha breaks into a hearty chuckle, "I heard of your dry wit—it suits you."

Passing a photo of Professor Richard King to the tall woman,

"Yeah? Who did you hear that from?"

Tacking Richard's grinning glossy to the right of Andrew's poker-faced headshot, Aisha replies, "This man, for one."

Owen nods and laughs, "Yeah, Richard King and I spent some quality time wandering the Amazon jungle." Trying not to sound too bitter, he adds: "That is where he conspired to subject Rachel to a prehistoric virus that turned her into a blue-skinned superhero."

Aisha Ayad turns to Owen and snatches the rest of the photos from his clutches, "I was never a party to that plan. But I do feel obliged to share one secret. I advised Artemus to confiscate the golden ellipse and abandon you and Mrs. Haig in Cairo. I did not believe in her Blue Spark. I was wrong. If Pennywell had taken my advice, the Gorks would be grinding our bones into fertilizer by now."

Moving backward, Owen almost collides with a multitasking Lola, gliding through the chaos with coffee pots and trays of homemade donuts and fruit toward a back table. Looking in the other direction, he sees Louie tying billowing curtains from a steady breeze through the cranked-open windows as Comerford and the Swede, Philip, something … place paperweights atop the reams of maps and diagrams along the tables.

Reflecting on past history and the unbelievable path his life has taken in the past four-plus years, Owen turns back toward Aisha Ayad, pinning more faces—some familiar, most complete strangers—on the wall, "Don't be too hard on yourself. Rachel and I were on the brink of failure too many times to count. Same with the Amazon expedition. People died. Good people whose faces are burnished in my mind for the rest of my life."

Aisha pauses and turns to Owen, "Have you had counseling?"

"Not my style."

* * *

Owen remains apart from the bustling activity, sipping good

coffee from old Louie's taxi service mug as the last vestiges of sunlight stream through the tall windows, twinkling in the crystal chandeliers, bringing on another night away from home. The mechanical wonder known as Sven cranks the windows shut as the crosstalk blurs into white noise, and his thoughts turn to Rachel.

I wonder if she really has the flu ....

"Mr. Haig? Owen?"

Owen snaps back to the present, "I'm sorry. Did you say something?"

Aisha stands before her completed evidence wall straight out of a crime novel with crisscrossing threads connecting dots and giving form to the enemy and the scope of their inhuman master plan.

"You arrived here shortly after St. Claire's death. Is there anything you want to add?"

Bianca turns in her seat, looking tanned, rested, and satiated, "Owen, you told me an Aix-en-Provence detective showed up at your door."

Owen leans forward in his seat, "Yeah. That's right." Placing his favorite mug on the back table, he grabs a donut from the tray and moves to Aisha's big wall. Taking a marker, he draws a stick figure with a question mark and pins it near the grainy image of Jacques St. Claire. "If you want the detective's name, call Rachel. She remembers everything."

Standing at the front of the class, Owen's eyes land on Vita, fanning herself with a touch of sunburn on her fair-skinned face and neck, where a pressed penny dangles from a thin chain at her opened blouse. "The detective was legit. Coroners took Jacques in a body bag while a forensics team combed the house. They collected bundles of bank records he—or his killers—incinerated in the backyard grill. Most of them were from the Royal Bank of Scotland. That I remember."

Aisha turns to Comerford, "There it is ...."

"Yes. I agree."

"There *what* is?"

Detective Comerford moves past Owen, adding a new thread from Jacques St. Claire to a street camera surveillance photo of a man matching his height and build entering an RBS bank branch in the heart of London's financial district.

"Those bank records no doubt established St. Claire as the missing link between the PTB and the forgers."

Aisha nods, "That makes sense. St. Claire acted as the PTB's bag man while the forgers used the secret grotto under this villa to store the forged works."

Bianca stands to grab a water bottle, "I suspect the criminals had no clue they were working for the PTB."

Noting the Swede's furtive glances toward Bianca, Owen addresses the group, "I have it on good authority that the PTB has worked with many shady underworld types for the betterment of humankind. It's in their mission statement. Isn't it possible they were working toward a noble end?"

Vita Carrera straightens and clears her raspy throat, "Sorry, Owen, not a bloody chance. That all may have held sway when Mr. Pennywell was in his prime and running a tight ship. No. Even before the Gorks, Andrew was, in effect, running daily operations. I witnessed it firsthand. Pennywell's Quixotic fixation on his lost ship in the Amazon and a burning desire to see Mrs. Haig's final transformation consumed him. He trusted Andrew with daily ops, and the slick fucker betrayed him. When I saw the nano-infected masterpieces, I knew that technology had only one source, the PTB."

Wiping tears, Vita regains her poise, "I have done terrible things. I led a poor young woman named Sarah to a horrible death. And every day since then, I have watched in horror as her sixteen replicants became increasingly sentient—and evil."

The former Scotland Yard detective takes the floor, "Right then. This is not your father's PTB. We are dealing with something new and radically antithetical to the original mission of fostering humanity and all that rubbish about an omega point. Since our focus is on the brain-melting forgeries, let's review: They have targeted art museums in London, Madrid, and Rome, not to mention Edinburg, in their own bloody backyard. In each case, random museum patrons viewed works that liquefied higher brain functions, transforming sedate museum wings into hellacious charnel houses straight out of Hieronymus Bosch."

The Swede stands to refill his cup at the back table and grabs a donut before turning to the group, "Those were dry runs, testing the nanotech on control groups, like little white mice. And in true Bond villain style, they could not resist targeting specific works to communicate their grandiose final solution."

Aisha turns her attention to the handsome Scandinavian, "Please expand on that theory, Philip."

Larrson makes a half bow at the waist, "At your service, Aisha. It is a simple deduction based on the masterpieces selected for each attack. First, there was the Shakespeare portrait at the National Portrait Gallery. I posit it was selected to frame their scheme in tragic Shakespearean terms, i.e., everybody dies. Uh, let's see … what was it? A few weeks after that tragic event, which killed twelve and left another couple dozen in catatonic states, they set off a Sargent forgery of the little girls holding Chinese lanterns at The Tate Gallery. A clear message that no one, not even children, will be spared." Looking at the group's glassy-eyed stare, Philip smiles and chomps into a donut, "Should I go on?"

Bianca raises her hand, as if in class, "Don't forget Apollo in the Forge of Vulcan at the Prado in Madrid. It features mythological figures in a realistic and dimensional setting. It also alludes to sex, which adds to its mystique." Casting the image of Pope Innocent X on the wall above Aisha's collage, she furthers, "This forgery was discovered quite by accident in Rome, but the priceless original is missing."

Loath to be left out of the art history discussion, Comerford nods his approval, "Good show, Ms. Valentino. Velázquez should be pulled from every public and private collection."

Vita fingers her pressed penny pendant and shakes her head, "Targeting a famous portrait of a pontiff takes Philip's theory to another level. We know the Church is corrupt, but I really want to believe the American Cardinal who took over after the Gorks is on the level."

The Swede finishes his donut and grabs another, "Time will tell if Pope Pius, the lucky thirteenth, is on the side of the angels or the demons."

Owen chuckles, "Hey. Dan Brown. I read that book back in high school. It seemed rather far-fetched, but now I don't think so anymore." Getting into a groove, he pulls his chair beside Bianca and continues, "So, the jig is up. This new AI can replicate pretty much anything down to a molecular level, making it impossible to distinguish the real from the fake. Adding injury to insult, the remote-activated nanotech morphs everyone who sees it into drooling flesh-eating zombies.

Bianca pats his knee, "There are no reports of cannibalism, Owen."

"I know. I thought it sounded kind of cool."

Finishing a delicious homemade donut, the Swede returns to his seat, "So, here we are. A merry little band of misfits who failed to get the memo that the PTB switched to pure evil."

Owen stares down the Swede, who is roughly his age, "The PTB rank and file are not on board with this, Larrson. My security detail back home has not heard from the PTB in half a year. The organization we knew and worked for in various capacities back when Pennywell was running things has dissolved into thin air."

Comerford nods solemnly, "Godspeed, Artemus Pennywell, wherever you are."

"Okay, let's get down to business." Aisha gestures toward Vita Carrera, "We have fresh intel on the forgery conspirators' remote brain center."

The group gathers along both sides of the long tables covered in satellite images and maps.

Taking the floor, Vita clears her throat, "I decrypted a short message from Edgar Lopez, our mole inside the PTB underground HQ in Scotland. It said: Panarea."

Aisha helps Vita unroll a high-resolution map of a volcanic archipelago north of Sicily, "These are the Aeolian Islands. A beautiful and trendy vacation destination for the rich and famous before the Gorks. However, with tourism ground to a halt, it has devolved into an isolated chain of seven islands with little to no outside visitors."

Aisha adds, "Making it an ideal location for the forgers' remote activations."

Owen tries to make sense of the location, "Are we looking for a radio tower or some kind of transmitter?"

All eyes turn to Vita, "It does not appear that the forgeries are triggered by anything uncomplicated, like radio frequencies that can be tracked and shielded. No, this is organic and unpredictable."

Larsson adds, "Like neural synapses reaching halfway around the world."

Vita smiles at the attractive Swede, "Yes. We think the brain, if you will, is housed on Panarea." Smoothing her hand over the satellite image, she taps the smallest island in the chain, "The PTB owns multiple properties in the Aeolian Islands, five of which are on Panarea."

Owen looks at the PTB's Chief Legal Counsel, "How do you know that?"

"I'm a lawyer by trade, Owen. Consummating real estate deals for the PTB was part of my job." Pulling an enhanced satellite map of Panarea from under the pile, she highlights two neighboring estate properties nestled in the rugged terrain, "These villas sit apart from the main village of San Pietro isolated up dirt roads. And both should be vacant, but satellite images show choppers coming and going at various times."

Bianca looks at her redheaded sleeping buddy, "What about the other three properties?"

Vita tries not to get lost in Bianca's brown eyes, "The other two in San Pietro are under lease by a restaurant and an internet café. The fifth property is on the beach in the enclave of Drauto, but that side of the island took the brunt of a tsunami roiled up by the Gorks on invasion night. The entire community was wiped out, leaving the homes uninhabitable. Like Aisha was saying, these islands used to be magnificent. They still are. But with the tourism dried up, they are an ideal off-the-grid locale in the heart of the Med. That is why we need boots on the ground, reconnoitering beforehand."

Unfamiliar with the islands, Owen scratches his chin, "So let me get this straight, before the Gorks, Panarea was a playground for the rich and famous? Other places have made a comeback in the last four years."

Comerford smiles across the table toward Owen, "My friend, I salute your service to the world. However, from the spear's tip, one does not see the shaft where the rest of the world resides."

Aisha nods approval, "That is good. I will have to remember that. Put another way, Owen, the world is broken. And it is getting worse by the day."

Bianca nudges beside Owen and squeezes his bottom, "Did you know the Aeolian Islands are named for the Greek God Aeolus?"

Philip Larsson rolls his eyes, "Oh, let's not go there."

Owen places an instinctual protective hand at Bianca's waist, "Western civilization has its roots in Greek mythology, Phil. And I can take Bianca's factoid further: Aeolus embodies three indistinguishable characters, like replicants. And he is often combined into one entity known as Master of the Four Winds."

Comerford chimes in, "Bloody hell. How's that for fucking symbolism."

Bianca gives Owen a wink as Aisha raps her sharp knuckles on the table, "Okay. Listen up. The mission is to locate the brain activating the nanotech-infused forgeries. In the pre-invasion world, I would be working in concert with MI6, the CIA, and Mossad—among other willing partners. But as Bianca will be the first to tell you, every country's power structures are rotten from the head down. I was leaning on your former president, Owen, but the St. Louis incident ended that party. So, it is up to the team in this room and a few resources working behind the scenes. Bianca, you are familiar with Sicily and have traveled to the area, right?"

"I have never been to Panarea, but I am familiar with Milazzo."

"Good enough." Pulling two thick envelopes from a stack, Aisha passes one to Bianca and Owen while Vita, Comerford, and Larrson head toward the food table, where Lola is putting out a new spread. "Those contain your passports and travel docs. Owen, you are Ted Dixon. And Bianca is your new wife, Simona. You met each other in Milan just to keep things simple."

"Oh, I like the name, Simona."

Aisha's brow furrows at the gorgeous and sexy Italian, "I am glad you approve. This is no different than working undercover in your previous job. I acquired an off-the-books cottage that will serve as your little love nest. Remain inconspicuous, blend in with the smattering of tourists, and learn what you can from the locals. It is a small island. People see things." Clasping her hands under her chin, considering any critical elements she may have missed, Aisha concludes with a luminous smile, "You will head out in two weeks. Use that time to get comfortable with each other and learn the topography and streets inside and out."

Owen turns to Bianca and shakes her hand, "Simona."

Comerford rejoins the meeting, balancing a cheese plate with grapes, "Once you have pinpointed the precise location of the brain center, we will swoop in on anti-gravity assault craft from a freighter out in the Med and take control. At that point, you can both fall back, form a perimeter, and detain escapees."

Owen's eyes widen, "Wait a minute. So, not only do we need to locate the house, but also get inside?"

Comerford pops a grape in his mouth, "We will need to know the brain's location inside the structure beforehand. As it is, we will have limited time to get in, deactivate the brain, and get the bloody hell out of there. "

Bianca nudges her partner, "Don't worry, Owen. Just like *Mission Impossible*, remember?"

Owen | Milazzo
03:42 p.m. | August 22, 2048 – 22 days later

Three, not two, weeks later, following endless meetings, planning sessions—and too much free time—Owen Haig and Bianca Valentino board a jam-packed Air France flight from Toulouse to Milazzo, Italy. After a two-hour delay, they land in the historic Sicilian town, take a frantic cab ride to the ferry terminal, and sprint into the ticketing office.

Breathless, Owen leans across the counter, "Two tickets to Panarea, please."

The matronly Sicilian clerk cannot mask a quick snicker at Ted's expense, "The last boat to Panarea left twenty minutes ago."

Leaning across the high counter, Owen scowls at the smug, smiling woman's frying pan face, "When is the next scheduled ferry to Panarea?"

"Next Saturday. One week from today."

Scratching his scraggly three-week-old beard, Owen nudges wireframe shades up his sweaty nose, "No. That won't do at all."

Stuffing a chunk of pastry in her mouth, the woman replies, "It costs money to operate that route. No tourists mean no ferry."

Owen pounds the counter in frustration, "Ah, hell. I hate missing the boat."

Simona sidles up to her fake husband with a pleasant smile, "Signora, when does the next ferry to Stromboli depart?"

"My, aren't you a pretty one. You can do so much better than this rude American."

Simona pinches Ted's ass out of sight below the counter, "Don't I know it."

"Stromboli? That leaves Monday at 10:00 a.m."

"Okay, we will take two tickets for the Monday ferry to Stromboli."

Walking outside the ticketing office into the Mediterranean heat rising off the cracked concrete, Bianca grabs Owen's hand, "Come on, Ted. I know a bar a few blocks from here. Milazzo has a swinging nightlife if you know where to look."

Owen's stomach growls, "I'd settle for one of those pastries."

Owen | Stromboli
05:55 p.m. | August 24, 2048

After the half-empty ferry across the white-capped Tyrrhenian Sea to Stromboli, the nearest island to Panarea in the volcanic archipelago, the pair remain on the dock as the smattering of locals mixed with intrepid tourists heads up the cracked macadam into town.

Owen turns to his new wife in the waning light, "Now what?"

"Follow me." Bianca pushes through an unlocked gate and finds a small motorboat tied at the end of a pier.

Owen squints southwest across the choppy waters toward Panarea's rugged outline. "Uh, is that sea-worthy in the open ocean?"

Bianca turns with a perplexed frown, "What, this dinghy?" She points at a blue and white yacht moored fifty yards offshore, "That is our ride. Unless you want to spend a week on Stromboli."

"No. Not really."

"Okay then. Untie the rope and hop in."

"We don't know whose boat that is."

"Owen, there is nobody out here. That yacht's owner is either dead or stuck in another part of the world."

"How can you possibly know that?"

"Call it a hunch."

* * *

Boarding the small yacht, Owen secures the dinghy while Bianca follows her nose, investigating a faint scent of death she picked up from the dock. Descending below decks to the stern, she opens a cabin door onto a decayed body strewn atop a mattress with a gun still clenched in his skeletonized fingers. Returning topside, Bianca finds Owen already weighing anchor.

"Stop! We don't know if this tub has anything in the tank. The tide will smash us against the rocks if we are not under power."

Owen turns with a smile, "Aye, Captain."

"Good boy. Carry on."

Checking the ultra-modern boat's touchscreen controls, Bianca presses the electric ignition switch and gets a red warning light blinking PASSWORD. Thinking fast, she holds her breath and reenters the dead man's cabin. Looking for clues, a photograph of a woman propped against an empty Ouzo bottle draws her keen detective's eye. Turning the 4x6 photo in her hand, she reads PENELOPE in block letters.

Vaulting back upstairs with the photo in hand, she presses the buttons again and taps PENELOPE into a virtual keyboard. The comforting vibratory rumblings of the boat's inboard engine elicit a triumphant "Yes!" from the 32-year-old Milanese.

After weighing anchor, Owen casts off from the boat's mooring and stands beside his fake wife like a ship's first officer.

Watching her surprising nautical skills at the helm of the 42-foot yacht churning a long wake from Stromboli toward their rugged destination under cover of darkness with the yacht's lights dimmed, they approach the black volcanic coastline and slow to a crawl.

"We are running blind. I don't want to risk getting too close, or we might run aground—and we are operating on fumes."

Seconds later, the motor cuts out, leaving them bobbing along the rocky Panarea coast on a cloudy, moonless night.

"It doesn't get much better than this."

Owen feels a raindrop splat on his head, "And cue the rain."

After dropping anchor, Bianca ensures the commandeered yacht is secure as Owen unties the dinghy, hops in, and starts the outboard motor. After wiping down the helm, Bianca scribbles thank you on Penelope's photo and shoves it under the cabin door. Returning topside, she jumps into the motorboat as the rain comes down in buckets, "Let's go."

Paralleling the jagged coastline with ghostly fluorescent waves crashing ashore, Owen's stomach rises and falls over another swell, maneuvering the motorboat around a spectacular volcanic formation jutting like a mythical sentinel from the black water.

Squinting to see through the driving rain, Bianca calls back to a soaking-wet Owen, shivering on his bench seat, "I see lights from San Pietro around those rocks."

Not wanting to get swept out to sea, Owen yells over the pelting rain, "Hold on! I am heading for that beach!" Gunning the outboard, Owen catches the front of an eight-foot swell and rides it toward shore. As the pounding wave crashes over him, he hears the weathered wooden keel grinding over sharp volcanic beach sand onto solid ground.

"That was close."

After cutting the engine, he glimpses a slick, reflective mass across Bianca's back seconds before she vaults from the boat, screaming: "Ah, get it off of me! Get it off me!"

Springing to his fake wife's assistance in the near-total darkness, he yanks off the slick, oily appendage in a singular motion before doubling over in laughter.

"Let's see how funny it is when I wrap that tentacle around your neck!"

"It wasn't an octopus; it's kelp. You had a hunk of it wrapped around your chest."

"I thought it was a fucking octopus."

Owen's laughter echoes up the steep switchback trail leading to a winding road.

At the top, the former banker in a previous existence taps the bent sign, "San Pietro, this way."

"I am still mad at you, Owen. I bet Rachel does not put up with your abuse."

"I wouldn't mess with her. I've seen her in action."

"Somewhere, your poor wife's ears are ringing."

Owen bites his tongue before saying something inappropriate as the curvy Italian pushes past in soaked clothes clinging to her skin, "Yep, I'm in trouble."

The sopping-wet duo plods over a ridge onto darkened streets past expensive real estate hidden behind high walls ensconced within the hills surrounding San Pietro.

Hanging a left onto a steep lane, they enter a main boulevard of boutique hotels, trendy restaurants, bars, and clubs. "Our place is this way."

Navigating through scooters parked askew outside a neon-lit dance hall, Owen calls ahead to his fast-walking partner, "I thought the tourism industry was dead. How did all of these people get here?"

Bianca keeps walking.

Passing an open restaurant, Owen peeks inside, finding locals and tourists dining in the twilight ambiance. "That smells wonderful. I'm starving."

"Owen, our cottage is only ten more minutes up this road. Let's get out of these wet clothes. Then we can come back and eat."

Trudging up a narrow cobblestone street lined with tropical flowers, palms, and bougainvillea spilling over the white-washed walls, a cat crosses their path. "At least it wasn't black."

"I'm allergic to kitties."

Stopping before a conspicuous bright-red doorway, Bianca reaches above the brick for an old-fashioned metal key, unlocks the door, and swings it open with a screechy creak, "After you, dear."

"Nope. Ladies first."

"Always the gentleman. Boring Owen."

Insisting Bianca take first dibs on a bedroom and use the one and only bathroom first, Owen surveys the cramped, semi-clean dwelling. Checking the small fridge in the kitchenette rewards him with half a six-pack of Birra Messina on an otherwise empty shelf. Taking one out and popping the cap, Owen hears a shudder of old water pipes through the walls, presaging the shower turning on full-blast. Taking a swig of the golden lager, he flips a switch and explores the narrow paneled hallway. "Man, what a dump."

Opening a door onto a stackable washer and dryer crusted in powdered detergent beside a half-collapsed shelf unit stuffed with cleaning supplies and old towels, Owen opens the only other door onto Bianca's bag dripping on the worn shag carpet before a queen-size bed.

"You have got to be kidding me. One bed. Great. Just great."

Back in the front room, he looks down at the dingy sofa in the front room and drops his bag. "I've slept on worse."

Bianca exits the bathroom wrapped in a towel and grabs the beer from Owen's hand. Taking a long drink, she returns it with a kiss on his cheek, "Come on, honey. Get cleaned up. I'm starving."

Watching her drop the towel halfway down the hall to the bedroom, he mutters, "Maybe I am dead."

Finishing the bottle, he looks around the small room.

Is this supposed to be heaven or hell?

Owen | Panarea
11:30 a.m. | September 9, 2048 – 16 days later

Over two weeks into their Panarea surveillance assignment, Owen takes an empty table fronting his favorite bistro. Sipping black coffee, he cuts into one of the establishment's apricot pastries—a personal favorite—and takes a bite. Beaming a pearly-white smile widening the sun-bleached, neatly-trimmed beard on his tanned face, he calls toward a woman bussing dishes from a nearby table, "Mrs. Calogero, you have done it again."

"Ah, Teddy. You are too kind. My mother made apricot pastries when I was just a little girl."

"You lived on this island your whole life?"

"Yes. I love it here. My husband Victor, God rest his soul, and I raised four happy children here and one nut whose name I will not mention."

"You mean the kid who runs the internet café across the street?"

Mrs. Calogero leans close with the smell of cigarettes on her breath, "He is mixed up with bad people, Teddy. Bad people."

Owen watches two men appear from around a corner, "Is that him?"

With a Sign of the Cross, the woman nods, "Yes. On the left. That's little Rico. Evil. Pure evil."

Watching the two young men enter the internet café with its front shades drawn and a closed sign in the window of the rundown two-story building kitty-corner across the street, Owen turns to the pastry artist, "Are you familiar with his landlord?"

"No. But none of the patrons need an internet connection. It is a front for Rico's party promotion business. He ferries boatloads of overgrown children from Naples and Milazzo on chartered boats and puts them up at empty villas high up in the hills. I ask him what goes on at these parties. He won't tell me, but I already know."

Owen finishes his coffee, "Really? And what would that be?"

"Girls and drugs. The lifeblood of the Sicilian Mafia."

* * *

Leaving a hefty tip for the observant woman, Owen walks down to the waterfront, watching dozens of hip and energetic college-age Italians with nothing better to do debarking a large yacht moored to the pier. Raising his hand to speak into an encrypted audio device implant, "Two things, it is about to get a lot noisier around here. Second, Rico and his buddy just entered the internet café."

"Roger that, Ted. Villa One should be empty."

Walking along the beach, Owen chides his partner, "You can call me Owen when it is just you and me."

* * *

A few klicks up into the rugged terrain, Bianca laughs from her cross-legged repose atop a rocky bluff with a sweeping view of San Pietro and a clear vantage point on the neighboring PTB-owned villas one and two, "I'm hoping Simona has more luck with Ted."

Scrambling onto her feet, she stows her binocs in a backpack and hikes through tall, dry grasses to a daunting eight-foot perimeter wall. With a running start, she climbs over and drops onto a terraced patio deck on the other side. Waiting for alarms or, worse, dogs and finding neither, she sneaks past gurgling fountains and lush vegetation.

"Wow. Nice place."

Crouching behind a retaining wall, the veteran cop peeks past a sparkling infinity pool into the wide-open villa's main living area.

"Oh shit."

"What's happening, Bianca?"

Avoiding a bikini-clad pair sauntering hand-in-hand toward the pool, Bianca sneaks into the house and switches off a security panel. "I'm in."

"Any trouble?"

"Nothing I have not seen before."

Checking every room in the echoing ultra-modern tri-level layout, she steps onto a balcony overlooking the pool and catches the eyes of one of the girls. Raising a finger to her lips, she backs away from the rail like she is meant to be there. Hurrying to the main floor, she checks an empty garage before exiting back the way she came.

"No brains in that place, just like the other villa."

"Okay, let's regroup back at the cottage. I owe you a dinner."

Bianca hops the wall and jogs down the dirt access road, passing a caravan of electric four-wheelers kicking up dust clouds and hauling a gaggle of giggling new arrivals in the opposite direction.

"You owe me more than that."

* * *

Owen finishes his sea bass to a plate of bones at their favorite San Pietro eatery as Bianca pushes her untouched pasta bowl aside and refills her glass to the brim. "Man, I'd kill for a hamburger."

Owen smiles, "When this is over, I may steer clear of Italian for a while. But the seafood is excellent."

Sloshing red wine on the table, "I grew up on cheap red wine and sticky pasta. I'm sick of it."

"What's wrong?"

"I have no one in my life."

"Come on, now. Be honest. There is not a red-blooded male on the face of this planet that would not have an interest in you."

"You don't."

"We have a good relationship. Why mess it up? I am taking you home before we cause a scene. Low profiles, remember?"

Bianca chugs her glass in protest, reaching for a refill as Owen pushes it out of her reach.

"Seriously, we need to leave. Now."

With a slurred head-turning laugh, Bianca rises to a wavering stance, "Okay, Dad. Let's go."

Owen glimpses Rico huddled with two swarthy colleagues at the restaurant's bar, "That's a new one."

Supporting his tipsy wife, Ted guides Simona outside and down the cobbled street as a trio of Euro brats whiz past on scooters too close for comfort before pulling to a stop outside a nightclub rejuvenated by a youthful injection of Rico's rambunctious recruits.

Faking a stumble over a curb, Simona cuts in front of Ted and pulls him into a darkened alcove outside a rollicking joint with a hypnotic repetitive beat thumping out its doors. Draping her long arms around his neck, she backs Ted against a wall and kisses him long and hard under the Mediterranean moonlight.

Pushing back, she hits him with an alluring smile, "You know what happens now?"

Still recovering from the kiss and unsure if he can walk, Ted's eyes widen, "No. What?"

Simona laughs, snapping back to sober on command, "Not what you—or your pants—are thinking." With a brown-eyed twinkle, she gestures at the row of parked scooters. "We will steal those idiots' motorbikes and scout the fifth PTB property in Drauto."

Owen shakes his head, "Vita said that place was destroyed."

"Vita can go fuck herself." Simona opens the rollicking club's front entrance, proffering a playful wink at a grinning doorman before disappearing into the crowd.

Ten steps behind his fast-moving partner, Ted peers into the thrumming dance club at the dizzying spectrum of lights and lasers illuminating a stew of intoxicated youth undulating and writhing as one to the pulse-pounding beat. Stepping across the threshold, the doorman extends a muscly arm, "Cover. You must pay if you want to come inside."

Pulling out his wallet, Owen thrusts a bill into the man's pudgy hand. "There. Satisfied."

The bouncer flips him off with a gap-toothed grin.

Feeling close to a million years old, Owen spots Bianca already with a fruity neon cocktail in her hand and leans in to yell in her ear, "I thought you said we need to check out that villa?"

Pulling from his grasp while bouncing to the syncopated beat, she kisses him again and laughs, "Not now, silly. We will wait until early morning. In the meantime, I want to dance."

Simona pulls Ted into the overcrowded dance hall before abandoning him at a cocktail table and melding into the throng of sweaty revelers bumping and grinding to an unrelenting percussive beat. Two young women amble up to Ted's table, sucking down fluorescent cocktails through weird curly straws, laughing, and giggling over the ear-splitting noise. Peering beyond the oblivious pair blocking his view, Owen watches Bianca amidst the scene, running her hands over a vivacious partier while bouncing her short black hair across her face to a staccato beat.

Far removed from any semblance of the only world he knows; Owen grabs a beer from a help-yourself ice bucket, recedes into the shadows, and takes a swig while maintaining a vigilant eye on his steaming hot date's erotic gyrations.

You know, just to make sure she stays safe and all of that.

Deep within the bowels of Owen's id, a Freudian sarcasm calls bullshit on his pleasure principle self-denial.

Yeah sure, Owen. If you say so.

Bianca | Drauto

12:25 a.m. | September 10, 2048

Following a 25-minute scooter ride out of Panarea well past midnight, Owen and Bianca whir along a deserted stretch of coastline before entering the decimated seaside hamlet of Drauto. Pulling to a stop at a crumbled intersection, Owen checks the boarded structures for signs of life, "My Spidey senses are tingling."

Fresh off her three-hour cardio workout, the sweaty and sober Bianca ignores the odd comment and wheels across an overgrown field before cutting down a long alley behind Drauto's shuttered commercial district. Owen revs his tiny electric engine, following in hot pursuit, zigzagging around piles of trash and darting rats. Rounding a corner, the pair skid to a stop on the crushed asphalt, kicking up gravel and dusty debris.

Surveying an erstwhile parking lot fronting a crumbled municipal structure in the village square, Owen notes tents of every shape and size encompassing a homeless encampment aglow with smoldering fires and the unpleasant smell of urine lingering in the early-morning stillness. "Jesus, San Pietro is just right up the road."

Bianca swipes her brow, "The trash has to go somewhere."

Owen kicks aside a syringe lying on the ground, "We need to find another way."

"The road leading to the villa is on the opposite side. There is no other way."

Riding single file, they glide between the tents, trying not to run anything or anybody over. Focusing on every subtle twist and turn, thankful for the quiet electric scooter's low hum, Owen stops at a dead end. "Shit."

Bianca pulls to his side and wheels 180 degrees, "This way."

Owen turns his bike around and locks onto an emaciated human being's bulging red eyeballs peering from a filthy open tent. Dressed in oily rags, the person raises their arms, whimpering incoherent words.

"I'm sorry. I cannot help."

Owen throttles forward, cognizant of wary eyes watching his wraithlike presence from slits in tents and makeshift hovels like a scene ripped from some medieval tale.

Breaking from the far side of the squalid, drug-riddled camp, the pair speed toward the sound of crashing waves, following an overgrown access road paralleling oceanfront estates. Darkened silhouettes of former grandeur rise and fall with the flood-ravaged topography left to rot since a Gork battle cruiser dropped from the sky a quarter mile off the rugged shoreline. The resulting tidal wave swamped Drauto, sweeping affluent residents out to sea on the hellish invasion night.

Riding side-by-side, Owen glances at Bianca, "We might be stumbling into a trap."

Bianca nods and pulls off the road under a thick stand of trees and vegetation. "Let's ditch the bikes and proceed on foot."

Out of habit, Owen pats his belt where a holstered weapon should be, realizing he left his 9mm at the cottage in a grate beneath the sofa with the rest of his valuables. "Shit, Bianca. What am I going to do? Hit them with a well-timed joke?"

Bianca lifts her top, showing off her perfect breasts and shoulder-holstered Glock, "Don't worry, honey. I got us covered in case things get hot."

Pausing to scan fallen trees and collapsed walls forming well-defined shadows across the dystopian scene, Owen turns to his partner, "You left me high and dry for three hours at that club. I hope you enjoyed yourself."

"I needed to blow off some steam, and you are no help. Also, Rico uses the party charters as a recruitment source for drug mules and prostitutes."

Owen frowns, "I suppose the ones who don't pan out end up drug-addled zombies at Camp Urine. Poor Mrs. Calogero must be beside herself."

Bianca hits Owen with a quizzical frown, "Who?"

"Rico's mother—nice lady—makes a mean pastry."

"Owen, do you hear that?"

"Hear what?"

Seconds later, a sleek chopper passes overhead at treetop level. "That."

Owen nudges her in the arm with a snickering laugh, "Who are you? Radar O'Reilly?"

"Who?"

Owen watches his sexy partner crouch forward, surveilling the villa estate where the chopper lands with its blades winding down. Still smarting from his latest pop reference falling flat, he mutters, "Rachel always pretended to get my obscure references."

"I'm not your wife, Owen."

Crouching low, Owen follows Bianca's advance to a retaining wall with a better view of three men exiting the chopper on an overgrown lawn fronting the dilapidated villa. "Why did we not come here first? The brain must be inside. Call in the cavalry, and let's get the hell out of here."

"Calm yourself, Owen." Bianca pulls a small device from a tight pants pocket and presses a button.

"Now what?"

"That signaled Aisha's people on a freighter 20 miles offshore. They should be on our coordinates within minutes."

"Why am I constantly kept out of the loop?"

"Owen, I love you like a brother, but you must stop thinking the world is conspiring against you."

* * *

Over an hour later, Owen yawns from their defiladed position. "It is half past four in the morning. Where are they?"

Bianca scans the parked chopper, catching the tell-tale glow from the tip of the chain-smoking pilot's cigarette. "Maybe something happened."

A rush of activity and loud voices break the quietude.

Owen and Bianca watch the men hustle out of the villa, hefting something between them on a beeline for the chopper as the cigarette man flicks his smoke and jumps into the cockpit. Seconds later, the rotors spin up for a quick take-off.

"They sure are leaving in a hurry."

"Good. Now is our chance. Let's go."

Knowing deep in his heart that Aisha Ayad's assault team is likely dead, Owen grabs his partner's shirt tail, "No. Bianca. We need to get out of here. I have a bad feeling about this."

Unholstering her Glock, she smacks Owen's hand off her shirt and takes a deep breath as the chopper flies off at high speed. "The mission is to take out that fucking brain. If no one is coming, it is up to us."

Trying to reason with the stubborn Italian who never quits, Owen shakes his head in defeat, "Okay. Hold on. Let's think about this. We can't waltz in there half-cocked. We need to formulate …"

A deafening noise and blinding white light precede a violent shockwave shattering the darkness.

Owen | Drauto
06:39 a.m. | September 10, 2048

Awakened by searing pain permeating his entire body, Owen's scorched eyelids peel apart, staring into a deep blue sky. Sensing frantic activity and hearing muffled sounds through his ringing ears, he tries to focus on a blurred form in a banana-yellow hazmat suit, yelling a muffled command while injecting something into his burned and bloodied leg, returning him to an opiate-induced altered state.

Hazmat-suited sailors from an Italian Navy frigate off Drauto lift Owen's limp body from the scorched Earth and position him atop a stretcher board. After strapping him down, they carry him into a waiting medevac chopper. Secured beside one other victim, a female, a team of medics run IVs and monitor weak vitals as the Italian navy airship rises above a smoking crater where a sprawling oceanfront villa once stood. Flying at a low altitude over San Pietro, the chopper breaks out across the open sea, buzzing a moored blue and white abandoned yacht on an emergency heading for the US Naval Air Station hospital in Sigonella, Italy.

Owen | US Naval Air Station, Sigonella
06:45 a.m. | October 2, 2048 – 23 days later

A tremor jostles utensils on Owen's bedside table as he snaps awake and pans his field of view out a window in his hospital suite toward acrid volcanic smoke billowing from an active Mount Etna.

Smacking exposed chapped lips from his mummified repose, Owen attempts to speak, "Nurse." Clearing his parched throat, he tries again, "Nurse. Somebody. Anybody. Hello?"

A blithe nurse wearing a white coat over her digitized camo uniform with a stethoscope slung around her long neck saunters to Owen's bedside. "Hello. I am Lieutenant Jane. How are you feeling today, Mr. Dixon?"

Owen tries to blurt out his real name as an orderly enters with a tray of meds and a pitcher of ice water.

Unable to take it any longer, Owen pulls the lid off the plastic pitcher and gulps it down his gullet, sloshing cold water on his bandaged chest and hospital bed sheets.

Swiping his wet mouth with his thick-wrapped right arm, he eyes the tall woman. "What did you call me?"

The woman checks her old-school clipboard, "We found a crispy ID in your pants that says your name is Ted Dixon from Akron, Ohio. As a fellow Buckeye, you wouldn't be carrying around a fake ID, would you? Uh, Mr. Dixon, you suffered first and second-degree burns over your entire body from a gas pipeline explosion on the island of Panarea. Beautiful place. I spent a two-week furlough there and never wanted to leave. Of course, that was Pre-Gork ...."

Owen grabs the Naval officer's arm, "What about my friend?"

Pulling from the man's slackened grip, Lieutenant Jane scans her charts and shakes her head. "I am sorry, Mr. Dixon. You are the only patient who checked in through our emergency services that morning."

Confusion mixed with fright and paranoia cause Owen to retreat into his wet sheets. "My skin is crawling with ants."

Lieutenant Jane checks his line before injecting another dose of morphine, "Here, this should help."

The drugs course through his veins, making him warm and sleepy, dreaming of Bianca.

Owen | Milazzo

02:18 p.m. | October 9, 2048 – 7 days later

Trying to figure out how to explain the last few months to Rachel and just get back home, Owen sits at an airport bar nursing a beer and catches his scarred and ruddy reflection in a mirror. "I look like a fucking mutant."

Incapable of tears, he chuckles at his weird predicament and looks down at a knapsack of donated clothes and toiletries Lieutenant Jane collected out of pity upon learning the backlogged American embassy wanted nothing to do with the discharged mystery man.

His head swimming with pain pills pilfered over his extended convalescence, Owen glimpses a sexy Italian woman pulling a wheeled suitcase through the crowd.

Reacting to the woman's curvy swagger, jet-black shoulder-length hair, and flawless olive skin, Owen jumps from the bar stool, chasing down her back-turned stroll through the bustling terminal, yelling, "Bianca, you're alive!" Grabbing an arm, he spins the woman on her high heels like a lunatic, staring into her mortified face.

The startled woman's expression transmogrifies into a grimacing sneer, cursing and slapping her assailant across his peeling red face.

Warding off another blow with a profuse apology, Owen parries the woman's heavy bag swinging toward his head in self-defense while receiving another salvo of Italian epithets before she storms off.

Wiping the woman's spittle from his cheek, Owen makes eye contact with a disapproving gaggle of gawking eyewitnesses.

"I thought she was somebody else. I'm looking for Bianca. Bianca Valentino."

The irate woman dispatches a burly cop cradling a mean-looking submachine gun to question her stammering and emotional assailant.

"Mi scusi signore. Fammi vedere il passaporto e il biglietto."

Flummoxed and catching the words passport and possibly ticket, Owen turns on the old charm and attempts to laugh it off, smiling and gesturing toward his bag propped against the bar stool, where he abandoned it in pursuit of the woman.

Looking between the enraged, well-dressed, upper-class woman and her downtrodden, despicable, disagreeable-smelling assailant, the no-nonsense airport security officer sides with the voluptuous lady, pinning the perp face down on the dirty linoleum with his knee pressed into the bum's reddened neck. Calling for backup, he checks the creep's jacket and pulls out a bag of smuggled pills.

The indignant Italian woman spits at Owen once more for good measure as backup arrives to arrest the pill-popping, drugged-out loser for sexual battery and a host of trumped-up narcotics trafficking charges.

Owen | Milazzo

02:00 p.m. | November 12, 2048 – 34 days later

Curled on a hard cot in his cell, Owen hears two guys down the block going at it for the third time since the break of dawn as Officer Alberto rushes past yet again, commanding them to knock it off.

Sucked of all pride and suffering physical and mental traumas beyond human endurance, Owen wills his aching body enshrouded under a coarse wool blanket to rise toward thick iron bars under pervasive fluorescence casting his cell in a soul-crushing greenish glow.

"I need to pee."

Scratching himself, he sees a new cellmate drooling down the facing cot six feet across the dank cell. Owen swings his feet onto the sticky concrete floor and stands at the urinal against the back wall, relieving himself while wiping his face with the back of his crusty and quaking hand.

After quelling the sodomizing sister act for the third time, the guard taps his nightstick against Owen's barred door.

"Dixon!"

Zipping his grubby trousers, an emaciated Owen sporting a four-week growth of scraggly beard pivots from the stinking urinal to face his jailer.

"It is your lucky day, Ted Dixon. Someone posted your bail."

Flabbergasted by the news, Owen retreats to the sanctuary of his cot, "Are you sure?" Overcome with rampant paranoia and reeling from narcotic withdrawals, Owen squints toward the tall, mustachioed Italian jailer while picking dead skin from his peeling hands, "It is illegal to trick me."

Officer Alberto chortles, "Come, my friend. One month was long enough. Let's get you cleaned up."

* * *

Shaved and showered, Owen exits the Milazzo city jail onto a busy street and rifles through his returned bag of grubby hand-me-downs. Ripping open an interior seam reveals a donated cash card he had the presence of mind to hide before leaving the hospital. Pocketing the card, he dumps the bag and heads toward the docks, where he and Bianca missed the ferry to Panarea by twenty lousy minutes. Piecing together a nightmarish series of events, he reaches a solid conclusion in his foggy mind.

The answers I seek are all back on Panarea.

Waiting in a long line inside the ticketing office, fingering the cash card, unsure of the balance, he hears a familiar, screechy voice, yelling, "Next!"

Looking like a different person than the one who berated the frying pan-faced ticketing clerk months before, Owen mumbles, "One ticket on the next ferry to Panarea."

Watching the woman run the card and print a paper ticket, Owen breathes easier as she passes the card and voucher across the counter. Almost home free, she pulls back the papers with a quizzical frown contorting her ample countenance, "Have we met?"

Owen grabs the ticket and his card, mumbling "No." mid-turn toward the exit.

* * *

Disembarking the loaded ferry, Owen scans the crowded pier in a vain search for the familiar olive-skinned pretty face that has become his unbreakable obsession.

She is gone. I lost her.

Trudging up cobbled San Pietro streets past carefree tourists and lovers on a gorgeous Mediterranean afternoon, he reaches the red cottage door. Running his hand above the bricks, his fingers tighten around the metal key.

Thank God.

Inside, he walks across the worn carpet, opens the fridge, and sees the six-pack of Birra Messina he bought the day before all hell broke loose.

Downing a beer in one long pull before popping the cap off a second bottle, Owen slides the sofa where he slept away from the wall and stares at the exposed floor grate.

Dropping onto his knees, he pries it open, peers into the spidery recess, and extricates a plastic bag containing Ted Dixon's forged passport, credit cards, and a thick wad of Euros. Basking in his first good fortune in months, Owen removes a second bag containing his holstered P365XL PTB Special Edition. Stretching deeper inside, his hand closes around a last bundle holding two extra magazines and a silencer Bianca gave him, just in case.

After reacquiring his cache, he shuffles to the back bedroom and sees his partner's bag in a chair right where she left it. Contemplating Bianca's flirtatious personality, a thought crosses his sleep-deprived psyche.

What do I really know about Bianca Valentino? What do I really know about any of them?

Draining the last drops from the second bottle, he tosses it on the floor, climbs into Bianca's unmade bed, and curls into the covers, ensconcing himself in her sensual muskiness before falling into a deep sleep.

Owen | Panarea

09:35 a.m. | November 25, 2048 – 13 days later

Shaved, showered, and wearing a pale blue button-down linen shirt over lightweight khakis and leather loafers from a fine Italian clothier along San Pietro's resurgent business district, Owen waits at his favorite table for Mrs. Calogero to bring his pastry and coffee. Rehearsing for the millionth time what he will say on his first call home in months, one day before Thanksgiving, he spies Rico, and the boys enter the internet café right on schedule.

Careful not to spill on his new clothes, Owen finishes his apricot-filled delicacy and washes it down with the sublime brew, "Perfecto, Mrs. Calogero. Perfecto."

Leaving a healthy tip, Owen dodges the scooter traffic and crosses the street. Checking to see if anyone is watching, he enters the shady establishment and closes the door behind him. As his eyes adjust from the brightness outside to the shuttered interior, he slides around a reception counter, hearing loud voices and strange activity from behind closed doors up and down a dark hallway.

From his right, Owen catches a burly fellow exiting a bathroom with a surprised stare, turning to anger on his large, stubbled face.

"What are you doing here?"

Owen closes the distance between himself and the stout fellow, "Oh, I'm just looking for a little information."

"You made a big mistake coming back here."

Anticipating the hulking fellow's frontal assault, Owen sidesteps his attacker, undercuts the creep's jaw, and sends him to the hard floor in one sweeping motion. With a second knockout blow to the neck, he turns out the lout's lights as two more men emerge from behind closed doors in response to the commotion.

Owen raises his fists in a classic boxer's pose, "Okay, boys, one at a time. Step right up."

"Enough!"

A shirtless Rico exits the first room and flings a towel around his neck like he has just finished a workout. Pushing aside his associates, he sizes up the intruder with an approving gap-toothed grin. "You made it back. Good for you."

Striking paydirt, Owen pierces the young criminal with a determined look, "I want some goddam answers." Kicking the guy moaning on the floor, he grits his teeth, "And I'd rather not fight all of you. I am tired."

"There is no reason for violence. We are in the entertainment business." Rico laughs and pats his dark associates on their backs, "I'll handle our guest. Return to your assigned rooms and finish cataloging the new recruits."

The heavy fellow scrambles onto his feet and snarls at Owen before hustling to join the others.

Owen mocks the dangerous thug, "Wise decision, my friend. No hard feelings." watching him retreat to assist his mates.

Weighing his options, Rico pulls up a chair and props his feet on an empty office desk, "Okay. Sure, why not? Have a seat, Mr. Owen Haig."

Owen nods and sits on a squeaky office chair. "Why am I not surprised."

Rico stares across at Owen, "One of the first things I learned upon aligning my business interests with the PTB was to know thy enemy."

Owen shakes his head, "Look, I just want to know what happened to my friend and why the villa exploded."

Rico shrugs his thin shoulders, "Your friend's whereabouts are unknown. As you can imagine, the PTB is very interested in locating her as much as you. She knows too much."

"I assume my other associates are also dead or hiding."

Rico nods, "More the former than the latter, I am sorry to report. The operation was a trap. Aisha Ayad and her valiant crew never made it off the freighter. They are all dead. The PTB detonated the villa in Drauto because it had outlived its usefulness. The plan was to time the explosion to kill you and Ms. Valentino at the same time, but like a bad penny, you keep turning up."

"Do you know who posted my bail?"

Patting his narrow chest, Rico smiles and lights a cigarette, "Uh, that would be me."

Masking genuine surprise, Owen stares at Rico's smiling mug through a cloud of smoke hanging in the stillness, "Why would you do that?"

"Because I knew you would return to my isolated island paradise." Pulling open a desk drawer, Rico removes a mean-looking snub-nosed revolver and a box of 38-caliber ammunition, "I own the local constabulary, Mr. Haig. Your death will be written off as another ex-pat junkie who tried to break into my business looking for drug money. Meanwhile, the PTB experiment proved a raging success. Did you know they performed a final test before detonating the villa? A single Cezanne killed over fifty people." Swinging the empty gun through the air, he laughs, "Well, technically, they killed each other, but I digress."

"Is that so?" Rising from his seat, Owen pulls his muzzled P365XL and aims it at a gobsmacked Rico, who spills the 38 caliber bullets all over the floor, cursing his carelessness.

Looking down the extended barrel at the frozen, wide-eyed kid, Owen shakes his head, "Your mother is very disappointed." before squeezing off three hollow-point rounds through Rico's chest and neck.

Moving out of view, Owen waits for the others with his prized weapon, poised and ready. Like a bizarre carnival game, the idiots exit the hallway with pants around their ankles and guns drawn as Owen picks them off with close-range shots to their heads.

Racking a new clip, Owen steels himself, waiting for the gorilla to emerge from the hall. At the last possible second, he feels a hot breath on his neck and pivots onto the behemoth, who grabs the gun by the muzzle as Owen squeezes the trigger.

A look of sheer puzzlement contorts the man's face, staring at the redness spreading across his white shirt as blood spurts from his mouth. Owen steps backward as the 300-pound human muscle pitches face down on the floor.

Ninety-nine percent confident the immediate threat is extinguished but cognizant of more knuckle draggers showing up at any time, Owen jumps over the dead men, kicking open doors along the nightmarish hallway and yelling like a girls' basketball coach, "Listen up, ladies! Get dressed and get out! You're free! But you better leave now! Let's go! On the double!"

Seizing the opportunity to reclaim their freedom, the young women in various stages of undress scream down the hall and through the front offices toward the light of day. In the last room, Owen finds a naked threesome hunched over a powder-covered metal tray. Thinking of his daughter, he kicks it aside and pulls them onto their bare feet, "Get the fuck out of here! Now!"

High as a kite, a waifish, dark-complected girl jumps on Owen like a monkey and kisses him. "Grazie! Grazie!"

Knowing time is dwindling by the nanosecond, Owen carries her through the office to the door and pushes her outside to join the fifteen other girls, drawing the stares of curious onlookers.

Retreating down the empty hall, Owen exits an exterior door onto a back alley and hops a wall on a beeline to the cottage to grab what he can and get out of Dodge.

Owen | Milan
04:38 p.m. | December 20, 2048 – 25 days later

Frustrated and furious at his abject failure to contact Rachel, who must be worried sick, a downtrodden Owen claims a spot on a stained sofa inside the noisy and crowded lobby of a dilapidated apartment building converted into a hostel for wayward travelers. Peering through the rogue's gallery of refugees, ex-pats, and fugitives—all with stories of their own—milling about the overcrowded interior decorated with cheap tinsel and Christmas decorations, Owen maintains a vigilant eye for the establishment's manager, who promised him the use of his lone functioning satellite phone.

A nasally fellow with a cigarette dangling from his lower lip expels a rheumy cough and plops on the sofa beside Owen.

Suffering physical and mental wounds that will never fully heal, Owen scooches to the edge of the cushion with a low groan.

Man, what am I doing here?

Appearing out of the semi-festive throng like a savior, the manager approaches Owen with a kind-hearted grin and holds out an old yellow satellite phone in his large hand, "Talk fast, signor. The battery does not hold a charge for more than a few minutes."

Accepting the grubby, handprinted bricklike phone with a large crack in its casing, Owen fumbles for a scrap of paper from his shirt pocket containing his home number back in Newport, "Grazie. Grazie. I owe you one."

Taking a deep breath, the wayward Owen Haig ignores the red-blinking battery icon and presses the numbers into the scratched touchscreen. As the phone connects, he holds it to his scruffy face and attempts to tune out the background chatter, hearing a familiar voice over the staticky connection.

"Hello?"

Hearing Rachel's angelic voice, Owen wipes away tears with his dirty shirt sleeve, "It's me. Owen. I am coming home."

Following thirty precious seconds of white noise over the line, her quaking voice fills him with despair, "Owen, you can't. They told us you had died in an explosion."

Hearing his wife's cries and wails calling out for Dave, Owen stares through the room full of strangers surrounding his misery before an even-toned voice resonates over the faltering connection, shocking him back to the grim reality, *"My God, Owen, we buried you."*

Feeling a proverbial knife's blade stabbing him square in the back, Owen fights to control burgeoning rage in the face of brutal betrayal from the one man in the entire world he thought he could trust, "Well, unbury me, Dave."

"You cannot come back here."

"Why not?"

"Owen, the PTB monitors our communications. I'm hanging up. Don't call again."

The connection dies as two men slinging beat-up luggage jostle past Owen toward the check-in counter, hearing their names called for the last available room at the inn.

In shock, Owen follows in their wake and returns the phone to the manager.

"Signor Dixon, we are out of rooms, but you can sleep in the lobby. It is the best I can do."

"No. I'll be fine. Thanks for the use of your phone."

Owen slings his pack over a shoulder and walks out the door into the working-class Milanese neighborhood, past old homes strung with dull, solar-powered Christmas lights and manger scenes scattered up and down the tree-lined street awaiting Baby Jesus' blessed arrival.

We'll meet again. Don't know where.

Don't know when.

Dame Vera Margaret Lynn

Chapter Six:

The Farewell

Rachel | Hilltop

06:15 a.m. | December 25, 2048

Three-year-old Hannah romps onto Rachel's bed with Piper close behind, jostling her awake, "Get up, Mommy! Get up! It's Christmas morning!"

Bedheaded and bleary-eyed, Rachel props on her elbows, watching her rambunctious daughter bouncing the black spaniel pup airborne on the springy mattress. "Aw, it's so early, Sweetie. Don't you want to sleep a while longer?"

"I can't, Mommy!" Snuggling the dog, Hannah beams at her mother, "I have to see if Santa remembered my wish."

Rachel reaches for her water as Piper pulls from Hannah's tiny grasp and curls against her paralyzed legs, "See? Piper is sleepy."

Hannah rolls her emerald eyes, "Mommmmm … get up. I hear Dave downstairs doing stuff already."

"Honey. He is getting ready for our guests. Uncle Stan is coming over—and your Aunt Shirley. Don't you want to see them?"

"I guess."

Rachel pulls her daughter into a tight embrace, so she won't see her eyes filling with tears, "Merry Christmas, baby girl."

Pressed against her Mom's t-shirt, Hannah muffles, "Merry Chrithmuth."

Rousting Piper onto the floor, Rachel scooches her useless lower half to the edge of the bed, "As long as you are here, you can help Mommy get dressed."

* * *

The tail-wagging rescue meets the retrofitted elevator descending to the sprawling Newport, Rhode Island mansion's main level. As the conical lift's glass doors part, Hannah jumps off Rachel's lap and sprints toward the great room, where the family Christmas tree pulses and glows to *White Christmas*.

Rachel rolls past heirloom ornaments and decorations, adorning traditional placements throughout the festive main floor, sparking memories of Christmases past while absorbing her daughter's disappointment.

Hannah turns to her mother with a teary-eyed frown, "Santa lied."

"Why would you say that?"

"I told him, Mom, all I want for Christmas is Daddy."

Rachel reaches out to her pouting girl, "You know, even Santa can't make that happen."

"Then what good is he?"

A resonant *knock-knock-knock* interrupts Rachel's reply.

"Oh, good God. I thought we said to arrive sometime after

Noon. Aunt Shirley never listens ….."

Rachel and Hannah hear Dave cross the foyer to greet the early arrival, followed by a resounding, "Ho! Ho! Ho! Merry Christmas!"

Hannah's frown turns upside down as Rachel's heart beats out of her chest, "Oh no. It can't be."

Piper beats Hannah in her plaid dress and patent leather shoes in a race to the front doors, letting in the chilly air. Sliding around Dave's tree trunk legs, hoping for a miracle, her beaming smile fades, replaced by a confused frown, "Who are you?"

Bundled in a tweed overcoat with a red scarf around his neck and a herringbone cap pressed atop thick charcoal curls, the distinguished old man bends down with a warm smile, "My name is Professor Richard King. And you must be Hannah. I have heard so much about you."

Dave smiles at the PTB refugee, "Come in from the cold, Professor."

Acknowledging the welcome with an ironic grin, Richard enters the expansive foyer, loosening his scarf, "Thank you for springing me from Scotland, Dave."

Noting Hannah's disappointment and Richard's cumbersome suitcase and a big, wrapped box on the porch, Dave pats the man's cold back, "Hannah, why don't you help the Professor with his coat and hat and then take him to your Mom. I'll carry your luggage to a guest room, Richard."

Hannah grabs Richard's large hand by a finger and pulls him inside with a half-hearted, "Okay. Come on."

"Lead the way, Hannah Haig!"

Wearing an untucked flannel shirt over denim jeans, Dave closes the front door behind him and proceeds across the turnabout and down the winding drive, regretting not taking an extra half-minute to don a pair of boots on the frigid Christmas morning. Passing through the open wrought iron front gates, he jogs on numb feet along the tree-lined sidewalk to a black SUV idling at the slushy curb in the tony Newport neighborhood and raps frozen knuckles on the driver's side window.

The driver lowers the smoked glass halfway, "You got it?"

Dave passes a thick envelope through the opening, "That is over three thousand—one hell of a fare."

"Thanks, Mister. Pleasure doing business with you."

"Tell no one about the man you brought here this morning."

The Middle Eastern rideshare driver shrugs an insincere chuckle, "Man? What man?"

* * *

Richard rocks back and forth in a comfortable recliner, cradling a hot toddy in his thick hands, watching Dave position a new log on the fire, sending a sea of sparks up the flue. "A real working fireplace. It was worth escaping Scotland to see that once more."

Dave chuckles, "Yeah, Europe is a basket case. Then again, so is the good old USA."

"What's it like here since the Gorks?"

Dave pokes at the fire with a heavy brass tool, "Uh, well, things are slowly returning to a semi-new-normal. We boil water even though they say it's potable. There is limited Wi-Fi and internet, but the grid comes and goes without warning. I'm surprised we have power this morning."

"Merry Christmas, right?"

"Huh? Oh yeah. That probably explains that little mystery." Returning the brass poker to its stand, Dave wipes his hands, "How was your flight?"

Richard rears back with a yawning stretch, "Weird. I have not traveled on a commercial flight since the 1960s." Taking a drink, the 126-year-old man leans forward, "Thank you for arranging my travel. They are no doubt looking for me as we speak."

"I need to tell you something, Professor," Dave checks to ensure Rachel and Hannah are out of earshot, "Owen is alive."

"Owen Haig is very resourceful. I am relieved and saddened by that news." Richard stands and looks out a frosty window, "Of course, returning here is out of the question for him. What a travesty." Finishing his drink, he turns toward Dave with a smile widening across his lined face, "And now I am a fugitive as well."

"Do you think they will come after you, Professor?"

"Since The Powers That Have my Blue Spark pharmacological recipe, my whereabouts are of little consequence. Andrew can go fuck himself. However, I worry for The Council. There is nowhere on Earth for them to hide that is secure from his wrath."

* * *

An awkward silence fills the space across the festive dining room table between Richard, nursing another toddy in a Shetland sweater over a fresh shirt and corduroys, and a frail Stanley Hobbes, who timed his arrival for the mid-afternoon Christmas family meal.

Admiring the elaborate piney centerpiece and flickering red candles, Richard's stomach emits an audible growl, "Do you celebrate Christmas with Rachel every year, Mr. Hobbes?"

Managing chronic pain behind another pill gulped down with a glass of water, Stanley Hobbes pulls his cancer-ravaged diminutive frame into a comfortable padded chair. Coming to grips with spending his last Christmas under the same roof as the man responsible for Rachel's Blue Spark, Stanley cleans his thick round spectacles with a napkin, "I have known Rachel her whole life. Her parents, Marcus and Miriam Alexander, were a wonderful couple who opened their doors to a little turd like me." Stanley coughs and sputters, grabbing a hankie from a vest pocket, "They recognized the special bond I had with their daughter from the start. I wouldn't miss spending my last Christmas with Rachel."

Richard pulls the chair across from Stanley, "Your lung cancer … Stanley … how long do your doctors give you?"

"Those quacks thought I would not make it this far. And since I am inoperable in this fucking new world, I have no choice but to sit back and wait for the end."

Taking in Hobbes' dire prognosis, Richard pulls a bottle from his sweater and holds it up, "Would you be interested …."

Hobbes raises a hand, stopping Richard in his tracks, "I know who you are …." Richard tries to interject, but Stanley points a finger, "Let me finish, Professor. I have no interest in one of your death-cheating alien wonder drugs, and I can never forgive you for what you did to Rachel. What kind of man subjects a six-month premature baby girl to a horrible drug experiment?"

Impressed by Stanley's refreshing candidness, "Rachel was chosen based on her Alexander bloodline going back to a Second World War pilot named Neil Alexander. I will not bore you with the details, Mr. Hobbes, but her Blue Spark transformation, which is now complete, allows you to judge my hubris at this very table. Otherwise, we would all be either dead or speaking Gork right now. I have heard their tongue, it is not palatable to the human ear."

Hearing laughter from the kitchen at Piper's latest doggy hijinks, Richard lowers his voice, "I understand how Rachel's Blue Spark treatments must have appeared from the outside looking in, but there was no other way to administer the drug. And as for these," Holding up the pill bottle, "they are not a cure for anything, let alone your obvious late-stage lung cancer. They will merely allow you to go out on your terms."

Stanley's face turns a whiter shade of pale, "Why are you carrying a bottle of suicide pills?"

"Mr. Hobbes, if I forget your name at some point throughout today's festivities, please do not be offended. My mind falters while my body remains on auto-pilot. I am also here to see Rachel one last time before venturing on to my destiny."

Rachel's Aunt Shirley bursts into the room in her Sunday best,

"Who is ready to eat!"

Richard stands out of his seat as the handsome woman sidles around the dining table carrying the Christmas ham atop a heavy silver platter, "Allow me, Shirley."

Enamored with the erudite and sophisticated Professor King, Shirley's face reddens, "Why, thank you, Professor King."

"Please, call me Richard." Lowering the tray onto the table, he recognizes the ham's familiar loaf shape camouflaged under a sugary glaze amidst a grilled medley of carrots, beans, and potatoes from the canned vegetable collection he noticed in the larder during his nickel tour of the Hilltop family estate. "This looks delicious. Nothing like a canned ham."

Rachel wheels into the dining room, holding a bottle of Bordeaux with a storied past, and parks at the head of the table. "Knock it off, Richard. It is a canned ham Dave traded for a bottle of homemade gin. If everyone gets food poisoning, it is Dave's fault."

Richard quells a Pavlovian response to the glistening meat, "Regardless of its origins, it looks delicious."

Stanley leans in to snatch a piece of crystalized glaze off the cooked meat, "Hmm. Richard, this might be the spot where the jockey kicked it."

Rachel slaps Stanley's hand off the tray, "That is enough out of you, Stanley."

Wheeling to the head of the table between the unlikely pairing of the two older men so integral to her life, Rachel reaches forward and takes each of them by the hand, "It means a lot to me that you two have finally met after all of these years."

Stanley's eyes widen, "Uh, Rachel, you are turning blue."

Still held in Rachel's grasp, Richard watches her Blue Spark mastery, returning her complexion to normal at will as her voice fills his head.

"Yes, Richard. I am in total control of my Blue Spark. Don't look

so shocked."

A subdued Hannah saunters in and takes a chair, with Piper trailing close behind as Dave appears with a heavy pitcher, filling water glasses. Following on his heels, Aunt Shirley reappears with a basket of homemade dinner rolls. "I hope everyone brought their appetites!"

Richard stands and pulls out the chair to his right for Shirley, "Allow me, Madam." prompting a snicker from Hannah.

"Madam. That is funny."

Sitting opposite Rachel, Dave places a roll on a snickering Hannah's plate to his right and taps the table, "Baby girl. Let's show some manners. Okay?"

Hannah rolls her eyes, "Okay, Dave. I'm sorry, Aunt Shirley."

Shirley passes the breadbasket to Richard, "No apology necessary, Sweetie. Having such a gentleman at our Christmas dinner table is a pleasure."

Dave laughs, "Hey? What am I? Chopped liver?"

Stanley snorts with a mouthful of bread, "Yeah, I'm with Dave."

Post-invasion lean years bereft of soft drinks, pre-packaged snacks, and high-calorie junk foods have reduced the 68-year-old Shirley to her 110-pound fighting weight for the first time since her mid-twenties. Turning to Dave with her trademark coy smile, she lifts her glass, "Of course not, dear. What would Rachel and Hannah do without you? Especially since poor Owen's passing."

The room falls silent as Rachel mutters, "I think I forgot something in the kitchen."

Rolling away from the table with tears streaming down her face, Rachel wheels past the sink full of pots and pans to the back pantry before allowing her emotional dam to break.

"Is there anything I can do, Rachel?"

Pulling blond hair from her face, Rachel looks through watery eyes at Professor Richard King, "No. I'll be okay. It is just that …."

"I know. Owen is alive. Dave told me."

Exhaling a long and cathartic sigh, Rachel shakes her head and tries to collect herself, "He called five days ago. I was so shocked by the sound of his voice that I didn't even say goodbye."

"He would be here if not for the damnable PTB."

Rachel shakes her head, "Everything is upside down."

Richard's tone darkens, "I warned Kobayashi not to play God before he created Andrew and The Sisters."

Rachel lifts a jar of canned beans off a shelf and sets it down with effortless telekinetic ability, *"I think we are all guilty of playing God, Richard."*

Glancing over his shoulder to ensure they are alone, Richard leans in and whispers in her ear, "How long can you keep this up?"

"The Powers That Be will never get their fucking hands on my daughter. I will hide her Blue Spark to the day I die."

Switching off the waterworks, she presents her old friend with an effervescent smile, sans telepathy, "Now then. It is Christmas, and I know a little girl who has patiently waited to open presents all day. Let's eat some shitty canned ham and get on with this charade."

"That's the spirit, my dear."

* * *

Getting his second wind after the big dinner, Richard slides the large box he ported all the way from Scotland into the great room and adds it to Hannah's teetering stack of gifts while Rachel, Dave, and Shirley clean up the dinner dishes in the kitchen.

Hannah bounds up, gushing at the huge present, "That's for me? Wow, what's inside?"

The über-observant Professor watches Hannah's green eyes brighten with an intense glimmer, plopping his creaky old frame into a cross-legged repose on the floor next to the precocious girl, "You will need to open it and find out."

Not to be outdone, Stanley pulls a box wrapped in old newsprint from a bag, "Hannah, I have something for you, too."

"Mom! I'm opening presents!"

Hearing what she thinks sounds like *"Go ahead and start without us."* from the kitchen, Hannah digs her little fingers under the yellowed newsprint and rips open the present as her angelic features crinkle into a frown, "An old book. Um, thanks, Uncle Stanley."

Seeing her less-than-stellar reaction, Stanley taps the antique volume, "You are holding a first edition of Lewis Carroll's *Through the Looking Glass* from 1872. I bought it in an auction when I learned your Mom was pregnant with you. I thought I would have more time, but you can handle it."

Richard nods approval, "Stanley, that is excellent. I understand you have a rare books emporium. I would love to visit it before I leave."

Stanley shakes his head, "I only open by appointment, but yeah, sure. Any time, Richard."

* * *

Dave plays Santa Claus, distributing gifts of all shapes and sizes to everyone, lounging in comfortable chairs around the room filled with Christmas cheer warmed by a crackling fire with drinks and snacks within hand's reach.

Recognizing shiny papers from Christmas pasts due to the scarcity of something as simple as wrapping paper in the frightening new world, Rachel opens a small box from Dave with Aunt Shirley looking on with bated breath. "Oh, Dave. Where did you get this?" Pulling out a sparkling sapphire pendant on a long silver chain.

Masking embarrassment, Dave proffers a nonchalant shrug, "I made it for you."

Aunt Shirley admires the sparkling necklace, refracting shades of blue across Rachel's blouse, "It suits you, dear."

Rachel returns it to the box, "You have no idea how right you are, Aunt Shirley. Thank you, Dave. It is lovely. Okay. Who goes next?

Richard, I didn't know you were coming until the last minute, but I did come across something … Well, you will just have to open it."

Richard places his toddy on a side table, growling a smile toward Hannah while scooping up the box, "I love presents!" eliciting giggles from the young girl.

Ripping open the gift, Richard peers inside and pulls out a stack of old Polaroids with a tear in his eye. "Oh my …."

Aware of an unspoken bond between Rachel and Richard, Dave smiles, "Come on, Professor, don't leave us in suspense."

Richard shows the group a photograph of a younger version of himself with his arm draped around a striking redhead. "Rachel … where …."

"Nina gave them to me before she passed. The one you are holding up looks like it was taken at your old desert base."

"Yes. Lost Cactus." Richard replaces the photos in the box, "Have you heard from Agent Flynn?"

Rachel shakes her head, "No. My guess is he is in hiding, like, uh …."

Dave tosses a box to Aunt Shirley, "Come on, Shirley, we need to pick up the pace, or we will be doing this until New Year's Eve."

Ensconced within a plush recliner, Stanley sips a glass of wine and calls across to Hannah, "Open that big one from Uncle Richard."

Richard turns and smiles at his new friend as Hannah tears into the three-foot square box.

With hands on hips, Hannah cocks her head sideways, reading the long name, "Thun-der-corp."

Richard rubs her blond head, "Outstanding! Cute as a button and whip-smart to boot."

Stanley chimes in, "Just like her mother at that same age, Richard. I cannot tell them apart."

Richard nods, "Yes. She is quite special, like her mother."

Rachel crunches a homemade pretzel, "Hey! I'm right here."

Hannah parts the lid and looks inside, "What is it?"

"Here, let me help." Richard removes the protective outer shell, revealing the top half of a boxy metallic craft. "It is a working prototype of a hypersonic delivery drone."

Stanley laughs, "It looks like a souped-up toaster."

"Very perceptive, Mr. Hobbes. Flying toaster is its codename."

Dave crouches beside Hannah, admiring the shiny silver drone covered in lightning bolt decals, "So this is what all the fuss is about."

"Yes, but the actual drones are much larger, of course."

Hannah smiles at her reflection in its shiny fuselage before giving Richard a big hug, "Thank you, Uncle Richard. I love it."

"You are welcome, Hannah. Oh wait, I almost forgot. It comes with a card from Julius Hart. Would you care to read it, my dear?"

Hannah holds the card in her tiny hands, "Um, let's see … *Dear Hannah* … Hey, that's me! … *Merry Christmas from the brand new Thundercorp Ranch down here in Texas. I hope you enjoy this prototype drone. You can play with it and see what makes it tick but be careful and tinker with it only under adult supervision.*

PS - Give your Mommy a big hug for me and remind her I am only a phone call away if she ever needs help.

Your friend,

Julius Hart"

Dave gives an approving nod, "Wow, Rachel. You never told me you are on a first-name basis with the world's richest man."

Rachel shoots him a sideways smile, "I have loads of secrets."

Stanley grabs a gift near his seat and opens it, "Hey, it's one of my old schooner mugs. Thanks, Rachel."

"You are welcome, Stanley. I know there must be four or five more around here somewhere, but I wanted to give you back at least one."

Stanley laughs and coughs, "Through high school and into her early twenties, before Owen came along, Rachel would show up at my bookshop in the wee hours of the morning. I'd make her a coffee in one of these mugs and listen to her crisis du jour. She invariably left with a mug still clenched in her hand. It became a running joke. Thank you, my dear girl."

Rachel wipes a teary-eyed smile, "You were a better listener than my shrink and always kept a light on for me. Thank you, Stanley."

"It has been my honor, Rachel."

Dave passes another present to Hannah, "Well, on that note, who is ready for a refill?"

With a Dave Special Gin Rickey in hand, Richard plops down beside Shirley, who regales him with tales from a long history of Alexander Family Christmas extravaganzas.

Half-listening to her aunt's embarrassing tales while perusing the rare book Stanley gave to Hannah, Rachel rolls her eyes, "Aunt Shirley, we never did the polar bear challenge in the swimming pool on Christmas Eve."

Stanley chortles, "Yes, we did. It was 2014. No 2016. I'll never forget Miriam's …."

"Uh, Stan, you want to not mention Mom's boob job in front of the whole family?"

Stanley raises his highball glass with a chortling laugh, "I don't have to. You did it for me."

The laughter and lively banter veer from slapstick silly to melancholy to downright bawdy into the late Christmas evening hours, pushing past midnight before the tipsy revelers stagger off to their guest bedrooms, one by one.

Checking on Hannah, Dave takes the well-preserved 173-year-old first edition from her tiny grasp, places it on the bedside table, and turns out the light, leaving Hannah to her vivid dream of venturing through the looking glass and finding her father.

Returning downstairs to check the house before bed, Dave finds Rachel wearing the pendant he gave her while flipping through Nina's old Polaroid collection before the smoldering fireplace.

Bone-tired, Dave drops to her side and massages her shoulders, "What are you looking at?"

"More of Nina Madsen's old photos. I miss her. She never recovered after her abduction."

Dave picks up a photo to change the subject, "Hey, check this one out. It is Artemus Pennywell with Richard and Nina. I bet they were real hellraisers back in the day."

Rachel holds the Polaroid into the light, "What is that in the background?"

Dave squints at the odd figure, "I don't know. It looks like a child wearing some kind of a bee costume?"

Andrew | PTB HQ
10:00 a.m. | January 11, 2049

Andrew leans back in Artemus' old seat at the head of a long conference table in the not-so-top-secret-anymore multi-level PTB HQ beneath Crichton Castle ruins at its epicenter, extending far into the Scottish Lowland countryside. Drumming his fingers on the table to a rhythmic beat stuck in his head like a broken record from something 12 blasted in the lab earlier that morning, the replicant straightens as a virtual screen brightens with the image of a hard-hatted human's dull mug. "Status, Watson."

Ed Watson, the beleaguered American engineer field-promoted to Project Leader tasked with completing four 60-floor multi-use buildings in the footprint of the former Petronas Towers, flips his hi-def feed onto the nearest hulking structure. "That is Tower One, Mr. Andrew. Ain't she a beauty."

Andrew's intelligent, gray-eyed gaze studies the riveted, bent steel outer framing meant to look like God only knows. "You finished the turd. Well done, Watson."

"I had to bring the hammer down on the local labor force, which we should have done from the start."

"Lessons learned, Watson. Show me more."

Watson widens the lens across frivolous and expensive architectural details overflowing with tropical Malaysian flora as he walks along a path to the site of a future restaurant filled with local carpenters amidst a racket of nail guns and electric saws, "The new steakhouse should be open by late Spring."

Moving farther up the path from the clattering racket, Ed flips the camera, "So, aside from chronic plumbing and electrical issues, the units in these towers are, for all intents and purposes, ready to lease out. The difficult task now is convincing Malaysians who lost family and friends by the thousands when Petronas was destroyed by the Gorks to return to life high up in a skyscraper."

Andrew frowns, "Humans are a superstitious lot. Do what you can, Watson. And good job."

Andrew swipes the feed as the Sisters enter the conference room single file and take seats assigned by their number around the conference table.

Andrew smiles, "Good morning, ladies. Status, Number 1."

"I have a present for you, Andrew."

"I love presents."

Producing an old-school smart device from her lab coat, Number 1 slides it across to her boss, "This is a prototype from the replicant factory in Milan."

Andrew hefts the shiny flat rectangle, "Late 20s smartphone design. Brilliant. But won't consumers expect the holographic-level technology they enjoyed before the Gorks fried every chip in the world?"

Number 2 interjects with a gentle hand on her sibling's sleeve, "The devices appear retro but operate in holographic mode. Place it on the table and tap it."

Andrew's light touch projects an AI-generated hologram of his handsome face rotating in space eight inches above the unit. "I'm impressed."

"The world is starving for easy access to their fucking internet."

"Careful, 16, your misanthropy is showing." With a second light tap, Andrew's image disappears, "And the brain-eating nanobots from our art project are embedded in this device?"

"At a sub-molecular level. Undetectable. We can activate the little killers via satellites when the time is right. No more brain centers at remote villas guarded by corruptible, dirty humans."

"How soon to market?"

"Even with the rampant supply chain and resource bottlenecks, two to three years at most. Since there is no viable competition, we will own the marketplace on day one."

"Let's move on," Andrew slides the prototype phone into his pocket. "I have a meeting with Julius Hart in one hour. He wants to purchase the International Outer Space Consortium and use its fleet of anti-gravity ships to get his Thundercorp project off the ground."

Number 1 turns to the CEO, "What will you do?"

Andrew laughs, "Oh, I plan to sell it, lock, stock, and barrel. We need the cash to finance our plans."

Folding his arms, he looks down the table toward Number 8, "I understand Professor King has grown weary of our shenanigans and flown the coup."

"We tracked his movements to the Haig family residence."

Andrew sighs, "No matter, we have his Blue Spark formula. Richard is on his own path now. I say, Godspeed to him."

Number 8 swipes her hand, manifesting a holographic 3D image of Rachel Haig above the conference table. "Speaking of the Blue Spark. Rachel Haig's superhuman celebrity status is now a worldwide phenomenon. Everyone wants what she has. I am working with our Asian pharmaceutical plant on a mass-produced Blue Spark drug *promising* to emulate her superhuman results."

"I vetoed that plan. Too risky."

"You worry too much, Andrew. Only a trial phase will receive an authentic Blue Spark jab to generate a global demand. The masses will get a placebo."

"Will it do anything?"

"It is guaranteed to turn them a euphoric shade of blue that I am told is quite pleasant."

Number 11 chimes in, "Some call it orgasmic."

Number 1 ignores her sister, replacing Rachel's image with a flashy Blue Spark logo, "Under the brand name Blue Spark, the placebo acts as a Trojan horse, releasing our killer nanobots into the users' brains."

Number 1 proffers a devious grin, "I know what you are thinking, Andrew. The nanobots trigger via a telepathic chain reaction. All it will take is one of us to set someone off, and the rest should occur …."

Andrew's eyes widen, "… at light speed. Brilliant. How close are we on this?"

"Same timeline as the phones. About three years."

"Can we sync the phone and drug attacks?"

"That is the plan, Andrew."

The PTB CEO stands, "Carry on, ladies."

Number 11 rises to address the table, "What about Edgar?"

Andrew smiles, "The Powers That Be require a human face. Keep him and the other employees fat and happy for the foreseeable future. And ladies, no more public executions. St. Andrews could have been a disaster."

Number 7 pouts, "We demonstrated our commitment to the Overlords. And we don't get out very often."

Andrew frowns, "Next time, just go shopping or take in a show."

A frustrated Number 8 stands out of her seat, "What about Owen Haig?"

Halfway out the conference room door, Andrew turns to the mother of his child, "It does appear that Mr. Haig and his Italian counterpart survived the blast on Panarea. So be it. Aisha and her group of traitors are dead."

Number 8 seethes with irrational rage, "What if the Haig's daughter was born with the Blue Spark?"

Andrew returns a disarming smile, "I am aware of that possibility, Number 8. However, St. Louis eliminated the United States as a threat and left Mommy in a wheelchair. My intel reports the little girl exhibits no manifestations of her mother's abilities. As long as that remains constant, Rachel Haig can raise her daughter in peace. I owe that to Artemus."

Number 8 smacks the table in frustration, "Why not kill them, Andrew? And why keep Vita Carrera locked in a cell?"

Andrew's chiseled face softens into a forlorn pout, "Where is your humanity, Number 8? Our Ms. Carrera and the Haigs have suffered enough. Moreover, even with the Blue Spark, one little girl poses no threat to us." Raising a finger, "However, my shoot-on-sight directive for Mr. Haig and the Italian detective stands. Just don't go out of your way. They are beneath us, and from the looks of things, you all have your work cut out for you."

Richard King | Lost Cactus
04:38 p.m. | January 22, 2049

Wanderlust rumbles past a ramshackle checkpoint gatehouse clumped with cacti, tumbleweeds, and gnarled perimeter fencing, grinding the final yards across desert hardpan and crumbled macadam on flat tires before skidding to a stop, inches from a half-collapsed building.

As the overheated engine sputters and quits, Professor Richard

King's wrinkled visage broadens into a grin behind the wheel of the vintage autonomous RV he coaxed and prodded on a fourteen-day American odyssey from the East Coast to the abandoned Lost Cactus Laboratory hidden in the southwestern hinterlands. Touching a St. Christopher dashboard magnet, Richard coos, "You can rest now, Wanderlust. This is the end of the line for both of us."

Pulling his aching body out of the captain's chair, King hunches to his unmade bed in the back of the cramped interior, drops facedown onto the thin mattress, and passes out.

* * *

Richard awakens in the dead of night to a skittering commotion outside the RV. Peering through a filthy side window, his keen vision narrows onto something lurking behind a prickly bramble.

Stumbling from the RV armed with a flashlight, sharp rocks stabbing through socked feet, he shines the beam on the lurker, "Who's there? Come out."

A mechanical whir precedes a broken-down bot entering a patch of moonlight.

Richard lowers the torch, "Alpha?"

The one-eyed, multi-armed survivor whirs and clicks, "I am g-g- g-glad to see you, Professor King."

"I had no idea Kobayashi abandoned you here all this time."

Alpha moves closer, "He left me. Everyone leaves me. I am expendable like trash. I survive. 1,250 days since your l-l-l-last visit."

Richard nods, "Was it that many days ago? Yes, I came here with Penny Pennywell seeking the cube on the first anniversary of the Gork invasion. I trust it is where I left it in the warehouse."

Alpha's cracked eyeball rolls toward the heavens, "I am a-a-a-afraid not, Professor."

Alarmed, Richard pivots toward the hulking silhouette of the vaunted and legendary Lost Cactus base warehouse.

"What happened, Alpha?"

"The Sisters hap … hap … pened. Theeyyyyy returned to their conception … birthplace … disaster … searching for… the cube, and poor, poor, poor Sarah. Nothing beats the original. They left mad. Empty hands. So s-s-s-sad for them."

Richard wavers on his feet, "The Sisters came here? Oh no. That is not good."

Alpha's arms extend and retract, undulating through the stillness as the glitchy bot spins on its low chassis and bumbles down Main Street through the heart of Lost Cactus, sending nocturnal beasties scampering for the tall grass, "Oh, fear not, my Professor King. King slash alpha-prompt, slash-dot-slash. I hid the … I took it … it is in safe claws. Mine. It's mine. I am speaking now … I am in the cube. Hello? Can anyone hear me/I hear everything …. I. I. I. Need a lift. Cowboys 27. Saints Zero. Zeroes and one. Nope. Nope. Nope. Not telling. 27 to ZERO. Zero to hero. There is a heartbeat. Never did it really die …. Stay with me awhile. Sarah. Let's find …."

Richard follows the glitchy bot spouting drivel into the night, stepping on every sharp rock past the broken glass front entrance of his former lab building. Huffing and puffing, Richard hastens his pace, keeping Alpha in sight as it leads him on a circuitous path to cottage row, settling on its bent and rusted metal haunches before Guest Cottage 27-0.

Richard catches up to the waiting Alpha and doubles over, gasping for air, his heart beating out of his chest, "You hid it here? They will find it. Sarah's DNA must be all over this hovel."

Alpha's arm telescopes and taps the old man's forehead, "Think. Think. Think. If I was a honey pot, where would I hide?"

Richard trains his flashlight on the bot, looking for loose wires or a booby trap, "You are speaking gibberish, Alpha. I don't follow."

"Oh, but you did. We are here. 27-0. Sarah's house. Did you know she died in my arms? Let's go inside."

Richard follows the broken-down bot into the tiny cottage. "So Mitsuo put the recruit up here while he completed the replication tanks in my laboratory."

Alpha ignores the observation, gesturing for Richard to sit his corduroy ass in the chair, "I made chicken and rice—e- e- e- e- eat ... it is good for your soul."

Richard King checks his watch, "Alpha, it is 2:30 in the morning. I have been on the road for two weeks. Can this ...."

Alpha places a bowl before Richard, "No more drivel until you eat."

Too tired to argue, Richard looks down at the bowl, "It is empty."

Alpha punctures the scientist's already compromised grip on reality with a subliminal suggestion, "Look again."

Beyond weary and unsettled by the robot's illogical behavior, Richard looks down at a piping hot bowl of chicken and rice.

"Alpha, how ...."

"Chicken and rice was Sarah's favorite. I miss her, Richard." Alpha finishes drying the cookpot at the kitchen sink and hooks it on the wall betwixt its friends, skillet, and saucepan, "I will take you to her and the cube on one condition ... I go, too."

"Deal." Richard picks up a soup spoon and digs into the brothy dish, "It is delicious." After consuming half the bowl, Richard eyeballs the waiting bot, "I am hallucinating all of this, aren't I?"

"Not everything. That's not chicken and rice; it is a time-released toxin. You have three hours to transfer your essence into the cube before l-l-lights out."

Alarmed, Richard stands from the rickety IKEA chair, catching himself from falling, "I feel dizzy."

Alpha escorts the wavering Professor back into the pre-dawn chilliness, "Your light-headedness is attributable to something other than my poison soup. Richard, you take a lot of drugs. How did you navigate 3,000 miles?"

Richard gazes at a morning star as an owl hoot-hoots from its broken window perch. "Wanderlust drove. I watched what used to be America pass by my passenger window. Beautiful and sad. More the latter, actually."

"Okie dokie, Professor. Better g-g-g-get to your lab before it's time to die."

Richard pulls from the bot's grabby clutches, "You hid the cube in my laboratory? It was destroyed in Kobayashi's fire. No one can go in there for 1,000 years. No life support."

Alpha rolls his cracked eyeball, "... What are we learning, Professor? Never doubt a robot. The Sisters could not go in there. They value their lives. Perfect place to hide a cube. And Sarah was already dead, like us."

Richard yawns and nods, following Alpha into his former five-story laboratory building, trudging along a once-familiar corridor piled with trash, feces, and crumbled drywall to a fireproof steel portal opening onto an emergency stairwell spiraling down a suffocating shaft to the subterranean laboratory level. At rock bottom, they push through another metal door into a pitch-blackness before Alpha's headlight animates long shadows across boxloads of lab equipment left in teetering piles down the hallway, "This way ...."

"Don't you dare tell me what lies ahead—I built Lost Cactus. I know the way." Pushing past Alpha, King stomps down the hall with his brain agog with a mishmash of disjointed memories. Jiggling a doorknob, he turns to the bot with a vacant-eyed stare, "This was my quarters. It's locked."

Alpha tugs Richard's cardigan sleeve, "Professor, that is a storage closet. You stormed past the door to your old apartment. There is no time for an old home week on the Lifetime network. Maybe in the next life."

Richard chuckles to mask his confusion, "Yes. Perhaps. We shall see."

The pair continue to the hermetically sealed double-door main entrance to Richard's former laboratory at the corridor terminus.

"My laboratory. My home."

Alpha extends a power saw appendage without fanfare, cutting through thick black and yellow striped hazmat tape that Viraj Patel's clean-up crew plastered across everything as Richard gapes at a warning sign hanging askew above the doors: *HASTE MAKES WASTE. Skull and Crossbones to infinity.*

"You know, Alpha. Mitsuo Kobayashi never asked to use my lab."

"I know. My former boss lost his way." Pushing the doors inward, Alpha gestures for Richard to cross the threshold, "But we cannot change the past. Affecting the future starts here. You go first. Someone is waiting for you."

Taking a deep breath of the toxic air, Richard enters his old laboratory for the first time in decades, seeing an animated three-foot bee-like creature with an elongated snout vault off a high lab bench, shattering glass labware across the floor on a beeline to his long lost friend.

"Doc! Is it really you? I never thought I would see you again."

Richard laughs with tears streaming down his face, "Bentley! Bentley Bee. Now I know I am hallucinating."

Bentley looks up at the man who breathed life into his genome, creating the one-and-only walking-talking bee, "Why do you say that, Doc? I miss you. I miss the old days."

Richard sinks onto a lab stool, his sad eyes filling with tears, chuckling at the comical little hybrid creature he created at the dazzling height of his scientific career, "You died, Bentley. A long time ago. I left here not long after when The Powers That Be closed us down for good. It was not my idea. Disclosure Day ruined everything. There was no need for a secret research base backward-engineering alien technology anymore. They gave me a shiny new underground lab in Scotland to keep me quiet, fat, and content. I was played for a fool. Only now, at the end of everything, do I finally understand the truth."

Bentley's form distorts and fades, "Good for you, Doc. My job is done here. We'll meet again. Don't know where. Don't know when."

Monitoring Professor Richard King's cathartic revelation and the fast-dwindling time to the end, Alpha illuminates the laboratory in a dreamlike fluorescence, leading Richard across the pocked and charred concrete floor, crunching glass, shrapnel, and humanoid forms melted beyond recognition strewn about the expanse to a cart where the cube rests under a single ray of light shining through the poisonous ether.

Richard collapses into his squeaky old office chair beside the cube, still in his cardigan, undershirt, and corduroys, gazing at his filthy, bloodstained socks as Alpha syncs him to the cube via the same injectable cocktail Mitsuo Kobayashi administered to Sarah years before.

With a robotic sigh, Alpha steps back as the cube glows to life, "Professor King, you and the cube are now one."

Richard's body shudders before falling still, "Are you coming, Alpha? I can't see ...."

The life force drains from Richard as his soul enters the cube, leaving his deceased form slumped forward in the chair.

With the rather simplistic task completed with no time to spare, the quad-armed bot works fast, cramming Richard's lifeless body—feet and legs first—into an empty black chemical barrel emblazoned with a bright yellow bee logo over Japanese Kanji script.

Next, Alpha hefts the heavy cube and drops it into the barrel, crushing it atop Richard's body with an audible snap, crackle, and crunch, "Oops. Sorry, Richard. Tight fit."

After soldering the round lid to a tight seal atop the barrel, the robot carries its burden across the former base to a busted side entrance in the massive Lost Cactus warehouse.

Rolling the bee barrel into the darkened interior crammed to the rafters with all the secrets the world can never see, Alpha pushes the scuffed and dented metal drum past a heaping pile of demolished blue X crates the Sisters ripped to shreds in their fruitless search for the cube and Sarah's remains.

At a nondescript section near the back of the warehouse filled with centuries of priceless religious objects, Alpha wedges the barrel between two crates stenciled Peter and John before shoving more boxes in front and on top, concealing Richard and the cube among millennia of crated relics and antiquities.

With his monumental task carried to a sad fruition, Alpha climbs into a crate and seals himself inside, oozing a gelatinous preservative before initiating sleep mode, where he dreams of a new and better world.

* * *

Engulfed within infinite complexity, Richard bodysurfs a splendorous wave bathing him in dazzling spectral brilliance toward a ravishing young woman in sparkling blue pajamas, extending a soft and supple hand, "Welcome, Professor. I am Sarah."

Paddy | PTB HQ
11:15 a.m. | March 11, 2049

Elevator doors shoosh apart onto Level C as Andrew leads his almost five-year-old son into the gleaming white underground laboratory.

Paddy tugs at his father's black sleeve, "Papa, what happened to Professor King?"

Andrew tousles his son's raven-haired mop top, "Richard decided to leave us, Paddy. He will be missed."

"I never see Mom anymore. Where is she?"

"Your mother and aunts are on special assignments visiting

wayward Council members hiding in interesting places all over the world."

"Hey, kid! Don't listen to your father! He is a psychopathic lunatic!"

Ignoring Vita Carrera's boorishness dangling from a rope above imminent death, Andrew sidles up to a back-turned Number 16, kissing her neck, "Well done, my dear. You outdid yourself."

Number 16 blows a long bang off her sweaty forehead with both hands wrapped around the floor end of the rope and pulley contraption, "Vita is heavier than she looks." Turning to face Andrew with a puffy-lipped smile and a black eye, "and she put up quite a struggle."

Alarmed by 16's black-and-blue countenance smudged with lipstick, cuts, and scrapes, Andrew's visage darkens with hatred at the vile redhead swaying above the aquarium. "Now, Miss Carrera, I gave you a chance, and you threw it back in my face. You left me no choice in the matter."

Resigned to her ignominious fate, Vita shakes her head with mocked pity, looking down at Andrew and 16 on the other end of the thick rope, "What kind of an asshole lets his son watch him commit murder? Think of the boy, Andrew."

Mesmerized by the violence about to happen right before his little face, a wide-eyed Paddy absorbs the redheaded lady's artful plea, staring up at her nakedness, dangling from a harness like a reluctant acrobat above the aquarium's blue-green water with the word traitor scribbled across her bare chest in red lipstick.

Internalizing an illogical rage, Andrew pivots down the long aisle toward the elevators, "Let her drop, 16. Goodbye, Ms. Carrera."

In a panic, Vita lets loose the final argument in her storied legal career: "The Overlords are using you, Andrew. Only a fool would not see that. You squandered the golden opportunity to lead the PTB into an enlightened future. For what? You are as good as dead. So is your stupid fucking son."

Seething at the former legal eagle's mentioning of his son proves the last straw for Andrew. Halfway to the lift, he turns and holds up a hand, pausing 16, poised to lower Vita into the algae-infested water, "We are all servants of someone, Miss Carrera. The Overlords will do as they see fit. Pity you will not be around to see it."

Fists clenched in anger at the realization that Vita struck a nerve, Andrew continues onto the lift, fighting an onslaught of remorse, as Carrera's last words stick to him like glue. "Damn her. She is right. I am wrong."

Left behind to watch the lady's violent demise, Paddy's deep blue eyes probe the aquarium's murkiness—a fixture in the underground lab from day one—teeming with schools of fish and exotic underwater plants, catching the scaly, gilled, aquatic beast emerging from the swaying plants like the *Creature from the Black Lagoon* with its wide mouth opening and closing, exposing razor-sharp teeth.

Engrossed in what is about to happen, Paddy presses his face against the thick glass, anticipating the violence—only this time with a living, breathing human instead of raw chickens.

"Are you ready, Paddy? Here we go!" Number 16 releases the rope, dropping Vita Carrera into the aquarium in a sea of bubbles, writhing and thrashing as the Amazonian sea monkey swims up and chomps into her long, kicking leg, whipping its head in a violent feeding frenzy, ripping her in two as Paddy watches the tank turn from green to red, mesmerized, and unafraid.

With her job complete, a bloodied Number 16 squats beside the little boy and puts her hand on his shoulder, "Okay, Paddy, the show is over. Did you complete all of your school assignments?"

"Yes." Pulling a paper from a shirt pocket, he unfolds it and shows it to his Aunt 16.

"What is this, Paddy?"

"Can't you tell? It's a drawing of me and the Overlords."

"How come it's just you?"

"Oh, that's because everyone is dead.'" Paddy refolds his drawing and shoves it back in his pocket as a piece of Vita Carrera floats past on the other side of the glass, "Can we have ice cream for dinner?"

Number 16 smiles and dabs her bloody lip, "Sure. Rocky Road?"

"Uh, no. I want Cookie Dough."

The lab goes dark as the pair leave to get ice cream. The satiated sea monkey retreats to its underwater cave, where a pressed penny pendant settles on the aquarium's sandy bottom near a dismembered finger still wearing a PTB ring.

Anastasia Gabreski | Upstate New York
11:43 p.m. | May 10, 2049

Number 11 creeps along the leafy exterior of the former PTB UN ambassador's secluded upstate New York farmhouse. Spotting an open window, the svelte replicant climbs past bird-patterned curtains, swaying in a moonlit late-night breeze, finding herself in a quaint breakfast nook.

Adjusting to the darkness, a bright kitchen light switches on, illuminating 11's stealthy form in a tight black jumpsuit with a knit cap pulled over dark bobbed tresses. Hands raised in mock surrender, 11 proffers a sheepish smile, "Good evening, Miss Gabreski. I thought I'd pop in and surprise you, but it looks like the joke is on me."

Sitting cross-legged atop a rustic farmhouse counter made of reclaimed barn wood with her cascade of blond pulled in a ponytail over light pink pajamas, Gabby points the long barrel of her grandfather's single-action Colt 45 Peacemaker at the sexy intruder and pulls back the hammer, "Don't you move."

"It was an ordeal to get out here, what with the roadblocks and curfews. America has gone to shit, so at least let me sit and rest." The wily woman pulls a chair at the cozy breakfast table and leans back in her seat. "Ah, that's better."

Not falling for the Sister's effortless charm, Gabby holds the revolver on the replicant, "Which one are you? I can never tell."

"I am Number 11."

Gabby nods, "Ah, what happened to your hair?"

"Andrew does not care for the color purple."

Gabby shrugs a smile, "Well, he is an asshole." while trying to stay calm and stop her hands from shaking, "I used to appreciate your desire to stand apart. I guess that was all an act." With a hard swallow down her dry throat, she slides her finger over the trigger, "I have a rule about uninvited guests !...."

With a subtle yet intoxicating wink, 11 infiltrates Gabby's brain with her hypnotizing blueberry gaze aglow from her smiling visage. "Now, Gabby, I want you to turn that mean-looking weapon around and place it between your lovely lips."

Tears stream down Gabby's terrified face, fighting to disobey hijacked synapses controlling her motor functions and placing the long barrel in her mouth against her will.

"That's perfect." 11 notes a dog bowl on the floor near a built-in refrigerator and a sink full of dinner dishes as she turns back toward the frightened woman, clenching the live weapon between her teeth, "Okay, Gabby, I am sorry, but it is time …."

Millard Lufkin | Cape Canaveral
07:16 p.m. | May 16, 2049

Aeronautics mogul Julius Hart opened his checkbook and acquired the decimated remnants of the once mighty International Outer Space Consortium, IOSC, from Andrew's cash-starved The Powers That Be. Uninterested in resurrecting the foolish and unnecessary space tourism industry, the visionary genius salvaged flyable anti-gravity triangular spaceships and retrofitted them into haulers transporting the skeletal framework of his spherical warehouses—or Thundercorps—off the ground and into geosynchronous orbits above every continent.

Julius Hart's promise to a starving world: five Moon-like satellites warehousing an endless bounty of goods delivered anywhere on the planet in under an hour via a fleet of hypersonic drones to downtrodden masses, eking out an existence amid ruined infrastructure where trips to the mall or Amazon deliveries exist only as faint memories of a pre-invasion past.

After participating in The Council's mass resignation protesting Andrew's malignant PTB leadership, Millard Lufkin got a second chance to follow his passion for space exploration from Julius Hart, who hired the former NASA astronaut and IOSC Administrator as project leader at the Cape Canaveral Thundercorp facility.

* * *

Lufkin sits alone on an observation platform a quarter mile from technicians and engineers prepping a cannibalized anti-gravity engine mounted atop a 100-foot tower for a test fire on a breezy Florida evening. After everyone retreats to safe distances from the Zone of Influence, Lufkin watches a deep blue radiate from the alien-engineered nacelle as his noise-canceling ear protection muffles the familiar ear-splitting hammering noise generated by the engine's alien inner workings. Sitting forward with a water bottle, he smiles as the tower holding the physics-defying masterpiece of backward-engineered alien technology disappears for a heartbeat before the sleek housing cracks, returning the tall A-frame centered in the zone to normal Earth gravity.

Lufkin chuckles into an old-school two-way radio, "Shucks, people. Let's get it set up for another test next week."

Returning to his office overlooking the historic Florida base after watching another failed test that taught his engineers more than success ever could, Millard ambles past his secretary's desk, "Evening

Margaret. You should go home. It's late."

The middle-aged woman who had been at Lufkin's side for years avoids his kind eyes, shuffling through a series of virtual schedules, "Julius Hart called again; he is eager for a progress report on the engine tests."

"Jesus, Margaret, which is worse, Hart or our old boss Pennywell."

Margaret clears her throat with an odd twitch, "I really couldn't say, Millard. Oh, your niece is waiting for you. I let her into your office; the poor dear looked tired. So hard to travel these days."

Lufkin's brow furrows, "My niece? She lives in Kansas. What is she doing here?"

"Why don't you go in and see? She is a pretty young thing."

Millard Lufkin, 120 pounds lighter and nearing his astronaut weight, gives Margaret a sideways skeptical look, "You have met my nieces and nephews. Which one are you referring to exactly?"

Margaret masks a flash of pain as a bead of sweat forms on her forehead, "Don't be mean, Millard. Just go inside. She is waiting for you."

Olivia Paquet | Paris
07:16 p.m. | June 6, 2049

Number 12 exits a women's locker room in a hip-hugging Nurse Ratched uniform, holding a tablet over a bloody spatter from its previous wearer shoved into a locker in her bra and panties with a broken neck. Striding down a third-floor corridor in too-tight sensible white sneakers along the east wing of Sainte Anne Psychiatric Hospital, she hears screams, curses, and incoherent gibberish emanating from locked rooms up and down the mildewy hall.

Approaching a deserted nurses' station, she draws the slack-jawed gape of a janitor ogling her approach while stroking his mop handle with a lascivious snicker. Piercing the lech's ugly brain as she passes without breaking stride, the foul fellow drops to his knees and dunks his oily head in the slop bucket, drowning himself in the filthy water.

Navigating her way through the over-capacity mental hospital, which reopened its doors to accommodate throngs driven to insanity in the cruel and ugly post-invasion world, she stops at Room 311 and checks her tablet. After a curt *knock-knock*, she breaks the door handle and enters the spartan room.

Beyond a urine-stained mattress, empty side table, and faded Monet print hanging crooked on a dingy wall, 12 finds the PTB's former Communications Director, Olivia Paquet, back turned and naked at a lone barred window feeding stale breadcrumbs to pigeons on the paint-chipped ledge.

Seeing the accomplished 57-year-old advertising trendsetter reduced to a pigeon-feeding mental patient, 12 suppresses a twinge of pity, announcing her presence with a fake smile while fingering a syringe in her pocket, "Hello, Miss Paquet."

Covered in cuts, bites, bruises, and lice sores peppering her shorn head, Olivia pivots onto 12's voice, "Who's there?"

Number 12 recoils at the bloody gauze taped over the gaunt woman's empty eye sockets with a startled gasp, "What happened to your eyes, Miss Paquet?"

"I could not take the ugliness a second longer, so I gouged them out with my plastic pudding spoon. It was vanilla. I hate fucking vanilla pudding." Taking a half step closer to 12, Olivia's head tilts with a sly, gap-toothed grin, "I know you. I recognize your smell. You are one of the Sisters. Andrew sent you, didn't he?"

Number 12 checks the door to ensure no one is coming, "Yes. I have to kill you, Olivia. I am sorry."

"Don't be. I'm ready."

"Okay then …." Olivia reaches for the syringe in her pocket.

"No! No more fucking shots! We do this my way." Spinning to the open window, Olivia yanks at a metal bar embedded in the crumbling sill, "Help me dislodge these stupid bars so I can squeeze through."

Number 12 raises an eyebrow, "Are you sure? It is only three stories down. You may not die on impact. I can also give you the shot, just in case."

"Damn you, woman. Are you going to help or not?"

With a furtive chuckle and a story to tell back in Scotland, Number 12 steps up and nudges Olivia out of the way before removing three rusted metal bars with minimal physical effort, "There. Let me help you …."

"No. You better leave. This place locks down when someone farts."

Olivia shoves 12 aside and dives head-first through the open window, plummeting three stories into the hood of the chief administrator's fucking electric vehicle parked directly beneath Room 311, sucking precious electricity from the hospital's lone functioning charging station.

Ernest Gann | Cambridge
10:16 a.m. | June 14, 2049

On a gray and rainy June morning, Professor Ernest Gann breaks into his former suite of offices on a shuttered section of the MIT campus. Working fast to avoid the lax security patrolling for looters, druggies, and vagabonds, the PTB Mathematician moves past desks, chairs, and work benches shoved askew amid trash, clutter, and broken equipment to a familiar old whiteboard defiled by a crude penis rendering. Pausing his infiltration to erase the board, Gann scrounges for a red marker and writes: ERNEST GANN WAS HERE in big block letters.

Pushing through the bleakness, Gann enters the pitch-black break room and flicks on his torch, casting the beam across empty tables, upturned chairs, and cabinets long ago plundered of anything edible or useful.

Continuing to his lab assistants' offices, where scores of students fine-tuned curricula, checked scores, and dropped papers, his light shines across a faded Anastasia Gabreski bikini poster still hanging on the back wall beyond gutted desks and file cabinets.

"Thank God no one had the heart to take you down."

Reminiscing on the good-natured student prank that culminated with Gabby's famous swimsuit poster forever enshrined as an unofficial math department mascot and good luck charm, he pushes aside trash and broken furniture to peel the poster from the cheap wood paneling, where it had hung for years, revealing a hidden wall safe.

Inputting a long passcode, Gann opens the safe onto a shielded hard drive containing the PTB's intelligence on the third fleet lingering in the Solar System—comprised of endless scores of enigmatic cubes.

With a heavy heart, the brilliant mathematician rolls the iconic poster in a tube and drops the drive in his vest pocket, retracing his path toward the Red Line—back in service for the first time in half a decade since the invasion, garnering more fanfare and hoopla than a fucking Moon landing.

Walking along the deserted underground platform past self-congratulatory signage heralding the reopened Kendall/MIT Station, Gann waits two hours before boarding a half-empty eastbound train, slumping into a window seat with a burdensome sigh. Clutching the tubed poster, he avoids eye contact with the scattering of dull-faced passengers, pondering which is more valuable: Gabby's vintage swimsuit poster or the hard drive it concealed. Tough call.

"Anybody sitting here?"

Gann double-takes onto one of the Sisters, his heart beating out of his chest. "No. How did you find me?"

The attractive young woman wearing a zipped Patagonia jacket over black yoga pants and pink running shoes with a Red Sox cap pressed atop her black bobbed cut plops into the aisle seat and crosses her long legs, "Gee, thanks, Professor."

Squeezing his quivering knee in her vice-like grip, she whispers in his ear, "Where you headed, Mr. Gann?"

Grimacing in pain, his eyes water, verging on tears, "I don't know."

Number 4 releases her nimble hand, "That's okay. I believe you. There is nowhere to go. We own the US government. They are useless, like the UN. You are all alone. Why don't you hand over the drive, and we can go our separate ways."

Cognizant that he was not leaving the train alive, Gann shakes his head, "No. Fuck you and your boss."

"Have it your way, Professor."

Gann sees the flash of a blade a heartbeat before it pierces his torso as the world goes sideways.

Tipping Professor Ernest Gann's lolling head and shoulders against the window, Number 4 avoids the bloody wound, digging her hands in his pants and shirt pockets before locating the tiny hard disk. Turning to the murder witness across the aisle, who watched the whole thing without a flinch, she raises a bloodstained finger to her ruby lips: "See something—keep it to yourself."

Numbed to the horrors of the modern world, the man averts his eyes out the window at the passing shitshow.

As the train lurches to its next stop, Number 4 slides the tube from Gann's slackened grip and hands it to the man before moving to the exit, "Here's a little something to brighten your day."

Dr. Gene Simmons | Playa Pavones, Costa Rica
10:16 a.m. | August 19, 2049

A lanky, bearded Black man with bright midday sunshine glinting off his receding close-shaved scalp pauses at the gunwale of a fishing trawler, offering a final salute to the captain inside the pilothouse before flinging his duffel into a bobbing plywood skiff, chugging alongside in the rough seas.

The man climbs over the side, gripping a swinging rope ladder, pelted by ocean spray whipped off the white-capped Pacific on his way down before dropping the last five feet into the skiff's bow with a bone-jarring jolt.

Wincing from a sprained right wrist, the passenger grits out the pain as the shallow-drafting skiff motors away from the larger vessel, bouncing across cresting swells toward the Costa Rican coastline.

The gritty helmsman wearing wraparound shades with a gnarled pipe jutting from his weathered face calls over the crashing waves and whining engine, "Hold on tight, Señor!"

White-knuckling the bow line, the passenger complies, focusing on the dark green mountainous stripe separating the deep blue Pacific and a cloudless azure sky looming closer with every crested wave.

After twenty more gut-churning minutes, the skiff leaves deep water behind, navigating a series of coral reefs into a sandy-bottomed crescent-shaped aqua-blue lagoon ringed with idyllic thatched abodes amidst the lush tropical environs, like a scene ripped from an old movie.

Hearing the chugging motorboat's arrival at the off-the-grid commune, ex-pats, ex-cons, and those craving a slice of Heaven far from the world's troubles, gather at the surf's rippling edge to greet Dr. Gene Simmons, formerly of The Powers That Be, and now a wanted fugitive.

Spotting a subset of familiar smiling faces amongst the crowd, Gene vaults into the waist-deep cerulean water on a sloshing path toward his eight ecstatic children, splashing and swimming out to greet their long-lost father. Scooping up the youngest in his sprained right arm, he kisses her head and trudges toward shore with more kids hanging on to his olive-drab fatigues, not wanting to let go. The oldest takes his duffel and leads the ecstatic family reunion back to the beach, where Mrs. Simmons stands tall in a red dress with her arms crossed and a smile on her lovely face.

"You're late."

"I'm sorry, dear. I got hung up at work."

Ed Watson | Kuala Lumpur
12:02 p.m. | June 24, 2050 – 10 months later

Number 8 bounces her birthday boy on a knee, "Mommy loves her little Paddy boy!"

"Aw, c'mon, Mom! You are embarrassing me in front of everybody."

"I'm just trying to entertain you until the show starts."

Paddy rolls his eyes, scooching from his mother's grasp and reclaiming his popcorn from Number 11. Looking at the half-empty container, his blue eyes narrow on the beautiful replicant, "Did you eat my popcorn, Aunt 11?"

Picking a kernel from her perfect white teeth, 11 smiles, "Maybe. What are you going to do about it, you little squirt."

Number 8 spit takes cream soda on the seatback before her, causing Number 1 to pivot around, "Hey. Knock it off."

Andrew enters the soundstage where Artemus Pennywell and Ping held their one and only live podcast to the world. Raising a hand, his authoritative presence quashes raunchy banter and horseplay among the Sisters and one bored little boy on his fifth birthday, "Well, well. We have everyone back in the same room. How nice. I missed you all and am grateful for your stellar work in the field. And now, with The

Council's sad dissolution, what a tragic series of unfortunate events ...."

Number 13 squirms in her seat, "Except Dr. Simmons. He gave me the slip in San Diego."

"No matter, 13, the esteemed doctor may have escaped an easy death for now, but with The Council's demise, we can proceed to the next phase."

Looking at none of the Sisters in particular, Andrew smiles, "Now then, did our test subject, er Mr. Watson, in Kuala Lumpur receive his shiny new smartphone?"

Number 1 beams, "Ed Watson has had a working prototype in hand for one week. He loves it. And now his cohorts are clamoring to get their hands on one. Reintroducing smart devices to humans will prove easier than dangling a bag of heroin in front of a recovering addict."

"Well put, Number 1." Taking a first-row seat beside the beguiling first Sister, Andrew places an arm around her shoulder, "Okay, let's call Mr. Watson and take our little nanobots for a test drive."

A 160-inch virtual screen materializes before the small audience onto Ed Watson's dull-faced mug noshing on a thick hunk of meat. Observing his abrupt realization of being watched via the phone's hi-def camera feature alighting, they look on with equal measures of apathy and fascination as he straightens and chokes down his last bite.

"Hello, Mr. Andrew. You caught me having a late meal. Shit, it is eight o'clock over here already. My apologies. I see you have the whole crew on hand."

"Yes. So sorry to disturb your dinner, Mr. Watson, but we have limited time and are eager for an update on The Turd. Have the plumbing and electrical issues been resolved?"

Ed rolls his tongue over his teeth, dislodging a chewy morsel, "Um, well, yes and no. A work in progress with no end, really. On a brighter note ..." the American pans his shiny new PTB-provided smartphone over and around patrons enjoying a late dinner amid a lush tropical setting, "The Palms restaurant is up and running. I was enjoying the prime rib when you called. Excellent."

Andrew nods, "I am thankful you enjoyed your last meal."

Looking back into the camera, Ed frowns, "Last meal? Andrew, I can never tell when you are joking. But hey, what am I thinking? Thanks for the new smartphone. I'm honored to be part of the beta testing. It sure beats my clunky satellite phone all to hell."

Andrew's expression never wavers, "Language Ed. We have my son with us. It is his fifth birthday today."

"His fifth birthday? That's a big one. I have two kids back home living with their mother. Hang on, Paddy, I have a little surprise." The camera feed bounces sideways as Ed moves between crowded tables toward a bright blue macaw's prehistoric stare from a gnarled wooden perch. The bird fills the screen as the group hears Ed's pleadings, "Say, happy birthday. Say it ... c'mon ... don't make me look foolish in front of the big boss ...."

"Happy birthday. Squawk. Happy birthday ..."

Paddy leans forward in his seat, chomping a fistful of popcorn, "Thanks, you stupid bird."

Andrew shoots his outspoken son a stern sideways glance before raising a hand to stave off further comment, "On that note ...."

Acknowledging her verbal cue with a wicked smile, Number 16 pings a satellite, bouncing a signal halfway around the world that awakens billions of mind-altering nanobots lurking within the smartphone in Ed Watson's sweaty hands.

Andrew uncrosses his legs and leans forward, masking rapt anticipation, "Cute bird, Ed. Hopefully, you have more than a talking bird and a crappy restaurant to show us."

Ed Watson, the crude American engineer whose multiple field promotions had him leading projects well beyond his limited expertise and intellectual capacity, twitches, and stutters, frowning into the screen like he's viewing a vision of hell, "I, uh ... I'm sorry ... What is that? Do you see it? It's making me mad as a hatter. I can't look away from it ...."

"Mr. Watson, are you okay?"

Watson's facial muscles contort his ordinary Joe countenance into a horrifying monster with veins bulging and bloody nostrils flaring as the nanobots shred his sanity and transmogrify his throbbing skull into a blender set to liquefy. Watson rips off his shirt and bellows a roaring tirade, "You are all rotten, disgusting pigs! Everyone must die. Die! Die!" The divorced father of two from Kansas City, Missouri, flips the nearest table, sending frightened patrons stampeding for the exits to escape the snarling, shirtless lunatic who grabs a waitress by the collar and rips her throat open with his gnashing teeth.

The cracked case of Watson's brand-new smart device lies askew amid splattered food and drinks mixed with shattered plates and glasses, autofocusing on the atrium's glass ceiling five stories overhead as a cacophony of screams, cries, and curses climaxes with a single gunshot that puts a merciful end to the chaos.

Andrew and the Sisters bask in the unabashed success of their initial test before Paddy breaks the silence, "Did anyone bake a chocolate cake for my birthday?"

Andrew smiles at his young son before turning to Number 16, "Kill the satellite link to the smart device before someone else picks it up. No reason to harm anyone else right now."

Standing from his seat to exit the soundstage, The Powers That Be CEO turns to the Sisters, "Get the Korean plant cranked up. We will need half a billion units ready for market before we go live."

Catching his son's disappointed look, "Number 8, check to see if Paddy's birthday cake is ready in the cafeteria."

Julius Hart | Thundercorp Ranch
11:09 a.m. | October 13, 2051 – 13 months later

After touring a bloated federal government project under

construction north of Dallas designed to mimic an ancient Mayan temple—for some damn reason—Andrew bids farewell to a clueless contingent of hardhatted windbags, embarking on a solo helicopter flight to the legendary Thundercorp Ranch, covering a massive swath of south Texas including Elon Musk's former SpaceX digs.

Adhering to circuitous flight restrictions taking him out over the Gulf of Mexico before finally landing on Thundercorp Helipad Number 9, Andrew powers down the chopper's blades while watching a silhouetted craft elevate above the hazy horizon, hauling a massive chunk of steel under its triangular girth. Andrew follows the impressive aeronautical sight into the wild blue yonder as an autonomous transport breaks his reverie, braking to a screechy stop to pick up the new arrival.

The vehicle takes Andrew on a bumpy ride across an expansive tarmac lined with gargantuan ten-story hangars with workers and drones swarming over former IOSC space tourism ships in various stages of repairs and retrofits before winding through the main campus to a gorgeous glass structure encompassing the Thundercorp HQ and mission control in the shadow of a towering spire emulating the Seattle Space Needle.

Briefed on Julius Hart's ambitious plan to build spherical warehouses in geosynchronous low Earth orbits around the planet, the surprising progress already achieved troubles the PTB CEO as he enters the bustling vaulted lobby where a trim and pretty A or B-Class model dressed to the nines in a knee-length navy-blue skirt and blouse beams a pleasant greeting, "My name is Lucy, and it is my honor to welcome you to Thundercorp Ranch."

Amused by the feminine bot's no-nonsense formality, Andrew nods, "It is long overdue, Lucy. I am in your more-than-capable hands. Lead the way."

Following the dazzling synthetic woman's long strides in three-inch red stiletto heels across the lobby, passing human and non-human Thundercorp employees, the pair cross a land bridge to a glass-enclosed lift up the dizzying spire to Julius Hart's penthouse offices perched high atop.

Lucy escorts Andrew into a conference room, "Mr. Hart is late, as usual. Can I get you anything?"

Intrigued by the advanced replicant's aplomb, on par with the Sisters, Andrew leans in and whispers in her ear, "Surprise me."

The beauty returns a coy smile, sliding long arms around Andrew's shoulders and swallowing him in a passionate kiss, "Surprised?"

Andrew takes a half step back, his heart racing, "That was illogical, yet pleasant."

"I hope so."

Andrew's brow furrows, "Sorry?"

"What do you think I am?"

Accustomed to having the upper hand, Andrew's brow furrows, "A very advanced B-Class. Kobayashi made some that proved closer to the Cs … I was unaware your kind ever made it into the public domain."

"Well, this is awkward. Nobody owns me. I am human. My name is Lucy. Lucy Lufkin."

Masking rank embarrassment, Andrew retreats behind the safety of a long conference table and takes a seat, "My apologies, Lucy, but why then did you kiss me?"

"You said you wanted a surprise. Don't worry; it happens more often than you might guess. My appearance leads to wrong-headed conclusions. You are not the first." Twirling with a flirtatious over-the-shoulder smile, "Now, if you will excuse me, Andrew, I will check Julius' whereabouts. I saw him earlier this morning …."

* * *

Nursing a coffee while watching another nimble triangle haul a swinging mass of girders and beams into the sky, shedding Earth's gravity with backward-engineered ease, Andrew turns onto doors bursting open as Julius Hart storms into the room in a light blue button-down tucked in a pair of khakis with his sleeves rolled to the elbows, "Tell Senator Murphy to go fuck himself. Yes. Use those exact words."

Ending the call with a satisfied smirk, the aeronautical genius Julius Hart, who had the ear of Andrew's predecessor, takes a breath and plops into a swiveling leather chair at the head of the table, "Big Andrew …. all the way from Scotland. You know I never got your last name."

"It is just Andrew. Like Sting."

"That's a blast from the past. However, even in our circles, traveling is a bitch. You are not on my schedule for today. Tell me … Andrew … what brings you to Thundercorp Ranch?"

The PTB CEO ignores the snark factor and palpable chill between the two powerful men and pauses to watch another triangle vaulting skyward with its massive payload swinging underneath, "I was already in Texas. The Powers That Be is charged with completing phase four construction on the new North Dallas federal building."

Older, wiser, more grizzled, but virile and fit with a youthful glint in his soft blue eyes with curly light brown hair touched with gray at the temples, Julius Hart exudes the outward appeal of an aging surfer with a mental acuity on par with a supercomputer. Hands clasped atop the table, Hart smiles at the unexpected VIP visitor, "Nothing spells disaster like the US government entrenching itself in a massive Mayan temple. What's next? Taxpayers sacrificed before a fiery government deity as IRS agents rip still-beating hearts from their chests."

Andrew chuckles and finishes his coffee, "You paint a vivid picture, Mr. Hart. I take it you are not a fan of the reconstituted US government."

"The American experiment ended in St. Louis with President Jackson's murder. Whatever this is," gesturing toward the limitless expanse outside the floor-to-ceiling windows, "is not the USA I grew up in."

"Nonetheless, Thundercorp Ranch is impressive. Here we are in a space needle. How appropriate."

Hart nods at Lucy's return, bearing a coffee and Danish-laden tray, "Thank you, my dear."

Pouring a cup before chomping on a sticky roll, "The Space Needle is a nod to my Seattle upbringing. My father worked for Boeing. He was killed in the first hour of the Gork invasion."

"I am sorry for your loss but thankful you survived."

"Well, look at us. A couple of survivors. Don't cut yourself short, Andrew. You have also come a long way since we first met."

"You have me at a disadvantage, Mr. Hart. When was that?"

Hart's eyes narrow on the ageless CEO wearing his signature black mock turtleneck over jeans and Western boots, returning a blank stare, "Oh, come on, you must be joking."

"I rarely joke, Mr. Hart."

"Julius is fine. Seriously, you, of all people, don't remember? Invasion night. The fucking Gorks were busy ripping Earth a new one when you and your old boss, Artemus Pennywell, boarded the evacuation ship at the spaceport in Toulouse. I was on the chosen list already aboard. I remember passing Artemus my flask of family bourbon. Old man Pennywell loved the sauce."

Andrew reaches for the coffee decanter and pours a cup, "Your memory is accurate; however, that was not me. That was Andrew, the valet. I am Andrew, chairman of the most significant organization in human history. I am quite different from that man in every respect."

Julius mulls Andrew's imprecise words, "I am curious, Andrew. How did you con a sharp old coot like Artemus Pennywell into leaving you as his CEO successor of the world's largest criminal organization?"

Andrew bristles at the veiled civility stretching thinner between the two men, "I believe I should take offense to that characterization, Mr. Hart. If The Powers That Be are a criminal enterprise bent on world domination, what prevents me from killing you and taking back my anti-gravity fleet of ships?"

"You did not want or need those ships. You know it. I know

it. Yet I paid a stiff premium to acquire the entire International Outer Space Consortium's portfolio—most of which is beyond useless—just to access that fleet."

Watching another liftoff on the horizon, "However, as you can see, the anti-gravity space tourism ships make damn fine space haulers, slicing years off my timeline. I now expect Thundercorps 1 to 5 to be operational by 2060."

Leaning back with his point made, he shrugs a sly smile, "I got the ships, and you got piles of cash. Case closed."

Andrew proffers a conciliatory smile, "You are spot on, Mr. Hart. But while you reinvent e-commerce for a world gone mad, The Powers That Be is stepping up and finishing projects on every continent. Far from being evil profiteers like yourself, we serve humanity."

"What about that PTB bullshit regarding fostering us to an Omega Point?"

Andrew shrugs, "Lofty sentiments from our former glory. Artemus Pennywell knew it was all PR nonsense. He paid it lip service. Nothing more."

"I don't know, Andrew. Pennywell knew in his heart that Rachel Haig epitomizes humanity's destiny. I have met her and her husband on multiple occasions. She is special. I also believe Rachel represents a giant evolutionary leap."

"Perhaps. Who knows what poor Rachel could have become if not for St. Louis. Quite a travesty. And as for the PTB's involvement in rebuilding our world, our focus rests solely on pulling eighty percent of Earth's population out of Middle Ages squalor."

"Andrew, I hate to be the bearer of bad news, but from an outsider's perspective, I see vast sums wasted on monuments to human stupidity and greed. My sources tell me folks are afraid your buildings will collapse. Some already have. The new tower in Prague is leaning like Pisa. If I were in your lofty position, I should be more than a little embarrassed to be associated with these ridiculous structures." Raising a finger for emphasis, "Meanwhile, I am employing people in real jobs doing real things. And they know Thundercorp is critical to improving their lives. People out there are starving for purpose, Andrew. Not to be stacked like cords of wood. Humans are not wired to sit around and wait for Big Daddy to toss them a crumb."

Andrew sighs, internalizing anger, "I am not here for your approval, Mr. Hart. I came to offer you an opportunity to embed your company software on my new smartphones rolling out next year. All that cheap Chinese-made junk warehoused inside your orbiting satellites won't sell itself or be very useful if no one can place a fucking order."

Julius Hart can't help but laugh. "Ah-ha. I wondered why you graced us with your royal presence. The mighty Andrew, descending amongst the commoners. You want to embed *my* Thundercorp app on the new smartphones you are churning out of factories all over Asia. Well, I could have saved you the trip. Turns out I have people and robots who are pretty good at producing cheap new phones, too."

Andrew leans forward with a sly smile of his own, "Using whose networks? The PTB owns every communication satellite in the sky, but the bandwidth is at a premium. If I am to get the world back on the digital teat, I cannot and will not accommodate a competitor's phone. That is non-negotiable."

Julius Hart stands out of his seat and walks to the door, "Quite all right, Andrew. My Thundercorps will not only warehouse and deliver products from Madagascar to Michigan and every point in between at lightning-fast speeds, but each one will stream free internet to the world. No one will want or need your phones. And no one will have to suck anything. Those days are done."

A pregnant pause ensues in the mental chess match between the two men as Lucy reappears, "Yes, Mr. Hart?"

"Our meeting is over. Please escort Andrew out of the building. And next time. I will require notice before taking an in-person meeting."

"Yes, sir. Sorry, Mr. Hart."

"Not your fault. Good day, Andrew. Safe travels."

Realizing failure for one of the few times in his lifespan, Andrew stands, "So the aeronautics wunderkind is kicking me to the curb."

"Nobody calls me a wunderkind anymore. As you can see, we are all business here at Thundercorp. Playtime is over."

"Yes, good luck, Mr. Hart." Andrew stands to leave with a wink toward Lucy, "Lead the way, once again, young lady."

Dropping her cordial demeanor, Lucy's tone darkens, "Did you tell Andrew about my uncle?"

Hart sighs and nods, "Lucy refers to your former IOSC administrator, Millard Lufkin. He died in his office at Cape Canaveral. We kept his passing a private affair, but I thought you should know since he was a former PTB Council member."

Andrew feigns heartfelt surprise with polished ease, "Millard was a good man and the driving force behind the International Outer Space Consortium. Artemus loved him like a brother. I trust his murderer will be brought to a swift justice."

Julius glances toward Lucy with a wink, "I never mentioned how Lucy's uncle died."

Connecting dots, half a step behind the conniving pair, "Merely an assumption based on today's cruel world, but you both have my sympathies. Lucy, your uncle, was indeed a trailblazer. As for your passive accusations, Lufkin followed IOSC with no animus toward me or the PTB. You should know that since he was under your employ at the time of his passing."

Following another awkward silence, Andrew turns to leave before pivoting onto the suspicious pair, "May I inquire about his cause of death? I know Millard battled heart problems."

Lucy jumps in to speak over her boss, "Someone crushed in the back of his skull."

Andrew's eyes widen, "Really? Such barbarism. What is this world coming to?"

Julius Hart's mind races, not wanting to let Andrew off the hook, "By the way, I almost forgot. I poached your logistics man. You hemorrhage good people, Andrew. It must be your inexperience managing humans."

Andrew shrugs, not taking the bait. "Viraj Patel? A competent man. Good luck with Thundercorp. It indeed looks very promising. Too bad we could not do business on the smartphone app."

"Yeah, hard pass on that one, Andy."

"Good day, Mr. Hart. No need to bother, Miss Lufkin. I can find my way back to the helipads."

* * *

Back behind the sleek and modern chopper's controls, Andrew powers up massive blades and speeds across Thundercorp Ranch, ignoring warnings not to deviate from the outbound flight corridor on a beeline toward Dallas, where his jet is gassed up and ready to hightail it back to Scotland.

Growling into his headset like a madman, "Get me Number 1 … I don't give a fuck what time it is … just do it!"

Leveling off at 5,000 feet, he hears Number 1's silky voice in his ears, "Yes, Andrew. How was Thundercorp?"

"An unspeakable disaster, Number 1. Cancel the smartphones. Refocus all resources on the Blue Spark rollout. How many test subjects are we up to?"

"I believe the final tally is 132 people from all races and walks of life scattered around the world."

"That will have to be enough. Get the recruits started on the full-strength Blue Spark injections ASAP."

"Andrew, the inhibitor serum is still in testing. Without a way to pause their mutations, most subjects will die within days of their initial transformations. It won't be pretty."

"Life is messy, Number 1. Those with the intestinal fortitude to gut it out represent humanity's last hope against the Overlords."

"Andrew … what are you saying?"

"I'm done with this charade. I pray it is not too late to set things right."

**What does not kill me
makes me stronger.**

Friedrich Nietzsche

Chapter Seven:

The Exposition

Rachel | Hilltop
01:15 p.m. | October 13, 2052

Dave places a sandwich in front of seven-year-old Hannah, "Quit making a stinky face and eat your lunch. And don't feed it to Piper the second my back is turned, young lady."

With an anticipatory Piper watching her every move, Hannah parts the homemade bread slices and mutters, "Eww." while inspecting the pinkish meat-like substance spread thin under a limp piece of lettuce smothered in mustard and mayo. "What is this, Dave?"

"It's liverwurst. Loads of protein. Now eat."

Stepping to the sink to handwash more dishes, Dave hears Rachel's staticky voice from his two-way radio used to keep in touch with his paraplegic better half while at opposite ends of the labyrinthine mansion, "Dave! I need help with the damn Wi-Fi! I thought you had it fixed!"

Hannah watches her stepfather's grumbling exit from the kitchen while flinging a wet towel over his shoulder. With the coast clear, she scoops the icky sandwich and feeds it to Piper. "Here you go, boy. Hurry up and finish before he comes back."

Upon rushing into the expansive and well-appointed second-floor media room, Dave finds a visibly agitated Rachel parked in her wheelchair before the massive screen frozen on a bright, colorful pixelated image.

"Dammit, Dave. You said the satellite connection was rock solid. I need to see this. It is important."

Dave scrutinizes the blurred image on the screen, chuckling, "This does not look like one of your soaps. Porn, perhaps?"

"Fuck you, Dave. You know I can kick your ass from this chair."

"You can do a lot of things from your chair."

"If you don't fix the Wi-Fi so I can see what the hell is going on, you can forget that ever happening again."

"Well then, I better get on it."

Dropping the dish towel on an empty theater-style seat, the jack-of-all-trades opens a cabinet and inspects the interconnected blinking gadgets amid a tangle of wires and cables he installed to replace the fried obsolete pre-invasion networking equipment. Locating the culprit, he unplugs a router and turns to a disconcerted Rachel, "Count to ten, Rach."

Rachel mutters, shaking her head while staring at her useless feet, "Owen used to call me Rach."

"Okay. Thanks for that mental image stuck in my head … nine … ten."

Dave plugs the cable back into the router and watches the screen spring to life onto a young Asian woman floating through the air with the greatest of ease.

"Oh, Mother of sweet baby Jesus, she is flying. What is this?"

Warding off another heady swoon, Rachel huffs and wipes tears from her eyes, "They did it, Dave. Those PTB fucks went and jabbed human beings with the Blue Spark."

With the remote forgotten in her right hand, Rachel gestures at the jumpy video feed playing in fits and starts, "Look at those people performing tricks and somersaults like trained seals." Leaning forward in her chair, "And it appears their skin is blue, too." Rachel tries to see through the noise and distortion, "This feed is terrible. Can you make it any sharper?"

"Sorry, Rachel. We are lucky to get this. It looks like they are inside some kind of empty soccer arena. Can't quite tell where that is. Do you know if this is a live feed?"

"It is happening right now. I can sense it within every fiber of my being. I was finishing my show and about to join you and Hannah downstairs for lunch when something called the Blue Spark popped up in the middle of the screen. Well, you can imagine my surprise. I clicked the link, and the screen froze."

"The PTB controls the satellites, but if the entire world accesses the play button simultaneously, it crashes the feed. Like if an entire apartment building all flushed their toilets in unison."

"You love that analogy."

Dave shrugs his shoulders, "It's apt, baby."

Ashen-faced and frightened for humanity, Rachel ignores Dave's attempted levity and turns to the herky-jerky presentation, "So the PTB is dropping the Blue Spark on the world without any preamble or fanfare. They just put it out there."

Still processing the latest apparent seed change inflicted by his former employer, Dave frowns at a new series of video feeds cascading across the screen, "Are you doing that, Rachel?"

"Nope. Something or somebody else is in control."

The dizzying presentation pauses on two women performing

aerial stunts above a gathering of slack-jawed onlookers on a crowded city street.

"That is the new Times Square."

Rachel nods, "The dark-haired young woman is Monica Grasso."

"How can you know that?"

"I hear her inside my head. She wants to be like me."

Noting Rachel swaying in her wheelchair as her skin turns blue, Dave lifts her in his arms and kisses her soft on the cheek before lowering her into a plush theater seat and removing the thin remote from her hand. "Let me see what else we can find."

"Okay."

Alarmed by Rachel's intrinsic connection to the paradigm-shifting spectacle, he clicks a new Blue Spark logo springing from the lower right corner of the 160-inch screen. The city scene transitions into a high-def close-up of a seductive woman's alabaster face shifting to a vivid cerulean blue, whispering: *"Transcend to a new human reality ... with The Blue Spark."*

Dave's face goes blank, muttering at the screen, "... must get the Blue Spark ...."

Rachel snaps out of her momentary funk and punches Dave's muscular arm, "Knock it off. This is not funny. The Blue Spark is a living nightmare."

"Ow, Rachel. You pack a mean right hook. I was joking, by the way."

"I know. You are a horrible actor." Slouching back in her seat, she stares at the ceiling, "Why would The Powers That Be do this?"

Dave's brow furrows at a wonky video of a middle-aged man elevating large volcanic boulders into the air all around him on a black sand beach with the surf crashing at his back, "How did the PTB evolve these people to your superhuman level so fast?"

Rachel feels the Blue Spark coursing her veins with a shiver down her spine, "They spiked Professor King's original Blue Spark formula with the prehistoric Amazon virus to create a potent new drug that mutates at an accelerated rate."

"Jesus. To what end?"

"Good question. Richard's original Blue Spark experiment was an attempt to shortcut human evolution. The PTB at that time was growing impatient, and when I say PTB, I mean our alien minders."

"I can't believe I worked for those guys for ten years of my life."

Rachel pats her new man's muscular arm, "It's okay, Dave. The PTB has changed a lot since Artemus Pennywell's death."

"You mean because Andrew is now in charge. That is one evil robot."

Rachel laughs, "The advanced replicants hate it when you call them robots."

On the screen, they watch as a young man leaps off the Eiffel Tower and soars over Paris like an eagle.

"The world just changed."

"Again."

* * *

Left to her own devices. Again. Hannah wanders outside and down the tree-lined neighborhood street with Piper marching in lockstep at her side.

"C'mon, boy, let's find something to eat."

Hector Gonzalez | St. Dymphna's
03:42 p.m. | November 20, 2052 – 38 days later

The phenomenal exhibition of a new and improved posthuman reality via a breakthrough drug called the Blue Spark ignites a worldwide craze for miraculous injections to transcend horrible lives and achieve the advertised elevated state of being. Following the über-viral Blue

Spark launch, PTB clinics pop up in metropolitan hubs in every country, with dispassionate, white-coated staff performing simple jabs of the fast-tracked new drug at an assembly line pace on downtrodden scores queuing up for miles.

With tell-tale gauze bandages taped to their arms and great expectations for what happens next, the injected masses watch in wide-eyed wonder as the Blue Spark jab morphs their outward appearance—depending on their God-given skin color—from light azure to cobalt within hours. In tandem with the promised pigment shift, they experience a euphoric high, dubbed the Blue Haze, while waiting in vain to fly like Superman, read minds, or bend spoons.

The Trojan horse injections release nanobots that breach blood-brain barriers, nestling amid billions of nerve cells where they await a pernicious telepathic signal.

* * *

Despite feverish attempts to decelerate the 132 viral megastars' out-of-control physical and mental mutations, 98 perished in the heady days following their spectacular coming-out parties.

The dwindling subset that survived Professor Richard King's original Blue Spark spiked with a gain-of-function enhancement of the prehistoric Amazonian super virus are spirited to St. Dymphna's, an abandoned psychiatric hospital for the criminally insane in the Spanish countryside outside of Seville.

Hidden from the public eye, deep inside a shielded wing of the sprawling PTB black site's fortress-like perimeter patrolled by shoot-first-ask-questions-later security bots, craven PTB scientists study the grotesque posthumans, performing vivisections on the short-timers, reducing the class of 132 recruits who ignited a worldwide frenzy to a final eight.

* * *

Effervescing a transcendent blue radiance, Hector Gonzalez, an athletic 23-year-old Spaniard who signed his life away for the chance to fly like Superman, indeed defies gravity, hovering above his padded cell's dank cement floor. More bored and lonely from his solitary confinement than frightened and dismayed by his altered state, he exerts mind control on a hapless rookie guard stationed at the cell block's entrance, compelling the rookie's bowels to let loose. Hearing the high-pitched, muffled curses through the thick metal doors and walls, Hector performs victory cartwheels, swirling dust motes in the hazy light shafting through a grimy barred window onto the dystopian world beyond.

"Yeah. Got him."

Within minutes, the vindictive guard, and his boss, both wearing protective gear, burst into Hector's cell and beat him within an inch of his life with nightsticks.

Bleeding dark purple and gasping for air, Hector shrieks at his tormentors, "Just kill me. Damn you all to hell."

The lead guard returns a cold stare from thick goggles under his foil-lined hazmat suit, "Shut up, you blue-skinned freak!"

Instructing the stinky underling with fresh-crapped pants to strap the bloodied and bruised Hector to the stained cot, the man in charge jabs thick, gloved fingers into Hector's chest, "The CEO is due to arrive any time. If you pull another stunt like that while he is here, I'll chop off your blue dick and shove it down your throat."

Hector gathers his wits, masking searing pain behind a defiant smile, "Aw, you say the nicest things, Edwin. Who names their kid Edwin?"

The smelly guard turns to his superior, "Should I give him another whack in the head?"

"No. Hector here will behave. But keep your fucking suit sealed so these mutants can't get inside your dumbass head. And for God's sake, clean yourself up; you smell like shit."

Hector can't resist one more jibe, "Literally."

The ridiculous, grumbling guards tromp out of the cell in unwieldy suits and slam the door locked in their wake.

The other surviving empathic Blue Sparks confined in padded cells along the far end of the nightmarish shielded ward absorb Hector's brutal persecution, cheering the Spaniard's resilience.

"They could have killed you."

Strapped tight to the wet cot, with blood and tears streaming down his face, Hector offers a telepathic reply, *"That was my plan, Lamar. No luck. Hey, Monica, are you still with us?"*

Curled tight in the corner of her cell, the young American woman who bit hard on a too-good-to-be-true opportunity to become the next Rachel Haig by agreeing to participate in a top-secret drug trial, chokes back tears, horrified by her hideous transformation, *"Yes. How many of us are left?"*

Overwhelmed with regret and paranoia, the surviving Blue Sparks count off in a telepathic group conversation.

The final eight of them.

Institutionalized out of the public eye and slated for vivisections at the merciless hands of psychopathic scientists, the Final Eight await torturous deaths, unaware that their viral day in the sun spawned a worldwide frenzy for the Blue Spark jab. The ensuing Trojan Horse injections embed the latent malicious nanobots into tens of millions of unsuspecting brains on every corner of the planet.

Andrew | St. Dymphna's
06:19 a.m. | November 21, 2052

From the backseat of their self-driving SUV, Andrew and Number 1 gaze out smoky windows in silence as the rolling monster bumps and jostles over the last few kilometers of its one-plus hour commute from an airfield outside Seville. Passing through the imposing gates of the erstwhile St. Dymphna's Penitentiary for the criminally insane, the vehicle pulls to a stop amid weeds, grasses, and saplings, reclaiming an empty visitor lot, fronting crumbling stucco facades of deserted administrative buildings under a thick matte of bird-infested creeping vines.

Number 1 takes Andrew's hand in hers to stop his exit from the driver's side backseat, "Are we doing the right thing?"

Andrew yawns before returning a grinning shrug, "My dear, these eight recruits represent the embodiment of the PTB's mission statement I swore to uphold when Artemus Pennywell presented me with the keys to the kingdom."

Number 1's beautiful face crinkles into a confused frown, "Andrew, you want to help these people on one hand while furthering plans that will lead to an epic mass casualty event on the other."

"Ah, your confusion is well-founded, Number 1. The Overlords' imminent return necessitated a swift escalation beyond Artemus' aggressive plan for Rachel Haig. And now, the eight Blue Spark survivors behind these walls represent a ray of hope for humankind. On the flip side, the Overlords demand their pound of flesh. Hence, the Trojan horse injections. Perhaps we may never have to trigger the nanobots."

Number 1 stares outside the car window at a flock of birds roosting in the trees, "Do you believe in God, Andrew?"

Andrew kisses Number 1's hand before letting go, "Yes, I do. We are both constructs of human ingenuity guided by advanced extraterrestrial influences, and in their hubris, our creators gave us free will. I attribute the miracle of our sentience to a higher plan. Like our makers, we are inconsistent and illogical, yet near-immortal and beyond perfection on a razor's edge between man and machine. We are more similar to the Overlords than our human friends."

"The Overlords are replicants?"

"No. The Overlords are more like hybrids. After eons of

sculpting Earth into their advanced civilization, a comet on an apocalyptic trajectory forced the Overlords' departure halfway across the universe with their essences stored in dull metal cubes well beyond the understanding of current human intelligence. And now, they desire to return and reclaim their former glory."

Number 1 smooths her hands on her thighs, "I feel so used, Andrew. The Sisters and I longed for their return, believing they were part of us."

"I am sorry, Number 1, but to the Overlords, we represent nothing more than pawns on a four-dimensional chess board."

"Andrew, enough secrets. What is the plan, starting now."

"Secrets are meant to be kept, Number 1. Do not share this conversation with your Sisters. Some of them are beyond corrupted with pure hatred for humanity. I have seen it. God help me; I have encouraged it. Here is the plan: continue paving the way for the Overlords' return while planting the seeds for future sabotage, hence the eight surviving Blue Sparks."

"I fear the Overlords plan to kill us after exhausting our usefulness."

"The nature of the universe is a constant state of flux. Nothing is set in stone."

Number 1 holds Andrew's intelligent gaze, "Andrew, will we go to Heaven after we die?"

"Our sins are incalculable—hell is a more likely destination for you and me."

Looking out his window at the rundown facility, Andrew sighs, "All right then. Enough navel-gazing. One Blue Spark inside this dump, a young fellow named Hector, has already realized his posthuman form. The other seven languish in altered states between their human form and quintessential posthuman transformations. Kind of like a clogged sink. Let's go."

"So, I am the psychic plumber making a house call?"

"Good one, Number 1. Your wit, albeit snarky, is the epitome of intelligence."

"Wait until they get my bill."

Exiting the vehicle and stretching in the pale morning light, Number 1 dons her soft leather overcoat and steps across the dewy lot in tight-fitting olive jodhpurs tucked into knee-high boots under an ivory blouse with her short black hair slicked back on her perfect head.

Catching up to Andrew's steady gait halfway across the lot, she grabs him by the hand, "Can you wait for me, silly Andrew?" masking trepidation while smiling past a stone-faced security man frozen at attention.

Squeezing Number 1's hand, Andrew exudes confident elan in his usual PTB windbreaker over a black mock turtleneck, jeans, and western boots, "Now then, my dear, let us see what dastardly scientific progress hath wrought on the surviving Blue Spark test subjects."

"What if I cannot help them complete their metamorphosis?"

Andrew pauses outside a crumbled brick mess hall, "Have faith, Number 1. You can do anything. These last eight Blue Spark mutants must transcend to their final posthuman forms. Otherwise ...."

Both replicants turn in unison as a high-pitched male voice interrupts their conversation.

"Welcome to St. Dymphna's, sir and madam! What an honor it is to have you here in person!"

Andrew leans into Number 1 and whispers, "Who is this man?"

"His name is Dr. Jon Benz, a sadistic bastard with zero scruples or morals. I suspect he is also a Nazi."

"Really? A Nazi?"

"You want genocidal maniac; go to the source."

"Got it."

Proffering a flawless smile, Andrew steps forward to greet the bald man beaming under thick round spectacles balanced on his crooked nose. "Hello, Doctor Benz. I am Andrew."

"Oh, we all know who you are, sir. What an honor. I trust the drive was not too uncomfortable. The Spanish infrastructure was bad before the Gorks. Now it is almost non-existent."

"The drive was enlightening, right Number 1?"

"I learned so much my head is still spinning." Number 1 steps forward and smiles, "This facility is surrounded by a lot of nothing."

Benz laughs and wipes his glasses with a hankie, "It is the ideal location to accommodate psychotic murderers, pedophiles, and rapists back in the day. Now, it is the perfect solution for our needs."

Following the vile little man through the doors of a long three-story brick building, they clank up banks of metal stairs to the top floor and proceed down a corridor past labs and offices abuzz with white-coated scientists engaging their genius-level intellects on uncovering the underlying mysteries of deceased Blue Spark drug trial participants' dissected tissues and organs.

Number 1 hears the screech of a monkey from a lab down the hall before it falls silent. Passing the open doors of an empty operating room, she absorbs agonizing screams and wails still echoing off the grimy walls from the ghosts of former patients plucked apart while still among the living, "Andrew, the walls resonate hopelessness and despair."

Dr. Benz turns and proffers a sadistic chortle, "We should put that in our brochure." Unlocking another door in the labyrinthine interior, he wipes his nose, "This way, please."

Andrew pauses before the good doctor, "Your nose is bleeding."

"It must be the dry filtered air in this place."

Crossing a third-floor bridge into an adjoining building, Dr. Benz dabs his nose and instructs his VIP guests to stand behind a safety line taped to the linoleum floor tiles before accessing a biometric pad mounted at eye level. After a grinding *kerchunk*, the heavy metal double doors swing open, and Dr. Benz gestures for Andrew and Number 1 to cross the threshold with an exaggerated bow, dripping blood on the floor, "Welcome to the freak show."

Upon entering the thrumming command center, an abrupt tension fills the stale air as pale-skinned white coats and armed security personnel stand to greet their CEO's arrival.

Andrew nods and smiles at the nervous PTB employees, amused by the palpable trepidation reminiscent of accompanying his old boss, Artemus Pennywell, on similar field visits in the old days.

"At ease, everyone. We are here to observe. Some of you have met my lovely companion … say hello, Number 1."

"Hello."

"How nice."

Moving past Dr. Benz and his leaky nose, Andrew stands behind a young security officer struggling to quell his shaking hand caught holding a paper coffee cup. Bending over the man's shoulder, Andrew studies the unmoving shape of a young female mutant huddled in the corner of her dark cell. "Who do we have here?"

The security man manages to place the brimming cup on the desk without spilling a drop before addressing Andrew, "Uh, sir, this is Monica Grasso. She is one of the final eight."

Andrew nods, "Grasso. Oh yes, an NYC recruit."

"Spot on, sir."

Dr. Benz stands beside Andrew with a bloody hankie in hand, "As you can see, we maintain around-the-clock surveillance on the subjects, from a safe distance, of course."

"Of course." Andrew pats the security man's shoulder, "Carry on, and please, finish your coffee."

Moving past other surveillance stations with a vigilant Dr. Benz trailing behind, Andrew studies the deformed blue wretches in varying states of repose as Number 1 cuts diagonal across the room, her attention drawn to the last bank of screens.

Andrew pauses at another station, "This poor chap is unrecognizable. I assume it is a male."

A shaky-kneed female guard monitoring the station slinks out of the way, glancing at her wide-eyed co-workers, unsure what she is authorized to divulge.

With an exasperated huff, Dr. Benz's patience crumbles, "Oh, for Chrissakes." elbowing the tongue-tied guard aside and pointing at the distorted human on the screen, "This is Michael Tran. Like Ms. Grasso, he was part of the New York trial group. And at 59, he is the oldest participant still with us and the last Asian survivor."

"Is race relevant? They are all humans, or, at least, they used to be human."

"My apologies, sir. Race and gender appear irrelevant—the final eight comprise four men and four women of varying races."

Andrew feigns consideration of the chief scientist's words, buying time for Number 1's telepathic connection with Hector.

"Dr. Benz, let's start by reviewing a list of survivors."

"Yes, sir." Pulling up a virtual screen, Benz swipes through the dwindled roster of Blue Spark trial subjects with smiling human faces accompanying names and short CVs. "As stated, we are down to eight: Monica Grasso and Mike Tran from the NYC performances. Then we have Hedy Olsen from Sydney, Australia. Lucia Sandoval from Brazil. Lamar Tate, our last Black recruit, Los Angeles. Ada Hansen, Norway, and Enes Kabek from Israel."

"Herr Benz, that is seven."

Dr. Benz steals a nervous glance toward Number 1, engrossed in the last station's data and security camera feeds, "Yes. Quite right. There is one more. Hector Gonzalez. He is the only Blue Spark trial subject who completed the posthuman transformation. Blue, but human, like us. Er, well. You know what I mean."

His curiosity aroused, Andrew joins Number 1 and examines the anomalous young man lying on a cot in a darkened cell. After a quick glance, he queries Benz without turning around, "Why is he restrained?"

Number 1 nudges Andrew, her keen blueberry gaze fixated

on purplish welts covering the kid's swollen face, "Better yet, who is responsible for his obvious injuries?"

As the tension percolates, an imposing figure eclipses Dr. Benz's fumbling attempt for an answer.

"My name is Edwin Goddard. I am the head of security at this facility. It is my job to ensure the staff's safety."

Andrew pivots onto the thick-necked PTB veteran, "Ah, yes. Edwin. We have met. Please answer the question. Why did you or your men beat one of my experiments?"

Fearless and defiant in the face of the almighty Andrew, Edwin's voice booms across the room, "The young man you are spying on is a 23-year-old named Hector Gonzalez. While he does not have the monstrous transformed appearance of his unfortunate colleagues, he is by far the most dangerous of the Final Eight. We should put him down while we still can."

Andrew's brow arches, "What do you mean?"

Edwin swipes up a 3D layout of the black site, "We are here. Gonzalez and his freaky friends are two wings removed and contained inside what used to be the maximum-security psych ward. The whole wing is shielded to protect us from their telepathy."

Andrew nods, "The psych ward operates as an inverse Faraday cage."

Edwin nods, "Yes, sir. That is spot on. However, it is not enough. They penetrate our minds at will."

Number 1 zooms a camera on Hector's swollen face, "He is saying something."

Edwin huffs an exasperated sigh, "Mind games, Miss. Nothing more. And yes, we had to get physical with the detainee and strap him down for his own good."

Number 1 moves before the hulking man who worked as hired muscle for the PTB throughout his career and pierces his mind like a hot knife through butter, "Take me to him."

***

In full hazmat gear, Edwin leads an unencumbered Number 1 toward the locked-down psych ward. "Are you sure, Miss? I can fit you with clean gear …."

"No. If Hector Gonzalez can control my mind, I might as well be naked. It simply will not matter anymore."

"What about me?"

Number 1 ignores the hulking man's question as they arrive at the cell block's cramped control room.

Edwin rousts a pair of somnambulant security guards who jump from their seats, seeing a fearless Number 1's lithe form standing before them without protection.

"This young woman is here to see Hector."

Seated before a board covered in blinking lights, the first guard snickers toward his comrade, "Uh, okay. Should Al get the mop and bucket?"

Edwin smacks the insubordinate underling's covered head, "Don't be a wise-ass. Do as you are fucking told for once in your miserable cock-sucking life."

"Well, since you put it that way, it is your funeral, lady."

Number 1 snaps her fingers, causing the man to wince in pain, "I think you need to learn some manners."

A grating alarm and blaring yellow lights accompany reinforced doors gliding apart onto the long, dark cell block.

"Wait here with your men, Edwin."

"I was hoping you would say that. The Final Eight occupy solitary confinements at the far end. Hector's cell is the last one on the right." The man at the control panel straightens and nods at the bewitching woman, "I can unlock Hector's cell from here if you give the signal."

Number 1 ignores the dolts and enters the corridor past empty cells, hearing the tortured cries of former inmates echoing within the haunted concrete walls.

****

Edwin and his two men watch the sexy woman's dark silhouette recede down the hall, "Is she for real, Edwin?"

"I am afraid so. Between the blueskins and the replicants, we are obsolete as shit."

Zooming a camera, they watch Number 1 read a manifest before tapping a bolted door and pushing it open, "Hey. How did she unlock that door!"

"She entered Grasso's cell. I thought you said she was here to see Hector?"

Edwin's eyes widen in wonder, "The shit if I know."

****

"Hello, Monica."

Uncurling her hideous hunched form and peering through mutant eyeballs, Monica Grasso rises before the beautiful woman, "Are you an angel?"

"No. Far from it. But I can help you. Come here, my love."

With her once delicate features transmogrified by the toxic after-effects of the Blue Spark drug, the 32-year-old Jersey girl recoils from the charming stranger. "If you plan to put me down like a rabid dog, just do it. I will not stop you."

Number 1 raises her hands and places them on the woman's stubbled head, oozing with cuts and sores, "You received a massive overdose of the Blue Spark, but you can control it, like Hector."

"Hello, Monica."

Monica's bulging eyes focus on the handsome young Spaniard sitting on the edge of her cot, "Hector, is that you? How did you get in here?"

"Monica, listen to this woman. She will guide you. I used my

Blue Spark to project my essence through solid matter. Have faith. You can do it."

Controlling his complexion from natural skin tones to blues, reds, and purples like a chameleon, he defaults to blue, "Let Number 1 enter your mind and show you the way. It is the fruition of the Blue Spark miracle we were promised. You can still become the next Rachel Haig!"

Monica closes her reddish eyeballs and turns to Number 1, "Okay. Whatever you are planning to do to me, just do it."

* * *

Dr. Benz watches Number 1's peculiar activity on a hi-def color monitor, "What is your girl doing to Grasso?"

Andrew answers with a malicious grin, "A little neural plumbing to make things right, you Nazi prick."

Benz pivots bloodshot eyeballs onto Andrew's imposing form, "What?"

Andrew points at the evil scientist, "The Blue Spark worked. And yet you arrested their transformations, leaving these poor people to die painful deaths in their hideous altered states. Only a sadist would do that."

"I acted on your orders."

"I never told you to kill the 132 recruits. I wanted them alive."

"One of your women, like Number 1, instructed me to do it."

"Which woman? I need a number, you ass."

"Number 8. She brought the boy, too. He enjoyed killing them with his freakish telekinesis, like a cat toying with a mouse before ripping off its head. Your progeny is evil personified."

An enraged Andrew snatches Dr. Benz by his sweaty head, squeezing with all his might and crushing the man's skull in a lightning-quick act of violence before dropping the evil bastard to the floor in a bloody heap.

The twenty eyewitnesses to the cold-blooded murder gape at Andrew as he waves blood-soaked hands through the air, descending the room into chaos. Overhead lights pop and catch the ceiling ablaze as the surveillance feeds fill with static before sparking and bursting into flames. The guards and white-coated techs run for the double doors through thick, noxious smoke engulfing the chaos.

Andrew wipes the servers clean with a telekinetic EMP before accessing the still-functioning intercom: "In one hour, this black site will be turned into a smoking crater in the Spanish countryside. I suggest fleeing as far away as possible. By the way, you are all fired."

Biohazard sirens blare, prompting scores of scientists, staffers, and guards to trample over each other in a panicked retreat for the exits.

* * *

Number 1 sits behind the control board and engages the first cell's locking mechanism, ignoring muffled screams, hollers, and curses from Edwin and the twin abusers incarcerated within as Andrew's calm voice resonates through a tinny speaker.

"How did you do, Number 1?"

"The Final Eight are liberated."

"Excellent. The drones are en route. We have 42 minutes to clear the area."

"I'll be right there."

Pushing a comm button on the control board, Number 1 coos into a mic, "Goodbye, boys. I'll see you in hell."

Julius Hart | South Coast Plaza
06:23 p.m. | December 23, 2052

Nebulous rumors and delusional predictions of the once-ubiquitous smartphone's triumphant return to a world subsisting without their proverbial digital crutches since the Gorkian invaders melted their precious devices in 2044 persisted throughout the intervening years. However, with most of the world's retail infrastructure looted to the bare bones and burned to the ground, only the most dewy-eyed optimists among the nanny-state citizenry believed a mass-marketed smart device would happen again in their sad and wretched lifetimes.

The reasons, though manifold, from busted supply chains to decimated factories and a paucity of innovation and natural resources, failed to dampen an unwarranted hope to once again possess a beloved phone to have and hold. They needed it. They wanted it. Life was harsh enough without their handheld access to the latest puppy dog video, viral teen sensation, or twenty ways to bake a potato. Not to mention immortalizing their burger or buns for strangers to ogle, and most important of all, ordering any and everything online delivered straight to their damn door without leaving the sofa. The invaders crushing EMPs ruined so much more than civilization. Entire lives uploaded to a digital realm were swiped clean, never to be seen again.

Based on the flimsiest rumors that a moribund tech giant reanimated to life and was about to make a big splash with a sexy new smart gadget, unhinged dreamers camped out days, sometimes weeks, in advance at defunct arenas and empty malls, with gauzy visions of laying their hands on a shiny new device. In eight long dark years, hopes were dashed every single time on the silicon shores of a dried-up industry decades away from anything resembling pre-invasion business as usual.

* * *

Amelia Stawicki hunches over the tiny sink in her vintage camper, rinsing knock-off government SpaghettiOs from her plate. Glancing at a small, framed photograph of Mom and Dad, who perished on invasion night eight years earlier, she chuckles, "Ugh, Mom, you would hate this shit. Believe it or not, this tasted worse than the canned government ravioli. I will never get used to eating cricket meal no matter how much sauce they drown it in."

Glancing at the ceramic dog dish on the floor in the narrow camper, she scoops it up and scrapes hardened chunks from the rim.

"Hey, Bilbo, your food and my food look and smell remarkably similar."

The tawny Chihuahua mix ignores her, fixated on the burgeoning bustle of people outside his little window on the world. Emitting an ear-splitting bark, the little protector hears a distant rumbling seconds before it sends tremors through the camper.

"Bilbo! That sounds like helicopters!"

Leaving a sink full of dishes, Amelia snaps a leash on Bilbo and ventures outside into the brisk late December Southern California air. Gobsmacked by how much the crowd had grown in the last few hours, the pair navigate a dense, smelly human stew peppered with Blue Skins sleeping for days in cars and campers fighting for elbow room with hordes of locals arriving on buggies, bikes, scooters, and horseback, morphing the normally-deserted parking lots encircling the defunct South Coast Plaza shopping mall in Costa Mesa, California into a chaotic carnival-like atmosphere.

Carried on a human wave toward the shuttered Nordstrom anchor on the upper-crust end of the massive mall, Amelia ignores palpable hints of looming disaster as Bilbo zigs and zags, pulling her forward while dodging footfalls on a beeline toward a line of fire engines forming a makeshift barrier in front of a crumbled parking garage as riot police mill about behind pre-positioned K-rails.

Somehow reaching the concrete barriers, Amelia nudges beside two surfer dudes unfazed by the threatening scores and deafening din closing in all around them. Amelia recognizes their type.

Not a care in the world. And why not? The ocean works just fine.

The younger beach bum with thick bangs hanging over his pale blue eyes gives her a too-cool-for-school head nod, "Hey there, looks like it's happening. Finally getting my iPhone on."

His ripped, handsome, sun-bleached friend notices Amelia's lithe form and fresh-faced smile. Standing a little taller, he shoves back on some lout invading his space while addressing his friend, "Apple is dead, you idiot; it will be some sucky satellite junk or another false alarm."

No stranger to the beach life, spending the last eight years camping up and down the Southern California coast in her deceased parents' camper, Amelia acknowledges the boys with a cute grin while an unimpressed—and possibly jealous—Bilbo pees at the boy's sandaled feet.

"Ah, nice mutt you got there."

"That's Bilbo, he is my protector."

Fighting to maintain a little safe space for herself and Bilbo as the unruly mob pushes her against the concrete barrier, Amelia employs the dude's tactic and pushes back on someone pressing against her firm ass. Acting calm as alarm bells go off in her head, she tries to interact with the boys, hoping they may help her and Bilbo when things go south, "You guys ever hear of Julius Hart? I arrived here a few days ago based on a letter from my cousin in Texas. She said Hart is planning something huge, uh, Thunder-something …."

An older couple presses behind Amelia as the man widens his stance, clearing space for his wife. Adjusting wire-rimmed glasses with a sweaty smile, he taps Amelia's shoulder, "Excuse me, miss, I could not help overhearing. Julius Hart's company is called Thundercorp."

Amelia glances over her shoulder before double taking onto the bright blue couple, "Oh yeah, that's right, Thundercorp. Thanks, mister. By the way, what's it like?"

The older woman's eyes narrow on Amelia, "What is what like, dear?"

"The drug … you know, can you like, uh, read minds?"

"If we had special powers, would we be here risking our lives in this crowd for a phone?"

"I guess not."

Searching down through a forest of legs and shoes, she spots the couple's blue-dyed cat on a rope leash sniffing at Bilbo, who had never seen a kitty, let alone a blue one, in his four-plus years. "Cute kitty, I … Ow!"

Amelia recoils from a sharp blow, clutching her hands over her head as a hail of rocks reigns down, igniting a nightmarish riot. Absorbing kicks and jabs, something heavy thumps into her back, knocking the wind from her lungs. Gasping for air with no room to move, she pulls her left arm up and realizes she no longer holds Bilbo's leash as the 22-year-old is pushed over the K-rail, leaving the boys and the couple behind. Stumbling onto her hands and knees, she tries to regain her footing and find her dog as terrified people pile over the barriers, trampling her beaten body as the porous police line fades backward. Knocked sideways, Amelia hears a familiar bark over the chaos before shifting her swollen gape onto a snarling blurred form— her little dog clearing space for her to snap back to consciousness and stagger onto her feet.

Her head swooning and crushing pain radiating from her left arm hanging limp at her side, Amelia moans and cries, grabbing her little man in her unbroken right arm as rival gangs form a mosh pit, screaming and cursing in Vietnamese, Chinese, Spanish, and even some English. Gunfire erupts over multiple fistfights as someone hurls a smoke grenade into the rabble of bloody, toothless fighters, bouncing Amelia and Bilbo between them like pinballs.

Nicknamed Stringbean by her late father, the tall and rail-thin Amelia Stawicki from the planned community of Mission Viejo clutches Bilbo tight to her chest as she takes another blow to the head. Searching for an escape through searing pain coursing her body, she sobs and smudges a dirty arm across her wet cheek. "Ah, Bilbo, what are we going to do? I am sorry, boy. I just wanted a fucking phone."

A strong hand grabs her from behind as she wheels around in

mortal, wide-eyed horror, screaming in a hoarse voice, "Get off of me! Get off of me! Get off of me!" before her swollen eyes widen enough to make out the sculpted face of a local firefighter extending his gloved hands.

"Come with me, miss."

Amelia stumbles over a planter, almost dropping Bilbo in her haste to reach the man who lifts her and Bilbo above the crowd toward a makeshift field hospital setting up inside the cordoned-off parking garage.

With her left forearm broken above the wrist, her face swollen and bleeding profusely from multiple wounds, Amelia Stawicki hears her savior speaking to someone, "I have a female in her early twenties with bleeding head trauma and multiple fractures ...."

Amelia feels herself lowering onto a stretcher as Bilbo is pulled from her arms moments before a warm opioid rush turns out her lights.

* * *

A Christmas miracle manifests in the debonair form of trillionaire Julius Hart, sporting a jolly Santa Claus suit and fake beard waving at the throngs as his pilot completes a low pass over the erstwhile South Coast Plaza in Costa Mesa, California. Jammed with people, just like old times, two days before Christmas, Hart reveled in the irony-laced symbolism upon choosing the former world-renowned prestigious shopping mall to announce a glorious revival of mass consumerism.

"We are getting reports of gunfire and riots on the mall's north side."

Hart laughs into his headset, "So what's new, Charlie. Our people have the 405 Freeway side secure, right?"

"Yes, sir. We are good to go."

Hart turns and gives a thumbs-up to his high-paid elves as his lead chopper swings around and lands in a cleared section of the long-abandoned Bloomingdale's lot, "Okay, people, let's get this party started."

Feeling the weight of thousands of human beings, elbow-to-elbow, across the lot, Bristol Street, and a row of high rises beyond, as well as those jamming up the adjacent stretch of 405 freeway, Hart clears his throat and saunters atop a ten-foot riser like a rock star as a virtual screen materializes sixty feet into the dusky December sky, "Merry Christmas, Costa Mesa! I come bearing the gift you have all been waiting for—the brand-new Thundercorp Smartphone!"

20-foot holograms of the simple rectangular devices people have missed more than television since the invasion animate above the enthralled crowds to an expectant chorus of oohs.

"Everyone gets a Thundercorp phone. I guarantee it." Already sweating in the Santa suit, Julius pauses for effect and takes a measure of the crowd's ability to comprehend complex ideas. Pulling down his fake white beard, he gulps a water before continuing. "I know you have waited eight long years for this moment to arrive. But I require patience and courtesy for your fellow countrymen, or this will not work. Demand for this unbelievable new tech is beyond belief. So here is what we are going to do. Everyone must obtain a chip implant—one per customer—matching a new smartphone. Check the big screen above my head for injection locations in the SoCal area. We are setting them up worldwide. It is a major undertaking that will take years to complete. However, because I picked this mall—the former epicenter of brick-and-mortar retail commerce in its heyday—as the location for my worldwide announcement, my people are setting up injection booths inside the empty department stores inside the mall. Follow the floating smartphone holograms, and remember, at the first sign of trouble, we are shutting down. So, let's keep this event on an even keel and maintain an esprit de corps for our fellow men and women. It is days before Christmas, after all …."

"Motherfucker! Give us the phones now!"

"I heard that. Somebody help that poor man understand the error of his ways."

Watching agents implanted in the crowd close in on the heckler, Hart continues without missing a beat, realizing the lack of instant gratification is going over like a lead balloon.

"Now then, I want you all to take note of the Thundercorp warehouses being constructed in low Earth orbits. Here is where your new smartphones will become a paradigm shift in e-commerce! Those of you old enough to remember, think back to the pre-invasion world. You placed an order on your phone or computer, then waited days, sometimes weeks, for your items. Well, not anymore. Each new Thundercorp smartphone has a built-in app that allows you to place an order and have it delivered via a hypersonic drone within an hour in almost every case. However, before you start running up the credit card like back in the day when credit was a thing, the Thundercorp warehouses are still years from completion," gesturing at a half-built moonlike sphere visible in the darkening eastern sky, he adds, "as you can plainly see.

The first Thundercorp is scheduled to come online in 2060. That gives everyone time to obtain a smartphone and reacquaint themselves with the digital world. The cloud is still out there. It contains everything up to the moment the Gorks wrecked the world. And now you will once again possess the hardware to view it and take advantage of its endless wealth of knowledge."

"Don't forget the porn!"

Hart peers into the crowd of faces and laughs, trying to single out the heckler, "Who is that guy?"

Amelia Stawicki | Costa Mesa, CA

02:05 p.m. | December 31, 2052 – 8 days later

Amelia exits the Bear Street metro bus stop on the outer edge of the South Coast Plaza shopping mall, once more a sad and empty reminder of how things used to be. Unsure where else to go after her release from the hospital, looking like a plane crash survivor with her head wrapped and a left arm cast to the elbow, she avoids trash and excrement littering the cracked and stinky pavement, circumventing weedy planters and a burned-out husk of an Italian restaurant, spying the old family camper parked all by itself in the middle distance, right where she left it.

Approaching her sky-blue four-wheeled sanctuary through a light mist swirling on a chilly and overcast New Year's Eve, she could not believe her eyes, seeing it looking the way she had left it a week earlier when all hell broke loose. Venturing closer, she spies a fellow sitting in one of her cheap folding chairs under the extended awning, smoking a cigarette and drinking Coke from a bottle.

One of *her* precious Cokes.

Amelia pulls an old-school fob from her torn jeans and unlocks the camper with a loud chirp, causing the man to jump.

"Oh, hello, Miss Stawicki, you made it back."

"Who the hell are you?"

"I work for Julius Hart. He heard about your situation, and honestly, he feels responsible. The event was a shitshow from the start. No conceivable method exists to make a major announcement without causing a riot. Everyone is on edge. It is getting worse. Through his limitless sources, he learned your story, how you lost your parents on invasion night. That made him feel even more terrible about your plight. With all of that being said, he wanted to ensure your home was in one piece upon your discharge from the hospital. Nice camper, by the way. They don't make them like this anymore."

"They don't make fucking anything anymore."

"Yes, too true."

Amelia steps forward, wary yet intrigued by the stranger and his fantastical story, "You expect me to believe that the world's richest man gives two fucks for someone like me?"

"Yes, mam. Yes, I do."

Stamping out his smoke on the crumbled pavement, he stands from the chair and stretches, "I do have a confession. I jimmied the lock to get inside your camper and ensure it belonged to you."

"You couldn't check the plates? They are eight years out of date, but the license number should still register as mine."

"Uh, no, mam. It was registered to some guy; I can't remember his name. Anyway, the DMV is not what I call reliable."

Amelia coughs and winces at flashes of pain from her broken ribs, "Yeah, they sucked then, and they suck even more now. No one cares. The road rules are a joke. It's like Mad Max on the highways." Scrutinizing the stranger and noting the heavy sidearm holstered at his beltline, "So, how did you know it was mine?"

"Luckily, your DNA is well represented inside and out. And when every other vehicle exited the lot, yours remained, along with a few others. People died, Miss. It was not good."

"Uh, yeah. I experienced the *not-good* firsthand."

"Yes, well, there is something Mr. Hart wants you to have." Trying to remain as unthreatening as possible before the gun-shy beanpole of a girl, with her head wrapped, black eyes, and arm in a sling, he opens the camper's door.

"Come here, boy …."

Bark! Bark! Bark! Bark!

Amelia's heart soars as she drops to her knees to greet her one true friend, bounding out the opened door and leaping into her embrace, licking her face with his little tail wagging, "Bilbo! I thought I lost you, boy!"

The man lights a new cigarette and blows smoke into the air, "It turns out the fireman who rescued you is a dog lover. I picked your dog up at his firehouse three days ago. Little Bilbo and I have become good friends waiting for your return."

Jettisoning her standoffish veneer, Amelia pulls the man into her long-armed hug and kisses him on the cheek, "I don't know what to say."

With her little friend jumping at her feet, she climbs into her camper, "Oh my, you didn't have to clean my mess, mister. It is never this clean."

"I had a local lady do most of the work."

Amelia drops into her favorite seat and motions for the man peaking inside to enter, "Come in and sit awhile."

The man stubs out his smoke and shrugs, "Don't mind if I do." Angling his large frame onto a pull-out sofa, he finishes his Coke and studies the bottle, "I work for Julius Hart, but even I can't get my hands on one of these."

Amelia laughs, "Please take another. I can get more."

He pops the lid on a second bottle and downs it in a single pull, "Wow. That takes me back to better times. How did you …."

Amelia strokes Bilbo, snuggled on her lap. "Mexico. But you have to know the right people."

"Ah. Of course."

The iconic opening notes of *Also sprach Zarathustra* reverberate inside the camper, causing Bilbo's ears to perk up.

"What is that?"

"That, my dear, is your smartphone's ringtone. You can change it to anything you like. Julius happens to prefer classical music."

"My smartphone? No way, mister. Are you kidding me?"

The ringtone repeats as the man leans back and pulls the thin device from his jeans pocket. Proffering it forward, he finishes his Coke and smiles, "You really should take this call."

Amelia accepts the ringing device and cradles it in her free hand like a precious gem. Staring at the blinking icon, she realizes she has never owned a smartphone in her 22 years, "What do I do?"

"Really? You are a young one. Tap the phone icon with your finger to accept the call."

Amelia complies and lifts the phone to her face, "Hello?"

"Hello, Ms. Stawicki. This is Julius Hart. How would you like to join my team?"

Amelia's eyes widen in shock.

"Did my man mention you can keep the phone? You earned it."

Amelia Stawicki | Thundercorp No. 5
12:01 a.m. | June 6, 2060 – 8 years later

Plucked from obscurity and van life at the tender age of 22, Amelia Stawicki rose through the Thundercorp executive ranks in the intervening eight years, becoming Julius Hart's headhunter extraordinaire.

Packing an incredible rags-to-riches backstory, she travels the world, convincing rudderless twenty-somethings to get off the sofa and join Thundercorp. The cream of the crop from the idling generation with latent potential pouring out their ears undergoes strenuous physical and mental boot camps to deprogram from previous sloven lives before multidisciplinary training and, finally, six-month deployments aboard one of the five geostationary orbiting warehouses nearing completion in low Earth orbits.

Dubbed *Hart's Death Stars* by nattering-nabob media, academia, and environmental groups, greedy governments view the naked capitalism with unmasked contempt while seeking to milk it dry to enrich their Luddite legislatures. Julius Hart's all-in wager on reinventing e-commerce nevertheless shocks moribund industries back to life after years of post-invasion inertia, spawning a new breed of innovators and entrepreneurs eager to reap the whirlwind of progress.

The non-believers can suck it.

* * *

Clutching a pad in her toned left arm, Amelia leads a jelly-legged class of wet-behind-the-ears Thundercorp graduates sporting lemon-yellow jumpsuits denoting their newbie status through monotonal corridors to their hangar bay assignment.

Recognizing the green-around-the-gills graduates' deer-in-the-headlights expressions upon experiencing space and artificial gravity for the first time, Amelia pivots and proffers a confident smile to the group, "This way, people. Any questions so far?"

"Yeah, I have one. What happened to our bags?"

Amelia notes the young man's nametag embroidered on his new yellow coveralls, "Alan Adamo from Provo, Utah. Good question, Alan. The shuttle was delayed due to a tropical system. Don't worry; your dorms come stocked with all the essentials and basic toiletries you need until your personal effects arrive."

Reading the nervous group, Amelia proffers a confident smile, "Come on, people, you are all part of history. Embrace the moment. This station goes operational in one week."

At the terminus of the corridor, she pauses to double-check her tablet, "Here we are. Beyond this sealed airlock hatch is Hangar Bay Guinevere. Your new assignment."

One of the recruits speaks up, "Guinevere? As in King Arthur?"

"Julius Hart is an avid reader. His idea was to differentiate parts of each Thundercorp using literary references instead of the typical alphanumeric naming conventions." Registering the blank stares, Amelia switches topics: "Who wants to repeat the Thundercorp motto?"

"Think different?"

"No, that was Apple back in its heyday."

"Alter perception."

"That's it. Good job, Emily. Emily Dickinson. Luckily, you were not assigned to Thundercorp No. 3; that warehouse uses famous authors. That could get confusing."

Refocusing the group's attention on a wall-mounted console

adjoining the 12-foot hatch, "Note the panel shows greens across the board, indicating Guinevere is under full pressurization and life support. Just like your training, boys and girls, only this is real life."

Alan raises a hand, "Uh, Miss Stawicki, what happens if the lights are green, but the bay turns out not to be pressurized?"

Amelia frowns, "You refer to the accident that took nine lives. Safety measures have since been upgraded. This hatch will not open unless the bay is pressurized, regardless of the lights. Got it?"

"Yes, Ms. Stawicki."

"Okay then, kind of important. Who wants to volunteer and be the first to access the hatch leading to your new workplace?"

"I'll do it." Alan steps forward, inputs his twelve-digit PIN, and waits for something to happen for a 30-count before turning to his fellow yellows with a perplexed shrug, "Nothing happened."

Amelia sighs in her pale-gray jumpsuit with the iconic Thundercorp lightning bolt logo above the left breast pocket, "Here, let me try."

A dumbfounded Alan rejoins the snickering group as the hatch opens wide like a camera's shutter.

Amelia smiles, "Anyone know what Alan did wrong?"

"He didn't press OPEN after inputting his PIN."

"Precisely."

Accepting good-natured ribbing, Alan enters the cavernous Hangar Bay Guinevere, gobsmacked by the gleaming squadrons of silver drones aligned by size inside the massive bay.

Amelia spots the chief mechanic through a sea of sparks and shouts over the echoing din, "Hey Bob, look what I brought you!"

The hulking figure turns and raises his welder's mask while extinguishing his torch in the shadow of an SUV-sized drone suspended from an intricate web of conveyors crisscrossing the gargantuan expanse.

"More fresh meat! I'll take it from here, little darlin'."

Amelia beams a broad smile at the grizzled space mechanic,

"You're welcome, you sexist fuck!"

Turning to the fresh meat, she proffers a comely smile, "Well, good luck to you all. I will check on your gear and light a fire under their asses if it's not already en route. Anything else?"

"Yeah. Can I go home?"

"Sure, Alan, the door is right over there." Amelia points at the sealed four-story doors on Thundercorp Number 5's thin outer shell holding back the vacuum of space 206 miles above home.

Number 1 | Tokyo
09:19 p.m. | June 13, 2060

Mingling with pols, dignitaries, and honored guests attending the viewing party inside the Japanese PM's private suite of skyboxes at the Japan National Stadium, Andrew and Number 1 pass time at a cocktail table nursing drinks as the Hiroshima Children's Choir finishes their performance far below on the infield grass simulcasting on the venue's state-of-the-art audio-visual to an SRO crowd of 120,000 gathering to bear personal witness to Julius Hart's paradigm-shifting Thundercorp launch event.

Number 1 checks the evening's entertainment program on the brand new Thundercorp smartphone from her pricey Hermès swag bag, "Let's see, here is the agenda, and yes, Andrew, those angelic-voiced kiddies are the last act before the main event. You could have looked for yourself if you didn't throw your bag in the trash."

"I didn't want it." Andrew sips a vodka tonic and gestures toward a load-bearing column marred by a long, crooked fissure, "Look at that, Number 1; while Hart receives unbridled adulation for reinventing e-commerce, our people rushed this structure's last phase to be ready for tonight, and the cracks are already beginning to show."

Weary of the PTB CEO's sour attitude, 1 empties her glass with a sigh, "Are we safe up here, or should we evacuate?"

Burdened with an odd sense of obligation, Andrew ignores 1's sarcasm, "The PMs and presidents drinking and laughing all around us in this suite are the same ones who gave up on rebuilding their ruined infrastructure and threw it in my lap. In hindsight, they were the smart ones … I should have listened to Viraj Patel when I had the chance."

Leaning closer to foil eavesdroppers amongst the glittery partiers, "I don't know what has gotten into you. A few years ago, you had my Sisters murder The Council in cold blood, but now you are worried about a fucking stadium?"

"I fear for humanity, though I hate it so."

"Great. What is next, quoting Macbeth?"

Fixated on ice melting in his highball glass, Andrew's voice lowers to a deep whisper, "By the pricking of my thumbs, something wicked this way comes …"

"Okay, that's it. I need another drink. You stay here and guard our table, Shakespeare."

Pivoting from Andrew's party-pooper persona with an eye roll in her elegant black cocktail dress, Number 1 parts the chic gathering, attracting wandering gazes toward a long bar overlooking the commoners, filling every seat in the gigantic former Olympics venue rebuilt by the PTB. Catching an overtaxed bartender's attention with zero effort, she senses a presence from behind and spins in three-inch heels onto the United States co-president, cradling an empty glass.

Gobsmacked in the face of such a beautiful creature, the old letch gathers what is left of his wits and blurts, "I'm looking for a refill of this damn fine Japanese Scotch whisky."

"Sorry?"

The tall, gray-haired socialist's face flushes in embarrassment, "You are not a server?"

"Nope. Not even close."

Recovering from another in a long line of infamous gaffes and faux pas, the creepy man shifts gears with practiced ease, "In that case, how is it that I have not made the acquaintance of a ravishing young woman such as yourself, uh, miss …."

Number 1 smiles, "You can call me Sarah."

"Well, it is indeed a pleasure, Sarah. My name is William Thorndike."

Number 1 glances around the room, finding everyone too enrapt with the open bar and unboxing their shiny new smartphone swag before extending her hand with a shrug and a coy grin, "I know who you are, Mr. President. I guess you are here to support Comrade Hart."

The lascivious old lush downs a new tumbler of amber-colored truth serum and chortles, "Comrade? Julius Hart is a massive pain in the ass, but the revenue from his outer space warehouse scheme will enrich us all."

"So, capitalism is fine, as long as it lines your pocket."

"Please call me Bill. And no, it is just that, well … I'm sorry, where was I going with that?"

Amused by the doddering old drunk, Number 1 leans close and deploys her wicked feminine charisma before whispering, "Let's not talk economics … where's your better half, Mr. President? Did she not make the trip?"

Too arrogant and dimwitted to sense 1's utter contempt and mockery but mindful of the first lady's presence holding court on the opposite side of the room, the president swivels with a conniving grin, "Uh, she is no doubt watching us from right over there."

Number 1 proffers a friendly wave toward the old biddy while leaning in to whisper in Thorndyke's hairy ear, "Not her, silly. I was talking about your co-president. What's her name?"

Rattled by 1's hotness in the black dress with her manicured hand lingering near his left thigh, "Oh, you mean, uh, what's her name … Stephanie Caldwell. She is back in DC doing the people's business."

Number 1 turns to collect her second martini from the bar, "Oh, I see. So, you take on the Veep duties, like state funerals and ham-fisted ribbon-cutting ceremonies, which is all this really amounts to …."

"Now, hold on a minute, I am not …."

"That's okay, Billy. Keep your dick in your pocket. Now the missus is looking a little peeved at the both of us."

"Why I never heard such, such …"

Number 1 sips from the long-stemmed glass while piercing Thorndyke's psyche with her hypnotic blue-eyed stare. Gathering a few nuggets from the empty recesses of the man's failing brain, she breaks a telepathic hold and steps back, "Hmm-mmm. A damn fine Vesper Martini, shaken, not stirred. More than I can say for you, Billy. Sorry about the diagnosis."

"Now see here, young lady. That is confidential …."

"Oh, now. Don't worry, Mr. President. You still have three months before the names of your children and wife fade into the ether. Well, nice chatting with you."

Returning to the cocktail table, Number 1 giggles like a naughty schoolgirl as Andrew eyes her with suspicion, "Why were you talking to that dickless wonder, Thorndyke."

"Oh, Andrew, don't be jealous. I was just having a little harmless fun. He has Alzheimer's, by the way."

"Ah, interesting. Maybe Thorndyke will forget about the thousands of so-called insurrectionists his uni-party has locked away in internment camps all over the US."

"Perhaps." Feeling giddy and light-headed from the drink and her political espionage foray, Number 1 runs her leg up Andrew's calf under the table, "Tell me more about the crack in the pillar."

"What is there to say?" Andrew meets Number 1's beautiful blueberry gaze, "I should have listened to Patel, but now it is too late."

"Andrew, we both know that when the Overlords arrive, these people will be the first to die. It will not matter anymore."

Andrew casts a furtive glance at the well-heeled assemblage, migrating toward the expansive open windows as the parade of adorable opening acts finally ends, and Julius Hart's Thundercorp presentation begins.

"We traveled all this way; let's find a spot and watch the show."

Noting palpable excitement among the elites, Number 1 spies King George's deep-set eyes drawn heavenward at pinpoint lights performing physics-defying maneuvers, eliciting breathless gasps from the murmuring audience at once familiar with anti-gravity but never as the centerpiece of a plan to reinvent the world's economies.

In rapt anticipation, the crowd falls silent as a sonorous hum vibrates across the chilly nighttime expanse, and a lone spotlight illuminates a silvery drone descending out of the darkness to a round stage centered in the infield.

Andrew observes Number 1's impressed reaction mirroring everyone else in the skybox as a dramatic holographic lightning storm cascades out of the night, accompanying a thunderous godlike voice resonating over the sound system's massive speakers: *"Thundercorp. A civilizational revolution."*

Right on cue, a portal on the drone's lit fuselage swings open, and a miked-up Julius Hart exits the craft to an ear-splitting standing ovation as lasers and spotlights shoot in every direction to Wagner's *Ride of the Valkyries.*

"Whew! What a trip! Hello Tokyo!"

Exhibiting a youthful agility, Julius Hart jumps atop a high podium and pantomimes conducting squadrons of gravity-defying drones pouring out of the night. Strobing colors and patterns, the deft delivery vehicles buzz around the arena in complex formations before peeling off and idling feet above hundreds of specific seats.

As the massive stadium shudders to its compromised foundations and supports, Julius Hart's handsome visage, lit in blues and purples, broadcasts on the jumbo screens, "I hope everyone brought their new

Thundercorp smartphones!"

The ecstatic crowd goes wild, holding up lit devices syncing together and animating Thundercorp lightning bolt logos striking around the stadium.

"Good!"

Pausing for effect and a drink of water, the hoarse-voiced Hart continues, "Now. Check the home screens on your new devices. If the basket icon is spinning and your phone vibrates, you are on the cusp of receiving one of the first-ever drone deliveries from space. But not so fast—let's start this party by directing your attention to the screens ...."

With a smirk, Andrew notes that Hart could not resist pandering to the VIP skybox attendees before the common folk get their taste of revitalized capitalism. Some things never change. "You know, Number 1, these drones are no different than the prototype I used to evacuate Pennywell from Scotland during the Gork invasion. Why, it's funny, I can recall ...."

Brrrrr-brrrrrrr! Brrrr-brrrrr! Brrrrr ...

"Hold that thought, Andrew. My new phone is vibrating."

Andrew frowns, watching Number 1 check the colorful home screen on the Thundercorp device held in her nimble fingertips.

"Ooh, I get a prize. Too bad you threw yours away."

"Yeah. Too bad ...."

"Aha!" The debonair King George bellows a hearty chuckle, parting the wealthy partiers with his buzzing smartphone held high.

Exhibiting sheepish smiles with new phones in hand, a Middle Eastern fellow and the Japanese Prime Minister join the king as their fellow VIPs, still checking their devices, form a loose circle to see what happens next.

Casting his aristocratic gaze around the room with a winning smile, King George assumes control of the situation, "Ah, it appears it is just the three of us lads who got the call. Good stuff, I say. Mr. Hart, bring on your delivery drone with all speed."

Number 1 parts from Andrew, "Pardon me, Your Majesty, make that four."

King George extends his hand with a broad smile, "Ah, please join us, young lady … a flower in the thicket patch."

Observing the affable monarch take command of the room, Andrew grins at Number 1, holding her own as part of the odd foursome posing for pictures as guests access the easy-to-use camera on their new digital toys, capturing the ad-libbed historic proceedings inside the open-air VIP skybox.

Just like old times.

With the photo session complete, everyone gives way for a shoebox-sized drone with no visible means of propulsion floating into the open-air suite and simulating a mid-air curtsy before a red-faced and embarrassed King George, who chortles and mutters, "Good show. Bloody good show …."

The British monarch and the spellbound audience watch as a compartment opens on the drone's smooth silver surface. A heartbeat later, a thin mechanical arm extends, clutching an exquisite gold fountain pen in surgically precise robotic fingers.

Tickled pink by the demonstration, George scrutinizes the pen before accepting it with a subtle nod, "Aha, good show. My father collected fountain pens; don't you know." Sliding it into a jacket pocket, he adds, "This will enhance his already prized collection."

Unpracticed in public speaking, but realizing the drone is broadcasting his face to 120,000 pairs of eyes inside the stadium and millions more watching on their new devices worldwide, expecting a royal profundity to mark the occasion, King George VII ad-libs for one of the few times in his scripted and choreographed life: "Empires rise and fall … on the capricious tides of global trade and commerce. These anti-gravity drones will serve humanity well by transporting much-needed goods to areas in desperate need and restoring at least a modicum of our former way of life. Well done, Mr. Julius Hart. Jolly good show."

Unsure of what he said but aware every word will be analyzed to the nth degree, he sees all eyes still upon him, "This event is not about me. It is for the people. Let's get on with it." Pivoting to the lithe young woman at his side, "You are next, my dear. Let us see what the drone has in store for you."

Number 1 smiles as the little drone inches sideways and proffers a Tiffany blue jewelry box. Accepting it from the tiny hand, she peeks inside and nods, "Quite a lovely gift. Thank you."

Keeping the contents to herself, she steps back and shrugs toward the Middle Eastern man, "You are next."

Far back in the crowd of photo-happy onlookers, Andrew watches the replicant's effortless aplomb amongst the well-healed humans.

God help her, my Number 1 is different than her Sisters. She is human.

* * *

Too important to stick around for the rest of Hart's Thundercorp production, King George and his retinue depart, followed by presidents and PMs with friends and families in tow, eager to return to their ultra-secure Tokyo hotels powered with reliable electricity and unlimited taps of clean and filtered hot and cold running water.

As a crew of multi-armed service bots flits from table to table, collecting glasses and picking up trash, Andrew and Number 1 linger at the bar overlooking the crowd peppered with people on the receiving ends of generous drone deliveries as Hart's presentation continues.

"So, what was in the box?"

Number 1 fingers the Tiffany box in her hand, "It is empty."

"That is a little strange."

"It is a strange new world, Andrew." Number 1 peers far down at Julius Hart under a spotlight on the stage as his presentation drones onward, "Let's hear what else Hart has to say."

"… Thundercorp is partnering with a new breed of industry titans who saw the potential years ago, ramping up supply chains and manufacturing processes on every continent. My orbiting warehouses are already stocked with every item you don't know you want or need. And here is the kicker: it is all available from the app on your new smartphones that come internet-ready out of the box. That is right, free internet access for everyone! No more glitchy Wi-Fi or wonky satellite connections. And no more governments picking winners from losers forced to settle for a lousy shared signal or, most of the time, dead silence.

Twenty years have passed since the Gork invasion ruined civilization. In that time, promise after promise was left unfulfilled or manifesting in half-baked new abominations like this stadium. Folks, I hate to tell you, but this arena was the best I could do to showcase the Thundercorp rollout for the masses …."

Andrew scoffs at Hart's diatribe and finishes another Vodka tonic, "What an ungrateful bastard. Now I see why this skybox cleared out so fast. They did not want to endure Julius Hart lambasting them in person before their minions."

"Knowledge is power."

"Damn straight, Number 1."

"And even though the PTB monopolizes the communications satellite industry, you seem unfazed that his Thundercorps will put us out of business. Why?"

"The Overlords will come soon enough. Let's live for today."

Andrew takes Number 1 by the hand and leads her into an unoccupied lounge with a plush and inviting sofa.

"Here? Right now?"

"I have made terrible mistakes that I cannot undo. Soon, this will all be gone."

Andrew presses his sexy partner into the luxurious cushions with a long kiss while lowering the strap on her dress as fireworks rocket into the night, marking the conclusion of the game-changing announcement as the crowd roars for its savior, Julius Hart.

Julius Hart | Thundercorp
06:02 a.m. | February 2, 2064 – 4 years later

By 2064, humankind had endured so much civilizational upheaval most Earthbound denizens took little notice of the lightning-quick construction of geostationary warehouse satellites dominating the skies. And after learning Thundercorp's satellites offer free internet, their presence was deemed nothing short of miraculous.

Within a breathtakingly short amount of time, Thundercorp's algorithmic ballet of merch-laden drones streaking to and from the massive spherical orbiting repositories proves a boon that nourishes and fortifies a new industrial age. Utilizing the robust Thundercorp lightning bolt app installed on every device, dormant mass consumerism reanimates into an addictive new craze, fulfilling the insatiable human desire to possess the absolute latest—whatever—at any cost—and have it delivered within an hour after the order is processed.

For a civilized world reconnecting to a digital teat for the first time in two decades, the incredible drones screaming down from the heavens are music to their ears while virtual carts overflowing with purchased crap deliver the ultimate buzz.

Julius Hart is a genius.

By contrast, aghast at Hart's stranglehold on e-commerce 2.0, the threatened ruling class bandies about ideas to recapture the upper hand before they lose complete control, from monopoly-busting and regulatory restrictions to creative new sales taxes and audits; they plot and conspire as Hart's army of lawyers battles them tooth and nail.

Eager to join the loose and disorganized anti-Thundercorp coalition, environmentalists and socialists representing vocal minorities of Earth's denizens preferring the post-invasion agrarian society taking root over the last twenty-odd years feign objections and personal injuries from the mere presence of the orbital eyesores. Not to mention the ceaseless white noise of drones buzzing overhead, mesmerizing, and agitating in equal measure the vociferous yet scant subset of humanity incapable of looking away or tuning out the din.

The oft-repeated memes that no one bothered to inquire if they were cool with Mother Earth's skies reimagined by Thundercorp and its greedy capitalist sonofabitch owner, Julius Hart, are discarded to the proverbial trash heap. The mob has spoken. They want their shit, and they want it now.

Rachel | Hilltop

04:19 p.m. | July 4, 2064

Contemplating raindrops pattering against bay windows overlooking Hilltop's wooded grounds, a chill goes up Rachel's spine, alerting her to her mother's presence.

"Hi, Mom. Yes. I am in your favorite spot in the house. The place where you could keep a lookout until you saw me sneaking back home through the trees in the middle of the night. I thought I was so clever. Now I know I was a fool."

Rachel's hand turns blue as she wipes tears from her eyes, overwhelmed with emotion, *"We should talk more often. I miss you."*

Catching movement through the leafy oaks, Rachel turns away from Miriam Alexander's glowing translucence, leaning forward from her wheelchair close enough to fog the glass, watching her 19-year-old daughter jog uphill through the wet and dreary late afternoon in purple rain boots, short shorts, and a sopping tee clinging to her tall, athletic frame with a long blond ponytail curling down her back from under her dad's old Red Sox cap.

Suppressing an image of a young and handsome Owen Haig

wearing that same hat, Rachel stifles more tears and pounds a balled-up fist into her useless left thigh.

I think I am going insane.

Radiating the same effortless vivacity from her stolen youth, Rachel watches her daughter splash puddles along the circular drive before disappearing from view through an open garage door.

Pulling a blanket over her legs and scooping an old paperback off the bay window cushion, Rachel exhales and pulls herself together as the all-to-familiar sound of the inside garage door opening and slamming shut reaches her keen hearing, followed by an *"I'm home!"* resonating up the stairs.

Failing to clear her throat after not speaking a word out loud all day, Rachel blurts, "I'm upstairs, Hannah!"

Feeling self-conscious, Rachel checks her reflection in the dripping window as Hannah ascends the mahogany curved staircase three at a time, hits the second-floor landing, and bounds down the long hall in the wrong direction.

"Hannah. I'm in Mom's sitting area."

Drying herself with a guest bathroom terry cloth towel, Hannah finally locates her mother parked in the wheelchair before the bay windows with an old IOSC blanket draped over her legs and a dog-eared paperback opened to a random page in her lap.

"There you are! Are you reading a book?"

"Yes, Hannah. Why are you so surprised? I am an avid reader."

Dropping the sopping Red Sox cap atop a throw rug at her bare feet, Hannah scrunches the towel over her messy blond head, "You were back when Mr. Hobbes was around."

"Enough about me. You are soaked."

"Uh, yeah. I got caught in a downpour. I should have known better. It is July 4th, after all."

"What does that have to do with anything?"

"It has rained on every 4th of July since Dad left."

A sheet of rain whips sideways against the window as the skies open, and a thunderous crack rumbles in the distance. "Well, that can't be true."

Avoiding getting dragged into another circular debate over something she knows is a fact, Hannah plops on the cushioned window seat knee-to-knee in front of her wheelchair-bound mother, "Guess what?"

"What?"

"I got a job!"

Rachel inches backward and closes the book without marking a page, "A job? You don't need to work, Hannah. We have been over this. I need you close."

"Why, Mom? I can't stay holed up in this mansion my entire life. I need to get out among the people. Some girls from my homeschool class, Cassie and Becky, got me a job working at their dad's new cafe."

"Wait a minute … as in Cassandra and Rebecca Smythe? Didn't their dad take the Blue Spark jab?"

Hannah leans against the window and rolls her blue-green eyes, "So? That was twelve years ago. Mr. Smythe's skin isn't even blue anymore. It was a big scam. You really have some weird shitty fixation with the fucking Blue Spark, Mom. I understand your experience, but you act like if I go anywhere near a Blue Skin, I will somehow catch it from them."

"Hannah, there is so much you don't know about the Blue Spark."

More thunder precedes Hannah's reply, "I know the first Blue Sparks could fly, just like you."

Fighting off the temptation to tell Hannah everything, Rachel scooches back into her chair, "The videos of people flying were a PTB deep fake operation to con ordinary folks like Mr. Smythe into taking a shot that turned out to be a dud."

"Why would the PTB do that, Mom?"

"I don't know, Sweetie. There are a lot of things I do not know."

Hannah pulls her Thundercorp device from a tight back pocket in her shorts and holds it up before her Mom, "My friend sent me a link to a Fred Beaman podcast that regurgitates the Blue Spark conspiracy theories."

Rachel smirks at the shiny, wet smartphone, "Well, we now know Hart's phones are waterproof."

Hannah laughs, "Uh, yeah. How about that. I love this thing, by the way." Waving a hand, her eyes widen, "Wait! I did not tell you the best part of the Beaman podcast."

Rachel sighs, "What would that be?"

Adopting a gossipy tone, Hannah leans in, "Well, get this. An original test group of people from around the world received a legit Blue Spark treatment. Here is the kicker … they mutated into monsters."

"Honey, that story has made the rounds since you were a little girl. Fred Beaman is the same windbag your dad and I listened to in the old pre-invasion days. The guy made millions by entertaining paranoid conspiracies. It figures that the second the world returns online, idiots like Fred Beaman crawl out of the woodwork and begin spewing nonsensical drivel without missing a beat."

Hannah swipes her phone closed, "Sure, Mom, whatever you say."

Exerting intense mental effort to suppress the Blue Spark coursing Hannah's DNA since her conception, Rachel forces a smile, "Now, tell me about this job. What would you do at this establishment?"

"I don't know … make coffee … bus tables … it really doesn't matter to me. I just gotta get out and meet people."

"How much does it pay?"

"Mom … just let me be. I don't care about the money. That will take care of itself …." A violent gust pushes the trees sideways, snapping branches and roiling swirls of leaves into the maelstrom, "Holy fuck. I got home just in time. Another crappy July 4th rainout, just like every year since Dad left. I think it is a sign from God that he is out there somewhere, still alive."

Rachel pulls shoulder-length ash-gray hair behind her ear and pierces her daughter with a serious-faced expression, "Rachel. When are you going to accept the fact that your father is dead? And we have, too, had decent July 4th weather since then."

"No, Mom, we have not." Hannah jumps onto her feet and races out of the room, "I'll be right back!"

Bounding back before her Mom, Hannah presents a small, framed photograph, "This was the last year it did not rain."

Hannah notes her mother's adverse reaction to the happy image of her three-year-old self smiling from ear to ear in her dad's embrace with a sparkler clutched in her little hand. "Geez, it is just me and Dad. You act like it is kryptonite or something."

"That was right after I got home from my accident. Stanley was there that day. So much time has passed."

Catching a blue tinge in her mother's complexion before it fades to a Vitamin-D-deprived pallor, Hannah flings the towel around her neck and peers outside, "By the way, where is Mr. Dave?"

"I imagine he is waiting out the storm at the butcher shop."

Hannah's stomach churns, conjuring images of another signature Dave meat-heavy dinner, "Ugh … not more mystery sausage … did I mention his cooking is turning me into a vegetarian?"

"Why don't you like him, Hannah?"

"I like him fine, Mom. Dave Poole is your guy. I get that. It's just that he is not my father, but he acts like he is."

Unprepared for Hannah's fresh-faced candor, Rachel counters with a mixture of hurt and surprise, "That is because he loves you like a daughter."

"Enough. You are weirding me out, Mom." Pulling an unruly wet strand off her face, "By the way, I was asked again today about my famous parents."

"Yes, honey, I know that happens, and I am sorry about that. "

"No. You don't know. And if you are really sorry, you will tell me once and for all everything that happened to you and Dad beneath the Great Pyramid in Egypt. And then, all about the Amazon expedition. And last, what happened in St. Louis."

Rachel leans back in her chair and yanks the blanket off her blue legs, "Hannah, watch this." Putting her effortless telekinesis on full display, Rachel elevates picture frames and curios before setting them down with a flick of her wrist.

"Mom, you are bright blue. Are you okay?"

"Yes. I am fine. Blue is my normal skin color. Sit back down for a damn minute. First, it takes tremendous mental effort to hide my Blue Spark."

"Then why do it? You are the most famous woman in the world. You can fly, like Peter Pan and Wendy."

"I can't anymore. And I suppress the Blue Spark because, as your father once told me in a heated moment, I don't want to be a freak show."

Hannah starts to speak, but Rachel throws up a hand, "Uh huh, you want answers. I'll give you answers. Egypt started with a visit from your grandfather, four times removed, and ended with a catastrophic battle for a golden ellipse deep beneath the Great Pyramid on invasion day. Soon after, we were roped into an Amazon expedition to locate a lost alien shipwreck."

Hannah sits wide-eyed and wondering what got into her Mom. "And St. Louis?"

"A terror attack that killed the president and left me paralyzed. If anyone presses for more than that, tell them to come to me in person."

"Dave won't let anyone near you. You know that."

"Hannah, Dave started out as my bodyguard."

"But he is much more than that now. You two are sleeping together."

"Yes, Hannah, we share a bed."

"Does he love you, Mom?"

"Yes, he does. And I love him back."

"What about Dad?"

Rachel returns her skin to a natural color and wipes at her swollen eyes, "I will never stop loving your father."

Hannah stands barefoot in her damp shirt and shorts and checks her Thundercorp phone out of habit.

"Dave does everything for us. We could not survive without him." Wanting with all her might to tell Hannah the truth, Rachel bites her lip and turns back to the rain hitting the windowpanes. "He allows me to focus on one specific task. I will say no more on the matter."

Hannah scoops up her framed photo and clutches it to her flat chest before leaving the sitting area, "Oh yeah … your big secret. I know it has something to do with the Blue Spark."

Rachel calls after her daughter, already halfway down the darkened hall, "Nope. Way off."

Hannah's sarcastic guffaws echo down the hall, "You are a terrible liar, Mom."

Paddy | Kuala Lumpur

04:53 p.m. | September 11, 2064

The brash, blue-eyed progeny of replicant origin deboards a sleek anti-gravity transport into the humid gloom and walks among the bloodied PTB troopers of his father's battered expeditionary force awaiting evac on the puddled airstrip of an old Chinese-built base.

Established as a paramilitary organization under the PTB's auspices conceived to quash uprisings, level insurrections, and eliminate provocateurs, Paddy surveys the injured men and women.

What a shitshow.

On his first solo overseas mission as the PTB's de Facto leader with his father MIA, Paddy squints through the mist at a caravan of black vehicles idling on the far side of the base. "I'm here. What the fuck are you waiting for?"

Tall and lean with an innate presence that attracts men and women like moths to a flame, Paddy pauses before a wounded soldier. Unbuttoning his charcoal gray jacket, he hunches down to address the grizzled soldier double his 19 years, "Give me the real story before I have to listen to the PM's bullshit account."

The man coughs and spits ruddy phlegm, "It is good to meet you, young Paddy."

Paddy proffers an engaging smile, "Likewise. Tell me your name and story. Spare no details."

The one-eyed mercenary leader considers the brash young man hunched before him with an earnest look on his chiseled face, "Uh, sir, my name is Colonel Vadim Petrov. Our assignment was to secure a perimeter around a smoking hellhole where the Turd once stood so the relief agencies and emergency crews could get through angry mobs of people. While the quake did little damage to the rest of the city, it shook our buildings apart like Tinker Toys. The Malaysians are not stupid. They know who built the damn things. We show up like assholes in PTB choppers and wearing PTB uniforms, aggravating an already tense situation. The locals began attacking us with chunks of cement, rebar, and machetes, whatever they could lay their hands on. We employed crowd-disbursing tactics, but they would not be denied their vengeance. We had to defend ourselves."

The man's attention wanders onto a flock of birds skittering across the concrete, looking for bugs and worms.

Paddy taps the soldier's arm, "Go on, Petrov. I need to know what happened."

"Yeah. It was a slaughter. We mowed the rioters down like animals before retreating to our drop zone to get out of there. They kept coming."

The Russian military man breaks down and sobs, "Big mistake. Big fucking mistake."

Paddy pierces the soldier's addled psyche with his glowing blue eyes, "Get ahold of yourself, man. Tell me what happened next!"

After popping another pill, the Russian steels himself to continue, "An armed militia had our extraction zone surrounded, turning it into a kill box. The people you see here on this tarmac are the only ones who made it out alive."

Knowing the answer, Paddy asks the soldier one last question, "What did the militia do with the ones left behind?"

Stifling more tears, the man grits his teeth, unable to erase an unbearable image from his mind, "They beheaded the captured and carved PTB into their bodies before hanging them from the Turd's mangled girders and beams like fucking Christmas ornaments."

"How many?"

"We started with 206 men and women."

Disgusted and angry, Paddy takes a quick count, muttering, "This will not go unavenged."

The pervasive drizzle turns to rain as Paddy glances toward the aristocratic Malaysian PM in a red business suit and heels clacking across the tarmac with a shit-eating grin as a staffer keeps pace, holding an umbrella over her well-coifed head.

Acknowledging the permanent damage wrought upon the PTB's veneer of invincibility after a routine 7.2 earthquake shook all four 60-story towers, aka the Turd, in the hallowed footprint of the former Petronas Towers to the ground in a fiery heap of ineptitude, Paddy makes a fateful decision: The PTB will no longer provide cover for corrupt governments employing slow-witted architects and engineers cutting corners with cheap labor, third-rate materials, and flawed emergency protocols.

Embracing his burgeoning charismatic leadership, Paddy

addresses his troops with the motivational authority of a seasoned field general. "The losses suffered here served a purpose. No more half-measures. From this day forward, you will exterminate all rebels and agitators with extreme prejudice and overwhelming force."

"On whose authority?"

"Mine."

"What about your father?"

"His guilt for the faulty structures collapsing in on themselves led to this unwinnable travesty. I will deal with him in due course."

Smoothing a hand through his wet, side-parted, jet-black hair, Paddy straightens a thin red tie and buttons his sharkskin jacket, pivoting toward the approaching Malaysian prime minister with a devilish smile and a fiery glint in his eye.

Rachel | Hilltop
02:45 p.m. | January 10, 2065

Hannah finishes combing her wet blond hair and unwraps from a bath towel, letting it drop to the tiled floor revealing bluish bruising below her small and pert left breast reflected in the bathroom vanity mirror.

Observing the one-inch spot lighten upon a delicate fingertip press, she frowns as it reverts to a darker blue.

When did that happen?

Angling a handheld mirror, she discovers similar bruises on the small of her back.

That's weird … probably from bumping into stuff at the cafe … it's tight behind that counter.

Solving the case of the mystery bruises, Hannah moves to her closet to retrieve a preselected outfit with a fresh-faced, mischievous grin.

Mom's old black cocktail dress. Perfect.

Slipping into the short black number while her blond tresses air dry, Hannah pads barefoot to an antique dresser, removes her Grandmother's pearl necklace, and places the heirloom around her neck. Looking sideways into the ornate dresser mirror to latch it closed, she notes another bruise below her right elbow.

Okay, this is getting stranger by the minute.

Stepping into black patent leather heels, Hannah stalls for time, hearing guest arrivals and someone practicing a wedding march on the out-of-tune grand piano downstairs while standing in muted daylight before her bedroom window on a wet and dreary Rhode Island winter day.

Pull yourself together, Hannah. Everything will be fine.

Pivoting toward her massive bookcase jammed tight with volumes handed down over the years, the twenty-year-old extricates the first edition, *Through the Looking Glass*, Stanley Hobbes gave her for Christmas when she was three.

Flipping it open, she removes a photograph of her Mom and Mr. Hobbes from happier times and ventures down the stairs without drawing too many eyes. Looking for liquid courage to get her through the day, Hannah traverses the crowded foyer and comes upon Dave's friend, the butcher, blocking her path.

"Hello, Hannah. I haven't seen you in a long time."

"Uh, yeah, hi, Mr. Abercrombie."

Holding a platter of hors d'oeuvre sausages, the heavyset fellow frowns, "How come you never come downtown and visit anymore? Dave speaks so highly of you. By the way, these are made from duck … care for a bite?"

"Duck? Oh, none for me, thanks."

Excusing herself from the *Butcher of Newport* with a fake smile, Hannah parts the crowd and sidles beside a tall, bearded man in a blue suit, pondering the odd selection of bottles on a help-yourself bar cart.

"Hello, Uncle Joe."

Rachel's forty-one-year-old wayward little brother turns with a smile, "Hi, Hannah. What's it been, like, five years? You look great, by the way. I would say you are the spitting image of your mother in that dress, but something tells me you already know that."

Acknowledging Uncle Joe's pithy observation with a sly nod, Hannah hefts a dark green wine bottle, "Elderberry wine. Preferred by discriminating hobos all over Newport."

Uncle Joe laughs and leans close to Hannah's left ear, "Someone should tell your Mom's squeeze that people go blind from homemade hooch."

Hannah laughs and pours a glass, "Well, it's either the wine or Mr. Dave's bathtub gin."

"Sold. Pour me a glass, too." Joe casts a furtive glance around the spacious foyer at wedding guests filling the spacious main floor, "This takes me back to the old days when Mom and Dad would hold their monthly dinner parties. Your Mom and I were sent upstairs early on those nights. Looking back on it now, I think old Marcus and Miriam were swingers."

Hannah hands Joe a glass before sampling the sweet wine, "You know Mom sees them from time to time. Like ghosts."

Glossing over any comment on his sister's paranormal life, Uncle Joe downs the wine and pours another, "Only one way to get through this day."

Hannah holds out her glass, "Do you think my Mom is making a mistake by marrying Dave?"

Joe wipes his eyes, fighting back tears, "I recognize what you are doing, Hannah."

"What?"

"That is Rachel's little black dress. The one she wore the day she met Owen."

"It is my personal protest. I am surprised you noticed."

"I may be the dumbass little brother who was never around, but I remember when your Mom met Owen Haig. He saved her."

Hannah bites her lip, "How long are you hanging around, Uncle Joe?"

"I'm leaving tomorrow. You should come with me. I am heading west. The open range. God's country."

"What will you do out there?"

"I got a job in Fort Collins teaching English at the internment camp." Sensing Hannah's dismissive reaction, "Don't judge, Hannah. Most of those people locked up are patriots and their kids need teachers."

"Good for you, Uncle Joe. Grandma would be proud you are finally putting your Ivy League education to good use."

"You should come. Your mother can't keep you locked up here forever."

"I can't. She needs me."

"Who needs who?"

Hannah and her Uncle Joe turn in unison onto a beaming Rachel, resplendent in an off-white dress in her flower-adorned wheelchair.

"Mom, you look beautiful."

"Thank you, Hannah. So do you."

Turning her bright green eyes onto her wayward brother, the forty-five-year-old paraplegic laughs, "And look at you, little brother. I am so happy you could make it … no date?"

Uncle Joe grins at his big sister's jibe, "I like to attend these Newport weddings stag." Scanning the crowd, he downs his wine and raises his thick eyebrows, "I plan to hook up with one of these old blue hairs before the night is done."

Rachel turns and seems to notice the SRO gathering for the first time, "I think the half of Newport still alive is crammed into my living room."

Hannah produces the old photograph and holds it before her

Mom's gaze, "I brought one more guest."

Rachel smiles at the image of herself and Stanley, "Aw, that is a sweet gesture. Hannah, be a dear and put it on the mantle with the rest of the family photos."

Hannah clutches the old photo and turns to Uncle Joe, "I will save you a seat." before moving to the great room where the ceremony will take place.

Joe Alexander watches his niece disappear in the crowd before filling another glass.

Rachel taps his sleeve, "I see you are off the wagon. Again."

"What's it to you, Rachel? The world is shit, and it keeps getting worse. I came to say goodbye."

"What?"

Feeling no pain, Joe points at Rachel, "You are making a big mistake keeping Hannah here like a fucking prisoner. I can tell she is miserable. Kind of reminds me of you. What am I saying? She is you."

"Joe, you don't know the whole story. I suggest you cool down and lay off the wine."

"Quit pretending you are like Mom, Rachel. You suck at it."

Desperate to calm her mercurial brother, Rachel pierces his mind, *"Joe. I have been protecting Hannah from the Blue Spark within her since birth. It will destroy her, just like what happened to those other victims. I am afraid, Joe. I don't know what else to do, and I am becoming weaker by the day. As for Owen, he is alive, the last I heard. I am sorry I kept all of this from you."*

Stunned by the revelations, Joe collapses on a stool, "Did Mom know about Owen?"

Rachel nods with more telepathy, *"I told her right before she passed away."*

Joe nods, mulling the new information, "And Dave?"

Rachel nods.

"Holy Mother of God, so this is a charade?"

"No. Of course, I love Dave. I would not marry him if I didn't."

With an irony-laced chuckle, Joe finds the gin bottle on the cart, "This requires something stronger than elderberry wine."

Expressing relief after sharing her burden with her baby brother, Rachel smiles, "Pour me one, too." With a quick punch to his leg, she adds, "Joe, you cannot tell Hannah. The truth will kill her."

Chapter Eight:

The Drone

Hannah | Thundercorp Ranch
02:35 p.m. | February 9, 2070

Hot, sweaty, and lost in her thoughts in a light blue cap and gown under a scorching South Texas afternoon sunshine, Hannah Haig inches forward in an alphabetized queue of Thundercorp graduates as *"Ruprecht Gzdinski, Logistics, and Supply Chain Management!"* booms from the PA to raucous hoots and cheers from the kid's family fan club.

Nearing the tented stage erected on the wide-open tarmac before the massive graduating class framed by stands of wilting family and friends in the shadows of behemoth hangars and the towering space needle, Hannah reflects on the last five years, beginning with Julius Hart dispatching his charming and persuasive star recruiter, Amelia Stawicki, whose inspirational story opened her eyes to human civilization's desperate need for a younger generation willing to participate in their own future. Beyond receptive to change following Mom and Dave's odd wedding and his incessant meddling, Hannah mustered a stoic resolve, seizing the perception-altering opportunity and storming away from the Alexander family Hilltop estate with her mother's pleading entreaties not to leave ringing in her ears. Over the five ensuing years of intense Thundercorp education and training, the icy estrangement with her world-famous mom widened into an irreconcilable family rift.

Glancing at cheering families enduring the heat, Hannah wipes away a tear, wishing her mom could see her now.

Perhaps she just doesn't give a damn.

Succumbing to her unappealing self-pity, Hannah almost misses the next name echoing through the humidity, *"Hannah Haig ... Artificial Intelligence, Advanced Automation Delivery Systems, and Aeronautical Engineering!"*

Hearing her name and impressive list of degrees reverberating across the massive gathering snaps Hannah from her reverie at the foot of the stage. Pausing to take in the moment with a deep breath and exhalation, the tall blond vaults up the steps and strides toward the beaming dean standing at the podium.

Degrees in hand, Hannah waves at the applauding strangers before shaking hands with a line of robed professors, feeling cool air circulating across the tented stage.

Reaching the far end of the air-conditioned platform, Hannah sidles next to the man himself, Julius Hart, for her official Thundercorp graduation photo-op.

Hart places an arm around Hannah and assumes a smiling pose for the zillionth time before the robot photographer, "Well done, Hannah. I assume your Mom is not here."

Juggling the stack of diplomas in her sweaty hands, Hannah sighs, "No. My friends in Newport tell me she is in bad health."

"Oh no. Is there anything I can do?"

Hannah shakes Hart's strong hand and smiles for the last pose, "That would be swell if not for Dave."

"Ah, the husband, none too receptive to my offers to help."

"I appreciate everything you have done for Mom, Mr. Hart."

"Hannah, wait a minute," Hart pauses as the next name booms over the speakers. "Whatever happened to the drone prototype I gave you for Christmas all those years ago?"

"It's somewhere at the bottom of Narragansett Bay."

"Ah, well done."

Takeo Hirohito, Aeronautical Reverse Engineering … echoes overhead as Hannah returns to her row of hot folding chairs. Glancing sideways at a section reserved for friends and family, she double-takes at a bearded man wearing mirrored shades and a Red Sox cap. Squinting through the glare, she searches the sea of faces in vain, hoping for a second glimpse of the familiar face.

"It must be the heat. I am seeing dead people."

Julius Hart | Beaman Studios
09:35 a.m. | March 11, 2070

Julius Hart relaxes in the comfortable guest chair behind a microphone across the table from the host inside Beaman Studios in Los Angeles, California. Willie Beaman, the spitting image of his late father, the legendary podcaster Fred Beaman, winks at his producer and lights a cigar, waiting for the canned intro music to stop before growling into the mike, "Our guest today is Julius Hart, the genius behind Thundercorp, already celebrating a decade of transforming civilization, such as it is. Welcome, Mr. Hart."

Poised and confident, Hart pours a glass of the family bourbon he brought as a gift for the forty-something second-generation podcaster before leaning into the mike, "Good to be here, Willie. You know I sat for many interviews with your father back in the day. It is good to see you are carrying on his legacy."

"Well, thanks for coming in person. I know travel sucks. I guess it helps to have your resources."

"It does not suck to be me if that's what you are getting at."

"Hah-hah, yeah, I bet. I have seen your all-female flight crew, Julius. I gotta ask, those women must be replicants, right?"

"I employ people, Willie. Real human beings. By the way, the robots in my warehouses look like fucking robots. We have eight-legged spider mechs, bipedal janitorial bots, and even little robots that wheel around the corridors like the ones in old Star Wars movies."

"What do those do?"

"Nothing. Just like the ones on the Death Star."

"So, let me get this straight: There is no robot sex in Julius Hart's future."

"I am not a fan of the whole replicant craze. Especially the latest Kobayashi C-Class models. They really creep me out."

Willie rears back in his father's chair with a raucous laugh, "Okay, all you replicants listening out there. You were just served notice by none other than Julius Hart." After a long puff fills the eccentric studio with cigar smoke, Willie's smile vanishes, "Okay. Enough bot talk. I have two things I want to get into with you, and my time is limited. First, the bourbon is fantastic."

"Glad you like it. This batch is part of the last bottling of the old Hart family brand from casks recovered after the invasion."

"What a shame. Okay, second, I am hooked on your fucking Thundercorp smartphones like the rest of the world. We are broadcasting with your device's video and audio and bouncing the signal worldwide using your warehouses in the sky. Way more reliable than the old PTB satellites."

"Is there a question in there somewhere, Willie?"

"Uh, yeah. Explain why you are not a monopoly that needs

a break-up after ten years of ruling the skies with your lightning bolt Thundercorp drones dominating the brave new civilized world of 2070."

Hart sips from his tumbler, considering his answer, "I get this a lot. Why me? Did I have help? Fuck yeah. The Powers That Be, for one. That is, the old PTB. Artemus Pennywell, the former CEO, was a fellow visionary keen on helping me realize my warehouses in the sky. After his death, with the world in tatters, I accessed his alien friends to reverse-engineer my drones to give them their physics-busting edge."

"So, you cheated."

"No. The technology is all open-source stuff. You could do it, Willie."

"Yeah, sure, if I had your smarts."

"No. If you had my imagination."

"Go on. I'm listening."

"You said so yourself. Traveling is a nightmare to this day. But truth be told, the world's infrastructure was crumbling pre-Gork. And now, two-and-one-half decades later, here we are in the Year of our Lord 2070, and things are worse than ever. So, even if a certain industry, like automotive, decided it was time to jumpstart the old assembly lines to pre-invasion levels, the roads are impassable. So, what good would that do?" Hart shrugs, reformulating his point, "Forget something as big as a car. Take the electric toothbrush; how would the average consumer purchase and receive a fucking toothbrush without Thundercorp?"

"Yeah, I remember Amazon tried drone deliveries. The damn things did not work."

"That's right, Willie. Everything works great in the test markets under tight protocols and perfect conditions. But that is not where the real world lives. If they could have figured it out, you would be having this conversation with them—more than likely an AI replicant spokesperson—but you get the picture."

Willie pours another glass, "Yeah, a lot drier and less entertaining."

Hart laughs, "No doubt."

Lubricated by the strong bourbon, Willie Beaman's wheels begin to turn, breaking into a sly-faced grin, "I get it. I get it. Thundercorp awakened the moribund industrial world with an electrified jolt. Hence, your iconic lightning bolt logo."

Hart chuckles, "Not exactly, but I like the visual. It makes sense."

"You are damn right it does, motherfucker! The progress is out there! Did you know they are dredging the Port of Los Angeles so the big ships can come in for the first time in decades?"

"No. I did not know that. That is an excellent indication that the top-down authoritarianism infecting human society since the Gorks has run out of gas. The dam was going to break at some point. I'd rather it be through Thundercorp and a groundswell of entrepreneurial energy than more turf wars, civil strife, looting, and murderous mayhem."

Willie takes another long puff and raises his glass with a boisterous guffaw that would make his father proud, "Let's hear it for the bug-eyed, smart-device-addicted consumer and their insatiable desire for the latest—whatever—at any cost—dropped in their fat laps with pinpoint accuracy by whistling drones in mind-boggling short amounts of time."

Hart smiles, "I could not have said it better myself. The new mass consumerism is the lifeblood of the world's economies. I call it Capitalism 2.0."

Willie checks with his producer, tapping a make-believe watch before zeroing in on one more topic, "What about the spoiled-rotten whiners screaming bloody murder when delivery of a useless bauble exceeds an hour?"

"You mean the one-percenters?"

Willie laughs, "Yeah. Okay. I get it."

"This may blow your mind, Willie, but Thundercorp delivers necessities to stricken parts of the world. Food, water, medicines, and even human and replicant assets administering to massive populations subsisting in a stone-age hell over the last quarter century."

Willie starts to speak, but Julius cuts him off, "Ten years after the first highly publicized drone deliveries screamed down from the sky, Thundercorp has made thousands of millionaires and lifted millions out of squalid conditions. Aside from manufacturing delays beyond our control or the occasional wayward drone, we are doing the Lord's work. If some ass with a stopwatch catches his package three seconds past an hour, he can apply for a full fucking refund, but remember, he is stealing from some bloke on the opposite side of the world."

"So, they can suck it."

"Precisely."

"And the women on your private plane are all human?"

"Yes, Willie. With their beauty only exceeded by their supreme intellects and talents. I don't like replicants. As a matter of fact. We should ban them so people can finally get off their lazy behinds and begin functioning like previous generations used to do."

Paddy | PTB HQ, Scotland

05:35 p.m. | March 11, 2070

"Yes, Willie. I don't like replicants. As a matter of fact. We should ban them so people can finally get off their lazy behinds and begin functioning like previous generations used to do."

Uninterested in hearing more driveling banter from the Willie Beaman live podcast coming through loud and clear from halfway around the world, Paddy switches off the Thundercorp smartphone in his strong hand before hurling it at a wall, shattering it to pieces.

"My father made a big mistake not taking him down when he had the chance."

Pivoting to a conference table, elbow-to-elbow with squirming and fidgeting advisers, Paddy's handsome face contorts into a dark scowl, "How soon until we are ready?"

His new one-eyed mercenary general, Vadim Petrov, charged with rebuilding an advanced quick strike force starting with the survivors of the Kuala Lumpur debacle, stands out of his seat at attention, "Sir. The launch date is in three weeks."

Paddy yawns and waves him off, "Sit down, Petrov. I loathe the military shit. I just want those motherfucking Thundercorps blown from the skies."

Another man makes his presence known with a throat-clearing cough before swiping open a schematic Thundercorp hologram and zooming in on a red glowing core, "We will launch coordinated surprise attacks on all five warehouses, blasting our way to the power cores where each strike team will initiate the self-destruct meltdowns, blowing them into trillions of pieces."

A woman speed reads through a series of screens before chiming into the planning session, "Our spies confirm the primary function of each Thundercorp defense is blasting wayward space junk and warding off the occasional curious alien craft from venturing too close."

Paddy clasps his hands with an evil grin, "So, Julius Hart left the Thundercorps defenseless from an Earth-based attack. A very foolish oversight."

Number 8 beams with pride at her beautiful son, "The Overlords will be pleased."

Hannah | Thundercorp No. 5
05:35 a.m. | April 1, 2070 – 1 month later

Resembling a luminous pea-sized sphere much smaller than the Moon to the naked eye above the Mediterranean and North Africa, Thundercorp No. 5 maintains a 360-mile-high geostationary orbit like its sister warehouses around the globe, abuzz with hypersonic delivery drones coming and going, dodging a succession of anti-gravity cargo ships waiting to offload.

Joining Thundercorp No. 5's complement of 4,000-plus talented humans on her first six-month drone specialist rotation, Hannah Haig kissed Earth goodbye, her close-shorn blond noggin brimming with five years of training and education.

Discovering her co-ed dorm assignment too rife with cliquey shenanigans, sexcapades, and towel-snapping silliness, the natural-born loner finagled a cot and set up living quarters in her one-woman drone workshop ancillary to Hangar Bay Guinevere's cavernous four-story maw on the thin outer shell of Thundercorp No. 5. Tuning out Guinevere's cacophonous din opposite the closed portal to her little domain, she settles into a work-sleep-eat routine in the chilly life support and temperamental artificial gravity, performing surgical repairs on the hypersonic drones. Preferring the company of the scorched, dented, and pitted physics-busting wonders, she keeps nosy coworkers at arm's length except for Alan Adamo, a veteran drone mechanic whose obvious crush she finds charming, and Maddie LeBoeuf, a winsome communications engineer whose affections prove irresistible.

* * *

Angling off the creaky cot, Hannah untwists her thermals, snugs a soft wool blanket around a snoozing Maddie, and pads barefoot across her frigid space to a messy workbench. Trying not to awaken her guest, she switches on a light and pulls up her top, revealing bluish splotches on her chest and abdomen in a telescoping mirror.

"Hey, Sweetie, you should have those blue bruises looked at."

Hannah pivots onto Maddie's half-lit nakedness, casting shadows against the bulkhead, "Oh, I always get these. The thing is, I can't tell if it is bruises or the skin turning blue."

"Could it be from your Mom's Blue Spark?"

"My Mother, the world-famous Rachel Alexander Haig, has told me a thousand and one times that I am a dud. The Blue Spark did not pass down to my genes."

Swinging her legs off the cot, Maddie tiptoes across the cold decking and caresses Hannah's cheek, "You are anything but a dud, Hannah Haig." pressing into her with a passionate kiss. Coming up for air with a devilish grin, her hands wander to Hannah's waistband, pulling skin-tight bottoms down smooth thighs past quaking knees. "Don't listen to her. The woman has lost it. Everybody says so."

Her head a swirling mass of contradictions, a breathless Hannah surrenders to the moment, propping back on her elbows atop the messy workbench under the voyeuristic presence of a half dozen drones in various states of repair as Maddie's frank and nimble tongue works overtime on her swooning psyche. Nearing a euphoric climax, a clear-eyed revelation breaks Hannah's spellbound ecstasy like a bucket of ice water, "Wait just a fucking second, Maddie, you are telling me every Thundercorp employee, including you, thinks my Mother—who twice saved the world—is ready for the nuthouse?"

Maddie gazes up from Hannah's spread legs, her soulful blue eyes aglow in faint light permeating the locked workshop, proffering an innocent-faced shrug, "April Fools?"

Hannah pulls up her pants and shoots the dark-haired siren a quizzical look, "Today is April first? I have already been up here for two months."

With the romantic moment fizzled into the thin recycled air, the lithesome comms expert stands with a sigh and licks Hannah's cheek before slipping into her light-gray jumpsuit and heading for the exit, "You need to get Mommy out of your head, Hannah. We can talk more later. I gotta go—it's a spacewalk Tuesday. Those antennae arrays won't repair themselves, and I can't be late, or the old man will chew out my ass." Maddie sticks out her tongue with a flirtatious wink, "And we both know that is your specialty."

Hannah watches her sexy friend slink through the opened portal before pulling on boots and a jacket, grabbing her kit, and stepping into Hangar Bay Guinevere on a beeline toward inner airlocks leading to the dormitories and shower facilities.

Almost home-free, without enduring the usual banter and small talk from peers working 12-hour shifts in the bustling hangar bay, a familiar voice breaks through the racket.

"Hey, Hannah Haig! Are you up for breakfast?"

Searching the ordered chaos inside the hangar bay, Hannah's weary gaze latches onto Alan Adamo, radiating a hopeful grin on his grease-smudged mug amidst wiry bundles dangling inside a drone's human-sized cargo hold.

"Sure. Give me half an hour. I'll meet you in the cantina after my shower."

"Need any help with that?"

"Nope. I'm good."

* * *

Washing down an egg scramble wrapped in a limp tortilla with a weak powdered orange drink, Hannah leans back in a plasticky fast food-style chair, feigning mock satisfaction with the robot cooking, "Ahh! Now I know how the astronauts maintained their trim figures."

Alan finishes his pancakes, checking the temperature of his boiling cup of joe, "Ow, man, that is too fucking hot. Enough about the astronauts, you are obsessed with the damn astronauts." Attempting his first sip from the steaming cup, Alan taps a finger on the tabletop to regain his tired friend's wandering attention, "Hannah … what's up with you and Maddie …."

With zero desire to entertain Alan's prurient curiosity, Hannah cuts him off, "What happens in *my* workshop, on *my* personal time, stays there. Besides, Alan, if you must know, Maddie and I are just friends."

Alan rolls his eyes toward fluorescent ceiling tiles, casting the cafeteria in an unappetizing greenish hue, "Yeah, sure, says the girl sleeping with the hottest woman on Thundercorp No. 5."

"You mean Maddie? I had not noticed." Tapping her chin with a far-off gaze, she breaks into a mischievous smile, "Wait just a minute … she is attractive—if you are into model-perfect bone structure, lustrous black hair, perky tits, and long legs."

Leaning across the table in the crowded employee eatery, Alan motions for Hannah to come closer, "Now you listen to me, Hannah Haig. I am trying to be serious. Nobody up here understands how a rookie like yourself lands your own private workshop—and Maddie fricking LeBoeuf. Word is that you are getting special treatment."

"Oh, I see. So that is why I get the cold shoulder treatment? I'm an only child. The dorm life scared the shit out of me, so I asked if my workshop could double as my quarters, and the supervisor said okay. As for Maddie, we really are just friends. I have never experienced anything like her, and if you really want to know the truth, I have no idea what the hell I am doing most of the time." Raising a titillating eyebrow, Hannah adds, "I like to let her lead."

Alan Adamo suppresses his wandering imagination, glancing around before continuing, "Look, I am one of the few original Thundercorp crew still up here after ten years. I know everybody and everything that goes down in this fucking warehouse. Did you know your dark-haired squeeze reports to Mr. Hart? Rumor has it they are close if you get my drift. And since his connection with your Mom is common knowledge… well … people talk."

"My Mom disowned me the day I left Hilltop. Like dear old Dad, I can never go back."

"I thought your Dad died years ago. It was in all of the media. They erected statues. It was a big deal."

Hannah shakes her head and yawns, "I don't think so. I can feel it in my bones. My Father, Owen Haig, is alive." Wiping her cold, runny nose, Hannah shakes a finger at her friend, "As for Maddie, I know she works in communications and intelligence. Case closed. Who she talks to down at the Ranch is her business … I never asked for special treatment. In fact, I spent five years working my ass off before coming up here."

"As a friend, I wanted you to know where you stood. That's all."

"How come you can stand being around me, Alan? Aren't you jealous of my obvious privilege?"

"No. You have been through a lot in your life. I respect that."

Hannah stares daggers at a catty group, whispering and looking her way, "Who knew it would be so high school working up here?" Hannah flips the bird at them with a chuckle before turning back to an embarrassed Adamo, slinking down in his seat, "Don't be such a wuss, Alan. The world sucks. Everyone has problems. I am far from special."

Noticing Alan's eyes narrow at something on her face between sips of coffee, Hannah grabs his hand, eliciting a static electric shock, "What? Do I have something in my teeth?"

"Ow! What the Hell?" Pulling back a stinging hand, his dark brow furrows, "I could swear your face turned blue for a split second."

Pushing back from the table, Hannah wards off a dizzying self-awareness in the noisy cantina and rises from her seat on jelly legs, "Thanks for breakfast, Adamo. I better get to work. My babies are waiting back at the shop."

Alan watches her go before grabbing the half-eaten burrito off her plate and shoving it into his mouth.

* * *

Self-conscious and sleep-deprived, thanks to Maddie, Hannah returns to her workshop, settles into an oversized leather office chair pilfered from a recent shipment, and pulls up holographic schematics with a bored yawn.

Twirling the illuminated complexities of a physics-busting baby awaiting her specialized expertise, the projection blurs before her watery eyes. Checking a clock, she swipes the hologram off, "What the Hell, I still have a half hour before my shift starts."

Checking her pale complexion in the mirror, she swallows another pill, snuggles into the chair, and falls asleep like an angel in the chilly recycled air to Guinevere's soothing white noise beyond the sealed door.

Hours later, hunched low with her bottom slipping halfway off the seat cushion and long legs splayed atop the messy workbench inside her darkened inner sanctum, Hannah clasps her hands beneath her chin, dreaming of Dad and a fiery comet's tail from a Fourth of July sparkler clenched in the waving grip of a happy-go-lucky three-year-old version of herself.

Gazing into her father's expressive face, dread washes over her as his winning smile fades into the ether a heartbeat before a violent detonation rattles Hannah from her dream. Coughing in the smoke-filled air, she curls tight and covers her head as shockwaves rip through the thin bulkhead, extinguishing lights replaced by nightmarish strobing life-support sirens wailing like wounded animals.

Pelted by debris, drone parts, and personal effects, Hannah reaches for her emergency kit, pulling a portable oxygen mask over her head. Feeling it seal to her neck and shoulders, she hears curses, shouts, and staccato gunfire from the opposite side of the hatch, followed by a volley of high-caliber slugs ripping through the wall. Diving for cover under the workbench, more rounds pepper the bulkhead behind her upturned cot.

Sucking filtered air through the ill-fitting mask, the angry voices fade as a sickening hiss draws her frightened stare onto venting plumes from split ductwork crisscrossing the ceiling in her destroyed workshop. "I gotta get out of here!"

Tripping past overturned drone parts and tools in the hazy, low gravity, she snatches her prized photograph from a toppled heap, jamming it into her pocket as more tremorous shudders reverberate through the stricken warehouse.

Stepping into cumbersome gravity boots and zipping an olive-green Thundercorp jacket over her orange jumpsuit, Hannah peers through the Swiss cheese door, ensuring the coast is clear before smashing her fist into the frozen door opener with the heel of her hand. "Ow! Fuck it all! Where are my dumbass gloves?"

Pushing out the bent doorway and staggering into the charnel house that was the four-story Hangar Bay Guinevere, Hannah casts a panic-stricken over-the-shoulder glance at outer space beyond a truck-sized hole in the four-story hangar bay door, already mended by Thundercorp No. 5's self-repairing translucent nanotech skin designed to patch tears from tennis ball-sized meteors and the odd chunk of space debris that gets past the lasers.

Holy shit. Holy shit! What is happening …

Spying a lit airlock through her smeared face mask, Hannah chunks across the mesh deck plates in the heavy boots on a diagonal path through the death and destruction. Her calves aching, only halfway across the hellscape of scorched and headless corpses hanging in the low gravity like three-day-old helium balloons amidst blazing hulks of drones spewing thick plumes of smoke, she glimpses the disassembled automaton Alan was working on earlier and diverts toward the delivery craft with a solemn dread. Rapping a fist on the frozen metallic fuselage above an iconic lightning bolt decal, she approaches the closed cargo hatch, "Alan? Are you in there?" On impulse, she grits her teeth and yanks it open, recoiling from escaping gory globules, revealing her friend's rictal death pose tangled in wires with half his head shot clean off.

Slamming the portal shut, she ducks under a viscous red glob floating before her mask, "Godspeed, Alan."

Tearing from a witch's brew of poisonous fumes blending with a foul stench of death under her leaking mask, Hannah struggles to the airlock as her oxygen runs out. Suffocating, she shoves a dead man sideways to reach the security console and enter her twelve-digit PIN, sucking the plastic mask against her nose. Watching the door whoosh open, she tumbles over the threshold and smashes it closed before ripping off the spent oxygen mask, gasping for air.

That was too close.

Crawling through the airlock, she pulls off the cumbersome boots, sprinting barefoot over another dead man along the narrow, smoky passage, descending at a shallow angle toward inner concourses lined with dorms, eateries, conference facilities, gyms, offices, showers, infirmaries, barber shops, communications, data centers, and IT clean rooms comprising the lower portions of Thundercorp No. 5's northern hemisphere. Sensing firmer footfalls on the grated decking, she notes the warehouse's artificial gravity growing stronger.

Sneaking her way toward the expansive mall levels encircling Thundercorp No. 5, she stubs her toe on an inert little bot parked in the middle of the corridor. Cursing a blue streak under her breath, she leans her back against the wall and pulls up her foot, massaging the bruised and bloodied digit between numb fingers. Shaking her head at the cute little four-wheeled bot, she runs a hand through her short blond hair, feeling a bloody gash for the first time. "Well, this is just great, bleeding head and busted toe."

Pulling her pills from a pocket, she swallows back two more and peers around the nearest corner, coming face to face with a framed Soviet-style Thundercorp recruitment poster. Hannah can't help but laugh, reading the bold Cyrillic headline on a graphic diagonal below a diverse group of chiseled profiles gazing heavenward.

"You, too, can live the dream! Work in space! Alter perception! Join Thundercorp today!"

Inhaling short, labored breaths of thin air, Hannah takes stock of her situation.

Okay, I know where I am. This is the main equatorial concourse.

The transport bays are only a few hundred stories up from here. Now, which way to the nearest fucking elevator?

The grated decking shakes and shudders beneath her boots as muffled hammer blows resonate from the floors above as Hannah watches a poor soul pitch over a railing and drop five levels into a planter with a gruesome splat.

Hannah hunkers behind a wall as sporadic gunfire and approaching footsteps precede a group of space-suited Thundercorp technicians running past her position. Rubbing soot from her stinging eyes, she spies Maddie. Timing her reach, she grabs her girlfriend's arm and pulls her into a tear-filled embrace, "Maddie! You are alive!"

One of the men in Maddie's spacewalking party stops and waits before waving a hand in disgust, sprinting to rejoin his comrades.

Pushing back with a look of sheer incredulity distorting her model-perfect face, Maddie scolds her naive friend, "Haven't you heard, Hannah? We're under attack by a bunch of whacked-out space terrorists! We saw them come up fast and blast their way aboard through the Northern hangars. The other Thundercorp warehouses are already blown to bits! You really need to stop taking those pills. You sleep through everything! Luckily, you found me. Now let's get moving."

Hannah pulls back, "Where? In case you didn't notice, I lost my fucking space suit."

Maddie laughs, "No silly girl. We are heading to evacuation shuttles on Transport Deck Merlin before they blow this ball to smithereens like the others!" Noting Hannah's shell-shocked stare, Maddie grabs her by the hand, "Come on, lover. I got you."

Hannah lets the tall brunette lead her by the hand like a little girl to a crowd of employees cramming into a bank of functioning elevators like sardines. Elbowing into a glass-enclosed lift brimming with frightened people, Maddie loses Hannah's grip, wedging inside with an outstretched hand, "Come on, Hannah. You can fit right here next to me!"

Unwilling to squeeze inside the over-crowded lift, Hannah shakes her head with a claustrophobic shudder, stepping backward as the elevator doors seal shut.

"I love you, Maddie."

Standing ramrod still as the left behind scamper in search of other elevators, Hannah curses hang-ups and phobias that plagued her whole life. Locking eyes with Maddie through the thick glass, Hannah reads her lips a heartbeat before an explosion fills the overpacked elevator with a smoky green billowing of poisonous gas. In a nanosecond, a barefoot Hannah transforms from a self-loathing introvert to an unrealistic superhero—emulating her Mom—attempting to pry the doors apart with her fingers as the anguished cries from inside ebb to silence and the huddled forms slump together in a motionless heap of 22 human beings and one replicant suicide bomber.

Jack-booted, clomping footsteps shake Hannah from the horrified shock of dear, sweet, and sexy Maddie's demise. Catching her first sight of a black-armored and masked soldier emerging from a pall of smoke lingering in the air, shouting orders at his troopers, Hannah takes off at a dead run down the deserted hall, ignoring commands to stop.

Vaulting over a jumble of crates blocking the half-opened freight elevator, she kicks and screams at the upturned boxes, freeing the jammed door and pounding the close button as a grenade clatters inside. On reflex, Hannah scoops and tosses it back out before it explodes.

With no time to revel in her successful escape, Hannah doubles over, coughing up sickening goop as the light strobes and the floor drops from under her bare feet. Plummeting hundreds of stories with the ear-piercing screeches of the elevator careening down the bent shaft for almost a mile before screeching brakes slow it to a bone-jarring, merciful stop.

Regaining her footing in the dark frigidness, the lights return, illuminating a bold red warning stenciled inside the closed elevator doors

WARNING: ENVIRO-SUIT REQUIRED
BEYOND THIS POINT!

Skipping her rookie orientation that included a guided tour of the gigantic warehouse comprising the two-mile diameter sphere's southern hemisphere, Hannah recalls her logistics instructor's sage words.

Only a suicidal fool would venture into the unwelcoming expanse without an enviro-suit.

"Yep, just like the sign says. But it sure beats getting shot, gassed, or shoved out an airlock."

Jamming frozen hands into her jacket pockets, Hannah kicks the door open button and enters the below-freezing atmosphere, hitting her like a sledgehammer, wishing she had the damn boots back.

Awestruck by the gargantuan scale shrinking her frail form to antlike proportions, her telltale breaths waft into the stillness. Swallowing back inherited acrophobia, Hannah steps from the elevator onto a two-foot wide bridge spanning an echoing chasm. Glancing into the inky depths below her numb feet, she wards off disastrous dizziness, hurrying the last few meters to an elevated six-way intersection.

Straining to see down each winding and inhospitable path, Hannah shivers in the unbearable coldness.

I am truly fucked. This was a mistake.

Frittering any sense of direction from the moment she stepped off the elevator, a metallic clack-clacking of sportscar-sized spider mechs skittering up precipitous shelving catches her eye. Watching the eight-legged robots removing merchandise from crates with stunning articulation, she takes deliberate footsteps along a snaking maintenance track. An abrupt whoosh of boxy silver drones on conveyor rails like a roller coaster whizzes mere inches overhead, causing her to duck. Her heart racing from the near miss, she watches them twisting off in multiple directions.

That almost ended things real quick.

Likening the interconnected alien environment to the complexities of a human brain, Hannah bumps into a membranous dead end. Her vision adjusting to the semi-darkness, she distinguishes a pattern of circular holes in the translucent obstruction. Adding a fucking torch to the list of things to have handy when everything turns to shit, the stubborn tech tests the weight-bearing properties of the holes in the wobbly vertical surface with an exhausted sigh before pulling herself upward.

It's nothing more than a scary see-through rock wall. No big deal. I climbed higher than this in gym class.

Ascending fifty feet in the low gravity, Hannah collapses atop more freezing cold metal decking. Resting and catching her breath, she stares high up beyond the disorienting conveyors, drones, and spider mechs twisting over, around, and between sentinel-like shelves, noting light shafts illuminating a massive swath of wall curving on an elegant arc high overhead.

The skin. Thundercorp's outer fucking skin. If I can reach an airlock ... climb inside a drone's package compartment ... I just might get out of this alive ...

Compartmentalizing her plan's minimal chance of success, Hannah rises and jogs down a narrow alley, pausing at the far end to recon before bumbling out into the open. With halted breaths and her lungs burning from the bitter cold, she peers up and down a wide-open boulevard lined with massive shelves and laments out loud, "Jesus, it never ends!"

Beyond wishing she had an enviro-suit and helmet in the wafer-thin atmosphere, Hannah hunkers to the opposite side, noting Aisle 64A as she sneaks past its barcode-studded shelves crammed with every conceivable gadget, device, appliance, garment, and toy, the titans of industry on Earth can design, market-test, manufacture, and dangle before craven, brain-washed masses. Confident she is heading toward the outer shell; she spot-checks stamped corporate marks in search of anything resembling a footwear manufacturer to help her frozen feet.

Midway down the cavernous aisle, she spies palettes of shrunk-wrapped boxes stamped with L.L.Bean logos. Taking a chance, she topples a heavy carton, digging stinging hands under a glued lid enough to pry it open. Groping inside, hoping L.L.Bean does not sell mousetraps, she manages a smile, closing her fingers around soft, knitted fabric, "Aha, what have we here?"

Yanking a thick wool sock combo pack out of the ripped box, she holds her treasure to the pale blue light, "Socks. Fuck yeah. That will work."

Collapsing onto the deck, she bites the packaging apart, freeing pairs covered in blue butterfly patterns.

Sliding the soft wool over her feet and ankles, halfway up her calves, she pushes down her jumpsuit pant legs and leans back with a satisfied smile, wriggling her toes to restart the circulation. "Cute and functional. Thank you, L.L.Bean."

Pressing to the end of 64A and about to stumble across another wide lane to 64B in her new socks, the unmistakable sound of voices punctuated by crackling shortwave radios ends Hannah's short-lived morale boost with a petrified gasp.

Shrinking into hard shadows cutting across the grooved decking, she crouches under a metal shelf lined with *Eddie: The Friendly Robot* boxes. Frowning at the ridiculous goofballs staring at her hunched form from clear plastic windows.

People buy these things? Aren't there enough robots on Earth already?

Venturing another peek at a quartet of menacing figures smoking and laughing in the dimness behind two back-turned kneeling men, she hears the leader bark a command in Russian, prompting his cohorts to execute the pair with single shots to the back of their heads.

Oh no. My God. Shit. Shit. And more shit. What are those bastards doing down here?

Enraged by the cold-blooded murders of two helpless Thundercorp employees, Hannah sees the terrorists scurry like rats amid the labyrinthine miles of aisles, searching for more employees to butcher in cold blood.

Of course, there would be more than just me down here.

With the coast clear, for the moment, Hannah dashes behind a line of drones and comes face-to-face with the glowing robot eyes of a spider mech performing business as usual. Emitting a loud squawk, the eight-legged bot draws the attention of a murderous thug emerging from the shadows, clomping across the deck toward her position with the red light on his laser-guided weapon swinging upward in his gloved left hand.

Pressing against a lightning bolt decal on the far side of a pitted drone, the Russian's voice resonates across the expanse. "Show yourself! There is nowhere to run and nowhere to hide."

Reckoning the twenty feet of open space between her exposed position and the relative darkness of Aisle 64B, Hannah makes a sock-footed sprint toward the defiladed shadows in full view of the laughing terrorist as shots careen off a shelf inches above her head.

Cursing a blue streak down the football field-length corridor with tears streaming across her ruddy frozen cheeks, Hannah realizes the Russian will have a clear shot before she can reach the far end as she trips on her loose socks in a rolling heap on the hard metal decking. Staring into the mile-high canyon of shelves, she waits for the end.

What was I thinking? Even if I could get up there, I would die without an enviro-suit.

Contemplating her unrealistic plan and imminent capture, a shoebox-sized maintenance drone whirs overhead on a collision course with her attacker. Pulling onto her aching knees, Hannah hears deep-throated screams and curses preceding the unmistakable stench of burning flesh.

Processing the last-second reprieve, Hannah watches the heroic little drone's return, hovering before her stunned stare with the white-hot tip of its laser drill still smoking.

An assertive male voice blurts from the compact, rounded fuselage, *"Hannah Haig! I need your help! You represent the last chance to save Thundercorp's legacy! We don't have much time! Follow me!"*

Hannah's mind races, watching the little airborne automaton wobble and turn into the shadows without waiting for her to reply, "Julius Hart? Is that you? I don't know what they told you, but I am nothing like my parents. The *Let's Save the World* gene skips a generation."

Pausing midair, the hi-def camera lens swivels back onto Hannah Haig's obstinate cross-armed pose, *"Well, I suppose you can stay here and most assuredly die."*

Stunned by Hart's blunt assessment of her chance for survival, an indecipherable yell pivots her toward the terrorist, staggering into view with his disgusting face burned like a marshmallow. Raising the large-caliber weapon, he eyeballs Hannah before firing three errant rounds. "Hannah Haig! Come on out of there. My superior would like to talk with you."

"Oh yeah? Who the fuck would that be, Satan himself?"

"The Powers That Be want you alive, Miss Haig. One way or another, you are coming with me."

Recognizing the crude, one-eyed Russian's plan to stall for time until his knuckle-dragging comrades can arrive, Hannah turns on a dead run toward the waiting drone as the evil man empties his magazine, ricocheting hot lead off merch-laden shelves in a fit of rage.

Hovering at the far end of 64B, the maintenance drone waits for the terrorized young woman to gather her wits and catch her breath.

"Amazing what a half-crazed, pot-shot-taking terrorist can do for the stamina."

"You can go fuck yourself, Mr. Hart."

The nimble drone spins 360 degrees, ensuring they are alone,

"Please call me Julius, Ms. Haig."

"Okay. Julius. Call me Hannah. In for a penny, in for a pound, I guess. How can I help you stop those assholes from blowing up No. 5?"

"That is no longer an option. The terrorists will use No. 5's self-destruct to blow it from the skies, like the others. The fail-safes were a compromise I made with The Powers That Be when first building my masterpieces. And now, their new leadership uses the core meltdown mechanisms to destroy everything I have built for humanity. However, the joke is on them; No. 5's self-destruct is offline. It's been that way from the start."

Hannah lets out a sigh of relief. "Well then, that is lucky for me, right, Julius?"

"Wrong, Hannah. They are no doubt already knee-deep in the process of rebooting the self-destruct protocols. The blast will deliver Thundercorp No. 5 back to Earth in a trillion burning pieces, just like the others, taking us along with it …."

"What do you mean, us? You are not talking to me from Thundercorp Ranch?"

"As fate would have it, I was up here consummating a deal when all hell broke loose. However, I can use this handy little drone to lead you to my position. From there, we can put our heads together and formulate a plan of action. Please accept my apologies. I'm a little tied up, or I would come to you."

Keeping pace through No. 5's gargantuan warehouse, Hannah rounds a corner in time to see the nimble drone shoot straight up access stairs, bisecting the echoing labyrinth and disappearing high above. "Oh, c'mon, how much further?" Hitting the spiraling metal steps, she winds countless levels to a maintenance dock where Hart's drone waits.

"Excellent, Hannah. Your Mother would be proud."

Bent at the waist, struggling to catch her breath, Hannah shoots the little flying robot a puzzled look, "Why? I have not accomplished anything except following your drone like a dog."

Ignoring her modesty, the drone beams a narrow light onto a

row of lockers along a bulkhead, *"There may be an enviro-suit inside one of these lockers, which would improve your situation."*

Sweaty yet chilled, Hannah unlatches the first locker, "Empty."

Repeating the process with the same result, Hannah wipes beads of sweat from her brow and opens the last door, "Hey! What do you know? An enviro-suit."

"See? I told you."

Stripping to her underwear and socked feet in the frigid darkness, Hannah slides her aching body into the form-fitting intelligent mesh suit, reading MARTIN below the lightning bolt insignia on the left breast, "Thanks, Martin, wherever you are." Donning the boots, gloves, and wraparound helmet, she smiles toward the waiting drone, "Much better. I was freezing. What now?"

"I am inside the small control room to your left."

Reinvigorated by the enviro-suit's warming caress, Hannah jumps through the low gravity to another wall-mounted security console and taps a gloved fingertip to activate the screen, "Julius, the screen is blank."

"The systems are down. It won't be long now. We need to hurry. Step back."

The drone wobbles forward and lasers a hole in the door wide enough for Hannah to duck through. Within the cramped interior, she finds the wealthiest man in human history duct-taped to a chair with a bomb strapped to his chest rigged for an ignominious detonation.

"Hannah Haig! In the flesh. I have not seen you since your graduation."

"Julius, what …."

"Now, Hannah. My time is short, as the rather rudimentary countdown clock taped to my chest indicates. We do not have time to worry about freeing me from this predicament. I know that. I accept my fate."

Hannah moves before her boss, not hearing a word, "How are

we going to get you out of this mess? There are so many wires. I can't tell what would deactivate the countdown or set it off. I could figure this out if I had access to my tools. I can try to …."

Julius cuts her off, "Hannah!"

Hannah cries into her space helmet, "Julius, everyone is dead. Alan. Maddie … if I could save just one person …."

"Ah, the beguiling mystery that was Maddie LeBoeuf. I will miss them all, but she was special to me."

Hannah coughs and laughs despite herself, "So I heard."

Hart's brow raises, "The bottom of Narragansett Bay, you say."

Hannah's mind clicks forward, two steps behind the brilliant aeronautics pioneer, "Sorry? Oh yeah, but not before I took it apart and put it back together countless times."

Hart proffers a brave smile through tears welling in his eyes, "Has anyone ever said you look just like your Mother?"

Hannah nods, crinkling her itchy nose inside the helmet.

"She loves you, Hannah. Don't give up on her."

"From what I have been told, the world thinks she is a crackpot recluse."

"Things are not always as they appear."

Julius Hart observes Hannah Haig's face turn blue before reverting to a luminous pallor inside the helmet. "Now, down to business … a memory chip inside my right forearm contains intelligence critical to rebuilding my satellite warehouses. Only with this data can Thundercorp rise from the ashes. I need you to get it off this marble, or it will be lost forever."

"What could possibly be stored in a small chip in your arm that is not replicated on a thousand servers down on the Ranch?"

"Does the name Richard King mean anything to you?"

"No. Oh, wait … curly hair and a big laugh. Mom loved him. He brought the drone to Hilltop that Christmas morning. We never saw him again."

"Hannah, The Powers That Be stole his life's work before casting him into the desert. His idea was to secrete the final phase of Thundercorp from the PTB. I once told a podcaster that Thundercorp's technologies are open source. Anybody could do it. I lied. The hyper-critical components, including the alien mechanics of the physics-busting drones, exist only here and one other place." Julius motions at his bound right forearm with a rakish wink and smile.

"How do we remove it from your arm?"

"I apologize, Hannah, but you may wish to avert your eyes while I utilize the drone's laser to extricate the chip."

Hannah backs against a wall as the drone hovers over Hart's right arm on command. Before initiating the gruesome procedure, he turns to Hannah, "By the way, that other place I mentioned is the drone at the bottom of Narragansett Bay."

"I kind of gathered it possessed a significance beyond an elaborate gift for a three-year-old girl's Christmas."

"Another one of Richard's ideas. Quite a brilliant thinker."

"Except I crashed it into the bay."

"How fitting and ironic. Richard would get a good laugh from that. By the way, I am using a neural transmitter he designed to telekinetically guide our little drone."

Hannah bites her lip with tears streaming down her face, "Julius, are you sure … " watching Hart hover the drone over his arm and activate the laser.

* * *

Her eyes welling with tears, Hannah tucks the bloody chip into a zipped sleeve pocket and leaves Julius Hart to his imminent fate.

Alone on the elevated maintenance dock, Hannah looks through her fogging helmet at a spider mech crawling from the darkness as Hart's voice resonates inside her helmet, *"Hannah, my dear, we need to move fast. This mech will carry you to an airlock under my telekinetic guidance.*"

Peering into the dizzying heights, Hannah's chapped lips curl into a smile: "Great minds think alike."

Mounting the eight-legged robot like a jockey, Hannah scooches into a shallow ribbed depression on its curved metal back, grasping her gloved hands into deep metal grooves while pressing her legs and boots into the smooth sides, "Julius, … I'm gonna fall off."

Without warning, the spider mech's legs unfold, raising Hannah ten feet off the deck.

"Hold on tight. Here we go!"

Hannah emits a terrified yelp, like riding a bucking bronco, as the spider mech skitters to the edge of the dock and gathers itself before vaulting twenty feet through midair, snagging clawed feet onto precipitous shelf ledges rising to gut-churning skyscraper heights high above her terrified eyes. "Oh shit. I'm gonna fall. I'm gonna fall."

"Hold on, Hannah. Your angels are watching."

Hanging from the near-vertical climbing machine, Hannah repositions thick-gloved fingers in the precious handholds, flailing her boots across the spider mech's ribbed abdomen for a weight-supporting purchase, yelling into her comm, "Angels?"

"You are unique, Hannah Haig."

Thick, bar-coded, gun-metal gray shelves jammed to the edges with crates, cartons, and boxes pass her helmeted gape in jostling ten-meter incremental blurs, lifting Hannah higher and higher. Catching on to the agile spider mech's rhythmic mechanical movements and settling in for the long climb, she lets her mind wander onto Hart's last comment, "You think I inherited Mom's Blue Spark. That explains a lot."

"Hannah? Are you almost there? The countdown is close to zero; I don't have much longer. To answer your question … your Mother … "

With No. 5's thin outer shell only two tantalizing levels beyond her reach, Julius' last words fade to static as his explosive demise tears apart the control room, blasting shrapnel and debris past her elevated position. Thrown off balance by the thudding shockwave, Hannah loses her tenuous grip, tumbling backward down the frozen spider mech before clutching a sinewy hose at a ball-jointed ankle. Hanging in midair, she scans past dangling spider legs at the lone mechanical limb clamped atop a shelf ledge high above her perilous swinging position.

How long can it hold?

Not wanting to find out, Hannah taps her helmet light in the darkness and free-climbs up the spider mech's swaying form. Halfway up the smooth thorax, a hot metal slug ricochets off the bot's shiny black side.

Dammit. The light gave away my position!

Tapping off her helmet light, Hannah swallows back sheer panic, swinging under the load-bearing leg seconds before a hail of bullets careens off the shelves and stricken robot. Pinned upside down, Hannah locks her arms around a thin metal bar, straining her core to wrap her legs over a strut as the strange sound of her anguished voice echoes inside the fogged helmet, "Mom. I'm sorry. I never should have left Hilltop."

A volley of ropes whooshing upward shakes Hannah from her inertia. Scanning a path up the ten-foot leg, she climbs hand-over-hand near the ledge and strains to reach it with all her might. Unwilling to surrender, she swings herself back and forth for momentum before letting go and catching fingertips over the sharp edge as more shots whistle past. Realizing the errant fire is meant to pin her down, not kill her, she has no desire to take a mistake up the ass and pulls herself onto the defiladed flat surface.

Wedging against stacks of boxes, she peers over the side at shadowy forms shimmying upward with alarming alacrity.

What would Mom do?

With a devilish smile, Hannah braces her body between unmovable stacks and the spider mech's clamped claw, pushing the metallic limb off the edge with a vicious scream, and sending the massive robot hurtling down upon the climbers.

Hearing the terrorists' wails and screams plummeting into the void, Hannah shrieks over the ledge, "That one was for Alan."

Taking retaliatory gunfire on her elevated position, Hannah ducks back, "Oh, shit, I think they are through pussyfooting around."

Scanning the stacks of boxes behind her for anything she can weaponize, the whip-smart drone tech latches onto cartons of Chinese-made holographic devices.

That could work.

Scooching sideways with her head down and light off, Hannah topples boxloads of the junky knockoffs powered by notoriously combustible pre-invasion batteries raining upon her enemy. Hearing the satisfying cascade of detonations, she screams a rebellious cheer ringing inside her helmet, "That one was for Maddie!"

Free-climbing the last two shelf levels, she hoists atop a crossbeam of the warehouse's intricate skeletal framework and balances along the narrow purchase to the nearest airlock built into Thundercorp No. 5's thin outer shell. After ducking inside, she checks her oxygen level and reseals the inner portal before releasing the outer hatch. Poking her head and shoulders through the orifice, a random thought crosses her mind.

Don't puke in your helmet. That is the first thing they teach you in astronaut school.

Hoping her enviro-suit holds up to the rigors of space, Hannah remembers her spacewalking girlfriend with a wan smile, "Goodbye, Maddie."

On the verge of her first spacewalk, the drone tech presses the com button on her sleeve and voices a simple command: "Z461201-A: Home. Z461201-A: Home."

Straddling the opening, waiting for her ride, Hannah gazes at North Africa and the Mediterranean below her boots as unsettling vibrations rattle her awkward position, "Come on, you little shit, time is wasting here."

Turning her head inside the sweaty helmet, she watches a toaster-shaped silver delivery craft emblazoned with lightning bolts gliding into view. Clearing her throat, she voices a second command: "Z461201-A: Open Hatch."

Bucking an infamous sci-fi movie precedent, the drone hovers ten feet off Thundercorp No. 5's glistening outer shell and pops its door open on command.

Adjusting her stance to launch toward the drone's open hatch, space debris from another destroyed Thundercorp smashes into No. 5, knocking Hannah off her footing and sending her cartwheeling head-over-heels into space. Hyperventilating into her helmet, she sees Earth and space reeling past on a sickening loop as unchecked momentum spins her away from the massive station amid a debris field floating past at over 18,000 miles per hour.

"Oh no. Shit! Shit! Shit!"

Hannah blurts into her comm: "Z461201-A. Please, help me, for the love of God! Z461201-A: Package Retrieval Mode. Execute!"

Drifting farther from Thundercorp No. 5, Hannah cries, "Please execute."

Oblivious to the life and death drama unfolding before its perfect AI vision, the drone performs an elegant corkscrewing path, snatching the limp human in a long mechanical gripper, depositing her into the package compartment, and pressurizing to frail human standards while zapping chunks of Thundercorp debris out of its escape trajectory.

Hannah hears the door seal shut, heaving into her helmet in the pitch-blackness and passing out moments before a raging inferno engulfs the small drone.

* * *

Shockwaves from Thundercorp No. 5's expanding nuclear

detonation hurl the streaking delivery drone off-course, spiraling through the night sky over vast reaches of the Sahara Desert. Passing under ten miles above Earth, the rugged drone's autonomous guidance systems reestablish control.

Blazing-hot in her enviro suit, Hannah awakens to the paralyzing embrace of the package compartment's force field engineered to shield delicate merchandise from fiery reentries into Earth's atmosphere. Unable to move her head, blue-green eyes swivel to blinding light outside a tiny portal, anticipating imminent death as the ear-splitting whistle reverberates through her vomit-splattered helmet.

None too keen to burn up or crash, the determined mechanical wonder avoids fate, stopping on a dime at a preset delivery altitude in a miraculous hover, releasing its precious cargo to normal ground-level gravity with a green indicator light and a loud beep emulating a passenger jet's seat belt sign.

Stunned by her traumatizing escape and the Earth-shattering consequences of everything that once was but is no more, Hannah swallows hard down her parched throat and rasps: "Z461201-A: Thank You."

A calm, cool, and collected British-accented feminine voice replies through her helmet's comm: *"Hannah Haig / Drone Technician 581321345589: You Are Welcome."*

Breaking the package compartment seal, Hannah piles out of the hatch, dropping ten feet atop a stark, sandy ridgeline. The lone survivor of Thundercorp No. 5 struggles to stand on jelly legs while removing her helmet and wiping gunk from her face. Breathing in fresh air for the first time in months, she watches Thundercorp No. 5's expanding streams of burning debris streak across the North African night sky into millions of fireballs.

Beckoning Z461201-A down to her reach, an exhausted Hannah pops the rounded nosecone, pulls up her location on the nav computer, and sets a new course for Tunis. Peeling out of the sweaty enviro-suit, she stifles tears, taking one last glimpse of where Thundercorp No. 5 dominated the sky before climbing back into the package compartment, leaving the hatch wide open to let the nighttime desert air caress her luminous pale skin splotched with blue patches.

Studying Julius Hart's microchip in her bloody fingertips as the drone speeds north above windswept dunes bathed in light and shadow, a foreboding sense of dangers yet to come engulf her body and mind.

"Sorry, Julius."

The lone survivor of Thundercorp No. 5, Hannah Haig tosses the bloodied half-inch silicon alloy wafer out the hatch where its quintessential alien-infused tech is lost forever in the endless desert sands, like its backup chip buried in the silt at the bottom of Narragansett Bay.

Chapter Nine:

The Purge

Paddy | PTB HQ
09:42 p.m. | April 4, 2070

The three-car tram whooshes from the tunnel and screeches to a labored stop at the arrival platform in the deserted underground PTB transport hub. As its doors slide apart, beleaguered PTB mercenaries who aided Paddy's narrow escape from Thundercorp No. 5 assist their faltering leader onto the grated metal platform.

Stepping back from Paddy's gruesome countenance, the first man swallows hard, nods, and salutes, "What would you have us do?"

"Nothing. You got me home. Your mission is complete." Paddy doubles over in a convulsive coughing fit before straightening eye-to-eye with his loyal band of killers, "You are free to go."

"What's next? The squads from the other Thundercorps suffered only minor casualties. Surely, there must be …"

Paddy raises a bandaged hand, "No. What happens now is beyond my control. I did what I was told. As have you."

Watching them climb inside the autonomous tram for the quick tunnel ride back to the heliport, Paddy coughs and calls, "You may wish to seek out treatment for radioactive exposure as soon as possible."

The last man back aboard widens his eyes in fear, absorbing the portent of Paddy's rasped words as the doors slide shut.

Alone on the platform, Paddy mutters, "Although I am quite sure it is already too late."

* * *

Dragging himself down a corridor of VIP guest suites transformed into the Sisters' lavish quarters in the new post-PTB reality, Paddy hacks an uncontrollable cough, spitting gobs of bloody phlegm across the smooth, clean floor tiles.

Reaching Number 8's apartment, the trembling 25-year-old turns the handle and stumbles across the threshold like a drunk. From the semi-dark entryway, his rheumy eyeballs latch onto his angelic Mother across the well-appointed space. Her lithe form draped over a white leather Eames lounge chair in olive shorts and a black PTB tee, he notices she is reading a book amid her eclectic interior design flair and fascination with eroticism as portrayed in art dating back to antiquity acquired over two-plus decades of world travel.

Turning her blueberry gaze from a sexy romance novel onto the dark silhouetted figure in her doorway, 8's effervescent welcoming smile fades, "Paddy … is that you? I did not know you were back."

Enduring another brutal coughing fit, Paddy waves her off, "How could you? Even the PTB relied on Hart's fucking warehouses for communications."

"Too true." Sliding a bookmark into her thick, raunchy tome

and placing it on a side table, 8 sits up, focusing on Paddy's gaunt and feverish appearance, "Something afflicts my favorite son."

Limping from the shadowed entryway, oozing wounds and burns marring his perfect visage manifest in gruesome detail in the room's daylight ambiance, "I'm your only son, Mother." Rasping another cough, he adds, "And yes, something afflicts me, as you so benignly put it."

Shocked and horrified by her handsome and debonair son's grotesque appearance, Number 8 stammers for words, "Paddy … what did they do to my beautiful boy?"

Paddy shakes his head, revealing a significant loss of his lustrous black locks. "Do you still love me, Mom?"

"Of course."

Suppressing shooting pains racking his bleeding gut, Paddy tosses naughty throw pillows from an upholstered bench, slumping atop and hunching forward in agonizing pain.

Barefoot, Number 8 hastens to his side, ignoring a mephitic decay mixed with metallic stench and damp putridness seeping through his blood and sweat-soaked clothes, "You are on fire."

Ignoring a dreaded sensation of skin sliding off his face, revealing his perfect skull, Paddy struggles to speak, "I am dying from acute radiation exposure, Mom."

"But how? The Thundercorps were set for self-destruction. Entering the reactor cores was not part of our plan."

Paddy lifts his head and proffers a sardonic smile toward his worried Mother, "Yes, the best-laid plans …" More coughs … "Hart was aboard the fifth warehouse at the hour of our attack. The men captured him with minimal resistance, but Thundercorp No. 5's self-destruct was offline. Without the time or manpower to restart it, the only path to accomplishing our mission required exposure to Thundercorp No. 5's nuclear reactor core."

Tears welling in her eyes, Number 8 starts to weep, "Could not anyone else have done it? Why you?"

"The men are killers, not nuclear physicists. It had to be me." Wiping a tear from his Mother's cheek with a bloodied finger missing half a nail jutting from thick wadded gauze, Paddy manages to laugh, "Even in death, Julius Hart got the last laugh."

Number 8 shifts from acute sadness to a burning rage, "This is Andrew's fault. He should have killed Julius Hart when he had the chance."

"My Father … never was one of us. And now, at the end of everything, he is missing."

Number 8 forces a smile, "So is Number 1. They are together somewhere, fucking like rabbits."

"Forget them, Mom. The Overlords are here."

Number 8's devious smile returns, "I know. We see them, Paddy. They speak to us. My Sisters and I will tip the first telepathic dominos, triggering the deadly nanobots embedded in the brains of millions who received the Blue Spark injections."

Obeying a voice in her head, Number 8 kisses her son's crusted cheek. "I love you, Paddy. Please forgive me for what I am about to do." Pulling him into a tight embrace, she snaps his neck, killing him instantly.

Professor Ian Dury | The Mojave Desert
02:00 p.m. | May 1, 2070

"I'm telling you, Ian, it was those crazy environmental terrorists. They hated Julius Hart and Thundercorp with a white-hot passion."

Spry 84-year-old Professor Ian Dury presses back in the cracked leather shotgun seat in Chet Anderson's old reliable internal combustion Toyota pickup, frowning toward his longtime friend and colleague behind the wheel, "Chet, you are wrong, my friend. It was The Powers

That Be. No one else had the resources to pull off an attack like that. Blowing up all five Thundercorps at once? Come on."

Wearing a ballcap and mirrored shades, Chet downshifts the vintage truck across a dry wash and up a rugged berm, "Thank God most of the debris burned up in the atmosphere with the larger pieces hitting mainly water or open spaces."

"A huge chunk took out a city block of Austin near the State Capitol."

"How did you hear that? Everything is down."

"I have my sources."

"You know what the worst part is, Ian?"

"No more crappy Chinese junk delivered to your door in an hour?"

"No. Well, yes, but I would say losing the internet all over again."

Ian chuckles, scratching his long gray beard, "Yeah, it had a good second act. What was it? Ten years of high-speed data transfer right in the palm of your hand. What did you do with your Thundercorp phone?"

Bouncing and jostling in the driver's seat, Chet grips the wheel and laughs without taking his eyes off the narrow desert track through the cracked and dusty windshield, "I gave it to the grandkids. By now, it is in a thousand pieces."

Ian props his arm on the rolled-down passenger door window and tugs the brim of his signature fedora, "Just like the Thundercorps. How fitting. I pitched mine in a garbage can. Without a snowball's chance of seeing another broadband signal in my lifetime, there was no reason to keep the damn thing."

"What about the PTB satellites? It was a crappy shared connection but better than nothing."

"The way I understand it is that the PTB left their satellites to rot as space junk in deteriorating orbits. Nobody cared because

Thundercorp cornered the broadband market and performed beyond all expectations."

"Let me guess, your sources told you that, too?"

Ian raises bushy eyebrows and shrugs, taking a long drink from his canteen as Chet steers into a sharp turn, navigating a series of switchbacks, kicking up a long trail of dust and gravel.

"Fucking terrorists."

"Think motive, Chet, it was the PTB."

Allowing the maverick archeologist and notorious contrarian to have the last word, Chet guns his truck atop a wide-open plateau past more boulders, scrub brush, and cacti before fishtailing to a stop at the precipice of a steep drop. Exiting the overheated vehicle, the men venture to the ledge overlooking a vast swath of California desert that had not seen rain in over a year.

"There they are, Ian."

Ian Dury squints at geometric shapes blurring together and reflecting the scorching midday sun with blinding intensity in the arid valley far below and into the hazy distance, "Jesus, Chet, has anybody attempted to count them?"

"A count? Good luck with that. More cubes appear out of thin air every day."

Ian raises high-powered binocs and focuses on the closest metallic cubes scattered across the hardpan. Without averting his surveillance, the famous archeologist addresses his younger colleague, now a widower in his 60s with two children and a brood of grandkids back in Los Angeles, eking out the best lives they can manage in the dystopian world. "I have seen one of these before, Chet."

"What are they, Ian?"

Professor Ian Dury lowers his binocs and places a hand on his friend's shoulder, "You should go home, Chet. Stay with your family."

"What about you?"

"Would you mind grabbing my pack from the back of the

pickup? I am going to stick around. I want a front-row seat."

Chet's voice raises with unmasked alarm, "A front-row seat for what?"

"Their return."

"You can't mean … no, wait. Are you serious?"

"Afraid so, Chet, old buddy. Like I said. Go home."

Andrew | The Farmhouse
02:15 a.m. | May 13, 2070

Andrew sits erect in a portable folding chair under a sea of stars on a moonless night, sipping coffee and watching a snake slither past the patchwork front facade of his farmhouse exile tucked away in a remote parcel of the Australian Outback northeast of Perth. Concentrating on the creature's intricate pattern of luminous scales glistening in the flickering light of his roaring firepit, he watches it disappear amid dry grasses toward a desiccated Acacia tree rustling in a chill early morning breeze.

The front door creaking open and shut precedes the feel of Number 1's supple arms draping over his shoulders and breaking his reverie.

"Andrew, are you coming to bed?"

Lost in 1's sultry grin and come-hither blueberry gaze, Andrew smiles at his partner in exile, "Not yet. I am watching the stars."

"What for?"

"Salvation."

Patting her über-human partner's firm chest, Number 1 relieves him of his cup of joe and collapses in a canvas folding chair beside him. After taking a long drink, she touches two fingers to her soft lips, "Andrew, we have been over this. What makes you think the Light Specters will return?"

Andrew's intelligent eyes glow in the sparking and flickering firelight, "I have committed heinous acts, Number 1, that led to the ruin of humankind. There will be no salvation for me in this life or the next, but I wish for the Light Specters to return and set things right."

Realizing sex was not in the cards—at least for now—Number 1 crosses her legs and tosses the cup on the fire, watching it snap, crackle, and burn in the blue flames.

A meteor shower streaks across the night sky as a pack of howling dingoes fights over a late-night dinner somewhere in the darkness.

"The Light Specters fostered this version of humanity from its nascent and primitive roots hundreds of thousands of years ago. They have witnessed the species' ascension to this tipping point. If my old friend Artemus Pennywell were here, he would call upon our extraterrestrial friends to seek the Light Specters' intervention." Poking at the fire with a stick, Andrew generates a sea of sparks rising into the night, "I betrayed the cause. They will not take my call."

"Andrew, my love, it is too late even if you muster the entire Council back into existence. My Sisters plan to activate the Blue Spark killer nanobots. I hear their final preparations. They are close." Leaning forward, trying to make eye contact with Andrew, who seems off in another universe, "Hey. Earth to Andrew. Billions of people are about to die."

Andrew shakes from his trancelike state and turns to Number 1 with an unreadable expression on his chiseled face, "But not everyone."

The Sisters | PTB HQ
05:48 p.m. | May 16, 2070

Pelting raindrops and gusty winds from a tempest off the North Sea buffets the rocky escarpment above Crichton Castle's ruins, billowing the fifteen Sisters' diaphanous gowns as they join hands, resolute against the forces of nature. Number 2 squeezes 3's soft hand, passing her effervescent smile down the line as a crack of thunder like Thor's hammer rumbles across the dark green pastures from the gloom.

"It is time!"

Coalescing their prodigious telepathy into a singular energized neural power, the Sisters awaken diabolical nanobots lying in stasis within the brains of unsuspecting Scots scattered throughout nearby villages and hamlets to Edinburg and beyond. With humanity's fuse lit, their hypnotic chant wafts across the grayness as their world-ending purpose spreads unchecked at the speed of light, engulfing every continent in the initial throes of murderous chaos in less than a minute.

Flush with the intoxicating sensation of ritualistic mass murder on a global scale, Number 4 releases 3's hand and tilts her head toward raindrops pattering her face and trickling down her perfect cheeks as the sound of gunfire echoes across the lush green Scottish countryside from the tiny hamlet down the lane.

Number 2 pushes wet locks from her glowing blue eyes, her wet dress clinging to her body, "What do we do now?"

With the blood of her perfect son still under her nails, Number 8 dances in the rain, grabbing 12 by the hand and twirling her in the wet grass. Wiping purifying rainwater from her blue eyes, she lets loose a rebellious yell, "First, we destroy the PTB HQ. After that, I will find Andrew and kill him."

Staccato gunfire mixing with sirens wailing in the distance drowns the cries of innocents clawing over each other to escape a world gone mad in a singular collective heartbeat.

Ewan Burns | Edinburg
06:00 p.m. | May 16, 2070

Hustling through the rain showers to the front stoop of his two-story flat, Ewan Burns unlocks the red front door, closes his umbrella, and places it in the heirloom stand. Wriggling out of his wet trench coat and hat, he hangs them on the hooks and announces his presence, "Aileen, I'm home."

Loosening his tie, he walks through the cozy living room, past the antique TV set serving as a side table and his favorite chair, entering the creaky, dark hallway lined with family photos leading to the kitchen.

"There is something peculiar happening out there. People are acting a little crazy. Aileen? What's for dinner, dear, I'm starved."

Pausing at the entrance to the kitchen, he looks across the butcher block island at his wife of ten years, back turned, hunched over the stove.

"Aileen? Did you hear what I said? Something weird is going on outside. The cops are everywhere."

Taking a tentative step onto the kitchen linoleum in his wet loafers, he repeats, "Are you okay, dear?"

Aileen Burns coughs and makes a weird little chuckle, turning to face her husband, "Hello, Ewan. I was making dinner when this happened."

Ewan Burns gasps, seeing his wife's face with a long knife plunged into her left eye socket to the hilt.

"I … I … had to do it."

Ewan watches her grip another long knife while slinking closer with a steady stream of blood dripping down her face, "Come here, Ewan. I won't bite. I promise. Everything will be fine …"

The 34-year-old childless woman vaults over the island and lunges at her husband, wailing and gnashing her teeth, intent on ripping him apart.

Vickie Schimmel | Rome
06:00 p.m. | May 16, 2070

"I can think of worse places to be stuck for the rest of my life."

Vickie raises her glass to the cheers and hoots of everyone at her rowdy table of US government dignitaries, functionaries, and lackeys taking over a cheesy tourist restaurant across a busy boulevard from the Roman Colosseum.

Hillary Snyder, an attaché stationed at the US embassy, leans back in a low-cut sequined dress, twirling saucy spaghetti and jamming a mouthful between her lips before reaching for her third Cosmo, "Ah, but Vick, what about poor old Harold, back in DC?"

Vickie turns to her drunk gal pal, "The senator is too busy getting blow jobs from his interns to know I am gone. What a prick."

A teetering military aide within earshot slurs a rejoinder toward Vickie, "Fuck you, Schimmel. Harry got you the Vatican gig, you ungrateful bitch."

"Jesus, Tony, how long have you been waiting to say that?" Vickie downs her cheap red wine and pours another. "I'll say one thing for my husband, the good senator from New York: he knows where the bodies are buried."

More snide remarks, dirty jokes, and gossip follow as a mid-level military attaché halfway down the long table grabs a shapely hostess and pulls her onto his lap as the embarrassed young girl slaps the ugly American's ruddy face and retreats to the kitchen.

"Careful, Jimmy. These Italian girls bite."

Vickie hears what sounds like a car backfiring over the usual Roman traffic din and coughs in the stale air, "Hey, you know what. You know what? I, Vickie Schimmel, have a meeting with his … Grrrrrrrup … Pius the 13th … tomorrow at eleven sharp. Should I bring him some leftover carbonara?"

A long-serving diplomat with a soft spot for anything that

screws his own country on Vick's left hammers the table with his fist in a pique of maniacal laughter, "Christ, Vickie, you made me pee my fucking pants!"

"Wow, Jack, get ahold of yourself. You look like you are about to have a coronary."

A series of concussive explosions rattle the restaurant's windows and upturn carts and drinks, collapsing a precarious wall of wine bottles to the floor.

"Hey! Free wine! Now we don't even have to pay the check!"

Matt Clyne, a sober, well-dressed man who had babysat more than his share of Vickie Schimmel's hedonism and debauchery working overseas for the State Department careerist, celebrating her new post as the Vatican's US Ambassador, sidles over and whispers in his boss' ear.

Vickie's blue eyes widen, "Really? When did this start?"

Matt shakes his head and shrugs. "Just a few minutes ago."

Vickie clinks her glass to gain her group's less-than-lucid attention, "Apparently, while we have been sitting in this shitty dump, the world has decided to fuck itself."

Two of Schimmel's young male secretaries in matching blue Italian suits pause their fondling of each other under the table at their boss's bizarre comment, "Ms. Schimmel, Doug, and I want to head back to the mansion."

"No one is going anywhere, motherfuckers!"

Everyone at the American table turns toward the manhandled waitress, reappearing from the kitchen with a long, bloody butcher knife clutched in her tiny grip.

A grizzled military liaison at the far end of the festivities rolls his eyes, "Easy there, little lady. Put the fucking knife down before you hurt somebody."

Screaming in Italian, the waitress rushes forward and plunges the knife into the neck of her assailant before jumping on the table, kicking dishes everywhere, and screaming at the top of her lungs.

Vickie pushes back in her chair at the head of the table but finds herself trapped with no way out of the confining little hole-in-the-wall restaurant. "What should we do, Hill. Hillary?"

Vickie watches her friend's face turn blue, coughing and gasping for air before jabbing a fork into her right eye and screaming in multiple languages.

"Hillary! What the hell did you do?"

A taxi crashes through the wall, crushing multiple people before the driver climbs out a window and rips at the trapped victims with bare teeth.

Matt unholsters his illegal sidearm and checks the mag, chambering a round, before hugging the wall toward the exit, extricating himself from the nightmarish dinner party, devolving into a charnel house with half on their backs, fending off insane colleagues' snapping and biting attacks. At the broken entryway, he looks back and finds his stoic boss, Ms. Schimmel, trapped amid the Hieronymus Bosch hellscape, meeting his gaze and mouthing, "Do it."

Matt raises his gun without a second thought and puts her down with a single shot between the eyes.

Retreating from the zombie fest inside the Italian eatery, Matt dodges more screaming people outside, fleeing for their lives and killing with abandon in equal measures. Making a beeline across the chaotic log-jammed boulevard, he heads for the Colosseum's ruins. Jumping the barricades and turnstiles into the ancient structure, Matt searches for a hiding place through the darkness as the ear-splitting whine of a passenger jet's engines screams overhead. Rushing to the nearest vantage point, he watches the stricken craft angle sideways before nosing over into a hillside in a fireball rising skyward. Climbing as high up as he can, Matt finds a perch and cradles his weapon, watching Rome burn at the end of the world.

Zhao Ming | Beijing
12:00 a.m. | May 17, 2070

Halfway through her twelve-hour night shift as a seamstress in Mr. Lao's sweatshop, forging cheap knock-offs of high-end fashion apparel, nineteen-year-old Zhao Ming senses a dramatic change in the room's temperature. Pushing back from her hard metal chair, she raises a hand and calls over the man, "I have to pee."

The stern floor supervisor produces a frustrated scowl, striding over with his splintery measuring stick swinging in a menacing grip, "Use your bucket. Get back to work."

Zhao swallows back a taste of bile in her throat and feels her body break into a cold sweat, hearing strange growls from her fellow laborers, "Please. I must stand up and get away. Something bad is about to happen, I …"

The man's face contorts into a cold, demonic grimace as the meter stick whips around and smacks her head, sending her crumpling to the floor.

Gripping the sides of her head and writhing in pain, Zhao snaps. Scuttling to her feet, she stumbles backward into the co-worker's table and feels her hand close around a pair of scissors.

"Get back to work!"

Zhao lunges forward and jabs the sharp end of the scissors into the vile man's chest through his left ventricle, causing a gusher of blood as the room erupts into an orgy of murderous chaos.

Her sixth sense that something terrible was about to happen manifests in horrible gore and violence as Zhao runs into the shadows, belly crawling across the dirty concrete and escaping through a warehouse door into a back alley receiving dock.

Struggling to breathe through acrid smoke permeating the stale, polluted air suffocating her frightened form, Zhao hears strange sounds from an undulating mass blocking her path forward. Unable to discern what makes it move, she rubs smoke from her eyes, picking out human bodies piling together into a singular mass, eating themselves alive.

Taking a wide berth around the sucking, biting, snapping, snarling, and chewing, Zhao ducks on reflex as massive explosions tear open the skies, punctuated by automatic gunfire and the nightmarish cries of injured people lying scattered amongst the dead filling the streets.

Fred Krakauer | Lower Manhattan
12:00 p.m. | May 16, 2070

Mayor Fred Krakauer peers beyond the ornate golden draperies framing his mayoral office windows, gaping from his commanding Big Apple view at thousands of New Yorkers streaming into the streets on an otherwise pleasant Spring afternoon. Mesmerized by the hordes' movements, burning, looting, and killing with sheer unadulterated abandon, the ear-piercing sounds of alarms and sirens exacerbate his already screaming headache.

"Worse than usual. Something is happening out there …."

Fearing another in a long line of riots that have plagued his entire administration with no end, he suppresses a heady swoon, like coming down from a bad acid trip, and barks through the closed doors for his top aides, "Sam! Laura! Is anybody out there? Somebody better tell me what in the name of Rudy goddamn Giuliani is happening to my city!"

Receiving zero response from the backstabbing pair, who must be on their early fucking lunches, he bellows for anyone to hear, "Where is fucking LaTonya? Why can't I get the police chief's fat ass on the phone? Good Christ, where is everybody?"

Turning his utter frustration onto a young Black intern who happened to be bringing a stack of papers to his office when all hell broke loose, Mayor Krakauer licks his dry lips and motions for the nubile girl in a slinky orange dress to take cover with him behind the desk.

Unsure of what to do, she complies and kneels beside Krakauer on the thick carpeting.

Hearing explosions and automatic gunfire shaking his frontal lobe like a bowl of Jell-O, Krakauer scooches closer and proffers a bizarre grin, "What's your name, kid?"

Flinching at more loud gunfire through the walls, she double-takes at the old white man, noting a familiar lecherous look in his eyes, "Cassie Jones, Mayor Krakauer. I'm a psychology major at NYU here on an internship."

"Psychology? You mean like a shrink?"

Growing more uncomfortable by the nanosecond, Cassie slides her bottom in the thin dress away from the old man while attempting to engage him in conversation until someone comes to her rescue, "Mayor. I know what this is. My sociology professor warned us about it last year."

Ducking for cover as a hail of gunfire blasts through the locked office doors, Fred pulls the frightened young girl into a tight embrace, "What? Tell me, dammit. What is happening to *me*?"

The sickening foulness of cheap cologne mixed with sweat suffocates her in his brawny grasp as another hail of bullets rips through the walls. Reaching a hand over her head, she starts to cry, "Oh no, this is terrible."

Sensing the end of his corrupt reign as NYC's Mayor, Fred pushes her back and jerks her sideways by her lace collar, whipping her head back and forth, smashing it over and over again into the edge of his solid mahogany desk.

Releasing his grip with a startled grunt, Fred watches the young woman slump forward as his brain melts to its primitive core functions. Taking heavy, labored breaths, he slides a clumsy hand over her smooth, tawny face and tips her lolling head sideways like a rag doll.

With his last vestige of humanity and higher brain function wiped clean by the activated nanobots that entered the Mayor's frontal lobe via a long-forgotten Blue Spark jab years before, Krakauer lays the dead girl flat, yanks down his trousers, and pushes himself on top of her.

The office doors blast open, and a pair of officers led by NYC Police Chief LaTonya Edwards burst inside with guns drawn, "Mr. Mayor! We need to evacuate. Now!"

The veteran officers with a better angle around the side of Krakauer's enormous desk look down at the 62-year-old man's poop-smeared bare ass grinding on a dead girl's prone form with her dress pulled up around her chest.

The first officer looks closer and heaves up his coffee and Danish, seeing the Democrat chewing at the deceased girl's face with her brain matter spilling onto the expensive carpeting from the back of her cracked skull.

"Oh, Jesus. What should we do, Chief?"

LaTonya Edwards steps around the mess and holds a scarf over her mouth and nose to keep from throwing up, "Just kill him."

The second officer raises his service revolver and puts the Mayor down like a rabid dog.

Staring wide-eyed out the mayor's window at the carnage and mayhem spilling into the streets from everywhere all at once, LaTonya breaks down in tears, "I … I … I don't know what to do."

Chet Anderson | Los Angeles
09:00 a.m. | May 16, 2070

Awakened by a low-flying fighter jet streaking overhead, followed by something akin to an explosion shuddering his bedroom, Chet Anderson bolts upright, scratching and grabbing for a glass of water as he whips open his blackout shades and sees smoke plumes from multiple flashpoints across the City of Angels. Hearing sirens and police choppers through the walls, he calls downstairs, "Hey, kids! Grab your go bags! We are getting the fuck out of here!"

Peeking from her bedroom door across the darkened upstairs hallway in her pink robe, Chet's daughter yawns and frowns, "What's going on, Dad? It sounds like one of the boys' World War 3 video games outside."

Chet offers his beautiful daughter a brave smile, "Julie, I need you to stay strong. Get dressed. Pack the kids up and meet me at the truck in ten minutes."

"What about Angie and her kids?"

"She is clear across town. If there is a God in Heaven, we will see her again. Right now, we must get ourselves out of the city."

Chet's grandkids pile in the back of his old Toyota pickup with its vintage camper shell attached amid prepacked clothes and survival gear.

"Let's go, Papa! Come on! The monsters are coming!"

Chet girds himself for the worst, opens the garage door, and puts his trusty old truck in gear, "Oh, man. What the hell is happening out here?"

Rolling down the driveway onto the tony South Pasadena street, they see hordes of former neighbors staggering about, some running and screaming from others covered in blood and guts.

Julia looks out her locked window and sees the neighbor's shades open and close as a crazed man smashes into the car door, snarling and growling like an animal.

Letting out a scream, Julia turns to her Dad, "Floor it. Just run them over. Oh my God. It's the end of the world!

Rachel | Hilltop
12:00 p.m. | May 16, 2070

Arranging homemade chips and canned bread and butter

pickles next to liverwurst and onion sandwiches on his and Rachel's plates, Dave Poole slings a hand towel over his broad shoulder, setting the plated meals atop colorful woven placemats on the kitchen table. Completing another ritualized lunch-making with two fresh lemonades, Dave positions the glasses in neat symmetry and admires his handiwork.

"I'd make a damn fine chef if I do say so myself."

The shrill din of the neighbor's house alarm ratcheting through the wide-open bay windows behind the kitchen sink breaks the former PTB security man's upbeat mood. Hearing the monotonous droning unchecked through the trees and drowning out the pleasant chirps, hoots, and whistles of songbirds nesting in the oaks and maples, he shakes his head, "Shit! More fucking squatters next door. The cops really need to get a handle on the vagrants. This is beyond intolerable."

Snapping his holstered sidearm to his thick leather belt, Dave turns a familiar corner in the mansion and calls upstairs, "Hey Rachel, the neighbor's alarm went off again. I'll be right back. Your lunch is on the table if you want to come down."

No reply.

Bounding out the back doors on the pleasant Spring day, a tingling sense of dread goes up Dave's spine, "That's weird. The birds stopped chirping." Passing through the former glory of Hilltop's backyard entertaining area and covered pool deck, he unlocks the side gate embedded in a fourteen-foot privacy hedge and tromps downhill through piles of decaying leaves, "Man, I have a lot to clean up out here."

Jogging down the steep, muddy hillside to the property line separating Hilltop from its closest neighboring home—a split-level Craftsman worth millions back in its heyday—Dave ponders why Rachel can never remember the former family's name.

Hopping a rotting wooden fence, Dave trots uphill through the neighbor's unkempt yard, overgrown with vines and brambles, past an indefatigable solar-powered generator. "That thing runs like a fucking clock."

Vaulting up the front steps onto a trash-strewn front porch, Dave peers inside through the home's wide-open front door. Drawing his .38, he breeches the shadowed interior, finding the front rooms looted with upturned, ripped-up furniture and sick graffiti covering the walls. "What a shame. I wish someone nice would buy this place."

Moving to a wall panel off the main foyer, he pries the metal door open and switches off the grating alarm, reducing the spooky interior to an unnerving silence.

"Is anyone here?"

Stepping across the creaky floorboards in his muddy boots, Dave peers down a long hall with doors leading to other parts of the 5,000-square-foot home on a rocky hillside lot with an ocean view. At the first door, he pushes it wide with the muzzle of his handgun and lets his vision adjust to the dark, noting sheets and pillows strewn about the stained carpeting accompanied by the foul odors of piss and crap, but no squatters.

Moving past more closed doors, Dave reaches a great room backlit with broken windows looking out on the overgrown backyard with a children's play fort rising from a twisting mass of greenery.

Hearing his breaths, Dave moves to the home's dining room and finds a bloody carcass covered in flies atop the formal table. "Oh, come on now … what was that? A dog?"

The sounds of cans and jars crashing to the floor draw Dave's attention through the dining room to a shuttered butler's pantry with a light visible through the slatted doors.

Feeling exposed and more than a little scared, Dave sees multiple shadows under the double doors of people hiding in the pantry.

Hesitating and unsure of himself, he clears his throat and assumes an authoritative tone: "I called the police. The cops are on their way."

Dave pauses, hearing strange noises in reply, more animal than human. "Come on out of there. You can be on your way. No questions asked." Cursing to himself and mad at his trepidation at what must be a couple of skinny addicts shooting up in the pantry, he grimaces and calls out one more time. "Come out of there! I can't have squatters next door to my home."

No reply.

"Fuck. Now what?"

Biting his lower lip and racked with indecision, Dave's anger at the world overtakes his trepidation. Checking his pistol, he reaches forward and grabs the doorknob. Bracing himself for what lies on the other side, he whips the doors open onto a tangled mass of naked people chewing and gnawing each other to death. A woman with part of her lower jaw bit clean off looks up with a dead-eyed stare and returns to biting a dripping piece of human flesh still clinging to a man's breast by some length of sinewy tissue.

Gobsmacked by the terrifying scene, Dave staggers backward in his muddy boots, coughing and shaking, unable to quantify the disgusting sight in his addled brain.

Out of his periphery, but too late to react, Dave wards off a naked man with an uppercut to the guy's chin, jerking the middle-aged fellow's wild-eyed head backward with an audible snap. From the dark, two more crazed people jump him from behind. Dave twists and turns, spinning one to the floor in a rolling heap as the clinging female digs her fingernails into his neck and shoulders and bites through his left ear with ululating abandon. Writhing in pain, Dave pulls her over the shoulder by her hair and slams her atop a coffee table as his gun skitters across the parquet floor.

Feeling a steady stream of blood pouring from his half-missing ear, Dave hammers fists into another growling and grunting attacker as more insane snappers—drawn to the smell of fresh blood—descend on his trapped position in the dining room. Kicking at another chomping pair, Dave hefts a dining chair like a lion tamer and moves toward his gun.

Throwing the chair at the nearest teeth-gnashing human and scooping up his sidearm in one fell motion, Dave feels a woman's terrible sharp teeth biting through his calf. Caving in her gray head with the heel of his boot, Dave drops two more with clean headshots, clearing a path to the exit and checking his six, retreating toward the front of the house.

Feeling a queasy recognition, Dave glances back at the well-dressed woman who bit his leg like a drumstick, recognizing the mature old gal as a wealthy neighbor. Calling back to the dead woman in a hazy state of confusion and despair, Dave yells: "Mrs. Simmons, I'm sorry for crushing your skull!"

Hearing more footsteps throughout the labyrinthine home interior converging on his outnumbered position, Dave beats a hasty retreat out of the front door and sprints back to Hilltop.

Halfway back up the slippery hillside, a man drops from a tree and tackles him in the mud, sending them both in a rolling heap back downhill into the thick weeds. Warding off the man's gnashing teeth with all his might, Dave beats a fist into the guy's nose until he hears the skull crush inward under the pulverizing weight of his broken right-handed fist.

Scuttling onto his feet with a singular purpose, Dave bolts through the back doors into Hilltop's kitchen, past the lunch table, and vaults up the stairs three at a time to Rachel's bedroom.

Suffering blood loss and in mortal pain from multiple bite wounds and a broken hand, Dave trips through Rachel's door and lands on his face. Pulling himself onto his hands and knees, he sees Rachel lying curled on the floor, facing away from him in front of her wheelchair, "Rachel! Holy fuck! Are you okay? Something terrible is happening. We need to leave! Now!"

Covered in mud and blood from head to toe, with his face filling with tears, Dave crawls to Rachel's side and turns her over with gentle, loving care. Looking at his wife through swollen eyes filling with tears, he sees a luminous blueness glowing from within as her body temperature soars, "Rachel. I have never seen you like this before."

Regaining consciousness at his words, Rachel raises a hand and touches Dave's dirt-smeared face, "Thank you for taking care of me. I love you, Dave, but it is over."

Rachel's head slumps sideways as she takes her last breath.

Crying and cradling her listless form in his arms, rocking back and forth, unable to accept her death, Dave watches her radiance fade to a dull blue-gray complexion, "I am sorry, Rachel. I am so sorry."

The sound of breaking glass precedes clomping footsteps, growls, hoots, and strange barks as the growing post-human horde breeches Hilltop's hallowed first floor into the foyer. Checking his pistol, Dave chambers his last round, laying Rachel sideways away from the bedroom door, and pulls himself over her in a protective repose, waiting for the end.

Hannah | Oslo

06:08 p.m. | May 16, 2070

Ducking her messy head under the cool sheets, Hannah snuggles closer, basking in Maddie's perfect face, smoky eyes, and flawless smile, "Good morning, Sleepyhead .... No spacewalk today. We can sleep in."

Maddie's expressive features transform into blue stars streaking over and around Hannah's reeling psyche as her Mother's voice clamors inside her pounding head.

"Wake up, stupid girl. It is not your time to die!"

Startling from her dream in a pool of sweat, Hannah's blue-green eyes snap open.

Something is wrong.

Running a hand through her short blond bedhead resting face-up on a pile of fluffy pillows between two new friends bookending her nakedness, Hannah checks Greta's snoozing form, kicking and twitching in her sleep before crawling over Jakob, avoiding upsetting a metal tray smeared with traces of white powder at the foot of the bed.

Standing and stretching on the cold wooden floor of the Bohemian couple's third-floor Grünerløkka flat, Hannah saunters to a window and ventures a peek at the normals outside coming home from work and school in the late afternoon sunshine bathing the clean and orderly Oslo streets in a red-orange glow.

Squinting through the haziness, Hannah notices people huddling on the sidewalks as unorganized bands of citizens storm down past, carrying rakes, shovels, and torches, looking for a fight.

"Well, that's a little fucking weird, even for Norway."

On the run from the PTB and grappling with survivor's guilt and PTSD since Thundercorp No. 5's ignominious end, Hannah pads to her new friends' tiny bathroom and plops herself on the cold toilet seat for a much-needed pee. Scrunching up her bleary-eyed vision under the blue-tinged LED light fixture, she scrutinizes her pallor and yawns.

This bathroom lighting sucks.

Moving to the narrow sink, Hannah fumbles for her pills, ignoring the odd blue reflection of the girl in the mirror. Choking down three uppers without the help of the suspect tap water, she nods and mumbles, "I'm still dreaming. This can't be real. I look like Mom."

Hearing the roar of fighter jets soaring low over the city, followed by a series of concussive explosions, Hannah reenters the darkened bedroom to peer outside and look at what the hell is going down. Growing more concerned by the burgeoning chaos, she turns sideways toward the creaking bed and sees Greta riding atop her boyfriend and grabbing at his throat. "Hey, you two. Knock it off; something is happening."

An odd gurgling sound causes Hannah to look closer, finding Greta choking the life out of the cute Scandinavian boy with a knotted bedsheet twisted around his throat.

"Greta. Stop it. You are killing him!"

Greta's animalistic response prompts Hannah's right hand to lift on impulse and, flush with an innate power unleashed from deep inside, knocks Greta off the guy with the flick of her wrist.

Coughing and gagging, Jakob rolls off the bed, rubbing his sore neck and staring at the cute blond he and his girlfriend picked up in a bar two nights before, "How did you …."

Hannah stares at her blue hand and shakes her head, "I don't know. It just happened."

Seeing Greta gathering to strike like a cobra, Hannah flicks her wrist again and smashes the girl's head into the wall, rendering her unconscious.

"That should hold her for a while."

Reeling from his close brush with certain death and gasping for oxygen, Jakob stares closer through the dimness, brushing back his thick blond hair with his piercing ice-blue eyes bugging out, "Why are you blue?"

Hannah shrugs her bare shoulders, searching for her pack, "My Mother is dead. That is why I am fucking blue, Jakob! Now, help me find my clothes. I need to leave."

Feeling horny after his girlfriend's choke job, the muscly Jakob crawls across the bed, smooths a finger through the leftover powder, and rubs it on his gums, "Hang around, Hannah. We can have more fun with Greta out of the way. I can call another girlfriend to join us if you like."

Pulling into her travel pants and yanking an I Love Oslo sweatshirt over her head, Hannah smiles at the strapping young man sporting a massive erection, "As tempting as that sounds, I think it best to leave before they catch up to me."

"You never said who is looking for you."

Hannah straightens her clothes and pulls into her boots, registering incalculable grief mixed with revelatory awareness coursing her transhuman neural pathways, "The Sisters. There are sixteen of them. They can't have me fucking with the Overlords' plans."

"Overlords? What the hell are you talking about? What will you do, Hannah Haig?"

Hannah shoves a few random items into her pack and flings it over her shoulder with a brave chuckle, "Ignorance suits you, Jakob. Never change."

Dressed and ready to go, Hannah bends down and kisses Jakob's cheek, "Thanks for your hospitality."

"Hey!"

"Hey, what?"

Jakob flashes his pearly white smile, "Your complexion is back to normal."

Hannah nods, flush with the knowledge and power hidden within her since conception, "I know. Goodbye, Jakob."

Moving to the door as gunshots blast through the streets, Hannah turns to the young fellow, "If I were you, I would be long gone before that bitch wakes up."

Professor Ian Dury | The Mojave Desert
07:11 p.m. | May 16, 2070

After an exhausting hike, Ian Dury reaches a passenger jet's smoking debris field. Noting the familiar star and bars insignia on an engine cowling attached to the broken back half of the blue and white United States Government fuselage, he squints into the fading light at a swept wing jutting skyward and what appears to be the remnants of the front half of the craft scattered in jagged chunks across the blackened desert hardpan.

Picking his way over and around scorched luggage, bags, garbage, and dismembered body parts littering the smoldering ground, he peers into an upside-down chunk of darkened passenger cabin punctuated in stark detail by the setting sun arcing shafts of orange light through portside windows.

"What the hell?"

Twenty feet above his reach, he sees a woman's headless body swinging downward from her belted second-row seat, dripping blood and sinewy gobs from her ripped-open neck and shoulders.

Adjusting his keen eyesight to the darkening ether as the sun dips below the jagged horizon, he flicks on his torch and shines it across blood splatters on the bulkheads and a twisted mass of bodies jumbled together between the rows.

"Ah, sweet Jesus. What happened here?"

A looming presence behind Ian breaks his rumination, pivoting to face a tall humanoid in blinding white robes floating three feet off the desert floor.

Bathed in the otherworldly being's radiance, Ian drops to his knees as a sonorous voice resonates across the space between them.

"The humans aboard this craft consumed each other like savage beasts."

Scuttling onto his feet, Ian shields his eyes from the brilliant entity, "Did you come from the cubes? I waited, but nothing happened. Then this plane fell from the sky. I thought it was a sign."

The being's luminescence intensifies, *"No signs. No miracles. The end of what once was but is no more is upon your kind."*

The being vanishes in a flash of light, leaving a gobsmacked Ian alone as a stiff, warm breeze blows blackened scraps across the dusky environs.

Emptying the last precious drops from his canteen, he pitches it into the flaming bushes, abandons the sad wreckage, and heads back to his camp.

Feeling like the last man on Earth, Ian tromps across the sand and dirt with his flashlight illuminating the path forward. Seeing monsters in the animated shadows of desiccated oaks and scrub pocking the winding hollow, he bellows at the top of his lungs, echoing angst and grief into empty box canyons and off sheer sandstone walls, stratified over billions of years, "I spent my life and career warning humankind that the advanced race who built the megaliths hidden in plain sight would return. I knew it! I goddamn knew it! They got rid of us, boy! It took them a whole day, but they wiped us out for good! I tried to warn them. No one listened. Now it is over."

After losing his way in the dark, Ian retraces his path to the elevated vantage point atop the plateau. With his last ounce of strength and crumb of sanity, he peers into the valley below, finding an abstract pattern of sand, brush, and rock formations resolving in light and shadow. No cubes.

"I missed it. Damn."

Collapsing beside his campfire's dying embers, Ian pulls a Mexican wool blanket over his shivering form and falls asleep under the starry expanse.

What's past is prologue.

William Shakespeare

Chapter Ten:

The Aftermath

Owen | Dolomite Mountains
02:05 p.m. | May 22, 2070

Owen Haig slings the axe over his head and brings it down in a cathartic release of energy, splitting the last log atop the leveled chopping stump amid splintered chips and bark. Propping his boot on the chunked surface, he grabs the firewood and tosses it in a wheelbarrow, ready for transport to a stacked cord near the secluded mountainside retreat. Wiping a soft cloth across his sweaty shaved head, the reborn man admires a raptor soaring on an updraft.

"Another beautiful day in the Italian Alps."

Living his second life, exiled from the cruel world, Owen shifts his gaze uphill beyond a stand of pines toward kitchen windows backing the multi-level hideout's elevated main floor, exchanging waves with a shadowed figure inside.

Thwacking his axe into the stump, Owen tromps across the sun-dappled pasture speckled with blooms to a rock-lined fire pit under an ancient chestnut tree draped with solar-powered light bulbs draped from its thick lower branches, creating a rustic wooded patio setting. Pouring a cup of Italian coffee from an antique blue enamel pot warming over glowing coals, he rests back in his rough-hewn Aspen rocker and takes a long sip before whistling, "Penelope! Come here, girl! I have a present for you!"

The German Shepherd rescued off the streets of Verona hears her name and looks up from a sun-drenched granite perch overlooking a gurgling mountain stream cascading down the rugged escarpment surrounded by miles of thick forests high up in the Dolomite Mountains in Northeastern Italy near the Austrian border.

Broadening an amused smile on his scarred and weathered visage, Owen watches Penelope romp through the tall grasses, sniffing flowers and chasing a fluttering butterfly before plopping at his boots with her lolling pink tongue and an anticipatory look in her intelligent doggy eyes.

Producing a sawed-off hunk of deer antler in his calloused hand, Owen presents it to his tail-wagging friend, "Here you go. Try not to gobble it up in one sitting."

Penelope snatches the gamey delicacy and commences chewing it between her paws.

"Don't tell your Mom, or you'll get me in trouble."

Penelope licks Owen's hand, bonding with her doting master, before gnawing the treat.

Standing and stretching his aching back, Owen ambles to the overloaded wheelbarrow, pushing it up the steep rutted path onto an expansive natural hardscaped terrace extending into the shadows beneath the cabin's rear half suspended into the thin mountain air on stilts.

Adding the split wood to his stack, Owen parks the wheelbarrow in his tool shed and enters the ground-floor mud room through an unlocked screen door. Sitting on a reclaimed paint-chipped wooden pew with the solid granite mountainside at his back, Owen pulls off his boots, picking up a muffled conversation from upstairs.

Pushing up his waffle-woven crewneck shirt sleeves, he splashes water on his face from a basin and dries off with a towel before climbing the creaky steps to the main floor in his socked feet.

Entering the kitchen, Owen nods and smiles at the visitor, Frederick Neumayer, a hale and hearty Austrian woodsman who has lived in the Dolomites his entire life.

"Hello, Frederick. It's been a while. What brings you to our little slice of Heaven?"

Circling the table, Owen kisses Bianca's cheek, less interested in the old man's reply than his woman's lovely face with what's cooking for dinner coming in a distant second, "Honey, you smell so good."

Bianca shoots Owen with her trademark sly grin, "You just plain smell."

"Well, that's what two solid years of chopping wood will do for a man—make him horny as a bear in heat, with a pheromone mixed with sweat aroma to match."

Comfortable with the hospitable couple's cheeky banter and familiar with their heartbreaking, harrowing backstories, Frederick chuckles. "You know, Owen. You remind me of a ski instructor I knew in the old days. The man had a wit about him. However, I believe his quick jokes masked a sadness."

"Oh, come on now, Freddie. What's past is prologue. Everything is good now."

Eye-rolling at Owen, repeating his favorite quote, Bianca freshens Frederick's mug, "I am not sure you understand the meaning behind that expression."

"Yeah. Probably not." Owen gives his well-read partner a playful shoulder squeeze before pouring himself a cup. "But all misquoted

Shakespeare aside, what do I have to be sad about?"

Bianca taps the chair beside hers, "Owen, would you sit still for a minute and let Frederick share his news—he has something important to tell us."

Owen plops in the wooden chair beside Bianca and places an arm around her toned shoulders. Kissing her cheek, he notes the vestigial scars marring her perfect olive-skinned complexion, adding a hint of sexy danger to her beauty. Ripping his eyes from his soul mate, Owen turns to the patient old man seated across the table, "Okay, Frederick, what's up?"

In his 90s, but with the stamina of a much younger man, Frederick pushes his ceramic mug aside and clasps his hands on the table, "Let me get straight to the point. I returned yesterday from Cortina d'Ampezzo. The town is in ruins. Everyone is dead." Shaking his head, trying to rationalize the horrible vision in his mind, he continues, "It is as if half the townspeople turned into rabid animals and attacked the other half. The carnage and chaos must have overwhelmed the constabulary in the first minutes. There is no one left in the beautiful town."

Owen's jaw drops, trying to quantify the man's words, "When …"

"Six days ago. I drove to the village for supplies and discovered dead bodies blocking the road, like the aftermath of a pitched battle." The old man removes his glasses and rubs his eyes, "So much death. So much blood. Madness. Just madness." Pausing to formulate his words, Frederick leans forward, lowering his voice, "I know this sounds crazy, but I felt a strange malevolence … I don't recommend using the roads anymore. Something is afoot."

"How do you know someone did not follow you here?"

"Not a chance, Miss Valentino. I hid my truck in the woods and took a backcountry fire trail home. After checking on my cats, I went to warn my old friend Salvatore."

"The horse breeder?"

"Yes, Owen, but I was too late. I liberated my favorite Maremmano from the stable and headed here. I hope one or both of you will hike back to the stables with me. I can't leave the other animals to starve."

"Sure, Frederick. I'll go with you." Owen turns to Bianca, grappling with the alarming news, "They did it. The hand-to-hand mortal combat matches the museum incidents. The motherfuckers figured out how to weaponize the nanobots from the forged paintings on a grand scale."

Frederick waves his hands, attempting to turn down the heat, "Owen, hold on, I do not know about elsewhere. With the Thundercorps down, there is no method of communicating long distance. Perhaps it was an isolated attack."

Bianca shakes her head, "No, Frederick. The plan was for The Powers That Be—or whatever evil they became—to take their killer nanobot technology worldwide." With an ironic laugh, she continues, "Never underestimate just how diabolical the PTB can be. First, they brought down the Thundercorps, saving the nanobots for after to maximize the chaos and confusion. Brilliant."

Owen's eyes widen, pointing a finger in the air, "Ah, wait just a minute here! Remember the Blue Spark jab? That is how they dispersed the nanobots."

"I hate to ask, but you never took the jab in 2052, right?"

Indignant, Frederick smooths his thick gray mustache, "Good Christ, no! My body is my temple!"

Pulling suppressed memories from the dark corners of his mind, "I witnessed what the Blue Spark did to Rachel. It was obvious from the start that the jabs pawned off on the world were not the same thing." Owen shakes his head, "Those poor people."

Bianca runs a hand through her thick black hair streaked with a shock of gray, harkening back to the year of the jab, "Owen, I was convalescing in Milan at the time with no idea if you were alive. There was so much misinformation and rumors about a Blue Spark miracle drug, millions lined up for weeks to be like Rachel Haig."

Owen suppresses memories of his previous life and concern for Rachel, leaning forward to look into the old man's worried eyes, "Frederick, stay here with us. It is not safe to go home."

"No." Frederick smiles through his mustache, "You are both too kind. I need to get back to my kitties. The wee ones count on me. But I will take you up on accompanying me back to the stables."

* * *

Soaking in an antique four-legged bathtub filled to the curved rim with piping hot spring water, Owen watches Penelope through his sleepy eyes, lying sideways on a pink shag bathmat, kicking her legs, and dreaming of God knows what.

Trees sway in the nighttime darkness, scratching against the panes outside the steamy bathroom windows as the door creaks open, revealing Bianca's sensuous form backlit in a light shaft penetrating the dim flickering candlelight.

Letting a towel drop from her midriff, the leggy Milanese steps into the tub and melds into Owen with a sultry moan. Probing nimble fingers under the hot water, she guides him inside with unbridled desire, rolling her hips to Owen's rhythmic thrusts.

"Remember our first night in Panarea? I wanted you to take me, Owen."

"I'm here now."

Sloshing water over the side, Bianca twists her nimble body, straddling Owen and giggling at his goofy-faced expression. Angling her head back and flinging her short black hair from side to side, she rises out of the water, pert breasts glistening in the candlelight, "… and making up for the lost time."

Owen pulls her close and kisses her soft lips, pressing deeper inside as a distinct noise shatters the moment.

Thwack-thwack!

Bianca sits up and checks Penelope, staring toward the bathroom door, looking nervous and emitting a low growl.

"What was that?"

Owen sighs as the romantic interlude fizzles, "Trees rustling, Bianca. We are fine. No one knows we are here."

"That's what worries me." Bianca stands out of the tub and wraps the towel around her dripping body. "Owen. Will you check downstairs? I am scared."

Standing out of the tub, Owen towels off and pulls up a pair of flannel pajama pants, padding barefoot and grumbling to the bottom of the stairs through the mud room and out the back door. Halfway across the terrace, he peers into the blustery, moonless night, "Anybody out here? Show yourself. I have a gun and am not afraid to use it."

Out of the corner of his eye and too late to react, Owen catches a human blur in filthy tatters vaulting from the tool shed and knocking him to the ground. Bleeding down his face from a forehead gash and terrified for his new family's safety, Owen kicks at the crazed attacker, crawling toward the door. The relentless and snarling middle-aged male latches onto his leg like a rabid animal, dragging him to the terrace edge with inhuman strength and toppling Owen down the steep incline.

Tumbling out of control, fending off gnashing teeth and scratching nails, Owen crashes against the cutting stump, feeling a sharp pain in his ribcage. Punching free of the lunatic with hazy memories of his old Krav Maga lessons in self-defense proving worthless in the melee moment, Owen pulls the axe from the stump where he had left it earlier and takes a wild backward swing, grazing the man's shredded torso enough to slow his advance. Stumbling backward to clear space and look for any sign of humanity in the man's lifeless eyeballs bulging from blackened sockets like sallow orbs of deadness, Owen gasps for air, taunting the man through gritted teeth, "Okay, you bastard …."

Gripping the axe handle like a baseball bat, Owen shifts into a batter's stance and waits for the next attack. The man, missing part of his face, does not disappoint, coming straight at him with a wailing and terrifying frontal assault, like a slow-motion fastball right over the plate. Waiting until the last possible second, Owen lops off the attacker's head like Carlton Fisk's home run swing in the 75 World Series.

Coughing and wheezing for oxygen with his heart beating out of his chest, Owen kicks the man to ensure he is dead before rushing uphill into the cabin, still wielding the axe like a firefighter, finding Bianca and Penelope huddling in the bedroom closet.

"Owen! Are you okay? You are bleeding!"

"Broken ribs and possible concussion; other than that, I'm just peachy. That was a nanobot victim paying us a visit. Judging by what was left of his clothing, he was probably on a backpacking trip in the mountains when his brain melted. There could be more out there. We need to keep things locked down for the foreseeable future. I am getting the old man and bringing him and his cats to our place at first light. There is safety in numbers."

"What about the horses?"

"Oh, good Christ, yes, the horses, too."

Owen drops the bloody axe on a towel and grabs his ribs, wincing in pain, scooching into the closet beside his two best friends, "In the meantime, can I sit here with you guys? I need the rest."

Penelope snuggles her head on Owen's lap as Bianca leans over and proffers a soft kiss on his bruised cheek, "Let me get you cleaned up."

Pope Pius XIII | St. Peter's Square
12:25 a.m. | June 1, 2070

The former Cardinal John Caldwell Montgomery of the Archdiocese of Chicago sits alone on a red velour gold-trimmed seat pulled from his official Vatican residence and situated on the intricate block patterns and travertine lines radiating from the Vatican Obelisk with the ornate dome of St. Peter's Basilica rising into the smoky Heavens at his back. Pulling a cigarette from his pack, he lights it, blowing smoke into the night while checking his solid gold mechanical Omega wristwatch with a tsk-tsk.

The Overlords are late.

* * *

Now in his twelfth year as Pope Pius XIII, the 72-year-old American came to prominence, taking up His cross and transforming from a backseater Cardinal into a vocal and outspoken critic of The Powers That Be and the new world order while pressing on as a tireless evangelical, rallying the despondent flock after the Gorks' botched 2044 invasion reduced civilization to a paganistic stone age. In the riotous, chaotic aftermath, mobilizing Catholics to help thy neighbors proved all-consuming, exhausting his keen intellect debating a faceless anarchical, hedonistic anti-religiosity spawned from resentful masses that believed a just God would have never let the Gork invasion happen.

Where was God when we needed Him?

With over half the Church lying in ruins worldwide, the decimated College of Cardinals took note of their courageous and controversial rising star, placing all of their unbroken golden eggs in his basket, even referring to him as a lower-case savior. The praise made Montgomery bristle at his feckless and cowardly colleagues in red, but he accepted the post with tearful resoluteness, knowing his dear old Mom looked down with pride at her boy.

As a poke in the eye to the mainstream do-gooders comfortable in their gilded palaces while their flocks' suffering continued unchecked, Cardinal Montgomery chose the controversial name Pius XIII after Pius XII. Feeling a prayerful kinship with the conflicted Pope who walked a nightmarish tightrope, fostering the Catholic Church through

Nazism, World War 2, and the initial throes of communism sweeping the world, he viewed his tenure as even more precipitous—one false move and the entire construct of organized religion would fall. He knew it. His enemies knew it. The devil tempted the desperate and afflicted, proffering miraculous and easy fixes, like a reinvented internet or a snake oil technology that would lift the world from its self-inflicted morass. The ultimate trick up the devil's sleeve manifested in the false promise of superhuman abilities and immortality via an innocuous injection. The Blue Spark. In his heart, the Pope knew that the jabs caused the Purge—a brutal and savage May day, two weeks earlier where over two-thirds of humanity ripped free of the mortal coil in a subhuman murderous orgy reminiscent of William-Adolphe Bouguereau's *Dante and Virgil,* only bloodier. Much bloodier.

In the Purge's bloody wake, with the world's governments dissolved into the ether and the rudderless third of the populace still alive, either starving and cowering in fear or terrorizing the countryside in murderous bands, the Pope stood as God's sentinel athwart sin and darkness. Alone and afraid, with scant papal staff and what remained of his vaunted Vatican Guard cowering in fear like the Twelve Apostles, Pius roamed the porous grounds by himself under a heavy pall of a burning Rome hanging in the polluted air as he prayed over the sick and dying. Powerless to stop armed militant groups from breaching the Vatican's inner sanctums and plundering the Church's history, he watched precious relics and artifacts carried off like looted sneakers by the armloads beyond the walls, never to be restored.

Pius' faith remained unshaken, born from an unquenchable belief that everything is according to God's plan.

Following a stem-winder homily in his native Chicago-accented English to shell-shocked hundreds at his first outdoor Mass in the post-Purge world, Pius XIII learned from rangers on horseback that strange newcomers who called themselves the Overlords were manifesting all over the globe.

Praying for guidance, Pius requested an audience with the newcomers, cognizant of a summit's implications for the beleaguered world.

In what could be a final message to his surviving colleagues delivered via old-school telegraph, an introspective Pontiff got straight to the point:

> *"I will negotiate an amicable peace to the best of my God-given abilities, but if I perish, the Church must go on. As priests, it will be up to you to minister to the sick and pray for their souls. There may be fewer of us than a month ago by a solid measure, but we, Band of Brothers and Sisters, must prevail. And now, it is incumbent upon me as humankind's ambassador to have an audience with the strange arrivals who call themselves the Overlords. I trust they are also part of God's plan from another time and place. What else is there to say? Pray to give me strength, and may God have mercy on our souls."*

> *Pope Pius XIII; His Holiness; Your Holiness; Holy Father.*

* * *

Praying for wisdom and courage, Pius XIII stubs out his cigarette, reflecting upon his namesake's secret negotiations with the Nazis as another meteor shower streaks across the chilly Italian night sky. On cue, the Overlords arrive in a bright flash, like lightning, illuminating St. Peter's Square in stark contrast. Blinded by their brightness, Monty, as some still call him, wearing a white cassock and skull cap, simple black loafers, and white socks, stands from his chair and takes three steps into the abyss. Allowing his vision to adjust, he lights another cigarette with shaky hands, scrutinizing the extraordinary delegation of twelve beings resolving from nothingness and floating toward him.

Blowing smoke through pursed lips, Pius raises a hand and

speaks with a gravelly authority, "I cannot float or walk on water like our Lord. Does that disappoint you, my friends?"

The incredible being at the center of the delegation settles onto the pavers, his large bare feet showing under flowing white robes glowing from within and silhouetting his ghostly form. Walking within long-armed reach of Pius' resolute stance, the hairless seven-foot humanoid proffers a peculiar grin, widening his porcelain Romanesque features like an animating sculpture while raising Pius three feet into the air. Meeting the Pontiff's steely gaze, the Overlord's sonorous tone resonates without moving his full lips, "Now you are a god. Does that please you?"

Swallowing hard, his feet dangling in the early-morning air like a marionette, Pius puffs from the lit cigarette in his trembling hand and blows smoke at the disrespectful humanoid's face, "There is only one true God, and it is not you or your friends. Please put me down."

The being's smile dissolves into a humorless shrug, dropping Pius to the pavers with a dismissive wave of his massive hand.

Regaining his footing, Pius catches his breath and smooths his cassock, flicking his glowing butt at the feet of the others, "Enough games. What do you want with my world?"

Another male from the contingent slides forward with visible agitation on his milky-white countenance, "Your world? I am afraid you are mistaken. We inhabited this planet when your forebears rutted naked in the wilderness like savage beasts. How peculiar and ironic that your species' demise resembles its primitive and violent beginnings."

Pius blanches at the cursed alien, "You are responsible for the Purge and the deaths of tens of billions of people. May you all rot in hell."

The leader extends his arms, turning down the heat between the ignorant and foolish human and his delegation, "Pope Pius XIII? Is that right?" Nodding without awaiting an answer, he continues, "Once more, you are misguided in your vitriolic attack. We take no credit or blame for the billions that perished. The Purge, as you call it, is a testament to your species' folly. An arrogant and misguided scientist within your kind co-opted our cubed technology to replicate sixteen sublime transhumans malleable to our cause. The sixteen progeny of his ill-fated experiment killed billions, not us. We came in peace while the Sisters cleaved over two-thirds of humanity from its roots."

Pius looks at his shoes, wanting another cigarette and contemplating the veracity of the leader's story while admitting to himself that it rings true.

Noting the Priest's grudging acceptance, the pleased Overlord continues, "The remains of the day following annihilation are yours to determine. Live or die, it matters not to us, but any attempts to interfere with the resurrection of our civilization will be met with swift and just retribution."

A glittering female separates from the group of twelve, assessing the plaza's history-rich layout, "You should be embarrassed, old man. These grounds consist of an amalgamation of materials applied in an ignorant expression of misguided architectural tropes. Your primitive civilization stole our brilliance while ignoring the underlying principles. Replicating without acknowledging the origins, paying little heed to the function underlying the form. Even more egregious, deceiving yourselves into believing the ingenuity manifested from your meager intellects. I posit your kind could never reach our exalted station if we allowed another million years to pass."

Unable to repress his humiliating anger, Pius pivots onto the conceited woman towering over him, "How dare you cast aspersions on this hallowed ground, inspired by a reverence for God and conceived and realized by magnificent architects, artists, and craftsman whose brilliance and talents were legendary."

The leader scoffs, "That is inaccurate. Look behind you, Priest. This obelisk at your back was stolen from a place you call Egypt over two thousand years ago. Given its hallowed position at the center of your plaza, your forebears recognized a significance underlying the design yet remained blind to its utility through a pitiable conceit."

Pius looks up at the Vatican Obelisk, indeed brought to Rome around the time of Christ before Sixtus V moved it in the 1500s to its current location. "That does not count! We have … we had … civilized the world, bringing peace and order to the planet. That is until the Gorks came. No one knew. No one knew." Pius falls to his knees and starts to weep.

The leader places an immobilizing hand on the disconsolate Pope, "Priest? Is it not a sin for you to lie?"

Quelling shameful tears, Pius shuns the being's painful hold on his arthritic body, forcing his watery gaze upon the Overlord's terrifying visage, "I do not lie."

Releasing the Pontiff with an expression bordering on genuine disappointment, the Overlord gesticulates his muscular arms around the plaza, "Vast storerooms beneath our feet contain records of off-worlders' incursions dating back to your antiquity and earlier. It is a fabrication to declare that the clumsy and infantile Gorkian invaders' attack was a surprise. You know better, Priest."

Cognizant that he may be the last person on Earth who knows The Powers That Be took possession of the Church's alien secrets and moved them to a secret location, decades earlier, Pius redirects the interrogation onto his radiant audience. "If you are our forebears, are you not also children of God?"

Growing weary of the pointless debate with the obstinate and frail old man, the leader proffers a heavy sigh, "Before the planet's cataclysmic upheavals erased us from Earth's memory, our genetic code mirrored your species. However, an advanced race hybridized with us at a crossroads of our civilization, transforming our kind into quintessential beings with telekinetic powers, freed from the shackles of corporeal existence. During this halcyon epoch, our technological advancements encircled the planet with magnificent monuments to our alien benefactors and engineering feats of computing, telemetry, astronomy, and infinite sources of pure energy."

The female hovers next to the leader, picking up their backstory, "That was until a cosmic force doomed our perfect world to ruin. We shed our physical forms and uploaded our essences to the cubes now reappearing across the planet, covering large swaths like hatcheries, waiting to project back into physical beings."

Pius interjects, "This may be a semantical argument at best, but what you so blithely refer to as your essences, I call souls, which harkens to the one true God."

Eleven of the glowing Overlords recede into the ether, leaving the leader alone with Pius XIII in the middle of St. Peter's Square.

"I read you, Priest. Your faith is shaken. How could your God leave this burdensome leadership in your weak, arthritic hands?"

Whispering a prayer, the Pope turns and stares up at the obelisk, "I admit I never understood the significance of this red granite monolith made by pagan architects. And yet, humanity revels in a sense of mystery and faith in the unknown. We see beauty without a need to pull things apart and assess their former function while nurturing a keen curiosity. That is enough. The rest we leave to our Lord and Savior. Not everything can or should be known."

Turning back to the Overlord, Pius smiles, lighting another cigarette, "You are correct. The Church knew of alien life long before its disclosure to the masses. But the miracle of the resurrection is sacrosanct. My belief is unwavering. I will not bend a knee to your kind."

The Overlord hisses his disappointment, shaking his sculpted head.

Pius notes the reaction and presses his thin and fleeting advantage, "Since the Purge, there are no longer enough of us to repel your arrival, but we will try. You see, you miscalculate whom you are dealing with. We may be too stupid to know when we are beaten, which perhaps is our God-given advantage. While your kind fled Earth when a comet loomed, we persevered through incalculable schisms, wars, and natural disasters. If not for the destruction of the Library of Florence, I have no doubt the mysteries of your departure and the structures you left behind would be common knowledge. That may be history's most egregious sin."

The Pope takes a long drag and blows it into the brisk night air, "We will fight. That is the truth. I cannot lie."

The Overlord's visage hardens, "Are you the last of your kind claiming a position of authority?"

Pius XIII manages a hearty chuckle, harkening back to his Chicago roots, "Let me be frank, kill me, and someone else takes up my shield and sword. Look to the Gorks, my radiant friend. They did not make it a single day. Other superior extraterrestrial forces have attempted to dominate through the ages, hoisted on their own petard."

"I do not understand the reference."

"It's Shakespeare, you ignorant buffoon."

"Very well." Having endured enough of the old man's insults, the Overlord leader thrusts his hands into the night sky, conjuring a swirling mass of nightmarish red wraiths descending upon the Pope and elevating him to the bronze cross high atop the Vatican Obelisk. Pulling his weak arms straight out, the mocking ghosts nail Pius' hands and feet to the solid metal cross before swarming off to inflict hell on Earth.

With the unproductive negotiation concluded, the Overlord hovers before Pius, forcing the bloodied and beaten mortal to raise his addled head and meet his menacing glare, "If it is your intent to martyr yourself, Priest, let it be so."

* * *

Pius regains consciousness as the thick metal cleats holding his hands to the cross begin to slip. Hanging from the dizzying height, the helpless man mutters another Hail Mary as a brilliant blue flash illuminates the predawn plaza.

Fearing the Overlords' return, Pius repeats: "Hail Mary, Full of

Grace …" as gentle voices reach his ears. Assuming angels prepare to carry him to meet Saint Peter at the Gate of Heaven, joyful tears well in his crusty, swollen eyes.

"Hector, be careful with him."

"I'm trying, Monica. The wraiths hammered metal rods right through his palms. What a mess. Hold on, your Holiness, I got you."

Pius moans from the searing pain and blood loss as a warm, comforting embrace separates him from the cross and lowers him to solid ground.

Lying prone, Pius struggles to focus on the blurry vision of a man and woman hovering over him, dressing his wounds in a thick gauze.

The woman pierces a long needle into his shoulder, "Don't worry, Father, this will ease your pain while we transport you to the base."

The man pauses to scan a wandering horde entering the plaza, "Monica, we have company."

The pretty woman studies the listless groups, "No hostiles—at least for now. Let's finish this up and get him out of here."

Pius feels the woman's supple hands wrapping his throbbing head, fixating a druggy gaze on her pert breasts under an army-green tee embroidered with a numeral 3. Trying to establish a coherent thought, Pius blurts out, "Who are you?"

The young man's youthful voice evokes confidence and a hint of pride, "We are the Final Eight."

The woman reaches across and smacks her partner's arm, offering the Pontiff an apologetic eye-rolling grin, "Two of the eight … I'm Monica Grasso, and this is Hector Gonzalez."

Automatic gunfire ends the introductions as the shell-shocked crowds disperse, searching for places to hide from their traitorous fellow humans, "Monica, we need to get the fuck out of here. Now!"

Looking down at a bloody and beaten Pope Pius XIII, Hector

shrugs his shoulders with a sheepish grin, "Oops, sorry, Padre. I better watch my language around the Pope."

The Overlords | The White House
05:35 p.m. | June 15, 2070

Miasmal fog permeates the stillness as kettles of vultures devour the fly and worm-infested rotting flesh and bones of tens of thousands lying twisted together in rictal death poses across the National Mall and Tidal Basin. Within the Beltway alone, over a million more grotesque mutilated bodies litter the streets, buildings, hotels, universities, museums, and eateries of the nation's former capital, where over seventy percent of the population, including most of official Washington, fell prey to the Purge.

The Blue Spark jab's false promise of a better life through the brain-enhancing miracle drug confirmed what shell-shocked survivors knew from the start: There are no miracles.

* * *

A trio of Overlords arrive on the overgrown White House lawn near the burnt-out airframe of Marine One and enter the ruins at 1600 Pennsylvania Avenue. Floating past indigent squatters cowering in fear under a profane vandalized life-sized portrait of a smiling Hillary Clinton overlooked by looters who either stole or burned everything not nailed down, they navigate the dark interior's former gilded glory to the West Wing, encountering zero resistance, as expected.

Pulling through a pile of mangled corpses twisted together in a bullet-riddled corridor splattered with dried blood and offal where a discombobulated last stand took place, they pause to check the deceased individuals' identities as rats skitter along the molded baseboards.

One of the Overlords tosses a dismembered forearm wearing

an expensive watch atop the pile and nods further down the darkened passage, "Their leader is not among these bodies. Let us move on."

Gliding above the blood-soaked plush carpeting, an Overlord waves a hand and parts locked double doors like the Red Sea, "In here."

The trio bisects a cleaned-out anteroom before entering the Oval Office, finding the co-leader of the free world slumped over the Resolute Desk with half his head blown all over the frame-filled credenza at his back with the .45 still clutched in his crooked fingers.

Pulling on his greasy, thinning gray hair, they peel the still attached half of his slackened face from the dried pool of blood on his blotter and lean him back in his fancy leather chair, his head lolling sideways with a one-eyed stare into oblivion.

An Overlord pushes a finger into the President's eye socket and digs out what's left of the eyeball as another Overlord swipes open a virtual screen to engage the retinal scanning software protecting the nation's last set of nuclear launch codes dated May 16, 2070. The date of the Purge.

Holding the still-gooey eyeball before the artificial intelligence, the beings wait as the algorithmic gatekeeper attempts to recognize the President's unique retinal pattern.

After a quantum reconstruction of the half-decayed eye, the scanner produces a crisp beep, opening a new screen with a long series of scrolling codes as a feminine computerized voice recites a litany of instructions and fail-safes incumbent on the President—or his successor—before launching a single missile from its silo.

The beings absorb the classified information before joining comrades pursuing similar intelligence from the world's former nuclear powers.

Hannah | Villa St. Claire
03:35 p.m. | June 22, 2070

Avoiding the Overlords' human concentration camps metastasizing over large swaths of Europe, Hannah tests her energized superhuman abilities by day, holed up in barns, empty rail cars, and deserted homes, awaiting the cover of darkness to travel. Realizing the boundless powers of her inherited Blue Spark, she defies gravity with ease like her dear-departed Mom on a southerly route from Oslo over Denmark, Germany, and Austria before tipping into northern Italy and the Provence region of Southern France in search of a storied villa—Dad's last known address.

Closing in on her destination, a large estate surrounded by vineyards and forests in the commune of Le Tholonet, she rises over the last physical barrier blocking her path—the gradual northern slope of Montagne Sainte-Victoire's rugged limestone ridgeline rising before her blue-green eyes. Flying to the top like a trapeze artist without a swing, she looks down at the moonlit, craggy rock formations contrasting light and dark as déjà vu stops her dead in her tracks.

Settling atop a lofty ledge overlooking the mountain's precipitous southern face and the Mediterranean sparkling on the dark horizon, she swoons with a heady familiarity.

"Mom and Dad were here."

Exploring the boulder-strewn heights, Hannah retraces her steps and stumbles upon a camouflaged aperture visible only from a specific sight line.

"Of course, Mom told me the story about the cavern where they met Grandpa Neil for the first time."

Turning a brilliant glowing blue, Hannah jumps feet first into the void, descending like an elevator to the slippery limestone beside a fast-flowing subterranean stream.

With an owl-like night vision, Hannah lowers her radiance and turns toward the silhouette of a decrepit airframe listing on its side a hundred feet downstream. Vaulting through the cavern's stillness, she lands on a broken wing and steps in her scuffed boots to the cockpit. Peering inside, she finds a skeletonized pilot still wearing its flight jacket with his skull propped against the busted canopy. Searching the tight cockpit, Hannah grasps a photograph and gapes at the black and white portrait. Startled by a familial resemblance to the beautiful woman smiling from the well-preserved image, she flips the silvery print, reading faint numbers on the back.

Searching for more links to the past, Hannah slides a hand inside the dead pilot's flight jacket and removes a yellowed envelope. Opening the brittle paper in her delicate fingers, Hannah recognizes her Mother's familiar longhand script."

"Mom had excellent penmanship."

Clearing her throat, she reads the letter to her deceased ancestor resting in the plane.

Dear Grandpa Neil Alexander,

I am returning Grandma's photograph to where it belongs with you in your final resting place. I am sorry it has taken so long to return it, but we went from weird to bizarre and back again before my Blue Spark destiny became a fully realized phenomenon.

You told me to have faith, and I did. Now, I am something of a celebrity accompanying President Lena Jackson on campaign trips around the country, lending my Blue Spark powers to rally public support in the strange new post-invasion world.

By the way, you have a new granddaughter named Hannah. Owen and I love her to pieces. She is the apple of his eye, doting over her when the PTB is not pulling him away on extended business trips. What did we sign up for? :)

With my Blue Spark on full display, I travel the country but keep little Hannah's inherited powers a secret. Even Owen does not know that my transformative DNA passed on to her. It requires all of my strength to maintain the secret. In the coming years, as she matures, it will drain my life force to keep her free of my burdens—the cross I bear as her Mother.

Why, you may ask, do I maintain this facade? I guess it is safe to say I do not trust The Powers That Be. I know that they will experiment on her as the first naturally-born transhuman. She is indeed remarkable. Someday, when I am gone and can no longer hide her powers, Hannah's Blue Spark will evolve far beyond mine—which is a good thing—she may have to save the world like her dear old Mom. Stranger things have happened.

PS—When Owen discovered my plan to return the photograph, he asked about your Black Scorpions flight jacket. I told him it belonged to you and perhaps someday to Hannah.

Thank you, Grandpa Neil, for helping us save the world (the first time), and I know I will see you again in Heaven.

God Bless,

Rachel Alexander Haig

Her eyes filling with tears, Hannah folds the letter and places it inside the cockpit on top of the photograph, her right elbow knocking Grandpa Neil's skull loose from his desiccated spinal column.

"Oops, sorry, Grandpa."

Wincing at her clumsy desecration of a hallowed final repose like a grave robber, Hannah examines the flight jacket, finding it as supple and wearable as the day Grandpa Neil put it on for the last time over a century before, save for its holed and stained left side. Hannah shrugs and pulls it off the remains, "Oh, what the hell. You certainly don't need it anymore, and I could use a jacket."

Louie | Villa St. Claire
05:15 a.m. | June 23, 2070

Settling in the predawn fog at Villa St. Claire's busted front gate, Hannah adjusts her pack straps and crunches across the gravelly circular driveway to the front door. Unsure of what lies within, she raises her hand and hesitates before giving the paint-chipped door a solid knock.

Biting her lip, checking her six, making sure she is alone, she hears movement from inside as the door inches open.

"Who is there?"

"Hannah. Hannah Haig."

The door creaks open another inch, "Please repeat."

With an exasperated sigh, she repeats, "Hannah Haig. Owen and Rachel's daughter."

The door swings wide, revealing an archetypical Frenchman, "Hannah Haig. You don't say? What a surprise. Please come in from the cold. You are turning blue."

"That is a long story."

"My dear, it goes back farther than you know."

"Is my father here?"

* * *

Louie brings two coffees to the butcher block table and slides into a seat across from Hannah, taking a long sip while contemplating the young girl's familiar face.

"You favor Rachel's beauty. Has anyone told you that?"

Hannah laughs and takes a long drink, "Oh, that is good coffee.

I can't remember the last time I had a decent cup. Yes, Louie. Everyone has told me that my whole life."

"You asked about Owen. He returned here in 2048 to take part in a PTB mission. That was the start of his troubles … he loved your Mother, Hannah."

"I remember celebrating the Fourth of July, and then he was gone." Hannah reaches into a pocket, pulls out her favorite picture, and passes it across the table. "We never saw him again. Dave said he had died a hero. I was three."

Louie fingers the photograph of a smiling Owen and a happy-go-lucky three-year-old Hannah grinning from ear to ear with a sparkler in her little hand.

Hannah smiles, "It was also my third birthday celebration. Today, I turned 25."

Louie slides the photo back across the table, "Happy birthday, Hannah."

"Did Owen ever return here to the villa?"

Louie raises an eyebrow, "Indeed, your Mother kept a lot from you. She had her reasons … No, Miss Hannah, your father couldn't return here to the Villa St. Claire. He was wanted by the PTB for trumped-up crimes and, as far as I am aware, remains a fugitive to this day."

Louie stands and moves into the great room with the first glimmering of morning light eking through the sparkling clean sliders, "However, he did contact me from somewhere in Italy in the early 2050s. Don't ask me how, but his resourcefulness was boundless. I hope and pray that it still is."

Hannah leans forward, hanging on Louie's drawn-out account, "Come on, Louie. What did he want? Do you know where he is?"

"Out of respect for your Mother—God rest her soul—I hesitate to tell you the next part of the story." Louie hefts a weighty art volume from its place in the great room and drops it with a thud atop the butcher block table. "Believe it or not, this book contains the answer you seek."

Louie flips through the pages, looking for a colorful spread featuring Diego Velázquez's masterpiece, *Portrait of Innocent X.*

"Ah, here it is."

Hannah leans forward, studying the vibrant color plate, "Looks like a mean guy."

"Looks can be deceiving." Pausing to formulate his words, the resilient C-Class replicant continues, "When Owen arrived at the villa for his last mission, he was assigned to work with an art forgery expert named Bianca Valentino. She favored this volume. Owen knew that. It was their secret connection." Turning the book toward the light, Louie smiles at Hannah, "Look closer, my dear. Tell me what you see."

Hannah lowers large blue-green eyes closer to the glossy page, "Oh yeah, I see it. Indentations of writing … of what … I guess numbers. Yes, a sequence of numbers."

Louie exhales, "Coordinates, to be precise. Bianca wrote them on a separate sheet, pressing into the page, hoping beyond hope that Owen would discover it and reunite with her someday."

Hannah frowns, "How could she know to do this before their troubles even began?"

Louie shrugs, "I don't know. Woman's intuition, perhaps. The fairer sex is one of life's enduring mysteries."

Hannah finishes her coffee and touches the book, "Now, why would she leave this information for my Dad?"

Louie meets Hannah's watery gaze, "They fell in love."

Hannah nods to herself, mulling the words in her head, and leans back in her chair, "Well, Mom married Dave Poole. I guess all is fair in love and war."

Louie smiles, relieved to have that nugget in the open, "Well said, Miss Hannah. Bianca's keen sense of foreshadowing prompted her to conceal the coordinates to her secret retreat high up in the Dolomite Mountains on this page."

Hannah examines the Papal portrait, committing the faint impression of the numbers to her photographic memory.

"So, somehow, this artwork carries a hidden meaning between them."

Louie nods, "Very perceptive, Hannah. However, years passed without any contact with Owen or Bianca, while the PTB kept this place under surveillance on the off chance that one or both would return. Of course, Owen and Bianca knew better than to do that."

"Louie, I'm tired. Please get to the point."

"Oh, I do apologize, my dear. You see, I do not receive visitors aside from the beggars and bands of highwaymen. They are a dangerous lot."

"I'm sorry, Louie. How have you managed to keep this place intact for over two decades? It looks perfect."

Louie smiles, "Olga and Sven do most of the work. They are patrolling the grounds. Perhaps you will meet them later today."

Entering the kitchen, Louie opens a catch-all drawer, "Let me finish the story so you can rest from your travels." Holding up an old Thundercorp phone, he smiles, "Owen left a voice message on this device in 2054. Would you care to hear it?"

Hannah's eyes light up, "That phone still holds a charge? Hell, yes, I would!"

Pressing the screen to life, Louie passes her the phone, "I had to tinker with the battery to keep it from dying and preserve the data."

Hannah scrutinizes the smart device, her hand turning blue, "This is an older model ... you know I worked for Julius Hart's Thundercorp."

"Really? The man was a genius."

"He died on Thundercorp Number 5. I was the only survivor."

"Yes, the malignant handiwork of The Powers That Be."

Hannah nods in agreement, activating the voice message as her Father's voice crackles from the old speaker:

Louie, this is Owen Haig. This message goes to a Thundercorp phone under your name. I hope you receive it. Here is the deal: if you are still in charge of the villa and get this message, I need you to do something for me. Find a book on the old Spanish painter Velasquez in the villa's library and search the pages for a clue from Bianca. This message is no doubt being traced. I will contact you again in one week. I hope you get this, Louie. I am desperate. I do not know how much longer I can survive in this world.

Hannah looks up and hands the device back to Louie. "What happened?"

"I discovered the coordinates in short order, but PTB agents intercepted the call and ransacked the villa, looking for the book."

"What did you do?"

"I gave them another volume with fake coordinates to somewhere in the Pyrenees. That was the last time the PTB darkened the doors of this house."

"Did my Father call back in a week?"

Louie shakes his head, "Two years passed before I heard back from Owen, a drowning man in an endless sea, but he managed to send an encrypted text mid-2056 to this same phone. Fearful of revealing the coordinates to anyone intercepting the text, I used a substitution cipher similar to a Caesar Cipher, but trickier to unravel to mask the coordinates when I replied."

"What happened?"

Louie arches his thick black eyebrows and shrugs, "I don't know if he received my reply, let alone decoded the coordinates. Or if he ever reunited with Bianca. They may both be dead by now, for all I know."

With a loud yawn, Hannah stretches her arms straight out, "No, Louie, my Father is alive. I feel it in my bones, but right now, I need sleep. Can I crash here for a few days before heading to the Dolomites?"

A smile widens under Louie's thin mustache, "Hannah, the

Villa St. Claire is your inheritance."

Hannah slings her pack off a chairback with Neil's old flight jacket stuffed in the outer pocket, "Which way?"

Louie grins, "The master bedroom is upstairs and down the hall on the left."

Hannah frowns, "Um, I can't sleep in the room where Mom and Dad slept. Too many ghosts."

Louie nods, "I understand. Take Bianca's suite—she favored that bedroom every time she visited the villa in the old days."

Hannah looks across the great room to the open door leading into the warm and cozy space before catching Louie off guard with a sly grin, "So, Louie, what did you think of Bianca? Be honest."

Scratching his neck, Louie considers the loaded question, "First, no one will ever replace your Mom. She was special. My heart broke when you informed me of her death."

Mulling memories of the sexy and beguiling Bianca, Louie cracks a grin, "However, I recall the day Owen and Bianca met. Your father put up a brave front, feigning indifference toward the radiant Bianca out of love and respect for you and Rachel. However, he was doomed from the moment he first laid eyes upon Bianca Valentino. I do hope he found her. The man deserves happiness."

Hannah wipes away a tear, "I want you to come with me, Louie."

"I was hoping you would say that. Get your rest. When you awaken, I will make breakfast."

Hannah slings the pack, and the old flight jacket comes halfway out of the pocket.

Louie's eyes widen, "That is quite a relic from the past. Where did you get it?"

Hannah turns with a sleepy-eyed grin, "It belonged to Grandpa Neil. I should have left it with him. It is not wearable. The light in the cavern was not good."

Louie extends his hand, "Let me see what I can do with it, Miss Hannah."

With her exciting and dangerous former life reduced to more domesticated concerns like dishpan hands, Bianca washes breakfast dishes in the sudsy kitchen sink under a wide open window on a gorgeous Summer morning. Pausing her chore to watch Penelope's frolicking doggie hijinks chasing birds across the mountain meadow, she peers further downslope toward the old Chestnut tree where Owen and Frederick drink coffee and trade stories, as they had done almost every morning—weather permitting—over the past seven weeks since the first goonie attack.

One of Frederick's cats jumps on the sink and nudges against Bianca's flat tummy under a loose floral embroidered blouse. Patting the tomcat's furry head, the former Carabinieri chuckles, "Hey there, little man. Catch any mice this morning?"

The tortoiseshell mix jumps off the sink and trots out the door with its tail waving like an antenna.

Bianca watches the kitty head down the steps to the mud room, "The power of suggestion."

Resuming her turn at dish duty, Bianca rubs a bare foot up her taut calf as a solid rap on the cabin's front door causes her to let a dripping glass slip from her hands, splattering soapy water everywhere. Drying her hands before unholstering her Glock, she checks the safety and sneaks through the front room as another *knock-knock* rattles the brass door chains.

Hearing muffled voices, Bianca squints out the filmy peephole, "Who is there?"

"We are looking for Owen Haig ...."

Undoing the door locks, Bianca turns the deadbolt, swinging the door wide and raising the gun in one fluid motion, "Who is looking for Owen Haig? Speak up, girl, or I'll blow your head off."

Turning a light shade of blue, Hannah's persuasive telepathy convinces Bianca to lower the weapon while showing her hands with a disarming smile, "You must be Bianca … I get it. Everything is fucked, but I am not here to do anyone harm. My name is Hannah Haig. I am Owen's daughter."

Flabbergasted, Bianca's brown eyes widen in shock and surprise, coughing a dry-throated chuckle at the pretty girl with windblown shoulder-length blond hair wearing an old flight jacket over an olive-green jumpsuit and boots, "Of course. Look at you! I should have realized when I opened the door and saw your face. You look just like your Mother. I apologize for the greeting at gunpoint, but the woods are full of goonies, we …"

A tall man strolls from around the bushes with an expectant grin under his thin mustache, wearing a black raincoat over a turtleneck sweater, dark pants, and a gray felt fedora with a small case clenched in his hand, "Hello, Bianca, do you remember me?"

Staggered by the sight for sore eyes she never thought she would see again, Bianca shrieks with unbridled joy, jumping down the short flight of steps into the C-Class replicant's surprised embrace, showering him with kisses, eliciting a blush response.

"Louie! How did you get here?"

"I came with Miss Hannah." Louie straightens his coat, trying to regain his cool aloofness following Bianca's PDA, "I mean to stay and help out if that is amenable to the situation here on the ground."

"I can't imagine why not. Now, come inside." Bianca ushers her guests into the cabin retreat with an exaggerated bow.

Hannah walks past her gracious host with an easy smile, noticing trace scarring on Bianca's otherwise exquisite olive-skinned complexion and model-perfect bone structure contrasting with her effervescent and welcoming smile.

After scanning the woods, Bianca shuts the door and resets the locks before pivoting to her guests with her arms spread apart, "How did you get here?"

Louie removes his hat, drops his case to the area rug, and glances sideways toward Hannah, "We flew."

Bianca's brown eyes widen onto the windblown, weary travelers, registering Hannah's bluish pallor while holstering her Glock, "Wait here. Let's surprise Owen. This will be fun."

Watching Bianca exit the front room, Hannah and Louie exchange nervous smiles, hearing their leggy Italian hostess in the thin blouse and denim cutoffs calling for Owen to help with the trash.

Hannah smirks and raises an eyebrow, "Well, she is as advertised. What a body. She must be twice my age but fit as a fiddle."

Louie nods, "Now you can see what Owen was up against."

Hannah hesitates before speaking, "Louie, I was in love too. Her name was Maddie. She perished in the attack on Thundercorp No. 5."

"I am programmed as a Frenchman, my dear. I perceived your unrequited grief the day we met. Thanks for the lift, by the way."

"No problem, Louie. It was a little awkward, but we are here. Can you believe I am shaking?"

"What on Earth for?"

Bianca reenters the room with a conspiratorial giggle, "Okay, he is coming up."

Louie looks around the spartan interior, "Should we hide?"

Bianca holds out her hands, "No. Just stand there. I want to see the expression on his face."

Half a minute later, Owen's booming voice resounds through the cabin as he stomps past the open doorway leading into the front room, "Hey Bianca, the trash is only half full. What the hell …"

With a double-take for the ages, Owen takes three steps backward and twists around the corner, staring at the pair standing side-by-side in the darkened front room. "Hello?"

Stepping into the warm morning light glimmering through an

east-facing window, Hannah holds back her tears of joy, "It's me, Dad."

Dropping the half-full reusable sack at his boots, Owen rushes forward and pulls his long-lost daughter into a tearful embrace. "I thought I would never see you again. Look at how you have grown. My God, you look just like your Mom. All of those years that passed."

"I'm twenty-five, Daddy." Reaching into her jacket, she pulls out the photo, "I was three the last time we were together. Remember this?"

Fearful of letting Hannah slip from his arms, Owen accepts the photo, trying to focus his watery eyes, "Oh my, yes. That was a good day. We had fun. Hannah, I am so sorry. I wanted to come home. I missed you and your Mom so much. They would not let me come back. All of this time has passed."

Swallowing hard and verging on more tears, Owen looks into Hannah's glowing eyes, "Any word from your Mom?"

Hannah steps back, creating a space between herself and her long-lost Dad, still touching his fingertips, allowing her Blue Spark to shimmer a brilliant cerulean, alighting the room in shades of blue, "She hid my transformation until the day she passed."

Witnessing his only daughter's transhumanism for the first time, Owen stumbles backward into a chair, weeping into fists clenched tight before his grizzled face for his dear departed Rachel.

Heartbroken for Owen's loss and disappointed with her frivolous and insensitive behavior, Bianca takes Louie's hand, leading him out of the front room, "Let's allow those two the time to grieve. I will show you around and introduce you to our other houseguests."

Bianca's mind racing, she gives Louie a playful squeeze, "How are you with horses?"

"Horses, Madam?"

Owen | Dolomite Mountains
06:02 a.m. | July 15, 2070 – 8 days later

Snuggled in her Black Scorpions flight jacket over a tee shirt and shorts in the chilly morning air, Hannah tromps down the trail in her untied boots through the wet grasses toward dim solar lights strung under the chestnut tree where the firepit casts a warm orange glow on her Dad's face in the predawn darkness. "Morning, Daddy."

Owen beams at his grown-up daughter, "Good morning, Baby Girl. Did you sleep well?"

"The couch is a little challenging, but I am finally getting real sleep. Must be the mountain air."

Owen pours a piping hot cup of coffee and proffers it in his outstretched hand, "Here you go—better than Starbucks."

"Sorry, what's that?"

"Ah, yes, before your time, I suppose."

"I'm joking. Of course, I have heard of Starbucks. We had one on Thundercorp No. 5."

Plopping into the wide seat beside her Dad, Hannah kicks off her boots and curls her legs under her bottom on the thin cushion. Accepting the half-filled mug, she takes a sip, "Oh, that is good, better than the swill I used to serve at Mr. Smythe's coffee shop in Newport."

Owen leans back and slides his right arm around his daughter. "Smythe ... that name takes me back ... you used to play with his daughters."

Hannah looks askance at her Dad, "You remember that?"

Owen shakes his head, "I have repressed most of the last two decades, but the old memories linger. How did you convince your Mom to let you take a job with Smythe?"

Hannah laughs, "Oh, she was pissed, but Dave convinced her to let me out of Hilltop."

"So, you say Dave and Rachel officially tied the knot. How

about that? Dave was a good guy."

"You don't seem angry or upset. Why not?"

Owen finishes his cup and sets it on a chunk of granite used as a table, "Because, by then, I had fallen head over heels for Bianca. It took me a while to come to grips with that reality, and I had years of pent-up rage and conflicting emotions in my prolonged exile, staying one step ahead of the PTB, but now here I am."

"Mom never stopped loving you, Dad."

"I can't believe she is gone."

The reunited pair sit in silence, watching the craggy heights looming thousands of feet above their elevation turn from violets and blues to pinks and oranges as the morning sun rises in the east. Owen takes his daughter's hand and watches it glow blue, "Rachel should have told me about your Blue Spark. It could have changed things."

"I knew Mom was gone the second the Blue Spark hit me like a ton of bricks." Hannah turns to Owen, "It's funny how I was able to compartmentalize odd blue patches and weird coincidences that became more frequent as the years passed."

"Why didn't you go home after Thundercorp?"

"The same reason as you and Bianca."

Owen nods, "The PTB."

"Dad, whatever is left of the PTB is allied with the Overlords. Beyond this cabin retreat you call home, a final war to preserve whatever is left of the human race has already begun. I can't stay here with you forever. My destiny is to fight those things and save the world."

Owen rolls his eyes and tsk-tsks his headstrong daughter, "Where have I heard that before."

"Oh, no, you don't. I am not like Mom. My powers extend well beyond hers. There is nothing I cannot do." Hannah eyeballs her Dad while elevating their seat off the ground, hovering in the wetness. Setting them back down, she points a finger, igniting a log propped against the firepit before flipping it atop the embers.

Unimpressed, Owen grunts and exhales, "Hannah, I watched your Mom battle evilness under the pyramids and disarm a prehistoric missile in the middle of the fucking Amazon. Her exploits left her paralyzed and in a deep depression. Her decision to become a superhero drove a wedge between us. You were too young …"

"I am not a child anymore. I can stay for a few months, giving me time to figure things out. And then it will be time to go."

Owen looks toward the cabin, "I know, Hannah. I struggled for so long to get here. I just don't want it to end."

Hannah smiles, "Dad, you have sacrificed enough. Just like Mom. And Bianca. You deserve some peace."

Eager to shift away from end-of-the-world talk, Owen chuckles and tugs on Hannah's flight jacket sleeve, "I can't believe Neil's old jacket is in such good shape."

"Louie cleaned and mended it before we left Villa St. Claire." Scrunching her cute face, Hannah flips an unruly blond lock behind her ear, reading Owen's mind, "And no, you can't have it."

Owen's face transforms into a faraway smile, thinking of the villa, "Ah, my old villa. I bet Louie kept the place in impeccable shape."

Hannah bites her tongue, reticent to tell Owen that they burned it to the ground before leaving for the last time so no one else could occupy it ever again.

Frederick | Cortina d'Ampezzo
04:43 p.m. | August 20, 2070 – 36 days later

Staying within eyeshot of Frederick's horse-trekking lead along a winding and precipitous backcountry trail through high-elevation Alpine wilderness, Owen guides one of Salvatore's sure-footed Haflinger saddle horses along an ancient path carved out of a boulder-strewn granite escarpment sloping at a dizzying incline to an abrupt drop and a frothy river cutting through a rift valley far below. Focusing on the 90-year-old guide-cum-sherpa entering thick pines up ahead, he muses on the toll his body has taken, robbing him of his swagger and leaving him reticent and afraid,

"Good Christ, I used to free-climb, but now I can barely stomach the altitude."

Longing for his warm bed with Bianca snuggled atop him like a blanket, a chill wind penetrates Owen's riding jacket, flannel shirt, and thermals. Quelling shivers in the thin mountain air, he adjusts his goggles and studies parting clouds, revealing rugged topography and the daunting path ahead in the waning light.

"Helluva way to get the groceries."

Nearing the end of the third and final day of their high-country journey from Bianca's secluded cabin hideaway to the former Olympic village of Cortina d'Ampezzo—a four-hour drive on a circuitous network of interconnecting forestry roads pre-Purge—Owen's ass aches from the hard saddle strapped to his mature horse's chestnut back with empty satchels slung behind him on a supply run before the first winter of a new and threatening world makes the arduous passage impossible.

Breathing easier as his horse clomps into the wooded cover, Owen pulls down his foggy eyewear and looks back at Hannah, crossing the curved granite face. "That's my girl."

A distinctive bird call breaks his reverie, prickling a sense of danger up his spine as he turns and eyeballs Frederick's raised hand through the woods, signaling a halt.

Owen pats his snorting horse and whistles the reply, "Shush, old boy, or you will get us both in trouble."

Catching the rehearsed signal through the gusts whipping past her, Hannah prods her light brown mare into a trot, joining Owen's halted position ten feet into the piney tree cover.

"What's up, Dad?"

Owen shakes his head, "I'm not sure. Frederick signaled to hold up."

Hannah motions ahead, "It could be more goonies roaming the woods. We shouldn't let him do all of the heavy lifting."

Owen's windblown visage widens into a wistful grin, "I feel like I am on another adventure with your Mom. Back then, I was the reckless one. These days, not so much."

Listening for Frederick's all-clear, he nods more to himself than his daughter, "I am older and wiser now. Let's wait. Frederick knows these mountains like the back of his hand and can shoot the whiskers off a marmot from fifty feet."

"That's fucking ridiculous."

Owen tips his Red Sox cap under a knitted hat, "His words, not mine."

Hannah shivers and shakes her blond hair bunched against the scarf around her neck under her Olympic ski cap with rose-tinted goggles hanging around her neck. "It will be dark in another hour. We'll have to set up a camp and get there in the morning."

Another chirp-chirp signals the coast is clear as Owen and Hannah follow Frederick's path through the idyllic forest, ducking under low branches and enjoying the relative silence.

Owen breaks out in a hearty laugh.

Hannah stares at her father's back, swaying from side to side on his mount, "What is so funny?"

"I was just thinking what an excellent father-daughter bonding experience this would be in another reality."

Hannah chuckles, "Yeah. I guess it would." Patting her beautiful six-year-old mare's chestnut coat, she switches subjects, "I like my horse. She has a pretty blond mane, just like me."

Owen laughs, "She sure does, Baby Girl. What's her name?"

Leaning back in the saddle and stretching her back, Hannah keeps a blue hand on the bridle and the other holding the reins, soothing her saddle horse with a telepathic serenity. "I named her Maddie."

Owen shifts in his seat, allowing his horse to pick its path, "Right. You mentioned her—your friend from Thundercorp No. 5. I'm sorry you never had a normal life."

Hannah pulls a pinecone off a branch and tosses it at her Dad's back, "Don't ever say that. Normal would have been boring. And we would be among the billions of dead. As it is, I will kick some Overlord ass and save the world."

Owen sees Frederick stop up ahead, inspecting something blocking the trail. "Sure, Hannah. First, let's loot and pillage like a trio of barbarians and return to the warm cabin."

"And a warm Bianca."

Owen turns and winks at his precocious daughter, "Yeah, that's right."

* * *

Hannah crunches through pine needles and branches to Owen and Frederick, hunched over a sheltered campfire, flickering oranges and yellows on their exhausted faces.

"I fed and watered Maddie and your two babies. They are tired and ready for a good horsey snooze."

Frederick coughs and nods, "The hollow should offer some protection from the elements and any nocturnal threats."

Owen raises his brow, "Like what?"

"Big cats, bears, wolves, and, of course, the goonies. Although they would be more interested in us than the horses."

Hannah plops beside her Dad, "How can these brain-dead people still wander the world?"

"I don't know, Baby Girl."

Frederick reaches into a pocket and produces a folded map.

"Okay, enough goonie talk." Unfolding the aged and wrinkled paper, he taps his finger on a remote point amid forested topography surrounded by mountainous terrain, "We are here. Believe it or not, under fifteen kilometers from Cortina d'Ampezzo."

Hannah points to a large body of water, "What's that?"

"Lake Misurina. A beautiful spot, fancy hotels, the works."

Owen's eyes alight, "Well shit, Frederick, why not check there first. It is half the distance."

Frederick shakes his head, "No. It is gone. I am sure of it. Six thousand people lived in Cortina d'Ampezzo. That is where we will find enough food to fill our bags."

Owen scratches his head and says aloud what everyone is already thinking, "What if everything is already looted?"

Frederick nods, "Then we starve."

Hannah yawns and stretches, curling herself on the cold, hard ground, using a rolled sweater as a pillow, "On that happy note, good night, boys. See you bright and early."

*　*　*

Under a blanket of stars, with the temperature hovering near freezing in the predawn stillness, the trio breaks from the woods onto a macadam lane across from a postcard-worthy three-story chalet perched on a landscaped rise amid an enclave of exclusive ski residences occupying the upper slopes above the outskirts of Cortina d'Ampezzo.

Seeing the dark outlines of an inert chairlift rising above the pines in the background, Hannah slides off her mount and ties Maddie to an iron gate at the bottom of stone staircases leading uphill to the primary residence with its sleek and modern four-car underground garage visible around a long driveway to the right. "I want to look inside."

Frederick starts to object, but Owen intercedes, "Hang on, Hannah, I'm coming with you."

Exhaling a vaporous cloud into the chilliness as sunrise illuminates the upper reaches looming behind him, Frederick lights his pipe, "I'll watch the horses."

Hannah opens the unlocked door and steps inside onto a beautiful woven area rug, with Owen following on her heels. Flicking on torches, the pair inspects plush furnishings, heirloom photographs, landscape paintings, etchings, and tapestries decorating the rustic Bavarian interior's exposed wood-beamed ceilings, carved moldings, and intricate detailed second and third-floor balustrades.

Pulling off her knit cap, Hannah winces at her reflection in a gilded mirror, removing a pine needle from her shoulder-length, dirty blond hair, "Well, I look a fright."

Practicing his Italian reading a placard arranged beside an expensive crystal vase overflowing with dried-out flowers on a priceless hand-painted credenza, Owen demurs, "Sei bellissima."

"Your Italian is terrible, and you are a big liar."

Stepping into the sunken living room atrium, they illuminate closed doors lining the upper floors before climbing up the opposite side and sneaking down a hallway decorated with vintage skiing paraphernalia.

"This is eerie."

Enamored with the chalet's former glory, Hannah casts an over-the-shoulder glance at Owen, "What do you think a room here would have cost back in the day?"

"A few grand a night. My old boss at Ford & Poole took his family to the Italian Alps on a ski vacation back before I met your Mom."

"Is that so …." Hannah reaches the hallway's terminus and kicks in the thick wooden door with her boot. Smiling at a surprised Owen, she raises a thick eyebrow, "Can't be too careful." Peering into the darkness, she gulps, "Oh my. Dad. You have to see this."

Looking over Hannah's shoulder, Owen shines his torch inside what must have been the chef's kitchen onto a knot of twisted skeletal remains with dried-out flesh hanging from the desiccated bones, like a nightmarish game of Halloween Twister.

Widening his gape across scraps of ripped clothing and dark

splotches and splatter patterns covering the walls, an alarmed Owen taps Hannah's shoulder, "Come on, let's get out of here." Suppressing a queasiness from his empty stomach, "I may never eat beef jerky again."

Hannah pivots, glowing a brilliant blue, "Dad, do you think it gets better in town? Come on. They are dead. They don't even smell anymore."

"I smell them."

"Cover your nose, you big baby."

Owen swallows back trepidation, following his daughter's transhuman glow into the kitchen, taking a wide berth around the dead, his boots sticking to the wooden floorboards.

Hannah flings open cabinets with her mind, finding nothing but pots, pans, plates, and platters before reaching a pantry door and perusing the emptiness within, "Damn it all."

Owen shines his light onto the shelving overhead. "When in doubt, look straight up."

Standing on his toes, he stretches his six-foot frame, reaching his hand to an upper shelf and pulling down a dusty wine bottle. "Chateau le something … there's more, but I can't reach it."

Hannah nudges her Father aside, "Allow me …" raising off the floor, she hands down another bottle, a case of crackers, and a block of cheese.

Owen fills a paper sack from a lower shelf, leaving the smelly cheese wheel behind.

"No coffee?"

"Sorry, Dad. Perhaps the Starbucks in town?"

"Very funny. Let's get the fuck out of here."

* * *

Breathing the crisp mountain air tinged with a strange odor under a robin's egg sky with morning dew evaporating into a ground fog along a deserted cobblestone lane angling toward the center of

Cortina d'Ampezzo, Owen lags behind Frederick and Hannah, walking his horse dubbed Flynn past a row of busted-out boutiques. Striking paydirt at a former upscale shop, Owen sheds his jacket and ties his horse to a signpost before calling toward Hannah and Frederick, "Hey, wait a second … I want to pick out something nice for Bianca."

Catching the eye-rolling pair's nod, gesturing toward a hotel at the end of the block, Owen grunts a reply, too focused on his task, crunching over broken glass and a dead body athwart the threshold. Navigating upturned shelves and elegant displays, he scrutinizes a row of lingerie mannequins and undresses one resembling Bianca's litheness.

"Sorry. I need this more than you do."

Adding the silky nightie to his saddlebag, a Hermés display catches his eye. Unfolding a black cable-stitched cashmere sweater, Owen blanches at the price before checking the tags and choosing a Size Small. Hurrying to the shoes, like a timed game show shopping spree, he stumbles upon knee-high leather boots in a size six. "She will love these."

Snatching fistfuls of designer yoga pants, undies, and tees on his way back to the front of the shop, he stuffs the loot into the saddlebag, unties Flynn, and hastens to catch up with Hannah and Frederick, cradling ceramic coffee cups in the shade of a hotel awning.

Keen to show off his finds, Owen notices the brews, "Hey. Is that …"

Frederick smiles, taking a long sip, "Yes, it is."

Owen's eyes widen, "We have not had any coffee in over three weeks. Is there more?"

Hannah nods, "Yep, the carafe in the lobby is full, but it's cold."

"I don't care, hold my horse."

Owen disappears inside.

Frederick asks Hannah, "Should we have mentioned the massacre?"

"No, he is on a caffeine quest. I doubt he will even notice."

Owen exits the hotel's revolving door with a cup in hand, "Oh boy, did I need this."

Hannah frowns, "Dad? Did you see all of the dead people in there?"

"Yeah, Baby Girl. Like Frederick said, this place is a dead zone. Let's locate supplies before we run into bandits or worse."

Scanning across the plaza toward Basilica Minore dei Santi Filippo e Giacomo, named for the Apostles Philip and James, Frederick notes Purge victims spread over the pavers where they took their last breaths.

"Perhaps this was a mistake."

Feeling exposed on the sunny street in the chic and trendy commune known for its lifestyles of the rich and famous après-ski high society reputation at the bottom of an Alpine valley along the winding Boite River, he looks back into the hotel. "Let's stable the horses inside before proceeding. There is a banquet facility toward the back. That should keep them safe and out of sight while we explore the town on foot."

"Frederick, how do you know this hotel has a reception hall?"

"It is where my wedding reception took place."

Owen finishes his cup and grabs Flynn's reins, "You never mentioned being married."

Frederick nods, "She passed a year later. Breast cancer."

"I am so sorry."

"Don't be. It was half a century ago. The world was a different place."

Leading the calm horses through the gruesome lobby, Frederick pulls ahead and flings open ornate double doors.

Owen shines his torch into the room, "Uh, with the doors closed, the babies will be in total darkness. Is that okay?"

Frederick pulls on his mustache, "Hmmm, I did not think of that."

Hannah hands her reins to Owen and elevates off the parquet floor to a crystal chandelier centered over the dance floor. Transmitting a controlled spark of human energy from an extended fingertip, the candle-shaped LEDs alight, refracting a festive ambiance. Looking down with a half-lit grin, she turns a lighter shade of blue, descending to the dance floor, "How's that?"

Owen feigns nonchalance, "Uh, let there be light."

Frederick nods, "Yes. Good show, my dear."

Gearing up for the village pillage, Owen retrieves extra clips for his PTB Special P365XL and pivots to a glowing Hannah, "Need I ask?"

"No, Dad. I don't need a gun."

Frederick slings two empty saddlebags over his shoulder and holsters his double-action Colt revolver. "Ready, my boy."

Taking a final check of the tranquil horses, Owen catches Flynn taking a dump on the dance floor before pulling the double doors closed and running a broom through the brass handles.

"Typical Flynn."

* * *

Finding picked-clean shelves, spoiled produce, and a foul-smelling, fly-infested butcher counter in a corner grocery, a dejected Owen pushes aside a cart, contemplating the posh restaurant across the street through the streaky, cobwebbed windows advertising meat and produce specials on faded poster boards clinging to the glass.

Hannah slings her empty bags on her shoulder and stands beside him, "What are you thinking?"

Owen smiles, "That this was a huge mistake. I see signs of life everywhere but not a scrap of food."

"I would welcome a sane human encounter right about now."

Frederick comes up behind them with a box of stale crackers.

"Have one, they're not bad."

"No thanks. Let's check Chez Empty across the street. If that joint turns up a big zero, I say, let's pack it up and head back. We can check more chalets on the way out of town."

"Agreed."

Splitting their tasks, like the previous Cortina d'Ampezzo establishments, Hannah heads for the kitchen while Owen checks the bar with Frederick standing watch.

Pushing through brushed metal swinging doors, Hannah glows to a subtle shade of blue, a beacon in the darkness.

Exploring past a built-in row of employee lockers, she opens one on impulse, flashing back to the ones on Thundercorp No. 5 where she found the enviro suit. Pushing aside a woman's jacket, her gaze lands on a photograph of a smiling little girl.

Closing the locker, she enters an expansive rectangular kitchen, her ambiance casting long animated shadows across commercial-grade appliances separated by marble-topped counters under magnetic racks laden with cookware and utensils.

Tsk-tsking a grease-splattered, thick-grated gas cooktop covered in grimy pots and pans, Hannah picks up a ladle and stirs a massive stockpot filled with a murky stew, watching a light-colored hunk rise to the surface before submerging. With an exasperated harumph, she drops the long-handled utensil and discovers more gut-churning culinary abominations as a prickling unease rises from her subconscious.

"Something is not right."

Examining the middle countertops through the darkness, Hannah's radiance reflects off a butcher knife chunked into a cutting board in a glistening puddle of blood.

Perplexed with a looming sense of jeopardy, her gaze lands back on the pot of murky stew with a startled gasp, "Oh shit. What was that?"

Grabbing the ladle, Hannah fishes the meaty hunk from the miasmic soup. Flinging it on the countertop, she covers her mouth to muffle her crying scream at the terrifying sight of the dismembered human hand lying palm-up with pasta noodles wormed around its bent digits. Stumbling backward, Hannah knocks a teetering stack of pots crashing to the floor. "Jesus, girl. Get a grip. It's just a hand. This town is littered with bodies."

Slowing her respiratory in the staleness, she scans the back of the kitchen, finding a bulletin board-lined corridor past the lavatories leading to the restaurant's storeroom. "In for a penny … in for a pound."

Venturing into the scary expanse with her flashlight held forward in her shaky grip, she pushes through the doors and casts the narrow beam across rows of shelving packed with cardboard cartons.

Lifting a heavy box, she rips it open and dumps a pile of military MREs on the floor.

Sifting through the packages, she can't believe her glowing eyes, "Pasta, soups, and casseroles … the mother lode."

Ripping open more boxes, she stuffs the lightweight aluminum pouches into her bags, unable to shake the grotesque image of the dismembered hand from her mind.

Clunk-clunk-clunk …

Startled by the noise, Hannah lifts her torch, "Who's there?"

Standing from her loot, she checks beyond the shelves, finding a thick metal door, like a bank vault, recessed into an old stone wall.

"Of course, the cold storage."

Clunk-clunk-clunk …

"I'm going to hate myself for doing this …."

Gripping the door's long handle, she unlatches the locking mechanism and pulls it open.

* * *

Resting his aching body in a chair at a linen-covered table across from Frederick, Owen pours the last drops from a half-empty bottle of Merlot found under the bar and tips his glass, "It's five o'clock somewhere."

Frederick raises his glass, "Cheers."

Hannah emerges from the kitchen, hefting two satchels, "You boys want to help or sit there and drink all day? The storeroom in the back is loaded with MREs."

Owen downs his wine and stands, "MREs? That will work. Let's load up and get the fuck out of Dodge!"

Frederick grabs his bags and follows.

"Dad?"

"Yes, Baby Girl?"

"Someone is using this restaurant. Hurry up. I do not want to be here when they return."

Sensing a dark undertone in her voice, Owen's brow furrows, "What? What did you see?"

Struggling to quantify the nightmarish image, Rachel collapses onto a barstool, "Don't open the door to the cold room."

Alarmed by Hannah's shift from cool, calm, and collected, Frederick upturns a table toward the front doors. "Hannah, get over here." Tossing his bags to Owen, he draws his revolver and barks at his companions, "I'll stand guard … get what you can, and then we got to go. Move it, young man!"

Alarmed by Frederick's overt reaction to Hannah's stare-eyed state, Owen grabs the empty saddlebags and stumbles through the kitchen and down the corridor to the storage room, his heart beating out of his heaving chest.

"Whoa, that is a lot of dehydrated dinners."

Checking the labels, Owen peruses a variety of dishes before loading them into the bags as a muffled clunk-clunk-clunk freezes the starving man in place. Dropping the last half-filled satchel, he raises his gun and torch, shining the light onto a thick metal door built into the spidery, stacked stone wall.

The cold room.

Ignoring Hannah's warning, Owen swings the door wide, dodging a goonie's bony-handed lunge by inches. "Jesus! That was close."

Lowering his gun, Owen notes the medieval-looking metal restraining collar around its neck attached to a heavy-duty shelf filled with human body parts ready for a cannibal barbeque. Taking a deep breath, his innate curiosity compels him to look into the bulging eyes with its gaping mouth stretched over a sadistic ball contraption strapped around its gnarly head.

Pondering its former life with genuine sympathy, he notices a missing left hand cauterized at the wrist.

"My God, who are the real animals in this strange new world?"

* * *

Toting saddlebags and a backpack loaded with MREs, a nervous Owen ducks behind a brick retaining wall, scanning empty windows above both sides of a twisting cobblestone lane. Sprinting on a diagonal to a broken storefront, he jumps inside, signaling an all-clear with the whistled bird call. Wiping sweat from his forehead in the late afternoon mid-sixties temperature, he reflects on the freezing three-day trek through the high country back to Bianca. "Please, God, just get us home."

* * *

Watching her father move with practiced stealth through the ruined village like an elite special force veteran, Hannah muses how many death-defying adventures he had experienced in his fifty-three years. "Mom, you must be looking down and wishing you were here."

Hearing the bird call, she vaults from her position and dashes up the street, keeping her Blue Spark in check.

* * *

Maintaining a vigilant watch from a looted candy shop as Owen and Hannah make their way up the street on full alert after the gruesome discovery in the restaurant, Frederick spots candy on the littered floor tiles. Reaching forward from his hidden position, he snatches a wrapped treat to satisfy his sweet tooth. Sucking on the bright green minty confection, an audible din of revving engines and loud voices reaches his hairy ears, looming closer with each quickening heartbeat.

Hunching around the side of the checkout counter, Frederick tries to whistle a warning, but the candy makes it impossible. Within half a minute, leatherbound bandits wearing helmets with skull masks covering their faces rumble to a stop on mud-splattered off-road vehicles outside Frederick's hunkered position.

Surveilling a skull-faced man dismounting like a traffic cop, Frederick watches him motion for trailing pickup trucks to stop.

Rattling chains and anguished cries draw Frederick's gape onto a caged individual inside a pickup bed. The traffic cop guy exchanges raucous laughter with the driver and taunts the prisoner like a caged animal at the zoo, clanking a baton against the metal bars as the half-naked, skin-and-bones woman wails and gnashes her teeth, clawing at the stick with her hands bound together and a leash around her neck.

Fuming at the inhumanity, Frederick raises his revolver, "This cannot go on."

* * *

Using the basilica's steeple jutting above the storybook rooftops in the picturesque commune as a landmark, Owen frowns, still blocks from the hotel.

"We're coming for you, Maddie, and Flynn. Hold tight, and don't pick on Frederick's nameless steed."

Checking the four-way intersection and scanning the windows, Owen bolts up the street, a block closer to the hotel, whistling for Hannah and Frederick to catch up.

Glancing at where Hannah should be, Owen grits his teeth in frustration, "What are they waiting for?"

* * *

Hearing the all-clear whistle, Hannah prepares to move forward as the roar of multiple engines resounds up the winding lane, stopping her in her tracks.

Sneaking behind a dead planter, Hannah watches in horror as the bandits parade human prisoners and caged goonies in the backs of pickup trucks through Cortina d'Ampezzo streets toward the River Boite outside of town, surmising the show of force is an unveiled threat to any lingering inhabitants considering an insurrection.

Half a block downhill from the lead four-wheelers, Hannah hears the screech of brakes as the procession halts before a trio of luminous Overlords. Watching the masked bandits collaborating with the imposing stark white humanoids, Hannah recalls the de-facto concentration camps spread across Europe, noting every invasion requires a traitorous lot willing to turn on their own kind.

A presence manifests out of the ether at her back as Hannah pivots onto a monstrous white being with a circumspect expression on his chiseled countenance.

Who are you?

Hearing the being's perplexed query invading her mind, Hannah summons her Blue Spark as gunshots ring out, sending the bandits scurrying for cover with others revving their engines and hightailing back the way they came.

The attack catches Hannah's interrogator off guard, giving her the millisecond advantage to blast him off a block wall before snapping his neck with a flick of her wrist. Tired of playing the victim and desperate to kick some ass, Hannah musters infinite human energy buried deep within every living soul and melts the being into a glowing puddle.

"Good, you can be killed. Thanks for the intel."

Hurtling over the chaos, she blasts bandit guards and yells for the prisoners to scatter before ripping a pickup door off its hinges and pulling the stupefied driver onto the street. Igniting the man's mask on fire, she settles before the caged goonie in the back, melting the lock and setting the poor woman free like a wild animal as six Overlords appear out of nothingness and surround Hannah's cerulean form.

"Hello, boys and girls."

The humorless leader tilts his head and raises a hand, paralyzing Hannah as the bandits regroup and move back onto the street with order restored.

***

Crouching behind a corner, wracking his brain for a way out of this mess, Owen senses someone emerging from behind, wheeling with his gun at the ready.

"Don't shoot, it's me."

"Frederick, goddammit, you were supposed to stay hidden—not shoot the place up like Dirty Harry. Now, what are we going to do?"

"Owen. Listen to me. The bandits had us in their sights the whole damn time. They drew Hannah into a trap before summoning the Overlords. I tried to create a diversion—killing a couple bandits in the process—but it did not work."

Owen scans the scene, shaking his head, "I can't lose my daughter again. What am I going to do?"

Seething with a burning, helpless rage, Owen gasps as a female Overlord places a crown on his Baby Girl's dirty blond head. "What is that thing? Dammit!"

Watching the situation deteriorate, Owen checks his gun, "Frederick, take the food, get your horse, and ride out of here. I am going after Hannah. Tell Bianca I love her."

Frederick glowers at his foolish friend, "Damn your stubborn soul. Now Owen, you know I can't do that …."

Thunderous cracks cut Frederick's remonstrative reply short as they witness the Overlords vaporized in nanoseconds by a surprise attack from a blue-skinned trio, landing on the pavement before Hannah's frozen stance. An attractive woman in form-fitting black tights, leaving nothing to the imagination, steps over a smoking corpse and removes the crown device from Hannah's head, staggering her backward, agape at her miraculous liberators.

"What happened … where … who are you?"

A tall and fit Black man in an olive-green army surplus jumpsuit and boots extends his hand with a bright smile directed at Hannah, "My name is Lamar Tate. Los Angeles, born and raised, baby."

Smacking his muscle-bound colleague's back, "And this strapping fellow is Enes Kabek, from Tel Aviv."

Heaping the miraculous last-second salvation atop a lifetime of perilous close calls, a relieved Owen leaves Frederick in his wake, sprinting down the street to Hannah and the blue trio, "Baby Girl, are you okay?"

The radiant blue woman cradles the brain lock device in her supple hands, gaping at Owen's worried face. "You are the world-famous Owen Haig! What an honor … my name is Ada Hansen. Oslo, Norway. We are members of the Final Eight."

Mindful of the traitorous bandits scattered among the buildings, Frederick continues past the reunion to the abandoned convoy with his revolver at the ready, discovering a frightened couple caged in the last truck bed. Catching his breath in the thin mountain air, he calls to the group, "How about one of you using your Blue Spark thing to free these folks?"

Impressed by the spry old-timer's physical stamina, Lamar vaults down the street and lands next to Frederick with a broad white smile, "Sure thing, Gramps." Melting the lock with the tip of his finger, the hip and confident young American opens the cage and steps back as the frightened pair scuttle past without saying a word.

Lamar winks at Frederick, shouting after the shell-shocked pair, "You're welcome!"

Catching movement under the filthy tarp in the cage, Frederick holsters his gun and leans inside, "And who might you be?"

An emaciated boy pokes his head from under the tarp, latching on to Frederick's kind eyes, "Lucas."

Realizing there must be more orphans amongst the decaying infrastructure, Owen turns to the de-facto superheroes, "This has the makings of a humanitarian crisis."

"We will transport young Lucas back to our base orphanage. He will be among friends."

Owen looks askance at the trio, "You have a base?"

Enes speaks for the first time, "You all must join us. Your presence is known. It is no longer safe. We caught the Overlords off guard. That will not happen again."

Owen raises his hands, palms out, "Wait just a second … let's all slow down … we also have a base. And that is where we are heading now. Thanks for the help, and good luck fighting the bad guys."

Grabbing Hannah by the arm, he pivots up the street toward the hotel, "By the way, Final Eight? Great name."

Hannah pulls from her Father's light hold, "Daddy. I have to go with them."

Frederick wipes tears from his eyes, patting Owen's shoulder, "You know she is right."

The Final Eight members elevate skyward with Kabek cradling the child.

Wrapping his arms around his long-lost daughter, not wanting to let her go, Owen kisses Hannah's blue cheek with tears streaming down his face, "How can I say goodbye a second time?"

"I have something for you." Hannah reaches into her pocket and hands him her favorite thing.

"Goodbye, Daddy."

Owen clutches the photo as his daughter lifts into the cool mountain air, joining her new allies and disappearing in a streak of blue.

"Goodbye, Baby Girl. Save the world and make your Mother proud."

Louie | Dolomite Mountains
11:32 a.m. | August 4, 2082 — Twelve years later

Louie tucks two folded pill packets in his suit jacket pocket and adjusts his tie before continuing down the short hallway and calling to Miss Bianca through her closed bedroom door, "Are you ready, my dear?"

"Just a minute, Louie. I'll be right out."

Standing topless in threadbare undies at the basin in the cabin's cramped master bath, Bianca Valentino checks her gaunt reflection in the mirror, dabbing a trickle of blood from her nose, ignoring the lump in her left breast and purplish blotches marring her rail-thin midriff.

"It sucks to die."

Limping past the four-legged tub and elevated window onto high tree branches, she opens an antique armoire, selecting her favorite Hermès sweater from a stack. Pulling the pilled black cashmere over her head with a heavy sigh, she brushes thinning gray locks off her face and steps into a short black skirt, padding across the worn floorboards to the closet for her designer boots. Weak and tired from getting dressed, she plops on the edge of her squeaky bed and slides her feet into the supple black leather. Gripping the left boot's zipper in her quivering fingertips, she tugs it upward, hearing an audible snap.

"Damn! Louie, I need your help!"

Standing outside the door, the C-Class replicant peeks inside, "Are you decent?"

"Just come here. The zipper broke, and my hands are too shaky to fuck around with it. Can you just help me?"

"Madam, need you even ask?"

Taking a knee in his black suit, his strong fingers zip the boot up her calf, covering an alarming-looking lesion.

"Miss Bianca, should I ...."

"No, it is fine. I can't even feel it. Thanks for everything, Louie."

Knowing everything is far from fine, Louie lowers her foot to the floor with a gentle touch. Propping the other boot on his thigh, he takes the unbroken zipper and closes it over leg bruises from tiny broken capillaries in her smooth olive skin to her bony knee.

Looking into Bianca's sunken eyes, Louie beams, "You will always be the same radiant beauty whom I met the first day you arrived at Villa St. Claire."

Bianca coughs a throaty chuckle, "You are a terrible liar. Nice suit."

"I have had it forever." Louie extracts the first small envelope from his jacket, "Shall I get you some water?"

"These are for the pain, right?"

"Yes, Madam. The pain."

Bianca takes the pills and swallows them down her dry throat, "Nope. I'm good."

Proffering a brave smile, Louie pats her bony leg, "Okay then, let's head outside."

Bianca stands off the bed in her three-inch heels, wavering with a heady swoon, "Whoa. The pills work fast. What will the other pills feel like? Will it hurt?"

Stifling guilt creeping through his synthetic brain, "I am not entirely sure, hence the reason for taking these first—no suffering on my watch. I suppose the high elevation and thin blood coursing your veins accelerated the narcotic effect."

"You sound like a doctor."

Down the cabin's creaky steps and out the mudroom door, Louie guides the sixty-six-year-old former Milanese Carabinieri across the sunny terrace before cradling her cancer-stricken body in his strong arms and carrying her down the uneven path to the patio fire pit under the old chestnut tree.

Removing a dead songbird and brushing leaves and needles off an old, stained seat cushion, Louie turns toward a stare-eyed Bianca,

"Why not rest in Owen's old chair for a while before venturing across the meadow. It is a remarkably agreeable Summer day."

Swallowing hard and forcing back tears, Bianca manages a sardonic grin, "Do we have time?" before waving Louie off and resting her bony bottom in the Aspen chair.

Desiring one last moment before the end, Louie sits beside her, musing on ashen remnants littering the charred granite fire pit. "Owen loved it here."

Bianca nods, "I miss hearing the birds. Owen loved the birds." her gaze shifting heavenward at a contrail billowing across the clear blue sky.

"Louie?"

"Yes, Ms. Valentino."

"Is Hannah still alive?"

The C-Class replicant monitors vitals while following her far-off gaze with a concerned frown at a missile's western trajectory. "She is the Final Eight's wild card. I hope so."

Sensing ominous tremors permeating the mountainside, Louie stands and extends a hand, "Perhaps we are running short on time after all."

Escorting the weak and unsteady Bianca across the Alpine meadow, the pair pause at the first limestone marker.

"Sweet Penelope."

Bianca squints through the midday brightness toward Louie with a slight slur in her speech, "Did Owen ever mention why we named her Penelope?"

Louie fingers the second cache of pills in his suit pocket, "Uh, no. Madam. I assumed it had something to do with Homer's *Odyssey*."

Bianca holds a soft cloth to her nose, soaking up more blood, "It was the name of our stolen boat to Panarea. Stolen time ..."

Louie scans more crisscrossing contrails, keeping the dialog as light as possible, "Is that so? You two had quite an adventurous relationship."

At peace with her destiny in the tranquil meadow, Bianca's life force dissolves, pulling from Louie's hand as he monitors her shortening breaths and faltering heartbeats. Stumbling past Frederick's plot, she collapses to her hands and knees atop rocky soil mounded in an oblong shape covered with new grassy shoots reclaiming the shallow gravesite.

Grabbing fistfuls of loamy Earth between her thin fingers, Bianca's dying eyes rest upon a lone purple bloom sprouting upward before the jagged limestone marker:

Owen Michael Haig
5-9-2017 ~ 5-9-2082

Standing resolute at a respectable distance, Louie scans Bianca's motionless form and reads her flatlined vitals with a grim nod. Crumbling the switched pill packets at his feet, he grabs a sack hidden behind Owen's marker and dumps out a plastic tarp before flinging the eco-friendly bag into the trees.

"I had to kill her!"

After wrapping her lifeless body in crinkled plastic, he lowers Bianca's body into the shallow open grave beside Owen's plot.

"Godspeed, my dear."

The lanky Kobayashi C-Class—the second of two replicants of an anonymous French taxi driver—makes the Sign of the Cross and hastens to bury Bianca Valentino under tamped-down dirt and rock, pounding her limestone marker into the loose soil with the back of Owen's old axe.

Ruminating upon whether an afterlife exists for the likes of himself, Louie hikes across the meadow with his suit jacket slung over his shoulder as a blinding flash engulfs the daytime sky.

Loosening his tie, Louie probes forward with outstretched hands to the Aspen chair, unable to witness the spectacular fireball expanding heavenward to the south. Settling back, he crosses a long leg, tapping dirty fingertips on the rough wood armrest, bathed in a ruddy orange glow with a brave smile under his thin mustache, awaiting the roiling superheated blast wave leveling thick pine forests at the speed of sound ...

"C'est la ..."

Chapter Eleven:

The Comet

Late Summer, 2082

Twelve years—less than a fraction of a nanosecond on an intergalactic timeline—after the Overlords' en masse return from their cubed self-exile, persistent sabotage by an anarchical last fifth of humanity led by a ragtag squad of blue-skinned transhumans shattered any hope of a coexistence.

Washing their hands of humankind in the blood of traitorous appeasers led by the Sisters, they cast the female replicants atop a proverbial funeral pyre as erstwhile superpower launch codes initiated countdowns in dead languages to an inglorious denouement.

Commencing with feckless fat cats and conniving cowards bunkered under an obsolete air defense headquarters deep inside a mountain on the North American continent already targeted by hundreds of nukes, the Overlords' systematic final solution launched every functioning nuclear missile from every silo, every submarine, every bomber, and every stockpiled warhead amassed by the shortsighted species for over a century to subjugate their fellow man.

Though collateral damage to the Overlords' rebuilt infrastructure proved unavoidable, their imperviousness to the radioactive fallout and a hundred-year nuclear winter afforded time to bulldoze vestigial remnants of humanity under a new Earth, shimmering to its previous glory.

What once was exists again.

Hannah | Corsica
07:00 a.m. | August 23, 2544 – 462 years later

A thunderous crack precedes a basketball-sized luminous orb materializing in an electrified hover above a windblown coastal pasture, scattering feral sheep descended from flocks tended centuries before by long-forgotten herders on Corsica's rugged eastern coast.

Calming a lone resolute ram, stomping its hooves, and shaking its spectacular spiraling horns, the orb divides into two lights, shapeshifting the second orb into a woman's naked form lying atop the tamped-down grass. Watching her first shallow inhalations of dewy morning air, rekindling the Blue Spark within her reanimating biological incarnation, the Light Specter forges an invulnerable mesh bodysuit out of rare elements from a far-off galaxy and places it at her side. Next, it conjures knee-high red boots and a vintage flight jacket at her twitching fingertips while conceding that sleeping beauty will require more than her inherited Blue Spark and alien armor to alter the course of history, yet she must prevail.

* * *

Blue-green eyes blink open to clouds floating across a morning sky as crashing surf and baaing sheep stir Hannah Haig from a timeless repose. Bolting upright, she casts her disoriented gaze upon her nakedness and the strange new world around her, like Alice awakening from a trip through the looking glass.

Where am I?

Stretching long arms with a loud yawn, she scratches her cold nose as dreams of sparklers and fireworks shooting across the night sky like comets fade to distant echoes. Removing wet grass from her shoulder-length blond hair, she reaches for a familiar-looking superhero costume, slinking her lithe form into it like a wetsuit as the intelligent woven mesh responds to her supple transhuman form.

Unfolding the vintage World War Two leather flight jacket, Hannah notes the off-model embroidered black scorpion patch with a wry grin before pulling on the boots under the flock's wary gaze.

Dressed and ready for whatever is to come, Hannah parts the tall grass to greet the fearless horned leader. Smoothing fingertips into the stoic creature's thick, mottled tufts of chocolate brown wool, Hannah gives the animal a reassuring pat, "Oh, you are a good boy."

Glimpsing baby lambs cowering behind suspicious ewes under an old oak tree, she laughs, "And a busy boy, too."

Scratching her imposing new friend's massive head, a fiery hellscape breaks free of her subconscious, flooding her mind with heartrending visions of the Final Eight's scorched blue bodies scattered across a smoking battlefield under a cast-iron sky.

Staggered by the cataclysmic recollection with salty tears running down her rosy cheeks, Hannah leaves the alpha male to watch over his family, hiking the eastern shoreline with the sepia-toned faces of her eight brave comrades projecting like vintage film reels across the rugged terrain.

Traversing slippery and treacherous volcanic formations, the wind-whipped sea spray from thunderous swells crashing against the rocks slows her progress as she reaches a sheltered cove with a sandy beachhead. Pausing to catch her breath, she watches shorebirds timing the tide's ebb and flow, advancing in search of morsels amid the polished pebbles and glassy bits before the returning deluge forces comical retreats.

That has to be a metaphor for something.

Revitalized by the Mediterranean sea air, Hannah removes her jacket and boots, wriggling her toes in the coarse sand, conjuring a childhood recollection of a day trip to Cape Cod with Dave pushing her wheelchair-bound mother down a boardwalk to a cotton candy vendor eking out a living in the post-Gork invasion world that was.

I wanted the blue, but Mom insisted on the pink cotton candy.

Allowing the receding tide to pull the sand from around her feet, Hannah wades farther into the surf as a hollow knocking sound draws her squinty gaze onto a glinting object bobbing against a fractured chunk of volcanic sea stack in a tangle of kelp. Intrigued, she sloshes across the shallows to the mystery object and scoops a US Navy fighter pilot helmet in her dripping hands. Dumping out water and a squatting crab, she reads the faded call sign Death Dealer along the barnacle-encrusted visor, mesmerized by the glittery blue paint job refracting the midday sun before tossing it back into the drink.

Pivoting her reverie toward the incongruent shape of an aircraft carrier jutting from the sea like an enigmatic tombstone of a past civilization dwarfed before a domed megastructure commanding the horizon to thousands of feet into the clouds, Hannah shakes her head, "The Overlords did it. They really did it."

* * *

Four centuries and sixty-two years after Hannah and the Final Eight failed to stop the Overlords from launching the world's nuclear arsenals in a two-week orgy of death and destruction, she shutters their brave faces behind a locked door in her mind with a sad smile on her purplish lips.

I wish you were here.

Wandering a windswept expanse uphill from the sea under gathering clouds, Hannah stumbles across trace evidence of a scorched concrete chunk sticking from the dirt. Seeing more broken pieces dotting the pasturelands, she takes careful footsteps toward rotted suggestions of erstwhile buildings at the heart of a former World War Two US Army airbase dubbed Alto Airfield—where her ancestor, Neil Alexander, took off on a last fateful mission in August of 1944.

Now what?

Casting her gaze over the ruins, Hannah finds the area teeming with plant and animal life that shrugged off radioactive fallout and a nuclear winter like a cheap suit. Under the curious scrutiny of squirrels scampering among the trees, she squats at the crumbled corner of a foundation and plays archeologist.

Placing both hands on the cornerstone, she closes her eyes, envisioning a bustling airfield circa 1944. Startled by her ability to conjure a past reality in three dimensions, Hannah pivots as a Jeep passes through her imperceptible form, kicking up a dusty cloud on a sunbaked main street lined with corrugated metal Quonset huts reflecting a blinding midday Mediterranean sun.

A boisterous gathering of fighter pilots draws her enrapt gaze onto the Black Scorpions squadron, smoking and drinking coffee in cheap lawn chairs on a grassy infield. Moving among the youthful faces epitomizing the Greatest Generation, self-conscious of her jacket's off-model scorpion patch, she eavesdrops on a stocky redheaded pilot, regaling his fellow warriors with tales of his latest dogfight over Italy.

"… so, there I was boys, providing air cover for a damaged B-24, trying to get home on one working engine. Did I mention the co-pilot flying solo as the pilot's head was blown clean off by AA shrapnel busting through the cockpit?"

A wide-eyed replacement pilot chimes in, "I know a guy who

knows a guy who was friends with the pilot."

Red melts down at the interruption, "Hey! Fuckhead! I'm telling a story here!"

Hannah snickers at the coarse language, and high-pitched squeaky voice as the man's face flushes with comical anger.

As if hearing her lilting laugh at his expense, the storyteller's pugilistic countenance furrows, staring through Hannah's ethereal presence with a noggin-clearing headshake while sparking another cigarette with a stolen lighter, "So, where was I? Oh yeah … the bomber was trailing a long plume of fucking black smoke, which draws a pair of Focke Wulfs like moths to a flame, coming out of nowhere with their 50 cals blazing … uh … blazing …"

"What's the matter, Harry? Finish the story."

"Just a minute."

Watching the one called Harry stomping around the group in her direction, Hannah panics, "Oh no. You can't see me. That's impossible …"

Breaking into a wide grin, the mercurial redhead looks right through her, "Captain! Tell these dolts about the FW-190s I shot down."

Hannah's jaw drops as the living and breathing incarnation of none other than her grandfather, four times removed, Captain Neil Alexander, strolls through her in an olive-drab flight suit and *authentic* Black Scorpions squadron jacket.

"Hi, Grandpa."

Hannah recognizes his shock of jet black hair and matinee idol visage from old photographs, standing tall and straight as if ripped from an Army Air Force recruitment poster,

Exasperated, Harry plops in a folding chair with the cigarette pursed between his lips. "Go on, Captain, you tell these idiots."

Neil's commanding voice rises over the background din, "My friend and wingman, the young and brash Lieutenant Harry Stark, scored a confirmed kill; however, the B-24 Liberator he was escorting crashed in the ocean with no survivors. Not sure about the second German craft."

"I shot it down, too, goddammit!"

"Perhaps, Harry. We'll never know." Neil turns and winks toward Hannah, gesturing toward a shady tree as a P-47 Thunderbolt roars overhead before banking out over the Med.

"You can see me?"

"I sure can. Neither of us is here. This is an illusion of your making. Well done, Hannah Haig."

Pulling an unruly blond strand behind her ear, Hannah stares spellbound and speechless at her ancestor.

"You look like your mother."

"So, I'm told."

Squinting through the brightness, the Army Air Force Captain, with seven kills under his belt, surveys the recreated Alto Airfield, "This takes me back." With a smiling nod toward Hannah, "Everything appears accurate, too, except for your jacket."

"Even the Light Specters make mistakes." Swallowing hard and not wanting to give away too much, Hannah hesitates to say more.

"We are far from perfection." Distracted by a bright speck in the daytime sky, Neil breathes in the salty Corsican air, refocusing his attention upon Hannah, "Do you know why you are here?"

"No."

"Please, have a seat."

Turning to find a lawn chair behind her, she shrugs, "Okay, why not."

Waiting for Hannah to get comfortable, Neil ruminates on the shady oak's complicated branches, "I remember this tree—one of the few not destroyed when the Allies liberated Alto."

Pondering the hazy sunlight filtering through the leaves, Hannah nods, "Beauty trumps evil, at least it used to …"

"It still can and will, Hannah Haig. The year is 2544. August, to be precise. Almost six hundred years to the day since Neil Alexander's last mission."

"Is that by design?"

Neil's rugged countenance darkens, "The Overlords' return has upset a universal consonance."

Hannah leans forward with a burst of recognition, "You, or Neil, convinced the Light Specters to save the world from the Gork invasion if Mom replaced the golden ellipse atop a beacon."

"A delicate negotiation, but yes. Only a handful of humans ever learned why Earth was spared from the Gorks. As a result of that fleeting victory, your mother, Hannah, proved humanity's potential to achieve its Omega Point and enter the universal community."

"The Overlords wiped out every human on Earth. I was there on the day of the final battle." Opening doors in her mind's eye, "I watched the Final Eight perish in a horrible fire. I died."

"Your friends perished, but you did not die. The Blue Spark embedded in your DNA allowed the transcendent life force within you to part from your mortal coil. While your eight friends survived heavy doses of the Blue Spark, emulating transhuman states, it proved insufficient to reach quintessence. You are the only one, Hannah."

"What do you mean?"

"Your inherited Blue Spark has evolved to a promised Omega Point."

"Great. Do I get a merit badge?"

Neil laughs, "How wonderful, the Alexander wit lives on. I was dispatched by the Light Specters to orient you to the reality in which you now exist. Like a flight instructor crash course."

Hannah grins, "Poor choice of words."

"Ah, yes. Enough idle chat. You reconstructed this airbase from your subconscious. Free your mind, Hannah. See what else you can do."

Hannah clears her throat and stands. "Okay. I'll play along." Smoothing hands down her sides, she takes a deep breath and closes her eyes, morphing into Neil Alexander flashing his trademark debonair grin.

"How's this?"

Impressed, Neil clasps his hands, "Excellent, my dear, like looking into a mirror."

Hannah transitions to a brilliant orb hovering above the stump.

Bathed in her ethereal glow, Neil offers a professorial nod, "You are wielding the innate human energy that makes you who you are. Every living being possesses it—the spiritual essence or soul—that leaves us at death and moves beyond an eternal horizon."

"You mean Heaven."

"Perhaps. Everything falls under God's creation. Your presence is according to His plan, not ours. We are energized messengers who made this same evolutionary leap long ago. And now you represent the crucible of your species' transformation."

Returning to her human appearance, Hannah shakes a finger at the Light Specter projecting Neil's form, "I did not ask for this."

"Nor did your mother. That is why it is called fate. Your transhumanism persuaded a skeptical intergalactic audience to bring you back." Pausing to ensure he has her full attention, Neil continues, "Hannah. This is paramount, and I need you to understand: You must defeat the Overlords once and for all so that humanity can begin anew."

Hannah throws up her glowing blue hands, "You are the fucking Light Specters. The most powerful beings in the universe. Why didn't you stop the Overlords?"

The spectral manifestation of Neil Alexander shapeshifts into Owen Haig's fatherly image, "Baby Girl. Sometimes, you have to fight your own fights."

Hannah shakes her head and holds out a hand, "That's hitting below the belt. Even with whatever I have become, what makes you believe I can defeat the Overlords now?"

Returning to Neil's visage, his projection starts to fade, "You really are a chip off the old block. I will impart the same wisdom Neil Alexander gave to your mother at her darkest moment battling her own demons and dark spectral forces arrayed against her: have faith."

Pausing to ensure the troubled young blond absorbed his deceptively sage advice, Neil switches gears, "The Overlords may appear indomitable, but they are not. They are nothing more than an algorithmic aberration abandoned to its own devices by a long-extinct alien race. Their cubed exodus into the cosmos left many doubting their artificial intelligence could return, yet it did. Never say never. And now they have corrupted the order of all things like a viral mutation. Resurrecting the human species rests on a razor's edge between infinity and oblivion. It all comes down to you, Hannah Haig. "

Hannah grumbles a sigh as Neil vanishes into the ether. "Faith. Easier said than done."

Alto Airbase returns to overgrown pasturelands with Hannah seated atop a wet tree stump in a steady drizzle as a massive airship passes through low cloud cover, bellowing klaxons, signaling its arrival, lumbering toward the multi-domed Overlord megalopolis dominating the eastern sky.

Rudderless, Hannah tromps downhill toward the coastline, surprising a squirrel nibbling a thorny thistle shoot. Acknowledging her presence, the tame creature hops on a gnarled branch and extends the weed in its little fingers.

Marooned in an altered state of reality, Hannah imitates her childhood hero, Lewis Carroll's Alice, accepting the soggy purple bloom between her thumb and forefinger.

"Thank you."

Rather than scurrying off to rejoin its nutty friends, the squirrel's beady black peepers lock onto her blue-green eyes for awkward minutes to see who blinks first. Surrendering with an overt blink as the drizzle morphs to steady rain, Hannah tucks the thistle in her jacket for safekeeping before morphing to pure energy and shooting skyward, avoiding the Overlord airship's detection.

The Overlords | Earth
01:17 p.m. | September 2, 2544

Dimming her quintessential manifestation to a glimmering sphere, Hannah left Corsica and embarked on a planetary recon of the Overlords' transformation of the only home humanity had ever known. Surpassing her worst fears, she discovers Earth's continents and oceans studded with their alien infrastructure. Meanwhile, the former world, including her hometown of Newport, Rhode Island, was gone, replaced with vast reaches of untamed wilderness and barren wastelands.

Finding only scant evidence of a former human civilization, like the aircraft carrier wreckage off the Corsican coast, Hannah bursts from place to place at incredible speeds. Surveying the African continent, she glides undetected above a massive complex in the Congo. Heading north, she explores the Giza Plateau, leveled back to a flat, arid desert. No pyramids. No Cairo, for that matter. Nothing.

Dodging ubiquitous Overlord mechs and drones, Hannah's attention turns to a thrumming power grid spitting electrified bolts into the polluted air over southern Turkey into Syria and Iraq. Horrified by the quasi-organic oily tendrils spiraling into the aridness in every direction, she veers north along a line snaking under the Black Sea and through eastern Ukraine, pinning another domed megastructure on the Northern European Plain rivaling the monstrosity visible from the Corsican shoreline she dubbed Atlantis.

Jesus, how many of them are there?

Scouting interconnecting nuclei and transport hubs throughout Russia, Siberia, China, Southeast Asia, and Japan, she dives below the choppy surface of the Pacific Ocean along a submerged line entwining the ocean floor like a sewn seam to a towering multi-domed complex balanced on stacks of gargantuan basaltic pillars reaching high above palm-covered volcanic islands and coral atolls dotting the deep blue ocean.

Floating amid schools of darting fish unfazed by her presence, Hannah wracks her transhuman brain, struggling to recall an oft-repeated Dave Poole conspiracy theory from her eye-rolling youth.

Oh, come on … it had to do with the South Pacific … what was the name? It sounded like a person … ah, that's right … Nan Madol.

A curious sea turtle swims to her glowing essence before gliding into the deep blue as Hannah scrutinizes complicated glyphs carved into megalithic columns rising from the sandy bottom to hundreds of feet above the waves, undergirding the resurrected Overlord complex.

The bastards rebuilt upon their ancient ruins and leveled everything else, with Mother Nature taking care of the rest.

***

Wishing she had paid more attention in world history and geography classes—not to mention Dave's crazy conspiracy theories—Hannah camps inside a shallow cave under a sea of stars on a cold, clear night in the Andes Mountains near Machu Pichu. Tuning out a thrashing hum from the bizarre tendrils strangling the craggy heights to a dizzying domed palace in the sky, she plans an early-morning recon with a loud yawn in her transhuman blond form.

Even a freak like me needs a little beauty rest.

Lying on her rolled jacket, she produces the pressed purple thistle from a pocket and twirls it betwixt her thumb and forefinger.

Scottish thistle … Scotland. The Powers That Be! That's what the little squirrel was trying to tell me. Come on, Alice. Grab a fucking clue!

Andrew | Former PTB HQ
05:32 p.m. | September 11, 2544

Hannah's radiant orb spins above frigid North Sea white caps and across the deserted Scottish coastline on a beeline toward her destination before shapeshifting to her human litheness and sticking a two-point landing. Adjusting the alien-tech superhero suit riding up her toned backside, she examines a felled stone wall crumbled into a weed and rock escarpment pocked with bird nests, seeing purple thistle among the scrubby grasses, acknowledging the symbolism, if not in reality, at least in her mind.

Mother Nature perseveres.

Placing wet hands on a massive stone with her nimble fingers splayed apart, Hannah projects a medieval castle to its 14th-century halcyon days on a strategic spot overlooking the River Tyne.

"You found the place."

Startled by somebody getting the drop on her, Hannah closes the image, pivoting onto a man with short side-parted dark-blond hair with a hint of gray at the temples, framing a chiseled countenance in a green PTB windbreaker over a black mock turtleneck, boot-cut jeans, and western boots.

"Yes, I did. Who might you be?"

"My apologies. We never officially met. My name is Andrew."

* * *

Leading his guest through a camouflaged passage under the collapsed wall and down a tunnel into pitch-blackness, Andrew stops before a damaged elevator and flips a light switch.

"Damn. That worked just an hour ago."

"They don't make evil underground headquarters like they used to."

Before Andrew can counter the cutting joke, Hannah beams natural light from her right index finger. "I'm a walking flashlight." Illuminating a bank of buttons, "I can do this with other body parts, too, but we just met, so … yeah."

Andrew opens the wonky elevator doors with a wry grin, "Duly noted."

Descending the damaged shaft through Scottish strata in the banging and clanking lift, the misaligned doors scrape apart, breaking an awkward silence.

"Watch your step."

Following Andrew, Hannah crunches her knee-high red superhero boots across broken glass, over and around upturned chairs, stools, and tables jumbled in busted heaps, blocking a central aisle under motion-activated, flickering fluorescents, casting twisted rows of smashed lab benches piled with thrashed chemistry equipment and crushed instruments and tools in eerie strobing lights and shadows.

Catching up to Andrew at a bone-dry floor-to-ceiling aquarium, Hannah peers through the cracked glass at trash and debris strewn about the sandy bottom. "What was this place?"

"This? This was an aquarium."

Andrew chuckles at Hannah's eye-rolling reaction to his little joke.

"I mean *this place*."

"Ah, yes. This used to be Professor Richard King's research laboratory. Richard was the PTB's chief scientist. Of course, that was hundreds of years ago. The damage you see is a consequence of the Sisters' misguided anarchic ecstasy following the Purge."

"The Sisters … Mom told me about them. She said one of them tried to seduce her."

"I am not surprised. Early in the Sisters' development, breaching taboos and sexual experimentation captivated their advanced intellects. How I miss those days."

With a raised eyebrow, Hannah snickers, "I bet you do."

Not taking the bait, Andrew taps the thick aquarium glass, "By the way, this aquarium was the home of a remarkable species from the depths of the Amazon, a mascot of sorts." Casting a wistful grin upon

Hannah, he adds, "A tale for another time."

* * *

Trailing Andrew through red double doors at the far end of the lab, Hannah enters a gymnasium-sized expanse replete with damaged pod-like structures, with some lying smashed on their sides at the base of a multilevel array of pillars rising high into the echoing space.

"This was the PTB Think Tank." Mounting a short flight of steps, Andrew peers inside a damaged three-person thinkpod still mounted atop a block, "These pods accommodated anywhere from one to ten people, providing total isolation to work a problem or invent something new. It was a pet project of mine back in the day. Artemus thought it a waste of money. He was right. They were seldom used for anything other than trysts or catnaps, but they did prove effective when sequestering oneself to ponder the world."

Jumping down the steps and moving farther into the darkness, he laughs, "Back when there was a world to ponder."

"My Mom told stories about coming here with my father for their indoctrination ceremony."

"The aforementioned inimitable Rachel Haig. A gorgeous woman ... Has anyone ..."

"Yes."

Moving to a solid black three-story outer wall covered in conduits and pipes, Andrew opens a breaker panel, flipping switches to power overhead lights and the ventilation system. Calling across the space to Hannah, "The HQ's shielded battery reserves could go another half a millennium. I can set the temperature anywhere that suits you."

"No. It is fine. Really, Andrew. I am pretty much immune to the elements."

"How about food? The PTB emergency supplies have an assortment of comestibles for just such an occasion. Although, I am not sure if a can of peaches is still good after 500 years."

Hannah laughs, appreciating her host's attempt to lighten the mood, "No. I rarely eat. Once again, it is not necessary."

Andrew waves his hands, "Yes. Yes. I know. You are not the same little girl I feared would overthrow the PTB with your inherited Blue Spark."

"You knew?"

Taking a knee to access an inset floor latch, he tugs a hinged trapdoor open, scanning the darkness before turning back toward a shocked Hannah, "Yes. Of course. Your Mother tried to conceal your Blue Spark from The Powers That Be. I don't blame her."

"You let me live."

"I decided the lesser of two evils was to allow you to mature, predicting a time like this would one day arrive. And now here we are!"

"Yep, here we are."

Wrinkling her brow, Hannah watches the mysterious man grab ladder rungs and lower into the eight-foot void with powerful agility before laughing despite herself as he makes a comical face poking his head and shoulders back out like a prairie dog.

"Come on, Hannah. There are things down here we need."

Following through the trap door to the bottom, stirring motes into the stillness, Hannah presses an energized finger to an antique camping lantern and turns the nob to full brightness.

Andrew jumps off the ladder's lowest rungs, brushing off cobwebs and dust, "That is quite a gift."

Taking in the natural limestone grotto deep beneath the Scottish pasturelands, she swipes a thick coating of dust from a black-and-white photo of Richard King taken at a much younger age amid a picturesque desert locale, "More of a curse."

"As you can imagine, the PTB amassed a lot of junk through the years. More than the Vatican. This is only a small portion. Most of it is in a warehouse at a long-defunct base in the American southwest."

"I am sorry, Andrew, but I doubt it survived the nukes."

Andrew squeezes around Hannah in the tight space with a cagey grin, pushing aside boxes to reach a ten-foot-wide draped rectangular shape, "We'll see about that."

Yanking off the sheet, the ageless replicant rolls and tosses it aside as Hannah's blue aura illuminates a massive world map.

"This was once used by Churchill and his planners when confronting pure evil. We shall put it to similar use. Be a dear and climb over to grab the other end. We need to …"

"Andrew, I got it."

Waving a finger toward the heavy and unwieldy World War Two artifact, Hannah elevates it up and through the trap door into the Think Tank. "What else?"

Scanning draped furniture, historical relics, and alien treasures, Andrew's gaze lands on Artemus Pennywell's monogrammed briefcase. Lifting it in a delicate grasp, he checks to ensure the spring-loaded locks are engaged before answering Hannah, "You are about the same size as the Sisters. Their wardrobes should be through there. Everything from flannel shirts and jeans to high-end European designer frocks. They had expensive and diverse sartorial tastes. While you do that, I will seek out my old office desk. There is something of importance locked inside."

Intrigued by the notion of wearing something other than her alien tech bodysuit, Hannah navigates troves of treasures in a circuitous path to reach the wardrobe racks, encountering a larger-than-life oil portrait of a distinguished older man with a bald head and intense gray eyes in a tailored black suit. "Andrew, who is this?"

"That is Artemus Aloysius Pennywell, the PTB's longest-serving CEO from 1952 to 2044."

Admiring the eight-foot vertical canvas in a gilded frame with an intricate inlaid peony design, adding another two feet to its height, she scrutinizes a golden Saguaro cactus bolo tie at the man's starched white collar, marveling at how the loose brushwork fools the eye into viewing the painting as photorealistic from even a short distance emulative of a

John Singer Sargent masterpiece.

"How old was Mr. Pennywell when he passed?"

"An irascible 134 years." Anticipating number-crunching calculations in Hannah's head, "Artemus took a life-extending elixir at a young and impetuous age. A move he later came to regret."

Acknowledging a touch of gray and subtle hints of wrinkling around Andrew's brown eyes that shift to elusive violets and greens in different lighting, Hannah shakes off an impertinent thought in her lonely mind.

"Andrew, you realize you are older than the canned peaches."

Searching into the shadows with the camping lantern, he nods, "My creator, Mitsuo Kobayashi, did not leave behind a manual. However, I am quite sure I have exceeded my warranty."

"How long have you been here?"

"Before the Purge in 2070, I lived in self-imposed exile in the Australian Outback with Number 1—the only replicant of a woman named Sarah to evolve into something more akin to your present state of being. I believe transhuman is the term used back in the day."

Pausing to collect his thoughts, "After the Purge, I returned to Scotland to stop her fifteen identical siblings from betraying what was left of the world. I failed. On the same day the Overlords launched the first nukes, I discovered my only son's grave. He died after taking down Julius Hart's Thundercorps. I could not return to Australia with the world thrust back into chaos. To this day, I do not know if Number 1 is dead or alive."

Hannah's eyes widen in shock.

"Andrew, I am the only survivor of Thundercorp No. 5. Your son was responsible for the deaths of thousands of people on those satellites, including my friends."

Andrew raises his hands in surrender, "Hannah, I am responsible for your Mother's wheelchair-bound latter years, but I had nothing to do with the Thundercorp operation. By then, I was also an enemy of the PTB. My son, Paddy, would have killed me as soon as look at me. I failed him as a father. That is why I was in exile in the first place … I am sorry …"

Fighting back the tears, Hannah reaches out with her hands aglow, "Please stop, Andrew. The version of me that survived Thundercorp No. 5 died long ago. It was part of her past, not mine. Case closed."

"No more secrets. We need to trust each other." Andrew's contrite expression morphs into a happy-faced grin, masking unadulterated relief, "You know what? There are cases of vintage wine in the food stores. Let's finish and toast the memories of those no longer here and our new partnership."

Hannah dives into the clothes racks, perusing the eclectic Number 11 collection, calling back toward Andrew with a winsome laugh, "A drink sounds good."

Watching the engrossed young woman rifling through the racks like a Black Friday shopper, Andrew unlocks his old desk. Opening a hidden compartment, he removes a two-inch cube he used in a former life to communicate with the Overlords before their return.

Exhaling a sigh of relief to have the crucial relic back in his possession, he tucks it into a pocket in his windbreaker. Ensuring his new partner remains otherwise distracted, Andrew scoops the monogrammed briefcase by the handle. Careful not to jostle the contents, he sidles through the crowded space and places the case in a conspicuous new spot behind Pennywell's portrait.

Stepping back to view the briefcase from different angles, he gives it a subtle nudge, just enough but not too much to cause suspicion.

* * *

Barefoot, in shorts and a thin lace blouse from Number 11's diverse wardrobe, Hannah stands on her toes, reaching high to draw a smokestack symbol over the words Arctic Circle near the top of the eight-foot-tall map propped against a wall in the erstwhile PTB Think

Tank, "Another factory ... God knows what they are making way up there."

"An Overlord snowman army?"

"Hilarious, Andrew. See, I am rubbing off on you."

"Andrew's humor was defined as dark to droll long before making your acquaintance."

Frowning at his third-person response, Hannah sips excellent 600-year-old Bordeaux from a paper cup, rechecking domes, generators, factories, and transport hubs indicated by half circles, lightning bolts, smokestacks, and Xs on every continent before pivoting to Andrew with a sly grin, "Here is the best part." Drawing a dome over Peru, she circles it and adds a star. "Overlord Central. Their fucking headquarters."

Andrew refills his cup before topping off Hannah, "You know that for sure?"

Hannah's lightheaded gaze swivels back to the map, downing the pricey red blend like lemonade, "Um, yes, pretty sure. Ninety percent."

Andrew reclines on a comfortable sofa salvaged from a pod, positioned before the map, twirling his half-filled cup, torn between Hannah's effortless natural grace and the symbols interconnected in a complicated grid across the vintage map.

"Do you know what this looks like?"

Capping the marker, Hannah drops it on the table and reaches for her wine, "No. What?"

"A brain. More of a neural network."

Plopping next to Andrew on the bouncy sofa, wine sploots from her cup, "Oh, damn, I really like this top."

Producing a cloth in his hand like a magician, Andrew reverts to valet mode, "Allow me." dabbing at the red stains across her chest as she folds a long leg underneath her and twists sideways to face Andrew.

Within dangerous proximity of each other with nowhere to go and their fates far from certain, Hannah leans into Andrew and kisses his scruffy cheek, whispering, "It's fine. I can get another blouse. 11 had tons of nice stuff."

Andrew withdraws his hand from Hannah's half-unbuttoned blouse, cognizant of her fragile psyche, "Right. How silly of me."

Wah-Wah-Wah, Wah-Wah-Wah …

Like a teenager caught making out, Hannah almost jumps out of her natural complexion, morphing to blue in response to the piercing alarm, "What the hell is that?"

Andrew tosses his cup, vaulting off the sofa to a wall-mounted old-school black-and-white monitor. Silencing the ear-piercing din, he turns to Hannah, "We have company."

"I'll check it out. Stay here!" Transforming to her energized state, Hannah shoots upward through solid rock to the dripping green surface world in heavy rain. Conjuring her superhero ensemble in place of the shorts and loose blouse, she keeps low, focusing on a surveillance drone three hundred feet downhill by the river, where it tripped Andrew's security perimeter.

How did you find me?

Hunkering behind a cut stone block, she keeps one eye on the drone and catches Andrew exiting the camouflaged tunnel entrance.

Gaining his attention with a tossed rock, she uses hand signals to prevent his ill-advised advance: *"One drone downhill near the river."* before raising a finger to her lips, pleading with him to hold his position and wait for it to move on.

Ignoring her wide-eyed plea to stand down, Andrew circumvents the drone, creeping to a closer view behind a sopping thicket as the rain turns to a torrential downpour. Catching telltale metallic glints of armor through the late afternoon gloom hidden in the woods along the river, he beats a hasty retreat to Hannah's position.

"You need to leave right now. There is no time to argue."

Searching Andrew's worried expression in vain for a glimpse of that droll replicant wit, Hannah shakes her head, "Andrew, we can take out one drone."

Andrew shakes his head, producing a thin remote from his drenched jacket, "That drone is the lead scout for an Overlord mech battalion hidden in the trees."

Hannah lifts her head, peering downhill, "Andrew, are you sure? Why don't they just attack if they know we are here?"

"I don't know, but we may as well exact a little revenge."

Pressing the remote, Andrew detonates preset C-4 explosive charges positioned amid the rocks and trees by the river in spectacular fireballs billowing hundreds of feet into the stormy skies above the Scottish countryside.

Enraged by her new partner's impulsiveness, Hannah grabs Andrew by his green PTB windbreaker, shaking him as flaming robot parts, branches, pelting rocks, and muddy debris cascade around them, "Why did you do that? I could have taken them out without drawing attention. Are you trying to get us killed? We have nowhere else to go!"

Andrew pushes back from the glowing woman in the torrential downpour, "You do, Hannah. Australia."

Pressing a slip of paper into her hands, Andrew sets off more charges, creating a ring of fire around the PTB HQ's miles-wide perimeter, "Fly away and leave this place. Never come back. I will hold them off."

Hannah scans the soggy slip, 'What is this? Coordinates? You aren't getting off that easy, Andrew—you are coming with me."

Ignoring his protests, Hannah throws her arms around the replicant in a blinding embrace, transforming their entwined mass to a spherical light blasting high above a cataclysmic stormfront flooding the British Isles and Western Europe, forever altering the continent's topography.

* * *

Failing to capture the elusive, energized enigma with the temerity to surveil their logical and orderly existence seemingly at will, Overlords drop through the rain amid smoldering tree trunks, busted limbs, and upturned clusters of thick twisting roots entangled with their decimated killer mech battalion's scorched and sparking robot parts wafting gray sooty smoke into the pallid dampness.

Piercing the surroundings with their ultra-keen vision, the investigators discover a hidden shaft descending into a subterranean multilevel expanse. Exploring the sabotaged spaces, finding no signs of life, they enter an erstwhile laboratory and proceed past an empty aquarium through red doors into a gaping auditorium with high black walls and broken pod like structures.

Sniffing the contents of a glass bottle, a curious Overlord turns toward a large world map, his dark, recessed gaze cogitating crude symbols from under a thick alabaster brow. Tilting his head at the South American continent, he notes an added emphasis on a half-circle glyph with an unpleasant foreboding.

Watching his six colleagues float, one by one, through an open trap door, he presses a finger to a reddish liquid in a thin paper cup and licks it with his gray tongue. Shaking his head in disgust, he follows the others through the opening, searching for museum-quality relics or carbon-based snacks, cowering among the ragged junk piles.

With the acidic taste lingering on his long tongue, the Overlord maneuvers around crates and draped furniture, pausing before a life-size portrait of an old man. Unable to look away from the subject's piercing stare, another Overlord nudges him aside, breaking the spell. Reaching for a thin black briefcase positioned behind the portrait at a calculated yet perplexing angle, the second Overlord places the attaché case on a cluttered tabletop with the wine taster looking on, noting the monogrammed AAP in solid gold scripted letters before unsnapping the locks.

Upon opening the hinged lid, the pair's black eyes widen in horror, realizing their error a millisecond before the briefcase nuke detonates with the power of ten Hiroshimas, incinerating the storied underground base to subatomic particles and collapsing the surrounding Scottish Lowlands countryside for miles in a deep concentric radioactive crater.

* * *

Beyond space and time, Artemus Pennywell laughs and raises a glass with his spectral friends.

Number 1 | The Farmhouse
11:32 p.m. | September 3, 2544

Outside a camouflaged compound sequestered in a vast region of unexplored Australian Outback hundreds of miles northeast of where Perth used to exist, a blinding flash pierces the night, manifesting two figures out of the ether, collapsing to the arid hardscrabble in a sodden heap.

* * *

A flash through window curtains billowing into the small bedroom elicits an audible hiss from the cat, stirring Number 1 from a restless slumber.

"It's just lightning; don't be such a scaredy cat."

Pulling covers under her chin, the brunette suppresses strange murmuring voices invading her perfect skull and tries to go back to sleep, counting off the seconds before a crack of thunder from another violent storm sends tremors through the patchwork facades of rusty corrugated metal, bricks, and stacked stonework constituting the ancient farmhouse where she had lived in total isolation for hundreds of years.

Puzzled by the lack of thunder shaking the old house to its cracked and leaky foundation, Number 1 sits up and checks a mechanical timepiece on the nightstand with a groan, "Ugh, it's only eleven-thirty."

Contemplating her lonely existence, she smooths a finger along the barrel of a loaded revolver beside the clock before reaching for her water.

Knock, knock, knock …

Almost fumbling the slippery glass from her calloused fingers, the startled brunette picks up the gun, tiptoeing through a labyrinth of halls and rooms before sneaking out a side door into the night. Stalking past the squeaking windmill and under rickety beams supporting a leaning water tank, she crouches behind a scrubby Acacia, surveilling humanoid forms lurking in the asymmetric dwelling's front porch shadows as a desolate hardscape rises from the darkness like painted backdrops from a staged production.

Aiming her weapon at the intruders, she hears the foreign sound of her own voice calling out, "Don't fucking move! State your business."

A silhouetted male figure pivots with a Cheshire Cat smile, "Which is it? Don't fucking move or state our business?"

With her long black hair pulled in a ponytail under an open flannel shirt, the strange new voice lurking within her replicant mind murmurs, *"About fucking time."* as an ebullient Number 1 drops the gun and rushes into Andrew's arms with tears streaming down her face.

"I thought you were dead!"

Soaking wet and dazed from having his molecules thrown back together like a tossed salad, Andrew staggers under 1's emotional greeting, "I could say the same about you. I did not know if you were still here, so I knocked."

Not wanting to release him from her long arms, Number 1's hand slides into his jacket and feels the cube in his soaking windbreaker pocket as her blue eyes draw onto his reticent young companion lingering on the porch.

"Andrew. You found her."

Hannah steps forward, allowing her skin to transition from a brilliant blue glow. "Hello, Number 1. I have heard a lot about you."

"You are both soaking wet. Come inside, and I will find you

some dry clothes."

"Go on, Hannah." Kissing the replicant's cheek, he passes the cube to 1 with a sleight of hand while motioning with his other hand like a magician, "I want to see what 1 has done with the place in my prolonged absence."

Waiting for the door to close behind the pair, Andrew scoops the loaded revolver from the dirt and gazes at the starry spectacle filling the night sky, focusing on a cosmic ghost's inexorable approach.

It is almost time.

Hannah | The Outback
07:26 a.m. | September 4, 2544

Listening for movement through the morning quietude, Hannah hears the bedroom door creak open seconds before a purring kitty jumps on the bed, staring yellow saucer eyes at her.

Hannah pets the jet-black furball with a non-threatening "Hello." as Number 1 peeks through the cracked door.

"Good. You are up. Get dressed. We are going on a hike."

Hannah's "No thanks …" goes unheard as the kitty vaults off the thin mattress to follow Number 1 down the hallway.

* * *

Tossing a daypack at a yawning Hannah, Number 1 weights a note under a ceramic mug for Andrew, spent and dozing in the back bedroom where she left him.

Breathing in the crisp morning air, Hannah tucks her straggly blond under a broken-in red ballcap, wriggling her toes in a pair of comfortable hikers. Shrugging into her pack over a green t-shirt with a screen-printed smiley face and a pair of dorky blue cargo shorts, she jogs past a chicken coop and raised planters covered in wire meshing, catching up with the ageless replicant along a meandering footpath away from the sprawling compound into the open desert. Syncing to 1's purposeful strides, Hannah admires the borderline surrealness of the Outback, stretching to the horizon like a romanticized landscape painting. Catching the sight of a long and colorful snake slithering behind a red rock, she ventures a word with her tight-lipped tour guide, "I guess you were surprised to see us on your doorstep last night."

Boots crunching over the graveled trail fill a prolonged silence before Number 1 stops and pivots to Hannah.

"There is something you need to know."

"Okay. I'm listening."

Wearing a faded Men At Work t-shirt with a revolver holstered on her right hip over cropped shorts showing off her long legs, Number 1 bites her lip and wipes a tear from her eye, "I believed for all of these years that a narcissistic psychopath named Paddy murdered Andrew. So, yes, I was surprised to see him. And you, for that matter."

Placing a firm hand on Hannah's shoulder, the fresh-faced beauty's eyes glow to an ultramarine intensity, "The door knock did not surprise me. Something survived in this part of the world ... hence the greeting at gunpoint. Whatever they are, they are an inhuman, vicious lot."

Hannah touches 1's hand, "How have you managed to survive out here all this time?"

"The Light Specters watch over me. They are integral to your presence here today. And now I understand that they kept Andrew safe through the centuries." Picking up a rock and tossing it at something in the brush, "I hear their conversations inside my head from time to time."

Peering at a column of smoke rising into the deep blueness on a distant ridgeline, Hannah sniffles and wipes at a tear, "I miss the old world."

"The old world was corrupt to its core well before the Gork

invasion forever changed things. The ensuing years were even worse. Perhaps the Overlords did humanity a favor by wiping the slate clean for a new beginning." Squinting through the brightness at the path ahead, Number 1 places her hands on her hips, "And now, to complete the circle, all you need to do, Hannah Haig, is kill the Overlords."

Toe to toe with the mysterious replicant, a gauzy recollection of her old pal Maddie's cavalier elan is replaced by a chorus of voices speaking in tongues within Hannah's psyche.

Number 1 squeezes Hannah's hand, "Are you with me? Snap out of it."

With a head-clearing shake, Hannah refocuses on the gorgeous dark-haired woman, leading her by the hand to a dizzying ledge where the trail turns technical, following precipitous switchbacks to the bottom of the rocky ravine.

Hannah tips the brim of her cap and peers into the depths, "What's down there?"

"Enlightenment. I won't let you fall. It's easy. You are going to love this place."

With her calves already aching before reaching the bottom of the echoing gorge, Hannah follows 1 down a rocky embankment to a fast-flowing creek gurgling and bubbling over smooth boulders.

"It's slippery, watch your step."

Hannah wades into the flowing waters, her boots sliding across the mossy rocks. Intent on not falling on her ass, she glances at 1's lissome form already twenty paces upstream, "Yep. Got it."

* * *

Miles up the winding streambed carving out the idyllic red rock gorge for millennia, Hannah pauses to catch her breath as 1 checks a stack of boulders on a sandbar at the confluence of a narrow side canyon tributary.

"This way, we are close."

Adjusting pack straps over her toned shoulders, Hannah reconsiders whether a rainy and dingy Scotland overrun by Overlord killer mechs was perhaps not so bad, trudging across the sandbar past the marker to keep up with her tireless trail guide.

With a lone circling vulture coming in and out of view in the violet-blue sky high above the steep canyon walls, Hannah follows up a series of waterfalls, stretching for slick handholds, hoping to avoid slithering entanglements. Pulling over a last massive boulder at the box canyon's terminus, Hannah lets herself slide down the smooth, wet rock and splash into a deep blue pool. Wading to a cascade pouring from a vertical fissure in the cliff thirty feet overhead, she shouts over the roaring water to a beaming Number 1, already perched on a ledge with her feet dangling in the misty air inches from the gushing torrent.

"Well, this is a pretty spot. Thanks for bringing me out here."

Standing on the slick purchase, Number 1 props a boot on a jagged outcropping and pulls herself up, straddling the icy flow pouring from the dark crevice at her back. "This is not it, silly girl—climb up here and follow me!"

Hannah's protest falls on deaf ears as Number 1 removes her pack and disappears into the jagged vertical crack, her voice echoing from within, "You will thank me when you see what is on the other side!"

Climbing to the precipitous ledge, a shaky-legged Hannah hugs the sheer wall and peers into the dark slot, expecting her vivacious companion to jump out and scare her.

Where did she go?

Testing the limits of her non-Blue Spark physical abilities—and her patience—Hannah grips her daypack strap in a wet hand and angles inside, sidestepping above the surging water along an uneven ledge into the void. Probing into the all-consuming darkness enveloping her sopping form as the opposing current flows past from deep within the cramped void, she ventures to a point where the gap narrows to a cat's whisker more than the width of her body. Quelling panic, Hannah pulls free of sharp outcroppings like lethal fingers clinging to her body and holding her back. Scraped and bruised, she verges on tears, sucking in her flat belly through impossibly narrow slots as icy water splashes over her face, mocking her resolve.

Quashing an implied temptation to morph into her energized Blue Spark manifestation, Hannah grits her teeth with a stubborn determination to do this like a real girl. Up to her chin in the dark, with thousands of tons of solid rock closing in on her fragile body, she realizes the gift of her Mom's sacrifice to shield her from her Blue Spark destiny for as long as possible so she could experience a mortal life.

Somewhere, Mom, you must be laughing your ass off right now.

Bracing against the fast-moving water rising over her neck and shoulders, Hannah takes one last gulp of air as her perilous footing gives way to nothingness. Losing her hat, she kicks her legs and swims toward a murky aqua glimmer as the narrowness opens onto an underwater expanse. Emitting bubbles, she comes eye-to-eye with a school of curious fish amid swaying aquatic plants seconds before breaking the surface, coughing out water, and gasping for air.

"Hey! I almost drowned in there!"

Leaning back on her elbows on the sandy shoreline, Number 1 waves a hand through the still air, "Sorry! I meant to ask if you could swim—must have slipped my mind."

Dog paddling to 1's naked repose propped on sharp elbows with her long legs stretched out at the base of a red rock outcropping, Hannah sloshes out of the water, shooing a prehistoric dragonfly flitting about cattails growing from the shallows amid darting minnows and wary-eyed frogs. Sopping wet and dead tired, she collapses next to her sexy, absentminded guide.

"That was fucking scary, girl."

"You did it without turning to pure energy. We are proud of you."

"Yeah, I did. Wait a second … We?"

Number 1 turns to her friend, proffering a sensuous grin, "Take off those wet clothes and relax. You earned it."

Catching her breath and composing herself in the serene setting, Hannah removes her smiley face tee, revealing scrapes and bruises. Smoothing back her wet blond hair, she lifts her gaze to red and ochre-striated cliffs rising high above, lit in morning rays turning to shadows all the way down to a lush oasis ringing the placid spring-fed lake reflecting the Australian sky at the bottom of the 300-foot-deep concentric chasm where she stands.

Wincing at a bleeding knee graze, Hannah frowns at her partner's perfect skin, "How did you ever find your way into this hole?"

Laying back on the warm sand with her arms folded behind her head, Number 1 gazes upward at a tiny point of light visible in the sky, "Hundreds of years is a long time to explore. This is one hole. There are other holes within a day's hike—drilled by those alien hybrid monsters."

Springing onto her feet with catlike agility, the brunette beauty wades barefoot into the water and backstrokes across the glassy surface, beckoning with her index finger for Hannah to follow, "There is something I need you to see."

Hannah swims across the lake to where 1 treads water with her long arms rippling the surface. "You have been a good sport, Hannah. The pay-off for your journey lies below."

Before Hannah can reply, Number 1 plunges headfirst into the depths.

Taking another deep breath, Hannah dives to where 1 waits in the clear waters, her lustrous black locks swirling around her like a mermaid, gesturing at an anomalous two-inch cube resting on the silty bottom.

Struggling to descend tantalizing feet to reach the mystery object, Hannah surrenders to her reality with a virtual "Fuck it!" transitioning to a luminous orb and lifting the strange artifact from the muck through icy waters lit in her dreamy cerulean glow.

On the sandy beach, kneeling over the cube across from a dripping Number 1, Hannah's complexion fades to normal as she touches its dull metallic surface.

"This cube once belonged to the Overlords. It wants to go home."

Hannah's eyes widened. "Is that what this is? Should we make sure there aren't any more down there?"

Ignoring the question, 1 touches the cube, causing a rippling effect between their faces, "I think it works."

"What was that? What is its purpose?"

"You ask a lot of questions."

Shaking her head with a genuine laugh, 1 looks back across the lake, "I can assure you that this is the only cube down there because I put it there for you to find. That was one reason I was excited to bring you out here this morning."

Her heart racing, Hannah surrenders to 1's blueberry gaze, "What was the other reason?"

"This …" Number 1 reaches across the dull gray cube and pulls Hannah into a sensuous kiss. "Hmm … electric."

Hannah touches water-wrinkled fingertips to her purplish lips, "Uh, I am flattered, but …"

"Poor silly Hannah. That was my way of saying thank you. What I meant by electric is this cube gave me a static shock when we kissed."

Standing tall and firm, 1 grabs her drying clothes, "We should head back while we still have enough daylight."

Confused by the mixed signals and the cube, Hannah pulls into her t-shirt, "Not the way we came, I hope."

Scanning an almost imperceptible trail winding to the top, the brunette pulls her wet hair into a ponytail over her bare back, "We can take the rim trail to the top and make our way home from there. Just watch out for the snakes."

Hannah ties her squishy waterlogged boots, catching a glimmering sheen on 1's curved lower back.

"I do not like snakes."

Dressed and ready to go, Hannah grabs her daypack by the strap and unzips it for the first time, "What the hell, Number 1, this is empty?"

With a coy smile on her lips, Number 1 drops the cube inside, "Not anymore."

Andrew | The Farmhouse

10:14 p.m. | September 4, 2544

Poking a bent spoon into a bowlful of mystery stew, Andrew glances through the flickering candlelight between Number 1 on his left and Hannah to his right at a rustic wood table in a dilapidated kitchen well after sundown in the Australian Outback.

"What did you say this was again?"

Spreading goat's milk butter on a chunk of crusty flatbread, Number 1 dips it in the dark broth and takes a bite, "Outback stew." with an approving look toward a voracious Hannah, already scraping her bowl.

"I cannot believe how hungry I was." Dabbing her mouth with a cloth napkin, Hannah scoops her empty bowl in both hands, "Anyone else for seconds?"

Number 1 sticks her tongue out at Andrew as a cut and bruised Hannah bounds across the dim kitchen with natural grace from an evolutionary gene pool to the mystery pot atop a thick-grated cooktop, "She likes my stew."

Biting his tongue instead of expressing the double entendre on the tip of it, Andrew nudges his late dinner aside, "You can finish mine,

Hannah. I do not believe this dish would have made the menu at the PTB HQ commissary."

Kicking Andrew under the table, Number 1 mouths, *"Is it time?"*

Andrew's eyes widen with a curt headshake.

Grasping his demonstrative not yet, Number 1 looks back toward Hannah in cut-offs and a holey Midnight Oil concert tee, transfixed by something out the window behind the kitchen sink.

"What's the matter, Hannah?"

"It is so dark outside. I cannot see the windmill."

"It is pitch-black on moonless nights. Be a dear and grab one of those bottles by the cutting board. I want you both to try my homemade vodka."

"Nothing a little stronger?"

"Don't be a wise ass, Andrew."

* * *

Half-listening to her candlelit cohorts exchanging gossipy tales from their salad days at an erstwhile The Powers That Be, Hannah sips another glass of the potent elixir the nubile Number 1 calls vodka. Smoothing a fingertip into melted wax pooling around the shrinking candle, she holds it close, mesmerized by its perfect casting.

"So, who put out Professor King's laboratory fire?"

Andrew pivots to a distracted and bored Hannah, "Ah, you are listening. I thought we lost you." Noting the young woman's relaxed posture, Andrew shrugs, "The lab fire ... my guess would be Number 11. She was always there to clean up the messes when one of poor Richard's experiments ran afoul of physics."

Number 1 sniffles, "I miss my sisterhood. Number 11 was such a sweetheart." Emptying a second bottle of the happy-face labeled craft vodka, the dark-haired beauty glances at Andrew with a raised eyebrow before launching into another story, "Let's see ... I guess it is my turn for story time. Okay, here is a whopper from the night of the Gork invasion when Andrew escorted Artemus Pennywell …"

Lightheaded and liberated from painful bumps, cuts, and bruises resulting from the daylong hike, Hannah sips her anesthetizing drink and raises her hand like she is in class, "Oh, hang on … I saw Mr. Pennywell's portrait in the PTB storage—my parents knew him well."

Number 1 raises her glass, "To Rachel and Owen Haig. A lovely couple who produced a sexy, adventurous, and brave daughter."

"Thank you, Number 1."

Andrew takes a drink, "To the Haigs."

Unsure of what Andrew is waiting for, Number 1 straightens in her chair, "Where was I? Oh yes. Andrew here," Rubbing a hand through his tousled auburn hair, "escorted Pennywell to the IOSC Spaceport in Toulouse to board an evac ship filled with VIPs …"

The candle flame dies, plunging the threesome into complete darkness.

"Who turned out the lights?"

"Are there any more candles, Number 1?"

"Try the cupboard."

Standing out of his rickety chair and probing across the kitchen, Andrew opens a crooked cabinet, pushing aside a giant furry spider hunkering next to a stack of plates before coming across another red candle. Smooshing it into the soft, waxy mass at the center of the table, he strikes a match, directing his solemn, uplit gaze upon Hannah, "It was my duty to ensure the CEO's safety at all costs. By the way, Julius Hart was also aboard that ship. "

"Yes, Andrew, you were the consummate professional valet. You came out of the evil closet well after the Gorks."

Lighting the replacement candle's crooked wick, Andrew turns on Number 1 with a steely expression on his chiseled face, "I could say the same about you, Number 1. At least I never participated in a ritual human sacrifice."

"No, Andrew. You will go down in history as the man who sold the world."

Observing the icy stare down between Andrew and Number 1, Hannah pours more vodka, "Come on, you two. Water under the bridge, right?"

Ignoring Hannah, Andrew breaks the impasse with a hearty laugh, "There it is. Well done, Number 1. *The Man Who Sold the World* will serve as our Bowie homage. It was important back in the day. It is good to continue a simple tradition even when everything else is gone. I was fearful we would not squeeze in a song title reference before the end of everything."

Leaning back in his chair with a satisfied grin, he nods toward Number 1, "*Now* it is time."

Noting nuanced changes in the good-looking pair beyond her keen perception throughout the meal and into the moonless night, Hannah fails to follow the couple's cryptic banter, conceding a paradigm has inexorably shifted.

Something has changed.

Downing her vodka, 1 sets the glass on the table, "Where was I? Oh yes. Damn, this story is taking forever. With the world going to shit and their International Outer Space Consortium evacuation spaceship under direct fire from a Gork battlecruiser, Andrew takes it upon himself to make a grilled cheese sandwich for Pennywell served on a silver platter … " Dropping all pretense of sexy sophistication in a shameless bout of drunken laughter, Number 1 punches Andrew's bicep, "You were there. Finish the story. I may pee my pants."

"Not sure what has gotten into you, 1." Screwing the cap atop the third happy-faced bottle, Andrew mulls how best to wrap up the non-sequitur of a story, "Ah, well, here is the kicker, Hannah. Our dear departed Pennywell was at wit's end after the day's catastrophic events, so he hurled the grilled cheese at a window—about a three on his temper tantrum spectrum, but there it is."

Hannah nods, "There it is." her furrowed brow fixating on almost imperceptible lights under Andrew's skin as the new candle's flame lengthens in a draft like someone opened a door.

Rubbing his chin, cognizant of Hannah's burgeoning awareness and delicate emotional state, Andrew glances at 1 for support, finding her preoccupied with undoing buttons on her flannel shirt, revealing hints of her sublime anatomy. "Oh, for God's sake. The grilled cheese story is allegorical: half fell to the floor, but the other half stuck to the glass like glue."

"Okay?"

Scooching his chair knee-to-knee with Hannah, the transformative man takes her trembling hands in his, "Don't you see? One side stuck while the other half fell." Searching for a modicum of cognition, he frowns, "Pennywell's action led to a random consequence. Come on, Hannah. I am telling you how to defeat the fucking Overlords!"

Tears roll down her cheeks as Hannah recoils from Andrew's outburst, "You are scaring me."

Number 1's face brightens, "Let me try, Andrew."

"Be my guest, Number 1." Andrew rises from the table and exits the dark kitchen.

Alone together, Hannah watches him leave, "I think he is mad at me."

"Don't worry about him. He has the weight of the universe on his shoulders."

The revelatory response falls on deaf ears as Hannah shrinks from a transformative Number 1's ethereal brilliance and piercing stare.

"Look at me, Hannah. It is time."

Hannah shakes her head, averting her eyes from the frightening new entity transforming from 1's beguiling feminine form. "No. I don't know you. And I don't want to go through your looking glass."

"You are already here."

Bracing against a churning dizziness while her heart beats out of her chest, Hannah fumbles to grasp a fork in her cut-up hand, making a clumsy stab through her teary vision at a chunk of meat lingering in the stone-cold stew at the bottom of her bowl. Pretending everything around her is normal, she examines the morsel on the fork's tines while suppressing an emotional release deep within her soul, "Is this chicken?"

The empathetic spectral presence observes Hannah's mental gymnastics with sadness, "The meat is from a desert death adder. But you know that. We used your knowledge, experience, and vivid imagination to construct a plausible reality where your Blue Spark transformation could evolve to its quintessence."

Shaking her blond head and refusing to accept the bizarre explanation, Hannah eats the succulent bite in protest, "Well, it tastes like chicken to me."

Things are not always as they appear, Hannah.

Startled by the unmistakable sound of her mother's disembodied voice, Hannah spits out the mystery morsel as the collapsing kitchen setting tilts on an invisible axis, sending her tumbling down an undulating surface that was the floor. Fumbling for a white-knuckled grip on the last solid purchase above nothingness, her legs dangle in a swirling radiance, hoisting onto a broken chunk of countertop like a shipwreck survivor cast adrift in an infinite expanse.

The scales fall from Hannah's eyes, reflecting a wondrous and incalculable interstellar spectacle.

"Oh my God. It is so beautiful."

Mesmerized by colorful light trails elongating past her illuminated face, her free hand waves up and down through twinkling space, accelerating to an incredible speed across cosmic waves before her tenuous grip separates from the chipped countertop, like losing a surfboard in an astral churn. Hurtling end over end toward a sinister black hole, a last-second tug slows her perilous spiral as Number 1's radiant imitator guides her by the hand through the entrance to a magnificent nebulous amphitheater.

"Look around you, Hannah … can you see them?"

Maintaining a dizzy-headed grip on 1's translucent shimmering hand, a warm and inviting communal light show fortifies Hannah's resolve.

"There are so many of them. Everywhere and nowhere. How can that be?"

Number 1 proffers a gracious smile, "You are among the Light Specters, Hannah Haig."

"Am I a Light Specter?"

"No. Your Blue Spark legacy liberated your essence to persevere beyond death for a purpose set into motion eons ago. Your transhuman evolution coincides with an impossibly narrow opportunity to destroy the Overlords once and for all so the human species can begin anew."

"I was never on Earth, was I? No primeval forests or sea turtles. No sheep and rams. No thistle-bearing squirrel or Outback farmhouse. It was all a mental construct leading to this … *whatever this is.*"

"Yes."

Morphing between pure energy and her transformational biological incarnation's obvious invulnerability to the vacuum of space, Hannah's mind opens to what was and wasn't since her reawakening, "Why Andrew and Number 1? Why not continue with Grandpa Neil's ghost or bring back my Mom? She had the Blue Spark. Is she here? I would like to see her."

"Your mother passed beyond the horizon where she watches over you, surrounded by the people she loves. She worries quite a lot."

"That sounds like her."

Number 1 morphs into her willowy human nakedness as Andrew appears at her side in his signature black mock turtleneck, jeans, and Western boots under a green PTB windbreaker.

"What troubles you, Hannah?"

"Okay, let's play dress up." Hannah shifts to her alien mesh bodysuit, red boots, and black scorpion flight jacket. "What troubles me is that I never met either of you … how could I know who you are or what you look like?"

Considering the honest question while rubbing his scruffy chin, "Five hundred years is a long time. Only replicant survival proved plausible in your psyche." With a chuckle, he slides an arm around 1's supple waist, "Even the late great Mitsuo Kobayashi had no idea how to calculate our lifespans beyond an educated guess."

Number 1 effervesces a radiant grin through the twinkling ether, "We appear as archetypical male and female representations from your subconscious."

Andrew raises his thick eyebrows and gives 1 a playful squeeze, "I, for one, never looked better."

Smacking away his wandering hand, Number 1 bites her lip, trying not to laugh, "Shut up, Andrew."

Hannah nods, "No wonder you look so much like Maddie …."

"I regret to say the real Andrew and Number 1 perished in terrible conflagrations along with every other living thing on Earth."

"So, I am the last surviving Earthling. What now?"

Andrew shrugs and grins, "History repeats."

Number 1 elbows Andrew, "That was beyond vague." Assuming an authoritative tone, she continues, "Allow me to expand on Andrew's rather simplistic answer. A massive comet's course through the Solar System mirrors one that struck Earth millions of years ago. An event that obliterated the Overlords' global infrastructure to enigmatic ruins obscured under thousands of years of human civilizational progress."

Andrew adds to 1's explanation, "The Overlords tracked the first comet's approach, allowing sufficient time to upload their essences, like software, to a cubed technology stolen from *their* alien creators. They escaped to the stars well before the cataclysmic impact." With a remorseful sigh, he continues, "Distracted by multiple threats, the Overlords' abrupt return surprised the Light Specters."

Number 1 shakes her head, "What is worse, we failed to prevent a corrupted The Powers That Be from conspiring to purge four-fifths of humanity. That oversight paved the way for the Overlords' comeback."

Andrew offers his svelte partner a consoling pat, "Now, now, Number 1. They won't discover this comet's destructive path until too late."

Paying close attention to the pair, Hannah arches an eyebrow, "How come?"

Andrew beams a sly grin toward Hannah's wide-eyed countenance, "Unlike the original comet's dead-on destructive path, the comet currently plying the long empty space between Jupiter and Mars is classified as a *near-Earth* comet, brushing past the Blue Planet at a tantalizing 1.5 million miles before continuing toward the Sun. At best, a cosmic event of this magnitude produces a spectacular meteor shower for the Overlords. Perhaps a few of the larger fragments make an impact resulting in the faintest chance of nominal damage—far from a global extinction event."

Number 1 takes Hannah's hands in hers, "But you, Hannah Haig, can shift the paradigm, diverting this comet onto a last-minute collision course with Earth, leaving the Overlord monsters with no time to escape."

Hannah masks a swooning desire as a heightened energy passes between their sparkling fingertips, "I am not trying to sound glib, but redirecting a comet sounds like a job for Superman. I don't know about you, but I last saw him in a comic book at Stanley Hobbes bookstore in Newport when I was a little girl."

Number 1 releases Hannah's hands, feeling an electric pulse through her transformative fingertips, "You are the Blue Spark. Only you can alter the comet's path toward Earth."

Discerning an unrequited chemistry between the women, Andrew crosses his arms and nods, "It is your fate, Hannah."

"And if I say no? Is that an option?"

Number 1 morphs to energy before splitting into eighths and shapeshifting to the courageous Final Eight, with Hector Gonzalez's heroic doppelgänger taking point, "Hannah. This is our chance to defeat the pasty white bastards once and for all. Don't let us down."

Andrew gestures at the onlooking spectral gallery, "The Light Specters endured internecine strife and tribulation for millennia, losing half our kind to abhorrent blackness due to irreconcilable differences over a beacon built to protect humankind by keeping a cruel and hostile universe at bay. We made sacrifices, partnering with many historical figures throughout human history to foster your species to the cusp of an Omega Point that came to fruition when your mother's Blue Spark passed to your inherited genes. Your refusal would mean that was all for naught."

"This is the real reason Mom hid my Blue Spark. She wanted to spare me from a fate only she could see."

"You must decide, Hannah. The comet is moving at over two million miles per hour, and time is running out to shift its path onto a collision course with Earth."

Hannah's body shimmers through the tight mesh bodysuit under the vintage flight jacket. "I guess the joke is on me, right?"

Dissolving the Final Eight back to her singularly elegant visage, Number 1 raises an eyebrow, "What joke?"

"The off-model black scorpion was from *my* memory of Grandpa Neil's old flight jacket."

"Yes."

"I see." Hannah spreads her arms, twirling like a ballerina, "And this hip-hugging bodysuit that rides up my ass was designed to protect me from a billion-year-old comet, not battling Overlord mechs like some kind of girl power comic book superhero."

Andrew reaches into his green windbreaker, producing the two-inch gray cube in the palm of his hand. "Your mission is elementary: Activate this cube at the center of the comet's nucleus before time runs out."

"That one little cube can shift a comet's path?"

"Size is relative, my dear. We have synchronized the extra-dimensional element within this cube's mechanisms to our objective."

Number 1 averts her gaze toward the ethereal audience with a pronounced sigh, avoiding the Blue Spark beauty's skeptical sideways glance.

"This cube is real?"

"Yes."

Sensing 1's reticence, Hannah frowns, "You could have just told me the hike was a test to see if I could make my way into a comet."

"I am sorry, Hannah, but our lovely hike together represents a fraction of the dangers you will encounter."

Hannah morphs into a glowing blue orb, "Can't I …"

Andrew clutches the cube in his hand, "No. That won't work at all. After traveling to reach the comet, what remains of your energized state will deplete upon traversing its violent electromagnetic atmosphere to the nucleus, leaving you dependent on your physical Blue Spark permutation. Since you are the first of your kind, we are unsure how your superhuman body will respond to the comet's harsh environment. You could perish within seconds of shapeshifting to your human form." Andrew nods and smiles, "No. That will not occur. You will likely experience intermittent failures, but your transhuman form should be fine. I want you to know what you are getting into, Hannah."

Sensing the Blue Spark blond's wavering confidence, Number 1 proffers a brave smile, "Please do not let Andrew's ruminations frighten you. Look around us, Hannah. We are surrounded by stars that go on forever. Your presence here at this moment in time is a miracle. The Blue Spark liberated your body, mind, and spirit to achieve the impossible." Smoothing a hand down Hannah's arm, "And in addition to protecting your beautiful human form, your alien mesh bodysuit will provide live data."

Number 1 brushes her thin fingertip back up Hannah's hand before tapping her on the left forearm above the wrist, opening a virtual readout already counting down past 02:49:17 on the left and a disconcerting empty field on the right. "Okay, pretty basic. From your intercept point with the comet between Mars and Earth, we calculate you will have about two hours left to reach the epicenter and activate the cube, but that means we need to move."

Watching the seconds tick off, Hannah's blueness deepens, "How will I know where to go or what to do?"

Number 1 gestures at the screen's blank right half, "By the time your boots hit the icy surface, this will fill with real-time tracking data measuring your distance to the epicenter while updating the comet's everchanging mass."

Andrew rolls the cube in his hand, "As long as this little gray cube is within short proximity to the epicenter before the countdown clock reaches zero …"

Hannah's eyes narrowed. "How short of a proximity?"

"A five-foot radius or less, obviously, less is better."

"Obviously."

Uncomfortable with Hannah's confused expression, Andrew adds, "Hannah, my dear, reach the center and activate the cube before the time runs out. It is that simple."

"Great. No pressure. What happens then?"

"The cube will warp time and space an imperceptible scintilla, unnoticeable to the universe, but enough to alter the comet's trajectory onto a hyper-accelerated collision course with Earth."

"The consequence of my action."

"Yes. Unlike millions of years ago, the Overlords will not have time to escape."

"What will happen to me?"

"If you are successful, the comet will bear down on Earth and impact within seconds after the clock reaches zero."

"Won't a massive comet destroy Earth while killing the Overlords?"

"The Overlords buried the former world deep underground, having the ironic effect of preserving it from the cleansing fire and brimstone in the aftermath of the cometary impact."

Hannah shakes her head and sighs, mulling a lonely existence among the stars until her eventual death with no one to mourn her passing. Or roll the dice and perhaps live on in a universal lore as the woman who saved the human species from extinction.

"How long will it take before life starts again on Earth?"

Surprised by the question, Andrew pauses to run the numbers before answering, "Life will, in fact, start over from scratch once the planet heals. The randomness inherent in that process could take a billion years—a blip on a cosmic calendar. Sentient life leading back again to humankind even longer. None of us will be around to witness that rebirth, but we have it on good authority that someone is waiting to fulfill that promise."

Hannah nods, "You mean God, right?"

A tight-lipped smile creases Andrew's handsome face, "Not necessarily."

Cognizant of the spectral peanut gallery awaiting her decision with bated breath, Hannah considers everything that once was while radiating her Blue Spark to an ethereal brilliance.

"Okay. I will do it!"

With mixed feelings upon hearing the young woman's decision, Number 1 materializes a glittery blue Naval aviator helmet with the call sign Death Dealer painted over a smoky visor and presents it to her courageous friend. "A helmet to protect that thick skull of yours."

"No barnacles ... thank you, 1." Pulling the helmet atop her head, she raises the visor and tucks short blond hair into the padded sides before embracing her friend and kissing her soft, glistening cheek, "You read my mind."

Andrew nods, "It suits you, Hannah. Something from your past. Number 1 will escort you back into the Solar System before propelling you on an intercept with the comet." Beaming with pride at humanity's star pupil, he places the cube in her glowing hand, "Good luck."

Hannah inspects the cube with an irony-laced laugh.

Andrew's brow furrows, "What's so funny, Hannah?"

"One of you better show me how to activate this thing."

Hannah's Comet

Hailing from the Oort Cloud in the Solar System's mysterious outer reaches, Hannah's Comet speeds on a near-Earth course like an out-of-control freight train at over two million miles per hour, streaking well past Jupiter on a fast approach to the Martian ecliptic plane.

Gaining speed and heating up as it enters the inner Solar System, its sixty-five miles of elongated, irregular-shaped nucleus composed of ancient rocks and a witch's brew of frozen elements streams spectacular dual tails of vaporizing dust particles and ionized gasses longer than the Sun's diameter, announcing its ominous arrival from the limitless darkness of space.

Enveloped in a turbulent, blurred atmosphere, the cosmic dirty snowball becomes visible to the naked Overlord eye in Earth's sky.

The Overlords

Calculating the enormous comet's near-miss path evokes a morbid fascination among the resource-starved Overlords, coveting its mining potential and clues to its mysterious origins at the Solar System's nascency.

Fascinating.

Averse to missing the rare opportunity to study a cometary event more massive than the planet buster that obliterated their alien-hybrid civilization millions of years earlier, the Overlords launch mech probes latching onto the icy surface like parasitic growths. The monstrous automatons smash into the nucleus, extending giant robot legs to travel across the frozen surface, drilling core samples and streaming scanned data back to Earth for keen, logic-driven scrutiny.

Buried in the data among the usual trove of riches found within a comet's nucleus, the Overlord scientists make a startling discovery: the deeper core samples contain spiked concentrations of compounds essential to the genetic code of all living organisms on Earth and beyond.

Synthetic hybrids of an ancient and long-extinct species of humanoid aliens, the Overlords register the latent threat to their existence—albeit in a remote and far-off future—launching a demolition mech tasked with shattering the comet to subatomic particles.

Self-preservation is paramount.

Hannah

"Thanks for the lift, Number 1. Wish me luck."

"See you on the other side, Hannah Haig."

"Yep."

Parting from her elegant, astral escort across the universe, Hannah's glistering sphere enters the Solar System at an impossible speed, threading the needle past Saturn and Jupiter on a sweeping convergence with the comet at a point in space between Mars and Earth.

Slowing on approach to the comet, Hannah's waning interstellar momentum completes a graceful arc up and around the luminous coma before penetrating its violent layers of electromagnetic waves and solar winds, siphoning the precious life force from her spherical transcendent state.

Stupid Andrew, must he be right about everything?

Shapeshifting to her superhuman incarnation, Hannah's descent comes in too hot toward the comet's inhospitable nucleus, dodging flying rocks and ice within the electric blue atmosphere's gigantic rooster tails of gasses, dust, and rocks churning in its spectacular wake. Quelling panic and pumping mental brakes, she strikes against a frozen berm and careens like a ragdoll across an ice sheet into a two-story sludge pile to a merciful stop.

Any landing you walk away from is a good landing.

Ignoring a stabbing pain in her side, Hannah scrambles to avoid a freight car-sized boulder glancing off the ice and rebounding into the blistering cold atmosphere.

Huffing an unnecessary deep breath in her disheveled and compromised Blue Spark state, Hannah straightens her dented helmet and brushes muddy ice off her jacket before checking the time.

01:56:21

Fumbling a pouch open midway up her calf on the outside of her right red boot, she verifies the cube remains tucked inside as a sharp pain drops her to a knee.

Unzipping her ripped Black Scorpion jacket, Hannah's shaky fingertips touch purplish wetness seeping through the self-healing alien mesh on her midriff below her left breast. Verging on tears, she scans the barren rock under the roiling poisonous atmosphere.

Fuck. Fuck, And more fuck. I am on a comet. What was I thinking? At least I did not lose the cube.

A tremorous thud draws her watery eyes onto light beams and illuminated debris clouds swirling beyond a curved horizon.

With her unresponsive telekinetic ability refusing to lift her frozen ass off the surface, Hannah takes long strides like walking on the Moon, hurdling icy rifts and razor-sharp outcroppings up the loose, jagged escarpment to the top before dropping to her flat belly to evade detection from a narrow searchlight beaming past inches above her helmeted head.

Scooching around a frosted black stone, she surveys the mile-wide crater to where a long, multifaceted, mechanized beast stomps across the mud and ice.

My kingdom for a pair of binocs.

Straining to see through the kicked-up vaporous pall, Hannah observes a massive centipede-like automaton doubling back on multi-jointed legs, drilling a Swiss cheese pattern from banks of lasers blasting away from its illuminated underside.

It appears to be looking for something, but what?

Angling sideways, she taps through her jacketed left forearm, ignoring the countdown clock and grimacing at the impossible distance to the nucleus epicenter almost directly beneath her position on the *You Are Here* diagram. Searching the crater for a telltale crevice leading to the comet's center, she sees nothing but icy mud, just like the rest of the 65-mile-long rock resembling a melted candy bar.

I should have asked more questions.

01:42:34

An ear-splitting sound revving to a deafening pitch twists Hannah's gaze through her dirty Death Dealer visor back on the centipede mech parked mid-crater seconds before it blasts a massive column of light from its glowing midsection through the rocky surface.

Shielding her blue-green eyes from the blinding brightness, Hannah waits for the din to stop before spying on the centipede's sideways scuttle, revealing a truck-sized hole through the strobing multicolored haze.

That's the way to the middle. I need to get down there.

Clambering halfway down the steep slope, Hannah dives for cover as a silvery metallic robot blasts retrograde rockets to slow its two-point touchdown near the centipede. Without a glance at the mech, it stomps toward the laser-drilled shaft and jumps feet-first down the rabbit hole.

Caught off-guard by the turn of events, Hannah's hand slips from its frosty hold as the precarious footing beneath her boots gives way.

Alerted to her tumble down the unforgiving icy scree, the centipede lights her stricken body as it bounces off sharp boulders to a rolling heap at the crater's rock-hard bottom.

01:28:03

Blinded by the mechanized centipede's probing light, Hannah swallows back painful bumps, cuts, and bruises, relocating her right shoulder and hitting the ground on a sprinting beeline for the rabbit hole.

Capturing the biologic's presence in its nightmarish beams, the centipede dispatches knee-high, eight-legged laser mechs like baby spiders on a skittering intercept.

Swallowing back searing pain with each loping stride, Hannah skids to a stop as the spider mechs form a tightening skirmish line around her.

Tired, hurting, and covered in icy filth, she lifts her helmet's scratched and smeared visor, wincing at the mech stand-off with a grinning, "Okay. You win." while raising her hand in a faux surrender, buying time to summon her unreliable telekinesis.

This had better work.

Exerting an excruciating right-armed sweep, Hannah blasts the bots from her path in a mangled heap and breaches their busted line. Thirty feet from the crumbling hole, a blow to her back knocks her face-first to the ice. Undaunted, she picks herself back up as a barrage of red, green, and blue lasers ricochet off her brilliant cerulean mesh.

Favoring her injured right arm, she takes two defiant steps back toward the trigger-happy little bots, "You want more? I'll give you more!"

Summoning her next energized sweep, Hannah raises her exposed left hand as a damaged spider mech swivels and fires its red laser, severing her pinkie digit mid-follow-through.

Clutching her bleeding hand and screaming in agonizing pain, Hannah grits her teeth, kicking and stumbling over the spider bots' smoking and popping carcasses to the hole's crumbling edge as the centipede mech rotates its central laser drill at the biologic intrusion from point-blank range. Radiating blue from within the crisscrossing lights, she gives the Overlords, who must be watching, a smiling, still-attached middle finger salute before taking a feet-first plunge into the abyss a split second before the thick laser slices a harmless chunk of comet into the tempest.

01:17:07

Pulling her injured body into a ball, Hannah radiates blueness down the fast-disintegrating shaft through a miasmic cascade deep inside miles of rock older than the Solar System.

With no bottom in sight, Hannah contemplates her inglorious end buried alive inside a comet's nucleus, or worse, shooting out the opposite side into open space as the craggy outline of a darker-than-dark detour comes up fast. Plying psychic brakes, she times a sideways lunge and catches a sharp-angled ledge with her bloody fingertips, almost pulling both arms out of the sockets. Scrambling into the intersecting void, the deafening roar of the shaft caving in knocks her off her feet under suffocating debris clouds exploding over her.

As the dust settles inside the shuddering pitch-blackness,

Hannah digs herself free, brushing black gunk from her ruddy cheeks on a sleeve while grimacing in pain toward the shaft, now sealed under impenetrable tons of rock. Casting blue light over the frozen cavernous expanse, she heaves a defeated sigh.

That did not end well.

Wandering farther into the vast open space inside the comet's nucleus, Hannah discovers twenty-inch rectangular footprints chunked in the ice. Expressing a weary grin on her ruddy, muddy face, she taps her sleeve to access the screen.

1209.725 feet … so there is still a chance.

00:59:58

Clenching her four-digit hand in the left pocket of her tattered Black Scorpion jacket, Hannah presses the lining to her wounded side to stanch purplish blood, shaking off dizziness and coughing ruddy phlegm. Pausing atop a jagged outcropping, she spits and scans the path forward into the thrumming space, tracking the Overlords' mystery robot through a descending series of grottoes past glistening veins and crystalized mineral formations interspersed with stratified black rock and ice. Lots of ice. Hunching through a vaporous borehole widened to the mech's girth, Hannah reaches the far end, catching herself at the top of a steep declivity.

Shit. That was too close.

00:27:24

Finding gouged divots down the frozen slope left by the Overlord's accommodating robot, Hannah's Blue Spark radiates, lowering one notch at a time, intent on avoiding another fall. At the bottom, she slips and slides into a sparkling crystalline ice forest, reminding her of giant icicles as visions from a former wintertime world conjure happy memories of sledding with her Dad.

Daddy, I miss you.

Almost making out a reply through the constant background noise deep inside the comet, a sharp crack shatters Hannah's reminiscence, eyes widening with the harrowing realization that she is on thin ice. Another crack opens a fissure, sending her careening down a frozen chute, smearing a bloody trail while digging her heels into the ice to a frosted stop at the bottom.

Crap. Let's leave that part out of my superhero legend.

Bent sideways by an unbearable stab from her injured left side, Hannah falls onto her hands and knees in a painful rictus as the familiar voice resonates in her ears.

Baby Girl, you are almost there.

Rolling onto her back, she wipes tears from her swollen eyes, hearing the unmistakable sound of Owen's voice as tiny luminous ice crystals fluttering in the ether land on her face.

"Thanks, Dad, I needed that."

Covered in cuts, scrapes, and bruises on her hands and face, Hannah scrabbles onto her red superhero boots and checks the *You Are Here*.

"48.623 feet. That's it?"

00:14:50

Breathing in through her stuffy nose and exhaling over purplish lips, Hannah Haig ponders the final leg of her odyssey, a robot-made ice tunnel aglow with the mech's strange strobing ambiance, in an odd way resembling the entrance to a hedonistic underground club back in her post-Thundercorp Oslo days.

Let's dance, motherfucker.

Ducking under and around long, dripping icicles, Hannah's blue aura pushes back against the red lights, breaching the hollowed-out space to a crouch at the tunnel's open end, overlooking a yawning black chasm. Across the bottomless void, the robot mech stands sentinel-like, its bulbous head and silver body spinning red warning sirens into the darkness like a bomb counting down to a detonation.

Piercing the mech's AI, Hannah's telepathy translates the predictable Overlord programming—similar to Thundercorp's drone language—and confirms her suspicion: The robot mech is set to explode *before* the comet reaches Earth.

Man, the Overlords are assholes.

Noting the mech's internal clock parallels her fast-dwindling countdown, she dims her luminescence to a light-blue glimmer, rolling sideways and tapping her forearm, measuring her distance to the epicenter.

Twenty-six damn feet! That thing is standing at the epicenter ... Now what?

00:07:56

Settling on a desperate ad-libbed attack plan, Hannah paces up the tunnel for a running start.

It's okay. I was never getting out of here alive.

Lowering the visor on her helmet over her grimy and determined face, she sets off like a speed skater, radiating a piercing blue through red strobes illuminating the icy tunnel.

Its detectors going wild, the once-stoic mech opens a ricocheting laser barrage, lighting up the chasm, ripping through Hannah's Black Scorpions jacket and glancing off her helmeted head and boots while taxing her superhero mesh beyond its limits.

Muscles burning, Hannah propels her injured body off the crumbling edge with a snarling scream, twisting her blue body in a lithe and graceful midair evasion of the mech's point-blank onslaught before a laser's white-hot beam gashes across her cheek and left eye socket through her melted visor, sending her reeling into blackness.

Plummeting down the abyss, fiery particles appear like sparklers before Hannah's compromised one-eyed gaze, conjuring a long-ago Fourth of July in her altered psyche.

Be careful, Hannah. Don't hold that sparkler so close to your face.

"I'm sorry, Mom. I should have listened to you."

Get moving, Hannah. There is still time.

Dropping like a rock through the frigid ether, Hannah's Blue Spark stops her plunge inches above a jagged, icy bottom and awakens miraculous God-given energy from every cell in her transhuman incarnation. Seizing her destiny, arms folded across her heaving chest, she rises undetected through the disorienting darkness into the deafening red strobing crescendo from the mech's freakish siren-shaped translucent head spinning like a centrifuge toward detonation.

One shot. That is all I will get.

00:03:39

Extending shaking, bloodied hands toward the bright and blurry red glowing robot, Hannah's tattered and injured body bursts to an ethereal radiance as cerulean lightning explodes from her palms in a gut-churning split-second, telekinetic takedown, blasting the walking time bomb off the epicenter into a thunderous cascade of ice and rock burying the mech's contorted form to its cracked bulbous head poking through frozen chunks of debris.

00:02:34

Screaming in agonizing ecstasy, Hannah yanks the battle-damaged Death Dealer helmet off her blond head and throws it into the chasm as she advances over the precipitous ledge and falls to her knees, bent over, vomiting, and coughing up blackish gunk spiked with the comet's poisonous atmosphere.

Pushing caked blond strands off her face, Hannah touches the long cauterized gash over her exposed left cheekbone to the scorched eye socket in a half-blinded stagger to the never-say-die mech's blurred form, restarting its ominous red lights, and ratcheting a banging beat to an off-kilter reverberation in a pitched and whining struggle to break free and resume its mission.

Clenching her four-fingered left hand into a tight fist, Hannah elevates a glistening boulder over the mech's strobing head, letting it drop with an affirming shatter as its threatening red glow and horrible din terminate.

Turning back to the epicenter, Hannah taps her arm, squinting her right eye at the blurred numerals ticking toward zero.

00:01:27

Dropping onto her hands and knees with singed hair falling over her scorched face, Hannah crawls toward the ledge. Sightless and out of time, she quashes panicky sobs as her numb fingertips probe for the robot's deep, rutted footmarks, indicating the epicenter she needs to reach. Feeling a linear impression on the frozen surface, she scrambles between paralleling footprints, hoping against hope with a hard swallow, groping down her right calf to retrieve the cube from its pouch. "Oh no. This can't be happening!" Grasping burned leather and tangled masses of long threads in her quaking hands, Hannah's heart sinks, "The cube is gone. It's over."

Hannah, you never needed the cube.

"Dad? Where are you? I can't see."

Hannah, honey, look within yourself … your Blue Spark alters time and space.

"I can't do it."

Come on, now. You warped across light years to reach the comet.

"I did that?"

Yes, you did. Now, Hannah, time is running out. You need to do it, and you need to do it now.

00:00:22

Squeezing her dying incarnation into a tight ball with her long arms wrapped over her battered legs bent up under her chin, Hannah concentrates her energized Blue Spark inheritance, curving time and space an infinitesimal degree as the comet disappears in a flash before reappearing on a collision with destiny to restore a universal consonance.

00:00:06 …

You did it, Baby Girl. You are the comet.

"Daddy, can we do sparklers when I see you again?"

I have one ready and waiting. Your Mom wants me to tell you …

00:00:00

The Overlords

A meteoric spectacle streaking across the polluted skies above their barren, colorless world elicits zero concern among the Overlords.

Nothing to fear.

An inconsequential handful of meteorites from the fast-approaching near-Earth comet result in only minor damage to their infrastructure.

Nothing to fear.

Imbued with the hubris of their long-extinct alien creators, the Overlords anticipate their planned cometary demolition while recalling mineral-laden probes from its frozen surface.

Nothing to fear.

Circumspect Overlords gape through massive observation windows high atop mushroom-domed megastructures as AI probe launch sequences commence milliseconds before the comet vanishes from the sky.

Nothing to …

Almost imperceptible reactions of dead-eyed Overlords precede a blinding white-hot brightness igniting the sky as Hannah's comet reappears and crashes into Earth just below the Equator, spreading vaporizing shockwaves at thousands of miles per hour to every corner of the planet.

Future Earth

With its feathery wings spread wide, a giant raptor soars across a crisp blue, star-filled sky above waves crashing against the rugged shoreline of an inland sea at the dawn of a new tomorrow.

Life on the third planet from the Sun rediscovers its way.

The End

Epilogue One

Hannah's distant memories of corporeal existence whither to cosmic dust blown across the fabric of time upon fulfilling the promise of her Blue Spark and resting beyond an infinite horizon with the eternal esteem of a universal community.

After eons of nurturing the healing planet, the Light Specters reach the moment in time to rekindle what once was and begin again. Call it destiny. Call it God's will.

It is how it is done.

* * *

An energized duo appears above rolling dunes overlooking an inland sea teeming with complex life on a resilient Planet Earth, recovering to its blue and green glory from a hellscape abyss. Fomenting a mighty gale on an otherwise splendid day, they blow away hundreds of feet of sand, revealing the uppermost portions of ruins buried under the desert terrain.

Exploring the vestigial architectural remnants of a past world, the sublime pair scans through sand and rock before locating a massive arched metal roofline constructed from an ageless alien alloy. Finding a riveted seam, they open a crevice wide enough for a human and descend into a cavernous expanse, their shimmering orbs illuminating troves of ancient history preserved in petrified crates stacked into the rafters interspersed among sections replete with biological and chemical knowledge critical for life. At a grotto of religious artifacts and relics, they exhume a barrel-shaped object, noting an almost imperceptible bee-shaped glyph on its side. Striking paydirt, they assume male and female humanoid life forms before rolling the heavy barrel into a patch of sunlight leaking from the fissure high above.

Conjuring a chisel in her hand like a magician, the female chunks its sharp tip under the embrittled lid and pries it open, revealing a one-foot metal cube amid crushed fossilized remains before her stellar gaze.

Assisting his attractive partner, the male extricates the perfect one-foot square object and sets it on the floor as the female ventures into the darkness, searching for a box marked *Alpha*. Smoothing a five-fingered hand over the cube's matte-gray sides, he smiles, producing a blue strobe intensifying into a powerful, solid beam projecting a human shape into the shadows. Observing the translucent blurriness take form and solidify into a physical human body, the female returns and taps the cube, completing the reincarnate procedure.

Careful not to disturb his trancelike state, the svelte couple study the fruit of their labors: a mature and distinguished male with a full head of charcoal gray curls wearing a pilled and matted wool cardigan over a mustard-stained undershirt and brown corduroy pants standing in a pair of holed and bloodied socks.

Amused by the man's expressive face and intelligent eyes, the woman reactivates the cube, this time projecting a feminine outline that resolves into a captivating young woman with a far-off and haunting blueberry gaze, standing tall and barefoot with shoulder-length jet-black hair over ice-blue, PTB logo-patterned pajamas.

The male waves a glowing hand before the man's deep-set stare before jolting him to consciousness with a simple finger snap.

Coughing and sputtering, the older fellow blinks watery blue-gray eyes around his strange new surroundings and rasps his first words in ages.

"Where am I? Is this a dream?"

"Hello, Richard. It is good to see you after so very long."

Shaking his head to clear the cobwebs after his Lazarus-like return, he widens a scruffy-faced grin, "Yes. That is my name. I am Professor Richard King."

With the lights coming back online one by one in his reconnecting neural pathways, Richard recognizes the dark-haired young woman in light-blue PJs standing to his right, "Sarah. Wake up, my dear. We made it."

Hearing her name spoken aloud, Sarah rouses with a frightful startle, "Where am I? Who are you? What is happening to me?"

The luminous female's graceful, calming presence takes the distraught Sarah by the hand, "Sit with me, Sarah. There are so many things you must learn."

Richard watches his cubed soul partner fall into the regal female's radiant embrace as the Light Specters' master plan unfolds in his mind, "I did not believe this day would come; however, your glittering naked presence liberating me and Sarah from the cube suggests humankind prevailed against all odds."

"Yes, Richard, we recognized humanity's potential, fostering your species through millennia, yet it was left to young Hannah Haig's Blue Spark to rid your world of a hybridized alien monstrosity."

"Kudos to Hannah. I met her once on a wonderful last Christmas day. At least for me … but I digress. However, while the Overlords were beyond pure evil, it was their cubed technology …" Adjusting to the darkness, Richard's gaze lands on the recognizable shape of a cracked skull peaking from the open barrel among jagged bone fragments.

"I am not really here, am I?"

The male's angelic visage widens into an effervescent smile, "Yes, you are, Richard. The cube replicated every detail from your final moment down to holes in your socked feet. You are you. There is no other you. Do not trouble yourself with the cube's origin. Suffice it to say, it did *not* originate with the Overlords. They stole it like they stole everything else."

Placing firm hands on Richard's shoulders, he proffers a warm and confident smile, "Forget the past. Plan for the future. And live in the present."

A hint of briny saltiness in the air wafting through the opening high above distracts Richard from a raft of questions filling his head.

"Is that what I think it is?"

"Let's go see."

Transported under the same midday sunshine that warmed his skin as a much younger man in a long-forgotten reality, Richard surveys structural remnants of the erstwhile Lost Cactus base he built in the post-World War Two American Southwestern hinterlands, "I used to be known as Doc when this place hummed with the prospect of discovery." Huffing a wistful sigh, Richard picks up a stone and tosses it into a clustering of odd-looking cacti, "Now it lies buried to its rooftops in rock and sand."

The sound of waves crashing in the distance interrupts Richard's introspection as his expressive face alights with a renewed sense of wonder at the unknown, "This was nothing but desert. Now, there is an inland sea right on the doorstep. How remarkable." An epiphanic shock widens Richard's eyes as a flock of reptilian seabirds squawks overhead,

"How long was I asleep? What year is it? Are there any others?"

"My dear Richard, the year is of little consequence and no, just yourself and Sarah—whose unplanned presence is most welcome nonetheless."

Richard stoops to pick up a shiny rock, "You can thank my old friend and colleague, Mitsuo Kobayashi, for playing God and uploading the original Sarah's essence to the cube."

"Yes, it would appear so, but Sarah's inclusion may also have been part of the plan from the outset. You see, Richard. It is time for humanity to begin anew."

Richard lowers to a knee to pluck a small purple bloom from a thorny stem, letting the words sink in before pivoting with a quizzical expression, "You cannot possibly mean in a biblical sense."

The glowing man looks down at Richard with an artful grin, "More or less, Richard, that is precisely what I mean. Plans are already in place, awaiting your keen knowledge, wisdom, and oversight. That is the purpose underlying your return to this hallowed place you created so long ago under the purview of an uncorrupted The Powers That Be. You are paramount to the endeavor." Reading an impertinent thought crossing Richard's racing mind, he smiles and adds, "But not in a conjugal sense."

With a nod, Richard stands and wipes sand off his corduroys, "That is perhaps for the best."

"Perhaps. However, procreation is critical."

Richard's brow furrows on the über-advanced human being, "Why yes, it is!" Wheeling toward the top floors of his former laboratory building jutting above ground, a boundless new energy courses up his spine, his brain swelling with thousands of new ideas, "There is work to be done here. Let's see ... I have the lovely and gracious Sarah to assist me in my old Lost Cactus laboratory, which I assume, with the help of the Light Specters, will work out just fine. So much to do ..."

Observing old Richard's unbounded energy and enthusiasm

within new Richard, the ethereal Light Specter manifestation injects a hint of modesty coupled with a peaceful serenity into the brilliant scientist's ego, "Remember, Richard, haste makes waste."

Looking back toward the arched roofline of the legendary Lost Cactus warehouse, where fresh air flows inside for the first time in eons, a spark of inspiration lights Richard's face, recalling a particular crate labeled with one word: *Bentley*.

"Can we bring him back, too?"

"Of course, Richard. A garden cannot flourish without a bee."

The luminous naked female appears, leading an enlightened Sarah toward them in the warm afternoon sunshine with Alpha trailing behind, ready to see what happens next.

Bibliography

Epigraphy

Chapter One:

Livio, Mario. "Did Galileo Truly Say, 'And Yet It Moves'? A Modern Detective Story" *Scientific American*, 6 May 2020, https://blogs.scientificamerican. com/observations/did-galileo-truly-say-and-yet-it-moves-a-modern-detective-story/

Chapter Two:

Parker, Nils. "The Angel in the Marble." *Medium*, 8 Jul. 2013, https://nilsaparker. medium.com/the-angel-in-the-marble-f7aa43f333dc

Chapter Three:

Ashcroft, Rachel. "What Does 'I Think Therefore I Am' Really Mean?" *The Collector*, 28 Oct. 2022, https://www.thecollector.com/what-does-i-think-therefore-i-am-mean/

Chapter Four:

Pessoa, Fernando., Zenith, Richard. *The Book of Disquiet*. Penguin Classics, 2002.

Chapter Five:

Tzu, Sun., Sawyer, Ralph. *The Art of War*. Basic Books, 1994.

Chapter Six:

"We'll Meet Again." *Wikipedia*, https://en.wikipedia.org/wiki/We%27ll_Meet_
    Again

Chapter Seven:

Nietzsche, Friedrich., Tanner, Michael., J. Hollingdale. *The Twilight of the Idols
    and the Anti-Christ: or How to Philosophize with a Hammer.* Penguin
    Classics, 1990.

Chapter Eight:

Wells, H.G. *The Time Machine.* Henry Holt, 1895.

Chapter Nine:

Carroll, Lewis. *Alice's Adventures in Wonderland.* Macmillan, 1865.

Chapter Ten:

"What's Past Is Prologue." *Wikipedia*, https://en.wikipedia.org/wiki/What%27s_
    past_is_prologue

Chapter Eleven:

Orwell, George. *1984.* Secker & Warburg, 1949.

Books

Charney, Noah. *The Devil in the Gallery: How Scandal, Shock, and Rivalry Shaped
    the Art World.* Rowman & Littlefield, 2021.

López-Rey, José., Delenda, Odile. *Velázquez. The Complete Works.* TASCHEN,
    2020.

Tipler, Frank J. *The physics of immortality : modern cosmology, God, and the
    resurrection of the dead.* Doubleday, 1994.

Videos

"Corpse Reviver Number 1 & 3 - Cocktail Masterclass." *YouTube*,
    uploaded by Behind the Bar, 16 Mar. 2020, https://youtu.be/
    InDoL8mmk0E?feature=shared

"Dante and Virgile." *Google Arts & Culture*, https://artsandculture.google.com/
    asset/dante-and-virgile/-AF79SI4-gGMKA?hl=en

"The exclusive island of Panarea." *YouTube*, uploaded by Riky & Trikki
    trips & curiosity around, 7 Jan. 2023, https://youtu.be/
    expgSSpnY08?feature=shared

"Eye of the Sahara." *NASA Earth Observatory*, https://earthobservatory.nasa.gov/
    images/150060/the-eye-of-sahara

"International Space Station, ISS, as seen from Earth." *YouTube*,
    uploaded by RichardB1983, 19 Jun. 2012, https://youtu.
    be/0yuQOO2jA1I?feature=shared

"Joe Rogan Experience #1284 - Graham Hancock." *YouTube*,
    uploaded by Powerful JRE, 22 Apr. 2019, https://youtu.be/
    Rxmw9eizOAo?feature=shared

"Riding To The Top Of The Gateway Arch In The Tram Car: What It's
    Like & What You Can See Of St Louis." *YouTube*, uploaded
    by GmaGpaAdventures, 2 Feb. 2020, https://youtu.be/
    kCJYaMMBUOk?feature=shared

"Timeline of Humanity." *Halcyon Maps*, https://www.halcyonmaps.com/
    timeline-of-human-history/

"The Ultimate Aeolian Islands Travel Guide." *YouTube*, uploaded by ViewCation,
    19 Sep. 2021, https://youtu.be/SpXRdDOQCVs?feature=shared

"William Shakespeare." *National Portrait Gallery*, https://www.npg.org.uk/
    collections/search/portrait/mw11574/William-Shakespeare

"Vatican documents show secret back channel between Pope Pius XII and Adolf
    Hitler." *YouTube*, uploaded by PBS Newshour, 7 Jun. 2022, https://
    youtu.be/T7fV1KOcR7U?feature=shared

Articles

Ashley, Steven. "Could an Industrial Prehuman Civilization Have Existed on Earth before Ours?" *Scientific American*, 23 Apr. 2018, https://www.scientificamerican.com/article/could-an-industrial-prehuman-civilization-have-existed-on-earth-before-ours/

Barras, Colin. "Transformers: 10 revolutions that made us human." *NewScientist*, 22 Oct. 2014, https://www.newscientist.com/article/mg22429921-600-transformers-10-revolutions-that-made-us-human/

Bourdin, Thomas. "What Is the Difference between Quarks & Leptons?" *Sciencing*, 25 Apr. 2017, https://sciencing.com/difference-between-quarks-leptons-8076741.html

Coxworth, Ben. "Scientists claim that 'self' can relocate to other bodies, or be made to include a third arm." *New Atlas*, 24 Feb. 2011, https://newatlas.com/brain-capable-of-redefining-peoples-selves/17951/

Curry, Andrew. "Gobekli Tepe: The World's First Temple?" *Smithsonian Magazine*, Nov. 2008, https://www.smithsonianmag.com/history/gobekli-tepe-the-worlds-first-temple-83613665/

Delach Leonard, Mary. "Wow! Take a look outside the hatch at the very top of the Gateway Arch." *St. Louis Public Radio*, 28 Oct. 2015, https://www.stlpr.org/arts/2015-10-28/wow-take-a-look-outside-the-hatch-at-the-very-top-of-the-gateway-arch

Dobrijevic, Daisy., Sharp, Tim. "How big is the moon?" *Space.com*, 7 Feb. 2022, https://www.space.com/18135-how-big-is-the-moon.html

Dowson, Thomas. "The Vatican Obelisk: Why is there an Ancient Egyptian Obelisk in St Peter's Square?" *Archeology Travel*, 22 Apr. 2023, https://archaeology-travel.com/street/vatican-obelisk-in-st-peters-square/

French, Paul. "Milan: Italy's Capital of Style Goes Noir." *Crime Reads*, 19 Apr. 2021, https://crimereads.com/milan-italys-capital-of-style-goes-noir/

Hardawar, Devindra. "You can buy a giant mech suit on Amazon Japan for $1 million." *Engadget*, 17 Jan. 2015, https://www.engadget.com/2015-01-17-do-want-kuratas.html

Harris, Pamela. "The Basics of French Country Decor." *The Spruce*, 31 Jul. 2023, https://www.thespruce.com/basics-of-french-country-decorating-452503

Kruesi, Liz. "All of the bases in DNA and RNA have now been found in meteorites." *Science News*, 26 Apr. 2022, https://www.sciencenews.

org/article/all-of-the-bases-in-dna-and-rna-have-now-been-found-in-meteorites

Lea, Robert. "Artificial gravity: Definition, future tech and research." *Space.com*, 20 May. 2022, https://www.space.com/artificial-gravity

Mcleod, Danielle. "Haste Makes Waste – Origin & Meaning." *Grammarist*, https://grammarist.com/usage/haste-makes-waste/

Netburn, Deborah. "We're in a crisis and St. Dymphna, patron saint of mental health, is having a renaissance." *Los Angeles Times*, 14 May. 2022, https://www.latimes.com/california/story/2022-05-14/praying-with-st-dymphna-the-patron-saint-of-mental-health#:~:text=%27"-,St.,Dymphna%27s%20Disciples%20meeting.&text=As%20the%20legend%20goes%2C%20Dymphna,a%20Christian%20mother%20in%20Ireland.

Nova, Michelle. "Spain: walling up madness." *Prison Insider*, 14 Apr. 2022, https://www.prison-insider.com/en/articles/espagne-l-enfermement-a-la-folie

Peres, Michael. "Gobekli Tepe is Rewriting Our Entire Understanding of Human History." *Thrive Global*, 18 Jun. 2020, https://community.thriveglobal.com/gobekli-tepe-is-rewriting-our-entire-understanding-of-human-history/

Rafferty, John P.. "Just How Old Is Homo sapiens?". *Encyclopedia Britannica*, 21 Jun. 2017, https://www.britannica.com/story/just-how-old-is-homo-sapiens.

Robertson, Cooper. "Gateway Arch Museum and Visitor Center." *Architect Magazine*, 22 May. 2018, https://www.architectmagazine.com/project-gallery/gateway-arch-museum-and-visitor-center_o

Rohan. "Symptoms of Radiation Poisoning: Causes, Treatment, Prevention all in One." *USUpdates*, 9 Feb. 2021, https://usupdates.com/symptoms-of-radiation-poisoning/

Scroope, Chara. "Naming Conventions". *Cultural Atlas*, 2021, https://culturalatlas.sbs.com.au/japanese-culture/japanese-culture-naming

White, Jenn. "St. Louis rally largest Obama crowd in U.S." *MPRNews*, 18 Oct. 2008, https://www.mprnews.org/story/2008/10/18/st-louis-rally-largest-obama-crowd-in-us

Zaid, Sareeta. "The Timelime of Humankind." *Intrepid Pea*, 2 Feb. 2019, https://www.intrepidpea.com/2019/02/timelineofhumans.html

Papers

Bele, Jean M. "Nuclear Fireball Calculator" *Nuclear Weapons Education Project*, https://nuclearweaponsedproj.mit.edu/fireball-size-effects

Bolter, Jay. (2016). Posthumanism. 10.1002/9781118766804.wbiect220.

Caire MJ, Reddy V, Varacallo M. Physiology, Synapse. [Updated 2023 Mar 27]. In: StatPearls [Internet]. Treasure Island (FL): StatPearls Publishing; 2023 Jan-. Available from: https://www.ncbi.nlm.nih.gov/books/NBK526047/#

Donitz, B. et al. (2021) 'New Frontiers Mission Concept Study to Explore Oort Cloud Comets', Bulletin of the AAS, 53(4). doi:10.3847/25c2cfeb.d7cfcc43.Lego S. Repressed memory and false memory. Arch Psychiatr Nurs. 1996 Apr;10(2):110-5. doi: 10.1016/s0883-9417(96)80073-2. PMID: 8935987.

McNamee MJ, Edwards SD. Transhumanism, medical technology and slippery slopes. J Med Ethics. 2006 Sep;32(9):513-8. doi: 10.1136/jme.2005.013789. PMID: 16943331; PMCID: PMC2563415.

Rose, Brian. (2021). The Vibrational Frequencies of the Human Body.

Websites

"A Dream in Panarea: Villa Lighea." *Engel & Völkers*, https://www.engelvoelkers.com/en-it/property/a-dream-in-panarea%3A-villa-lighea-4530260.1492572_exp/

"Aeolus." *Wikipedia*, https://en.wikipedia.org/wiki/Aeolus

"Astral projection." *Wikipedia*, https://en.wikipedia.org/wiki/Astral_projection#:~:text=Astral%20projection%20(also%20known%20as,physical%20body%20and%20travel%20throughout

"Carabinieri." *Wikipedia*, https://en.wikipedia.org/wiki/Carabinieri

"Comets." *NASA*, https://science.nasa.gov/solar-system/comets/

"Corsican Sheep Offer Exotic Horns, Fine Wool and More." *Creatures Corner*, https://creaturescorner.com/other-livestock/corsican-sheep-offer-exotic-horns-fine-wool-and-more/

"Cortina d'Ampezzo." *Wikipedia*, https://en.wikipedia.org/wiki/Cortina_d%27Ampezzo

"Ecclesiastical titles and styles." *Wikipedia*, https://en.wikipedia.org/wiki/
Ecclesiastical_titles_and_styles#:~:text=Pope%3A%20Pope%20
(Regnal%20Name),%3B%20His%20Eminence%3B%20Your%20
Eminence.

"Eden Course." *St. Andrews Links Trust*, https://standrews.com/golf/courses/eden-
course

"808 Mineral Water." *808*, https://www.808.ms

"Electroencephalography (EEG): Preparation, Results, and Cost."
eMedicineHealth, https://www.emedicinehealth.com/
electroencephalography_eeg/article_em.htm

"Extra dimensions." *Wikipedia*, https://en.wikipedia.org/wiki/Extra_
dimensions#:~:text=In%20physics%2C%20extra%20dimensions%20
are,on%20the%20Kaluza–Klein%20theory.

"Hoist with his own petard." *Wikipedia*, https://en.wikipedia.org/wiki/Hoist_
with_his_own_petard

"Influence of light on premature babies." *Draeger*, https://www.draeger.com/
Content/Documents/Content/whitepaper-lighting-in-nicu-en.pdf

"Inside the Brain." *Alzheimer's Association*, https://www.alz.org/alzheimers-
dementia/what-is-alzheimers/brain_tour

"Japan National Stadium." *Wikipedia*, https://en.wikipedia.org/wiki/Japan_
National_Stadium

"Kirby Morgan® KM37 Helmet." *Dive Commercial*, https://www.divecommercial.
com/brands/km37-helmet/

"Kuala Lumpur." *Lonely Planet*, https://www.lonelyplanet.com/malaysia/kuala-
lumpur

"Maremmano." *Wikipedia*, https://en.wikipedia.org/wiki/Maremmano

"Mecha." *Wikipedia*, https://en.wikipedia.org/wiki/Mecha

"Milazzo, Sicily; a city of three parts: ancient, medieval and modern." *Sicily
Visitor*, https://www.sicily-visitor.com/places/milazzo.php

"Nan Madol." *Wikipedia*, https://en.wikipedia.org/wiki/Nan_Madol

"Naval Hospital." *US Navy*, https://cnreurafcent.cnic.navy.mil/Installations/NAS-
Sigonella/About/Tenant-Commands/Naval-Hospital/

"Near-Earth object." *Wikipedia*, https://en.wikipedia.org/wiki/Near-Earth_
object#Near-Earth_comets

"Nuclear Flash Goggles." *Russomilitare*, https://russomilitare.com/product/opf-russian-soviet-chameleon-uv-ir-nuclear-explosion-goggles-steampunk

"Python." *Colt*, https://www.colt.com/detail-page/colt-python-425

"Ready to help the littlest ones." *Fresenius*, https://www.fresenius.com/ready-to-help-the-littlest-ones

"Ride of the Valkyries." *Wikipedia*, https://en.wikipedia.org/wiki/Ride_of_the_Valkyries

"St. Peter's Square." *Wikipedia*, https://en.wikipedia.org/wiki/St._Peter%27s_Square

"Through the Looking-Glass." *Wikipedia*, https://en.wikipedia.org/wiki/Through_the_Looking-Glass

"Viking Funeral." *Genius*, https://genius.com/Butcher-viking-funeral-lyrics

"World's Most Advanced Broadband Satellite Internet." *Starlink*, https://www.starlink.com/technology

"Zeptosecond - the smallest time unit ever measured." *BBC*, https://www.bbc.co.uk/newsround/54631056

About the Author

Author and artist John Hopkins' curiosity for what lies beyond common knowledge shapes his imaginative, character-driven storytelling. Following his muse, John created ***Lost Cactus***, a comic strip set on an off-the-grid top-secret research base—think Area 51. The strip's quick wit, fearless lampoonery, and supernatural mythology expanded into a shared universe of science fiction short stories and novels. Sequels and graphic novels featuring the expansive world-building of **Lost Cactus** and **The Powers That Be** shared universe are in the works.

Stay tuned and keep an eye on the sky.

johnhopkinsauthor.com